BLOOD & BONES: JUDGE

Blood Fury MC®
Book 3

JEANNE ST. JAMES

Jeanne
ST. JAMES

———

Acknowledgements:

Photographer/Cover Artist: Golden Czermak at FuriousFotog
Cover Model: Jeremy Mooney
Editor: Proofreading by the Page
Beta readers: Whitley Cox, Andi Babcock, Sharon Abrams & Alexandra Swab
Blood Fury MC Logo: Jennifer Edwards

———

www.jeannestjames.com

Sign up for my newsletter for insider information, author news, and new releases:
https://www.authorjeannestjames.com/

Character List

BFMC Members:

Trip Davis – *President* – Son of Buck Davis, half-brother to Sig, mother is Tammy, Runs Buck You Recovery

Sig Stevens – *Vice President* – Son of Buck Davis, mother is Silvia, three years younger than Trip, helps run Buck You Recovery

Judge (Judd) **Scott** – *Sgt at Arms* - Father (Ox) was an Original, owns Justice Bail Bonds

Deacon Edwards – *Treasurer* – Judge's cousin, Skip Tracer/Bounty Hunter at Justice Bail Bonds

Cage (Chris Dietrich) – *Road Captain* – Dutch's youngest son, mechanic at Dutch's Garage

Ozzy (Thomas Oswald) – *Secretary* – *Original* – manages club-owned The Grove Inn.

Rook (Randy Dietrich) – Dutch's oldest son

Dutch (David Dietrich) – *Original* – Owns Dutch's Garage, sons: Cage & Rook

Dodge – Helps manage Crazy Pete's Bar

Whip – Mechanic at Dutch's Garage (formerly known as the prospect Sparky)

Rev (Mickey) – Mechanic at Dutch's Garage (formerly known as the prospect Mouse)
Shady – *Prospect*
Easy - *Prospect*

Stella – *Trip's ol' lady* - Crazy Pete's daughter, owns Crazy Pete's Bar
Autumn (Red) – *Sig's ol' lady* – Accountant for the club's businesses

Former Originals:

Buck Davis – *President* – Deceased
Razor Stevens – *VP* - Deceased
Ox – *Sgt at Arms* – Deceased
Crazy Pete – *Treasurer* – Deceased
Tin Man (Tinny) – Deceased

Others:

Syn Stevens – Sig's sister
Silvia Stevens – Sig's mother, Razor's former ol' lady
Tammy Davis – Trip's mother, Buck's former ol' lady
Bebe Dietrich – Cage & Rook's mother, Dutch's former ol' lady
Clyde Davis – Buck's father, Trip & Sig's grandfather, deceased
Lizzy – Sweet butt
Max Bryson – *Chief of Police* – Manning Grove PD, Bryson brother
Marc Bryson – *Corporal* – Manning Grove PD, Bryson brother
Matt Bryson – *Officer* – Manning Grove PD, Bryson brother
Adam Bryson – *Officer* – Manning Grove PD, Brysons' cousin, Teddy's fiancé

Leah Bryson – *Officer* – Manning Grove PD, Marc's wife
Tommy Dunn – *Officer* – Manning Grove PD
Teddy Sullivan – Owner Manes on Main, Adam Bryson's fiancé
Amanda Bryson – Max's wife, owner Boneyard Bakery
Carly Bryson – Matt's wife, OB/GYN doctor
Levi Bryson – Adopted son of Matt & Carly Bryson (birth mother: Autumn)

Prologue

____

THE END

JUDD CREPT through the used car lot, keeping low and to the shadows, ducking behind each car he came to until he spotted the one he was looking for.

He grinned and his dick was already hard in anticipation.

At sixteen and not yet a member of the Blood Fury MC, he wasn't allowed to touch any of the club's sweet butts, unless his pop gave his permission. Like Buck had done for Trip when he was fourteen and got his cherry popped by one of them. In front of everyone.

Judd didn't want his first time to be in front of the club members because he didn't need them heckling him as they watched. Just like they did Trip.

Fuck that.

Instead, he found a way to pop a nut on his own. At least in a snatch and not his own palm. *That* he'd done more times than he could count. Sometimes him and the other boys would hide under the exec committee table during parties and watch when one or more of the brothers used that table to bang one out with any female they could find.

His fist had gotten some good workouts while watching some of that.

He'd tuck that shit away and remember it when he was in his bed at night, too. It gave him plenty of spank bank material.

It was his time. Trip lost his cherry at fourteen. And Judd was now sixteen. It wasn't fucking fair and none of the girls at school would let him down their pants.

It wasn't like he hadn't tried.

He was too tall and gangly, and they called him a loser. They also called him dirty, even though he wasn't.

The girls would say nobody wanted to let white trash like him touch them. Because if they did, no other boy would ever want to touch them afterward.

Well, fuck them.

He didn't want one of those snobby-ass bitches, anyway. All he wanted to do was blow a load deep in their cunt, not marry them. Or even date them.

They probably preferred to take it up the ass anyway, so they could say they were still virgins.

Right.

He blew out a breath and slid his hand down the hard-on under his jeans. He'd stolen some wraps from the pharmacy in town and had a couple tucked into his front pocket.

He was ready.

He had also stolen some money from the cash register when the clerk was distracted by Sig tripping and knocking over a display of sunglasses.

Judd slipped him a five for doing it. Then Sig had demanded more. But Judd told the twelve-year-old he could fuck off. It hadn't been worth any more than five since he only had to knock something over while Judd did the crime.

Sig threatened to tell the clerk if Judd didn't give him a twenty. So, he popped Sig in the mouth, making him bleed. The kid accepted the five and shut the fuck up after that.

Judd needed the rest of the money since tonight was the night he was going to get what he'd been waiting for.

He popped his head up from behind a Chevy and glanced around the dark sales lot. At midnight, no one was around. He just wanted to make sure the pigs didn't roll by and see him, fucking up his plans.

He moved closer to the old Dodge Caravan and peeked through the side window.

His heart pounded so hard, he could feel it all the way to his dick.

She was in there. Waiting like she said she would.

Because the cunt wanted the cash.

And he wanted the cunt.

With his blood racing through him, he jerked on the handle to the sliding side door of the minivan and carefully pulled it open, trying to be as quiet as possible.

"Got the scratch?" Molly asked.

He could hardly breathe enough to answer, "Yeah."

She held out her hand with her long nails and lots of dumb bracelets on her wrist. "Let's see it."

"I got it," he told her, worried she'd snatch it right out of his hand and go tell his pop. Then he'd get busted right across the mouth—if not worse—for trying to fuck a sweet butt when he knew he wasn't allowed to.

But fuck Ox. All he had to do was tell one of those patch whores to fuck Judd and they'd do it. And he wouldn't have to pay them shit.

"How much do you have?"

"What you wanted." He was getting annoyed. She let any of the brothers fuck her for free and now she was getting picky?

He would be a future Fury member. She needed to learn a little fucking respect.

"You'll get it after."

She held out her hand again. "Least show it to me."

"Fuck you, Molly."

"No, kid, you want me to fuck *you*. So, scratch or no snatch."

"You're a fuckin' whore, you know that?"

"If I wasn't, you wouldn't be getting ready to lose your virginity."

Heat rushed into his cheeks. "Ain't a virgin."

"That's not what your fist says." Molly laughed.

Fucking laughed.

Fuck her.

"Show me what I'm payin' for first."

"I'm sitting right here."

"You know what I fuckin' mean."

Molly sighed loudly, like this was a chore for her. She shoved up her short denim skirt, opened her legs and spread her pussy with her long-nailed fingers. "There you go, kid."

He couldn't see shit since it was so damn dark in that minivan, even with the vehicle's interior light. But it was a free place to go and Molly had access to all the car keys on the lot since she worked there as a receptionist during the day.

Judd climbed into the van and slid the door almost closed. He left it open just enough for the overhead light to remain on. He pulled out the money, waved it in the air and then shoved it back deep into his pocket.

"Shut it all the way so the cops don't spot us in here."

He frowned and shut it, engulfing the whole van in darkness.

"How do you want me, kid?"

He wanted her to stop calling him a fucking kid, that was what he wanted! He was fucking sixteen. He wasn't a kid anymore.

But he had no fucking clue on which way would be best in the back of a minivan. He'd seen a lot of fucking in his life. And he'd seen women getting it in all kinds of positions.

But he knew this would be once and done for the fifty bucks he was paying, so he wanted to pick the position he'd last the longest.

Trip hadn't lasted long his first time, which was one reason he was ribbed so hard afterward by all the brothers. Judge didn't want that happening to him.

"Just pull your fucking pants down and sit on the seat. Christ, kid. It's not rocket science."

Judd quickly undid his belt buckle and his jeans, shoving them all the way to his boots.

"God, you're just a gangly thing, aren't you? Nothing like your pop."

"You seen my pop naked?" Judd wondered if his mother knew. Or if Trixie even cared.

Not answering, Molly moved off the seat, waited for him to get settled, and then she shoved her skirt up even higher.

A smell wafted to him that made his nose wrinkle. Is that what they all stunk like?

So fucking gross.

But fuck it. They were there. He had the scratch and wraps. He was doing this.

He pulled a wrap from the front pocket of his jeans and handed it to her. With an annoyed sigh, she took it, ripped it open and rolled it down his dick.

He almost lost it when she did. That did not give him confidence in his staying power with what was coming next.

Maybe if he concentrated on the smell, he'd last longer. Yeah, that's what he needed to do. He inhaled deeply and almost puked.

Maybe that wasn't a good idea.

With that rot, maybe this whole thing wasn't a good fucking idea.

Fuck it. He was doing this. He could be pickier later.

"Wanna see your tits," he demanded as she began to climb on his lap.

"Not for a fifty."

"How much more?"

"'Nother twenty."

She was fucking crazy. He'd seen them before at the warehouse. They weren't worth a fucking twenty. *Fuck it.*

He held his breath as she wiggled herself into place, grabbed his dick, holding it where it needed to be and...

And...

Fuck. Fuck. Fuck!

He groaned as his load shot out of his balls and into the wrap before he was even able to stick it in. "Fuck!"

The bitch snorted.

Judd didn't find any of it funny.

"Wanna eat me out, instead, for that fifty?"

He tried not to gag. "No."

Molly shrugged, climbed off him and yanked her skirt down. "Better luck next time, kid." Then she dug into his jeans and yanked out the money he had tucked in the pocket. She slid open the door and disappeared into the dark.

He dropped his head back onto the seat, closed his eyes and blew out a breath. He just paid fifty bucks for something he could've done himself.

He yanked off the full wrap and tossed it onto the van floor with a curse. Then he yanked up his jeans and climbed out.

He was still a goddamn virgin.

He had already told Trip and Sig he was getting some tonight with Molly. Now he was going to have to lie.

He cautiously made his way out of the car lot, crossed the railroad tracks and hoofed it two more blocks home.

When a pig mobile raced past him, he hid behind a bush. His night had already gone to shit and him getting caught out after curfew would just be the fucking cherry on the...

Yeah, cherry on the virgin.

He blew out a frustrated breath and kept going. His pop wouldn't care if he was out after curfew, but he'd care if 5-0 brought him home.

Last time the pigs dropped Judd off, his pop beat him with a belt. Not for being out late, but for getting caught.

So now Judd was more careful. *Way* more careful.

As he turned the corner, he froze.

Their whole street was full of pigs. Not just local 5-0, but ones who were heavily armed, wearing all kinds of protective gear and hunkered down behind their vehicles and facing the old, run-down duplex they lived in. They looked like they were headed to war.

What the fuck was going on?

Did the neighbor in the other half of the house beat the shit out of his wife again? Even in all the times they'd shown up next door, he'd never seen a response like this before. Maybe this time he'd killed her instead of just giving her a black eye or a broken arm.

Judd ducked behind an overgrown bush and peeked through it.

What the fuck? The pigs were all focused on *their* front door, not the neighbor's, who shared the same porch.

Judd's heart began to thump. The pigs had their lights off, no sirens, no radios, and weren't saying a word.

Holy shit. Maybe they were arresting his pop for killing Razor and Tin Man.

His mom told him that Ox had shot Razor between the eyes in retaliation for killing the club prez, Buck. And then Tin Man tried to take Ox out for killing the man's brother. Judd's pop blasted Tinny right in the chest, dropping him right where he stood.

So, yeah, maybe all the 5-0 out front had something to do with that since it only happened a few days ago.

Maybe somebody snitched.

And if somebody snitched...

He needed to sneak around back, get into the house and warn his pop.

But as he made his way through the dark, sticking behind the shrubbery, he came out behind the house, only to see the same shit as out front. Too many pigs, wearing vests and carrying high-powered weapons. Plus, a couple more local cops.

There was no way to get to the back door. They'd stop him first.

Something huge was going down.

Glass breaking at the back of the house, and a flash bang that scared the shit out of him, had him hitting the ground hard. A whole bunch of shouting quickly followed, the sound of doors being busted in at the front and back, shouts that included the words "arrest warrant," and pigs moving everywhere.

Holy fuck!

Judd was afraid to move, and he couldn't follow them in, anyway, because some of the pigs remained standing guard outside. Probably to make sure his pop didn't escape out the back. He watched the pigs, who had their guns drawn, enter the house, shouting to one another as they cleared each room.

Almost all the windows were propped open since it was ball-sweating hot out and the fucking piece of shit house they lived in didn't have air conditioning. Because of that, he heard everything like he was right inside along with them.

He crawled forward, the dead shrub scratching his arms, his fingers digging into the dirt, so he could get a better view of the back of the house. But he wanted to stay where the local oinkers wouldn't see him. Because if they saw him, they'd probably nab him.

Where the fuck were his parents?

Where the fuck was Jemma?

Had they left town and not told him?

Had they left town and left him behind because he was in some damn minivan trying to get his cherry popped and they couldn't find him?

Maybe they left town and just didn't want him anymore.

Through the open windows, he heard a scramble of feet, more shouts, then boots rushing up the steps.

"Gun! Gun! Gun!"

"Put the gun down!"

"Put it down."

Holy fuck!

Judd couldn't breathe and was frozen to the ground.

"PUT THE FUCKING GUN DOWN!"

"Fuck you!"

"Let her go, Scott. You don't want to do that."

"Fuck you, pigs!"

"Let her go."

"Put the fucking gun down and let her go."

Who? Who was *her*? His mother?

"She's just a baby, you won't be able to live with yourself if something happens to her."

Jemma.

His fucking pop had Jemma.

Judd forced himself to keep his mouth shut and keep from shouting out to his pop.

"Let her go, Scott. We can do this without any of you getting hurt."

What was Ox doing?

"Will let 'er go when you get the fuck outta my house."

"Let her mom take her. We'll get them both out of here safely."

That motherfucker was using Jemma!

"This isn't going to end well if you don't let her go."

Judd needed to get upstairs. He needed to get Jemma.

"You really want us to shoot you in front of your kid? Is that what you want? To show them how much of a hero you are? Scar her for life?"

"Fuck you! Ain't takin' any of us."

"We don't want anyone but you, Scott. Wife and kid can stay here. But we have a warrant for your arrest and we're not just going away. Let's do this without getting anyone hurt. Including your little girl."

"How come you gotta bring a pig army to deal with one fuckin' man? You all pussies?"

Judd didn't hear the answer or even if there was one, but he knew why. His pop killed people and didn't think twice about it. He'd kill all those pigs without even blinking.

But it pissed him the fuck off that he was using Jemma. His baby sister was only five.

Worse, Judd could hear her crying even from where he was lying on his belly in the dirt.

He could also hear his mom throwing out pot shots at the pigs. He wondered if Trixie had encouraged Ox to use Jemma as a shield.

If she did...

Judd's jaw shifted and his fingers curled into his palms, his dirty nails digging in painfully. If she allowed her own daughter to be used, Judd was running the fuck away and taking Jem with him.

"Ma'am, take your daughter from your husband."

"No, you fuckin' don't, Trix. Stay where you're at. It's a fuckin' trick. You know how these fuckin' pigs are."

"Get the fuck out of our house," Judd heard his mother shriek. "Get out! This is our property! You got no fucking right to be here!"

"We're here to serve a warrant, ma'am, and we're not leaving until we do." The pig sounded pretty fucking calm for the situation. "So, let's make this quick and painless and stop scaring your daughter."

"You're the ones fuckin' scaring her with all those fuckin' guns drawn."

"Scott, this isn't going to end well."

"Yeah, it ain't, no matter what fuckin' happens."

When a sharp crack was heard, Judd's heart leapt out of his chest. "NO!" He jumped to his feet and began to sprint toward the back door.

Someone hooked him around the waist and pulled him to a halt. He began to struggle but was put in a hold that was not only painful, but made it impossible to break free.

"Lemme go!"

"Calm down, kid. You can't go in there."

"That's my sister!"

"She'll be fine."

"No, she won't!"

More shouts and boots stomping on the bare floors were heard. His mother was shrieking and his father bellowing out non-stop curses.

It sounded like a cluster-fuck.

But somehow through all that craziness and even through the pounding in his ears, he heard it.

Jemma screaming. Crying. Calling out Judd's name.

Judd lost all his strength and went limp in the pig's hold. His head dropped and he blinked back the tears that threatened to escape. "Jemma," he whispered.

The pig's radio squawked, and a voice announced Ox was in custody with just minor injuries. The woman and child were unharmed. Hearing that made him breathe a little easier.

"Lemme go!" Judd yelled, pulling on the arms preventing him from getting to his sister.

"You need to stay out of the way. If you don't, I'm taking you into custody."

Judd bit back his, "Fuck you," and nodded his head instead.

The pig slowly released him and as soon as he did, Judd ran toward the front of the house. The pig ordered him to stop.

He only slid to a stop when he saw a bunch of the military-like 5-0 surge from the house with his father in cuffs. However, it took a few of them to handle him because Ox wasn't going without a fight.

As Judd went to move toward them, an arm hooked him around the neck, cutting off his air. "Don't get any closer or you're going to end up just like your old man."

Judd forced a "Fuck you" past his crushed windpipe.

"Got a great future ahead of you, asshole. Just like him. Just give yourself a few years, if you live that long."

Fuck you. Fuck you. Fuck you, you scum-suckin' pig!

As they tried to drag Ox down the porch steps, his pop did a reverse head-butt and slammed the pig behind him in the nose. Blood gushed from the oinker's face and there were a bunch of yells, a raised metal baton and then it cracked his pop alongside his already bleeding head.

Ox dropped to his knees with his head hanging. The only thing keeping him from collapsing all the way to the concrete was the pigs hauling him back up. When they did, he spat a big, bloody hocker in one of their faces.

Judd shouted as everything became a blur. His father was shoved to the ground, a shin was pinned to his throat, and someone yelled, "Get a hood," as they shoved his face into the concrete.

Another one yelled, "Seems like someone earned himself a spit tax."

And then several of them began kicking his pop's ribs and stomping on him with their boots.

Judd's "No!" only came out as a squeak because of the arm pressing on his throat.

A flash caught his attention and he saw his mother, Trixie, rushing out of the house, screaming like a wild woman, her blonde hair flying behind her and her face twisted as she launched herself at one of the 5-0 beating up his father.

Another pig grabbed her, threw her to the ground and tried to pin her down, but she kept fighting. She was snapping with her teeth, clawing and spitting, too. Local 5-0 quickly jumped in and got her cuffed.

When the dust settled, his parents were both detained with their wrists and ankles bound, and screened hoods pulled over their heads. 5-0 dragged his father to a car, while a couple of them carried his mother.

She was still screaming but his pop was quiet as fuck, which was so unlike him.

Had they killed him?

One of the uniformed oinkers was yelling at Ox, "Double murder charge, resisting arrest, agg assault on several police officers, enough drugs in plain sight for a possession and intent to distribute charge. Illegal firearms. The list is fucking endless, Scott. You aren't ever seeing your kids again. Probably better for them, anyway. It'll give them a better future than an animal like you would ever give them."

The pig loosened his grip just enough for Judd to catch his breath. "Lemme go!" he cried. "Lemme go!"

"Who can come get you and your sister?"

"No one!"

"If you don't have anyone, Child Services will take both of you and most likely split you two up."

That couldn't happen. They'd run away first. He was not letting Jemma go anywhere without him. "No! I'm sixteen and old enough to take care of her 'til they come home."

"No, you're not. And your parents aren't coming home any time soon. Both will be going away for a long time."

What? "Even my mom?"

"She's getting charged with agg assault on a police offi-cer, and there were enough drugs in the house to be charged for that, too. You probably won't see her for the next five to seven years."

Holy shit. That can't be true! He couldn't raise Jemma by himself for that long. He didn't have money. He didn't even have a damn job. He didn't have shit. The only thing he had was what his parents had provided. Which wasn't much but it was something.

Now he'd have nothing. How was he going to take care of his baby sister?

"Got family close by we can call?" another pig asked as he approached with a pad and pen.

Judd blinked. Who the hell would want to take him and Jemma in?

The only person he could think of was his pop's sister.

But before he could tell the pig that, another oinker came out of the house carrying Jemma, whose face was ravaged from crying.

Holy shit.

Judd ripped from the pig's grasp and as he got closer, Jem spotted him and screamed, "Judd!" extending out her arms to him.

He snatched his sister out of the pig's arms, and she clung to him, snot running out of her nose and tears an endless stream down her cheeks. "It's okay, Jem. It's okay. Promise. Gonna take care of you. Don't worry."

The slam of car doors had him turning and watching the pig mobiles tear down the street, one carrying their mother, the other their father.

He squeezed Jemma tighter. He had no fucking clue how he would do it, but he'd do everything he could to take care of her.

He just hoped he didn't fail.

Chapter One

RUBBING his dog's ears was the next best thing to soothe his shit, right after the rumble of his straight pipes. Having that power between his thighs, the control of where his sled could take him in his hands, and the wind in his long beard was unmatched.

Jury, his American Bulldog, and his fucking kick-ass Harley were his saving grace. They kept him grounded when shit got a little twisted inside him.

It didn't happen often, but it happened.

And everything that happened on that mountain when they'd dealt with the Shirley Clan a couple of weeks ago was still haunting him. But then it was still fresh. For all of them.

He had a hard time sleeping after seeing what he saw up there. What those inbred hillbillies had done to Sig's woman, Autumn, had disturbed him to the core and he was having a hard time shaking it.

But Autumn had survived, was now safe and was sticking around to stay with Sig.

Hard to believe that fucker could hold onto a woman like Autumn—or Red, as Sig called her—but he was. But then, they were both fucked up, so maybe they were perfect for each other.

Sig was on the club run without her since she recently popped out a kid and wasn't in any shape to join them yet.

But she would.

Now Trip had Stella riding on his sled as his ol' lady and Judge didn't doubt Red would be riding behind Sig. Maybe come spring since this was the last planned run of the year.

If Judge hadn't been such a stupid fuck, he might have his own ol' lady on the back of his sled, too. But he fucked up badly and even though it'd been years, he wasn't ready to have another woman as his backpack.

Not one he could trust.

It was one thing to have a bitch riding him, another to have one riding with him. He preferred the first to the second.

At least, that was what he fucking told himself.

Cage, as Road Captain, was leading the formation through the back woods, hills and valleys surrounding Manning Grove, making sure to avoid Copperhead Road, which ran past the lane leading up the mountain to the Shirley compound.

He couldn't get all that shit that happened to stop bugging him. *He* was the club's enforcer. *He* wore the patch stating he was Sergeant at Arms. *He* was the one ultimately responsible for not only keeping everyone's ass in line but protecting club property.

He'd failed.

He'd fucking failed.

No one had held it against him.

But he held it against himself.

He hoped this three-hour, cold-as-fuck ride would clear his fucking mind, but it hadn't. Now he wanted nothing more than to head home, smoke a big fatty and maybe fall into some easy pussy.

Like most of his brothers, he had the phone numbers of all the willing sweet butts and female hang-arounds programmed into his cell.

All he usually had to do was send a text. After that, it wasn't long before he'd get a knock on his apartment door and when he opened it, willing snatch would be waiting on the other side, usually wearing a wicked smile and carrying a bottle of something strong in her hand.

Mentally, he began to go down his contact list to see who and what he was in the mood for.

Whoever it was, needed to blow his mind so he could forget—at least for a little while—about that fucking mountain, those inbred Shirleys and how a nine-month pregnant Autumn looked after they found her strapped to that bed in the compound.

So fucking caught up in his thoughts, he was surprised when they hit the town limits and headed down Main Street.

He didn't miss the fact everyone walking or driving through town stared at them rolling by. While the Grove's citizens were getting used to the return of the Fury, it didn't mean they all liked the idea.

Most of them didn't.

Trip was right, they needed to keep their shit as clean as possible to avoid hassle from the town council or even Manning Grove PD. *He* needed to keep his shit clean with them, too, since his business's survival counted on it.

He mindlessly followed the formation into the large municipal parking lot at the center of town and one-by-one, all his club brothers crab-walked their sleds back neatly in line next to each other, so they only took up a few parking spots.

He backed his next to Ozzy, and then Rook rolled his on Judge's other side.

Ozzy wore a huge smile as he jerked off his goggles.

"Can't get any fuckin' better than that 'cept for a fat, wet and hungry pussy. *Meeeeeow*."

Judge wondered if he would end up nuts deep in Lizzy later and if Judge should cross her off his list of ball-emptying potentials.

"Shit's gettin' to be blue ball weather, though," Rook stated after jerking down his face mask, heeling down his kickstand and yanking off his leather gloves.

"Don't be a pussy," Dutch griped in his gravelly voice as he walked past them, tugging on his long salt-and-pepper beard. "Us Originals never cried about a lil nippy nuts. You young fucks ain't made like we were."

"Yeah, bet you rode your sled two miles up a hill in five feet of fuckin' snow just to get your dick wet," Rook razzed his father.

"When your ma was still 'round, got my dick wet all the time. And the bitch could suck a knob off a fuckin' door."

"Christ," Rook growled, dropping his head and shaking it.

"Well, it's fuckin' true, boy. If it wasn't for that, never woulda made her my ol' lady and had her squirt you and your brother out." He waved a wrinkled, age-spotted hand and kept moving toward the front of the line where Trip, Stella and Cage were waiting. "By the way, havin' you two trashed her fuckin' pussy. Worst decision ever!" he shouted back over his shoulder.

Ozzy, another Original like Dutch, snorted and slapped his gloves on his leather chaps-covered thigh. "Fuckin' old man. Always was a pisser."

"Yeah, he was," Judge mumbled, sliding the key from his Softail Slim. He loved his sled. He'd had it customized after he bought it new to make it look even more badass than it came from factory. He'd traded in Ox's old sled he'd rode ever since he was old enough to be able to keep it upright. Which was not long after that fucker went to prison.

He'd also wore his old man's cut, but with his own name patch on it. Trip had him rip off the old diamond 1% patch on the back and remove the Original patch on the front, too. So far, only Ozzy and Dutch could claim they were Originals.

He didn't give a fuck about ripping those two patches off. Those were the two reasons that caused the Fury to burn to the ground in the first place.

Nothing but murder and mayhem...

When Whip and Rev strode by, Rev asked, "You assholes comin'?"

"Not yet." But that was his plan for later. He just needed to pick a place to plant his cum.

"Yep." Ozzy dismounted and chased after them.

"Fuck," Rook said softly next to him, which had Judge glancing at the man who was now standing in front of his own sled, a black beanie yanked over his head, dark sunglasses on his face, and his hands on his hips.

"What's up?"

"Fuck, man, look at that piece of fuckin' ass headin' this way. What I'd do to stick my dick in that..."

Judge's gaze slid from Rook to the object of the man's attention. With a quick glance, he noticed a woman walking in their direction—her face a bit pale, her eyes a bit wide and worried, and her hand tightly gripping a little girl's—had caught every male with a dick's attention.

Judge's jaw got tight at a couple of catcalls coming from his brothers which made the blonde move a bit quicker, dragging the girl, who looked about five, along with her. The girl also had blonde hair just like her mother.

Or who he assumed was her mother.

"You comin'?" Rook asked him, his eyes still glued to the very generous hips and thighs heading their way.

Judge could tell, even with her walking swiftly and stiffly, she couldn't control the natural rock and roll to those hips.

Nor the bounce to those tits, which were the perfect size for a man to be smothered to death. While wearing a smile.

They were just how he liked them. Tits, ass and pussy big enough to get lost in.

And this one had it all.

Problem was, she had a kid attached to her and she looked scared as fuck.

"You go on. Be there in a sec," Judge mumbled.

He didn't miss Rook's grin. "Aimin' high, Judge. But she's haulin' some baggage with her."

Judge didn't answer, he only kept his eyes locked on someone a fuck of a lot better looking than Rook.

Rook snorted, shook his head and wandered off, following the rest of his brothers as they headed toward Dino's Diner.

Judge tugged on his knit beanie, pulling it lower over his head, but kept his eyes on the blonde. Out of the corner of his eye, he noticed she was walking a direct line to an old silver Honda SUV. As they got close to it, she let go of the girl's hand and then screamed, "Daisy!" as little legs became a blur.

"Oh fuck," Judge muttered as the little snot monkey came tearing toward him.

"Daisy!" her mother screamed, now in a panic, and almost took a header herself right onto the pavement.

"Oh fuck," he muttered again as mom caught herself and kept hauling ass after her lightning-quick daughter.

But those stubby legs outran those fucking long, *wrap-those-around-my-ears* legs and got to him before she did. Though, Judge *might* have enjoyed watching those tits bounce out of control beneath her open coat as the woman scrambled to keep up.

"Hi!" was screamed up at him with a big smile and a sloppy wave.

"Guess your name's Daisy," Judge grumbled, looking

down into bright blue eyes and a whole bunch of sass. One little hand was plugged onto one equally little jutted out hip.

"How d'you know that?"

Judge jerked his chin up at the woman who was finally catching up. "That your mom?"

Daisy glanced over her shoulder and frowned. "Yeah."

"That's how I know. Was screamin' your name and you ignored her."

Daisy rolled her eyes. "She's *alllllways* screamin' my name."

"You give her a reason to scream your name?"

The little girl dug the toe of her tiny light blue sneaker covered with daisies into the pavement, making some beads on her laces jingle. "*Nooooo.*"

"That don't sound convincin'," Judge told her.

She shot him a bright smile. "I—"

"Daisy!" the blonde, curvy woman yelled, blindly reaching for her daughter as she kept her eyes glued on Judge, who hadn't moved from his sled. "We have to go." She sounded out of breath—whether she was out of shape or because she was scared of him, Judge didn't know—as she grabbed her daughter's arm and tugged.

"*Mommmmma,* I'm just sayin' hi!"

Another tug. "You said it, now we have to go."

"He didn't say hi back yet!" she screamed.

Judge winced. *For fuck's sake,* that kid was going to be a handful.

"Hi, Daisy," he said, biting back a snort.

She glanced up at her mother, "Now *you* say it."

Mom acted like she didn't understand. She probably wanted to disappear into the blacktop. "Say what, sweetie?"

"Say hi!"

Blondie blinked and her mouth dropped open slightly. "Umm. Hi." Color tinged her cheeks.

"Now *you* say it back," Daisy demanded from Judge.

"Know how this works, kid," he told her.

"Then say it!"

Christ, the kid was going to grow up to be a dominatrix. He lifted his gaze from the mini-me to her mother. "Hi."

"I'm so sorry she's bothering you," she said quickly. "Daisy, let's leave this nice man alone."

"Far from it."

Her just as bright blue eyes flipped from her daughter up to him. "What?"

"Nothin'."

"*Mommmmmmmmaaaaa*. He hasn't told me his name yet." *Holy fuck.*

"She's not normally like this, she's just tired and needs a nap."

"No, I don't!" *Stomp.* "If he doesn't tell me his name, then he's still a stranger and Aunt Heather says I can't talk to strangers. So, if he's a stranger, I can't talk to him. So, he *neeeeeeeeeds* to tell me his name so I can *taaaaaaaaaalk* to him!"

Blondie rolled her eyes just like her daughter had done and it was kind of cute. "Good lord, child, you're going to give me an aneurysm."

Daisy blinked up at her mother. "A what?"

"Never mind, we have to go."

"No!"

"You need to listen to your momma," Judge told Daisy.

"Don't wanna 'til you tell me your name."

God help the man who got saddled with that demanding woman. Though, if she grew up looking like her momma, most men might tolerate the attitude. And some other men might not like it and try to beat it the fuck out of her. "If I tell you, you gonna listen to your momma?"

Daisy's lips pressed tight.

So did Judge's.

Then the little girl stomped her foot once more with a loud huff.

Judge swung a leg over his sled and got to his feet.

Daisy's blue eyes went wide as she took in his height. "You're like the giant in Jack an' the Beanstalk!" she whispered in awe.

"What's the giant's name?" Judge asked her.

"Momma, what's the giant's name?"

"I... I don't know, sweetie."

"It can be your name," Daisy decided with a sharp nod. "What is it?"

Judge squatted down beside her and looked her directly in the eyes. "You sayin' we won't be strangers if I tell you my name?"

Daisy nodded her head like a little fiend. "No! Then we'll be friends."

Judge glanced up at Mom, who was nervously chewing on her bottom lip. "Not sure your momma will let us be friends."

"I'm not askin' her!"

Judge's eyebrows shot up. "How old are you?"

Daisy lifted a hand with all her stubby fingers spread wide. "Five!"

"Then you always gotta ask your momma everything first."

"Oh... please," her mother groaned, "not everything."

Judge's lips twitched and his eyes dropped back to Daisy's. "My name's Judge."

The little girl made a face. "Never heard that name before."

"Bet you heard a lotta names in all five of your years."

"I have." She nodded. "A lot." She pursed her little lips and searched his face. "Now we're friends, can I touch your face?"

What the fuck? "Why?"

"You look like a shaggy doggy. An' I wanna pet you 'cause I'm not allowed to have a dog." She huffed again.

Judge pinned his lips together. After a few seconds he had his shit together enough to say, "Not sure you touchin' a stranger's a good idea."

"You're not a stranger now, Judge," she reminded him with so much sass, Judge could taste it.

"You're right. I'm not." He pushed to his feet. "'Nother time, Daisy. Sure your momma don't want you touchin' men you just met."

"Then next time."

Judge met the bright blue eyes of Daisy's mother. "Yeah, maybe next time."

As he looked down at the woman, he noticed her hand shaking as she reached once again for her daughter.

"You afraid of me?" Judge asked softly.

He didn't miss her throat move as she swallowed. "Should I be?"

"Probably," he muttered under his breath.

"Sorry?"

"Nothin' to be afraid of. Ain't gonna hurt you." He flipped his eyes down to the little girl at her side. "Or your girl."

"Okay, well... N-nice meeting you."

He didn't even try to bite back his snort. *Liar.*

Lies otherwise known as polite bullshit. He hated fake. He wanted real. "Why was it nice?"

Her grip tightened on her daughter's shoulder. "I... I'm not sure what—"

"Said it was nice meetin' me. What was nice about it?"

Color flushed her cheeks again. "You... you were nice to my daughter."

"She's got quite the attitude. She get that from you?"

The woman's mouth dropped open. And after a second, she snapped it shut. "We need to go. Sorry for bothering you..."

He pointed to the rectangular patch on his cut. "Judge."

"Judge," she finished, snagging Daisy's hand in a tight grip and yanking her along as she rushed across the parking lot.

"Hey, you got a name?" he called out.

His answer was the slamming of a car door.

He waited with his arms crossed over his chest as the silver CRV sped out of the lot.

Then Judge smiled.

Until he saw it had New York plates.

That meant she was just a tourist and not new in town.

"Fuck," he muttered, smoothed out his beard, and grimaced.

He shook his head and headed across the street to the diner, bracing for his ass to be ridden hard for striking out.

Chapter Two

JUDGE GAVE his girl a little gas and cursed himself for riding his sled to work today. The weather could go either way in December and today was definite nutsicle weather. In truth, it was time to park the Softail for the winter. Which sucked. But in northern Pennsylvania, it was reality.

At least all the Fury members could park their sleds inside a huge shed on the farm. It gave him a little comfort to have it nearby in case of an unseasonably warm winter day since he preferred his sled over his Expedition. Unfortunately, he needed his Ford for two reasons. Bad weather and for hauling around the dogs.

Usually their American Bulldogs, Jury and Justice, were with him and Deke at Justice Bail Bonds during the day, so one or the other had to drive a cage to haul their hairy, farting asses. Most of the time, Deke got stuck doing it.

Today was one of those days since he'd had an itch to straddle his big girl even if the weather was as cold as a witch's tit.

The rumble of his straight pipes rattled the shop windows along the strip mall as he headed through the parking lot toward Walmart at the opposite end of the shopping center. He needed to grab another box of wraps.

Since going up that mountain, he'd been burning through them lately because he'd been burning through sweet butts.

There wasn't a lot of pussy hanging around The Barn yet. A half dozen or so.

Usually when one showed up and stuck, she told her friends. That meant soon there'd be more. Until then, unless he searched elsewhere, he was stuck with who they had. And he really didn't want to search elsewhere.

That could get fucking sticky.

Sweet butts knew the deal. Some hang-arounds did, too, though they held out more hope of sinking their claws into a brother and wearing a "Property of" cut.

If Judge looked for pussy outside of the MC, he'd want to keep it casual and usually women had a problem with casual. Might start off that way, saying they'd be fine with the arrangement. Until they weren't.

And then it got to the sticky part. The part where it took an industrial strength scraper to scrape them off.

So, for now, if it wasn't a sweet butt who knew her place within the club, then it was his fist. Or his Fleshlight, which he preferred over his fist, sometimes even over pussy.

No need to kick anyone out of his bed after busting a nut into that. No wraps needed, either. Just a little soap and warm water for cleanup.

But still... He needed wraps because Whip's ex-girlfriend Billie, who decided to stick around after Whip tossed her cheating ass to the curb, had made him an offer he couldn't refuse for tonight.

And, *fuck it*, he jumped on it because Billie wasn't a clinger. She'd stick around only long enough for them both to get off a couple times, and then she'd jet before even having to be told to get the fuck out. She also kept her pussy clean. That was a big fucking stickler for him and had been ever since he'd been sixteen.

Only problem with Billie was, she wasn't Judge's type at all, so she had to work a little harder with her mouth to get him ready. Good thing she sucked dick like a pro.

She had short black hair, loads of crazy makeup to give her that dark, goth look, and her clothing was the same dark style. She had all kinds of piercings—which Judge kind of liked, especially the ones in her tongue, hood and nipples—and she liked it rough.

The last part he didn't mind. To a point.

He wondered how Whip met her. Because he didn't seem the type to be into that, either.

Judge mentally shrugged. He was pretty fucking sure some of his brothers had some hidden kinks. He didn't give a fuck as long as they weren't directed at him. While he didn't mind double-tagging a woman, he wasn't taking dick in his mouth or getting it up the ass himself.

Judge turned his sled down an aisle and spotted an empty parking spot.

That wasn't all he spotted.

A silver piece of shit CRV with New York plates.

Behind it was a woman who was definitely his type.

He didn't like little.

He didn't like petite.

He needed tall and solid—since he was big himself—and lots of flesh to hold onto as he pounded it out. He loved to grab handfuls of tits and ass and to shove his face between thick thighs. If he could still breathe while eating pussy, she was too thin for him.

Fuck. Blondie was what he'd been hankering for. Not someone like Billie.

And though he was there to pick up wraps, he doubted the woman with the overflowing cart of groceries would be willing to share one with him.

And that was a fucking shame.

But he wondered how long she was staying in town and if he could convince her otherwise.

He slipped his sled into a spot in the next row, dismounted, and wove around a couple of cars to stand behind her.

"Need help?"

She squeaked, dropped the bag she'd been holding and a can of something rolled out, bouncing off his boot. He nabbed it. Cranberry sauce. The jellied kind he loved when his aunt had served it at Thanksgiving.

He hadn't had it in fuckever.

In fact, he'd love to smear that shit all over the blonde's huge tits, which looked even bigger in that tight V-neck sweater she was wearing, and lick it the fuck off.

Damn.

No time to get a raging hard-on. She was scared enough.

"That's a fuck of a lot of food." She'd already loaded a few plastic bags into the back of the Honda and still had a cartful. Maybe it wasn't just Daisy and her and she had a big family to feed.

If so, there went his fucking fantasy.

"Y-yes."

"Feedin' an army?"

Color rose into her cheeks and he liked seeing it. But the problem was, it wasn't because she was embarrassed, it was because she still seemed to be afraid of him.

Or at least worried.

Maybe she should be. While he tried to concentrate on her full cart of groceries, he kept imagining what she'd look like naked as she rode his dick, those tits of hers bouncing like two watermelons in the back of an Amish wagon.

Her brow furrowed. "Um... Christmas is coming up."

That didn't tell him what he needed to know. "Here to visit with family for the holidays?"

"Y-Yes. Something like that."

When he held out the can of cranberry sauce to her, he again could see her hand shaking as she reached for it. Instead of letting it go right away, he let his fingers brush hers. She snatched the can from him, quickly breaking the contact.

He jerked his chin toward the cart. "Why ain't your man here to help you?"

"He... He... He..." Her lips, which would look good wrapped around his dick, pressed flat.

"Got a stutter or somethin'?"

She shook her head. Her next inhale was like watching two huge balloons inflate under her open winter coat. Her expression became painful. "He's... gone."

Judge's brow dropped low. "What d'you mean, gone?"

When her blue eyes hit his they were filled with turmoil and he felt that to his fucking core.

"He's just gone."

What the fuck did that mean? "He get the cancer?"

She frowned. "No."

Judge began to gather the handles of the bags in his fingers until he had almost all of them. He lifted them and set them into the back of her SUV.

"I..." She grabbed two of the last remaining bags and tossed them with the rest. "I need to get back."

Judge made sure to grab the last one because once all of her groceries were loaded, she had no reason to stay.

And he wasn't done talking to her yet. He stared at the bottom lip caught between her teeth as she stared at the lone bag in his hand with almost a conflicted expression.

It pissed him off that he'd been nothing but nice to her and her girl and she still acted afraid of him.

Why?

Because he was big? Or because he was a biker?

"I need to go. I have frozen items that..." She plucked the last bag from his fingers, tossed it into the back of her CRV and slammed the hatch shut. She yanked her purse out of the cart, dug her keys out and shoved it securely over her shoulder. Judge did not miss her tucking a key between each finger.

A technique women tended to use to protect themselves when walking alone to their cages.

Was he that fucking threatening?

When she went to roll the cart to the nearby corral, he stood in front of it, blocking her path and putting a hand on it.

"Where's your girl?"

"She's... with my sister."

"That who you're visitin'?"

"I..." Her eyes narrowed and her mouth got tight. "Thank you for your help. But I have to go." She released the cart's handle and went to the driver's door, climbing in and immediately starting the SUV. "Thank you for putting the cart away."

Well, damn. "Hey, what's your name?"

His answer was the door slamming shut. He was still standing behind the cage with the cart, so she couldn't reverse out of the spot. Instead, she put it in drive and pulled forward through the empty spot in front of her.

"Fuck," he muttered as she sped away.

He still didn't know her fucking name, why she was in town or how long she was staying. Instead, he had nothing but an empty cart, that he did not need to haul the single box of wraps he was buying.

A blacked-out Ford F250 pulled up next to him, and the dark-tinted power window whirred down.

Deacon grinned at him. And he wasn't the only one

amused, so were the two dogs. Jury whimpered in the passenger seat, her tongue hanging out of the side of her mouth.

"Strike out again?"

Fuck.

"Means she ain't for you, cuz."

"Thought you were headed back to The Barn."

"I am. Just wanted to ask you to get a box of wraps for me, too."

"Coulda texted me."

"Coulda, but spotted you across the parking lot talkin' to that blonde again and decided to watch."

"Great," Judge muttered under his breath.

Deacon chuckled. "Grab me a box of Magnums."

"You don't fuckin' need Magnums."

"And you won't need any wraps if you keep strikin' the fuck out." The window rolled shut and Deke pulled away.

Asshole.

"You didn't have to do this, Cass."

Cassidy put the last of the bags onto the counter and turned toward her younger sister. "Yes, I did. It's the least I can do."

Heather shrugged one shoulder and began to unpack a bag. "You're not obligated."

"I feel bad crashing here. And you paid, I just did the heavy lifting." Her sister hated grocery shopping, so that was the least Cassie could do to help out around the house.

"You're my sister."

"Yes, and you're my baby sister. And it's not just me staying here, it's Daisy, who can be hell on wheels."

"What does that mean, Momma?"

Cassie frowned, not realizing her daughter had snuck into the kitchen. When her daughter was quiet like that, she worried. Normally Daisy made sure *everyone* knew where she was and why.

Heather snorted. "It's fine."

"I don't want to cramp your style... Interfere with..." Cassie raised her eyebrows and didn't finish since big ears were now settled at the kitchen table with a coloring book and crayons. Daisy might look like she was occupied, but Cassie knew her daughter was absorbing every word like a sponge.

"Yeah, well... We'll just get you two ear plugs for the time being," Heather teased.

Her twenty-eight-year-old sister had only married her husband a year ago and since Tyler was forty, they'd decided not to wait to start a family. That meant, they'd been working on it and now with two more people in the household...

"Tyler's parents are coming, right?" Cassie asked.

"Yep. And his brother, sister-in-law and nephew."

"So that's nine of us for Christmas." She shoved a gallon of milk into the already full fridge. "I hope I got enough."

"If not, we can do another run. We've got plenty of time and space since I've got an extra fridge plus a full-size freezer in the garage for when Ty hunts."

Cassie paused. "What about..."

Heather's hand stilled and her blue eyes hit Cassie's. "I talked to Mom and Dad yesterday..." She shook her head.

"I had nothing to do with it," Cassie forced the whisper past the lump in her throat.

"*I* know that, but they refuse to believe it. They don't understand how you couldn't have known."

"I didn't know!"

Heather came over to her and put a hand on her arm.

"Cass, I know. I know you would never do anything like that."

"I'm their daughter. Why don't they believe me?" Her parents not having her back hurt more than everything else that happened.

Heather shook her head again. "I don't know. You would've been," her sister mouthed the word *arrested* before continuing, "too, if the," she mouthed *investigators*, "thought you were. They found no," she mouthed *evidence*, "of that."

No shit. Cassie knew all of that. When everything went down it had been the scariest moments of her life. The rug had been pulled from under her and she had been left trying to make sense of it all.

"But the 'rents are getting a lot of sh— *crap* from people they know because of it. Maybe once that all dies down and it's old news, they'll see things more clearly."

If it took for everything to die down and become old news, Cassie wasn't sure she'd ever forgive her parents. They should believe her now. Currently, they were blaming Cassie for everything that happened and everything *they* had to deal with.

Like being ashamed and embarrassed.

Well, she was ashamed and embarrassed, too.

Because of that whole damn thing, she also had to leave her job and her home in New York and come to Manning Grove to avoid some of the shit that had splattered all over her.

She'd already decided she wasn't going back there ever again. She'd need to find a fresh start for her and Daisy elsewhere. A place no one knew who they were. Or who she'd been married to or who Daisy's father was.

She just didn't know yet where that would be.

In the meantime, her sister and brother-in-law, Tyler, were kind enough to take them in. Cassie just felt bad about putting them out. Especially since they were still in their "honeymoon" phase.

She turned and glanced over at her daughter, who was her clone. It was during her own honeymoon when Daisy was conceived.

At the time, Cassie couldn't have been happier. She had a loving husband, a baby on the way and a good job that made use of her vet tech degree. She thought things were perfect.

And they were.

For a little while.

She needed to stop feeling sorry for herself, deal with the hand she was dealt and find a way to move on. However, there was no going back to New York, her job or her marriage.

And, apparently, the disgraced daughter couldn't go home to her parents, either.

With a sigh, she stuck her hand into another shopping bag and pulled out a can of cranberry sauce. One that had a huge dent in the top. She rubbed her finger back and forth over the indentation, thinking about the big biker who had approached her in the parking lot.

Judge.

She'd only been in town a week and she'd already run into him twice in just as many days.

She turned to Heather who was putting away a couple boxes of cereal. "Do you know anything about some sort of local motorcycle club?"

Heather closed the cabinet door, turned and leaned back against the counter. With their similar looks, there was no doubt Heather was her sister. Both were tall, blonde, and curvy like their mother. Daisy would end up the same.

"In the last year, there's been talk about them and I've seen them around town. So far, they haven't created any trouble. At least, not that I've heard. Did some of them bother you?"

"I saw a bunch of them yesterday in town and Daisy ran up to one to introduce herself."

Heather snorted. "That doesn't surprise me."

Cassie sighed. "Yes, this is why she'll end up being abducted from right under my nose. She'll flag down the da — *darn* van and hitch a ride just so she can tell them stories or tell them how they should drive since at five she's already a backseat driver with all her years of driving experience."

Heather's smirk died as she slid closer along the counter and asked softly, "Were they rude?"

"Who? The bikers? Besides a couple of catcalls, no. But I only really talked to one."

"The one Daisy ran up to?"

"Yes."

"You talkin' about Judge, Momma?"

"Judge?" Heather asked, frowning.

"Yes! Judge is my friend now. He's gonna let me pet his face."

Heather's eyes shot to Cassie's. "He is, huh?"

Cassie pinned her lips together and gave her head a little shake.

"Yes! Momma said I wasn't allowed to last time because we only just became friends. But next time, I'm allowed."

"You are?"

"Yes!" her daughter shouted needlessly.

"Why would you want to pet his face?"

"'Cause he's got *allllllllll* this long hair just like a dog! And Momma won't let me have a dog!" She ended her complaint on a loud huff.

"Well, young lady, I don't think petting a man's beard is appropriate," her aunt told her.

"I don't care if it's not a... pah... apopiate."

"Do you even know what that means?" Heather asked, clearly smothering a laugh.

"No, an' I don't care, 'cause I'm doin' it next time I see Judge."

"You need to ask me first, Daze," Cassie reminded her spitfire of a daughter.

Daisy rolled her eyes.

"And if I give the okay, then you'd have to ask Judge after that." But it would never get that far because there was no way Cassie was giving Daisy permission to touch a stranger like that.

Her daughter turned back to her coloring and said, "He'll say yes."

"Don't be so sure."

"*Mommmmmmmma!*"

"Oh good lord," Cassie groaned. "If he says no, then that's the final answer."

"He won't."

Cassie *hmm*'d.

"He won't!" Daisy screamed.

"Inside voice, please."

"That *is* my inside voice." Unfortunately, that was true more often than not.

Cassie sighed and turned back to the last of the groceries.

Heather reached out and stopped her. "That can wait." She jerked her head toward the door to the back porch.

Cassie glanced at her daughter. "Aunt Heather and I have to run back out to the car. You're going to sit right there and color, right?"

"Mmm hmm," came the answer.

Cassie made a face and Heather slapped a hand over her mouth to muffle her laugh. They headed out the rear kitchen door and stepped into the attached sunroom.

"Seriously," Cassie started as they stepped away from the

door so Daisy wouldn't hear them. "She's not enough to make you want to rip out your womb?"

Her sister laughed. "She's a trip."

"Just wait a couple more weeks and you may stop trying to make one of your very own."

"She's no worse than we were."

"Were we like that?" Cassie asked, surprised.

"You tell me, you're the older sibling."

"I don't remember being so outspoken."

"Cass, you're no introvert. Neither of us are. We're just like Mom." Heather walked to the other side of the small sunroom and turned. "Have you heard from him at all?"

Cassie grimaced. "No. And I really doubt I will."

"Damn. This is crazy."

"I know. And until he signs the divorce papers, I'm stuck. All our assets were frozen, my car was taken, our house was taken. I have no money! Not even my own. And I'm afraid if I start a new bank account, that will be frozen, also." Why she was rehashing all this, she didn't know. But sometimes she needed to vent, otherwise she might crack.

"What are you going to do?"

"Well, I need to decide whether I'm staying here in Manning Grove or going somewhere else. But I don't know how to do that after losing everything. Even if I had money, I can't buy anything because it'll be seized!"

She had even lost her damn dignity.

Cassie bit back a frustrated sob. Heather already knew all of this, it was why she so generously offered up her home when their parents refused to help.

At least temporarily.

And it wasn't like her parents owed her anything. They didn't, but still... If Daisy was ever in a bind, she wouldn't slam the door in her daughter's face.

But she also didn't know if she wanted to settle in Manning Grove. From what she saw so far, it seemed nice, but she questioned living in a town and raising her daughter where a motorcycle gang existed.

She didn't know much about MCs but from what she did know, they were normally a rough and violent lot. She'd seen the Hells Angels and the Pagans in the news before. She knew gangs like that were nothing to mess with.

And Cassie didn't want to live in fear. If it was just her, she could handle it, but she had Daisy who didn't fear anything.

"Cass, we love it here. The schools are good. It's a great town to raise Daisy in. Find a job, and once you put away enough money, find a place of your own."

"I'm afraid any money I'll earn they'll seize."

Heather shrugged. "So, don't open a bank account yet."

"Well, what do I do with a paycheck?"

"Cash it."

"If they don't garnish it first to pay back his debts. I could end up working for free. And that wouldn't help me get my life back in order."

"*Oooooor* you could find a job that pays you in cash until your divorce is final or that little situation is settled."

"It's not a *little* situation and I can't get a divorce until he signs the damn papers."

"Right. And therein lies the problem." Heather groaned. "I'm so sorry, sis. God, I loved Dennis, too. I thought you two were perfect for each other."

"You weren't the only one. I feel so stupid for not seeing what was right in front of my face."

"It wasn't in front of your face, Cass, so don't blame yourself. As soon as you realized there was a major problem, you kicked his ass out."

"I should've sold the house immediately." She didn't because she needed a place to raise Daisy, and while she discovered the one problem, she didn't know about the even bigger one.

"You didn't know."

"Fuck," Cassie bit off. "How could I be so blind?"

"Those types of people know how to hide things well. You're not the first wife to be duped and you won't be the last. At least you and Daisy have a roof over your head, and we love having you here."

"For now."

Heather shrugged again. "For as long as you need."

"I'll go out and start searching for a job."

"It's going to be tough since jobs aren't plentiful up here, especially ones that pay under the table. I doubt the Amish are hiring since they usually raise their own workforce."

"Maybe Daisy and I can go panhandle at the center of town." Cassie laughed. "She could talk anyone into throwing us a spare dollar."

Heather laughed, too. "Not sure the police would like that since they do their best to keep this a family-friendly, wholesome place."

"Yeah, and Daisy would be sent up river for resisting arrest. I could see her running from them and screaming 'fuck the police!' at the top of her little lungs."

Heather bent over, howling.

Cassie was laughing so hard, she was crying. But it felt good. It had been a long time since she'd been able to simply laugh like that.

Most of the time she wanted to just sit in a corner and cry. Normally, she was not the self-pity type of person.

"*Mommmmaaa.*"

Cassie wiped the tears away and saw her daughter standing in the open doorway. "Yes, baby?"

"What's so funny?"

"Your momma told a joke," Heather answered Daisy, moving toward Cassie. "We'll be right in."

Daisy harrumphed like an eighty-year-old woman and

disappeared back inside, slamming the door shut behind her.

Heather jerked her into a hug. And while Cassie appreciated her sister's support, that hug made the happy tears turn sad.

"It'll all work out, I promise," Heather murmured into her hair. "There's nowhere to go now but up."

Cassie sure as hell hoped so.

Chapter Three

THE FRONT DOOR buzzer sounded and both dogs tore from reclining at Judge's feet out to the front of the shop in zero-to-sixty seconds flat.

"Yo! Just me," came the holler. Not that it was needed, the dogs' barks were enough of an indicator who was walking in. Right now, they were whining and yipping. If it had been a stranger, their barks would be more serious.

Judge tipped his office chair back, looked up at the ceiling and blew out a breath. Then he scraped a hand over the freshly buzzed hair on his head.

Deacon leaned against the door frame to Judge's office. "Damn, hope you didn't pay a fuckin' dime for that buzz job. It's as short as my nut hairs."

"Didn't think you had any yet. Or that your fuckin' balls even dropped. The other night Billie was tellin' me she went to suck 'em and couldn't find 'em."

Deke grinned. "Don't get what she saw in Whip, but whatever. Glad she stuck around. When I'm itchin' for some weird shit, she's always into it."

"She told me that to find your balls, she needs to jam a finger up your ass." Judge jabbed one of his thick fingers into the air. "Then she's gotta hurry up and catch 'em in her mouth before they disappear back into your vagina."

"Damn, look at you usin' all the big words, like vagina. Can you even spell it?"

"Yeah. D-E-A-C-O-N."

Deke snorted, dropped his head and shook it.

Jury and Justice pushed past Deke and back into the office. Jury immediately planted her head in Judge's lap for her required ear scratches.

Judge never denied her. She was the only steady bitch he ever wanted in his life. She'd never fuck him over like the two-legged kind.

"Any leads on that asshole?" Judge asked him.

Deacon moved into the office and dropped onto the couch along the opposite wall, kicking his boots up on the armrest and crossing his ankles. He twisted his head to stare at Judge, while Justice immediately jumped up and settled all eighty pounds of bulldog on Deke's chest.

"Damn, dude, how many times I told you, you ain't a Chihuahua." But like normal, Deke didn't push his dog off, instead he wrapped his arms around Justice holding him close. "Just watch the junk," he warned the dog and turned to Judge again. "Yeah. Talked to a couple people in Williamsport who said they saw him. Gonna head back that way again tomorrow. Plus, gave them my number in case they spot him."

"Got three days left to get his ass in front of that judge, Deke."

His cousin shot him a thumbs up and began to ruffle Justice's ears. "Who's a *gooooood booooooy*?"

"You, if you catch that fucker."

Deke raised an eyebrow. "Have I ever failed you before?"

"You wanna fuckin' list?"

Deke grimaced and kissed Justice on the nose. The dog, in turn, licked Deke's mouth.

"Fuckin' dude." Judge fake gagged. "He licks his fuckin' balls all the time."

Deke shot him a smile. "Don't be a hater."

"For him stickin' his tongue in your mouth? Or for him bein' able to lick his fuckin' balls?"

"Both."

"Probably put peanut butter on yours."

Deke snorted. "Which is it? I don't have any, or I have 'em and make buckeyes outta them?"

"What the fuck are buckeyes?"

Deke's brown eyes went wide. "The peanut butter balls dipped in chocolate... Wait... Mom never made 'em for you?"

"If she had, wouldn't be fuckin' askin'."

Deke grinned and folded his arms under his head. "Well, damn, Mom *does* like me better."

"Maybe. Maybe not. Ever get the shits after eatin' any of those buckeyes? Maybe that's why she never made 'em for me. I could be the son she never had."

"Damn, that's fuckin' cold."

"Anyway... Get that motherfucker and drag his ass in. Got a call 'bout an hour ago from a bail bondsman up in New York."

Deke pushed Justice off him and sat up. "For what?"

"Got a fucker who skipped on him and he figured since we're licensed to hunt, he'd throw the job our way. White collar crime. Shouldn't be hard to nab his ass. Can probably find 'im out in front of Starbucks drivin' a Volvo."

"Why us?"

"'Cause the wifey also skipped town."

Deke shook his head. "Yeah, and?"

"Yeah, and... She landed in Manning Grove."

"So, she's not on the lam."

"No. My guess? She's here probably puttin' things in order for him. The bondsman's figurin' the hubby might show up soon, if he's not in town already."

"Sounds too easy."

"No shit. And he offered twenty fuckin' percent of the bond if we get his ass. All we gotta do is hold him 'til the bondsman gets down here to haul him back up to Rochester."

"We got nowhere to hold someone."

"Sure we do. Not one of the rooms in the bunkhouse out at the farm got windows. We could throw him in an empty room and lock him the fuck in."

Deke pursed his lips and ran a hand down his long mohawk braid. "Sounds like a plan. Want me to sit on the wifey? Or find the other asshole first?"

"Door number fuckin' two. Time's runnin' out on him first. We got more time on this new one. But the bondsman's gonna email the address of the fugitive's sister-in-law. He's pretty fuckin' sure that's where wifey ended up. I can swing by there later and see what I see. Maybe confirm she's there and then, if needed, get Easy to sit on the house on overnights."

"Easy's trainin' with the vet on the Easy Bake Ovens," Deacon reminded him.

"Fuck," Judge growled.

"Yeah. Someone needs to know what the fuck they're doin' when we start..." Deke covered Justice's ears and whispered, "When we start incineratin' you-know-whats." He released the dog's ears.

"Fuck."

"Yeah. Right now, Shady and Easy are learnin' how to run the furnaces while the state paperwork's bein' processed."

"How fuckin' hard can it be?"

Deke shrugged. "Regulations and shit, I guess. But it's

more than that. Maintenance, required paperwork and other shit, too."

Judge's hand began to rub Jury's ears even faster at the thought of having her turned to ashes when she...

Fuck, he wasn't going to think about it. Not now.

"Got a name and shit?" Deke asked, switching back to the original topic, since he, like Judge, didn't like talking about their dogs ever needing to be cremated.

"He's emailin' me all that. Names, pics, along with the address to the house wifey might be holed up in."

"How soon?"

Judge frowned. "Shoulda had it by now."

"Did you check your fuckin' email?"

Judge cocked an eyebrow at Deke. "That what I gotta do, asshole?"

Deacon smirked. "Yeah, you gotta open your email to be able to read 'em."

"Thank fuck you're so fuckin' smart."

"Check. I'm curious what they look like. I can keep an eye open when I'm out and about. And send the pics to everyone else. Just in case. More eyes, the easier it'll be to spot 'em."

"Was plannin' to do that already. Don't act like you're the only one with a fuckin' brain in this place," Judge grumbled as he leaned forward and shook the mouse to his PC and woke up the screen.

The photo on his desktop screen always made him pause. It was the day he and Deke went to pick out Justice and Jury from the litter. They'd been eight weeks old at the time and cute as fuck.

Deke had gone to look at the pups after his old Doberman died. For the fuck of it, Judge went along, not planning on coming home with a little girl of his own. It was the best thing he'd done in a long time. He couldn't imagine life without her now.

He double clicked his email icon and a full inbox popped up.

What the fuck? He had like thirty new emails. He hated computers. Deacon was better with them but using one was necessary for the business they were in. So, he suffered through it.

However, he must have forgotten to check the business email in...

A week.

Shit.

"It there?" Deacon asked.

Judge quickly scrolled through the junk mail and some random inquiries, until he found the one from the bail bondsman in New York. "Yep."

He double clicked the email and it opened, filling his screen. It had a bunch of attachments, which included copies of the bond and all the paperwork. Then in the body of the email it listed some names.

Fugitive: Dennis LANGE – LKL Rochester, NY.

Wife: Cassidy LANGE – LKL Manning Grove, PA.

It also included an address for Heather and Tyler Douglas.

"So, last known location for the wife is right here in town on Fourth Avenue at the Douglases. Know 'em?"

"Nope." Deacon scratched at his beard. "They on the good side of the tracks?"

"Yeah." Manning Grove had a small seedy area on the other side of the tracks. It included a sketchy rooming house. It also was the area Judge had grown up in. At least until he was sixteen. And it was where the Fury-owned Grove Inn was located. The town council had been trying to "clean up" that area for a long time, but it had been a slow-fucking-go. They acted like it was some kind of ghetto when it was only lower income families and more affordable rentals.

"Pics?"

"Yeah," Judge murmured and clicked on the first one. Dennis Lange's photo popped up large and in living color. He didn't look like a hard-core criminal. In fact, he was wearing a suit in the mugshot. He clicked another photo and a smaller driver's license photo popped up. The man had to be in his mid-thirties. His hair was neat, he wore glasses, no tats. Just a typical nine-to-five sucker.

No prior record, either, from the info Judge skimmed over.

"Fuck yeah, bet this asshole drives that fuckin' Volvo, stops at Starbucks every morning, then makes an excuse to work late every night and is dickin' his secretary."

"You can tell all that from his photo?" Deke ribbed.

"Fuck yeah." Judge tapped his temple. "Can see right through these assholes. Don't ever think they'll get caught 'til they do. Then they get a high-dollar lawyer and get a fuckin' slap on the wrist."

"Well, he skipped, so thinkin' it wasn't gonna be a slap on the wrist. More like a slap on the ass when he's bendin' over and takin' it up the poop shoot in the joint."

"Yeah, he probably don't like dick up the ass. From the pic, it looks like there's a stick up there already takin' up all that tight real estate. Damn. Virgin ass. No wonder he skipped. Wasn't ready to get his ass cherry popped."

"And if he's a pretty boy, he probably would."

"You're better at judgin' that than me," Judge murmured, closing the pictures and double-clicking on the next one marked *C. Lange.*

The large color photo opened, and Judge's head jerked back, his mouth opened and he blinked.

What the fuck?

What the fuck!

Holy fuck!

Bright blue eyes stared back at him.

He shifted the photo over a little with his mouse and glanced again at the email.

Wife: Cassidy LANGE – LKL Manning Grove, PA.

Wife.

Cassidy Lange.

Last known location: Manning Grove, PA.

No fucking shit.

Wife.

He squeezed his eyes shut and his hands automatically went back to Jury's blocky head. She groaned in encouragement as he rubbed her ears.

The woman he saw in town was fucking with his head. Shouldering in on his thoughts.

The woman who caused him to cancel his "fuck date" last night because she was what he wanted, not Billie.

Because...

She...

Fuck.

He opened his eyes again and wasn't imagining it. Was he?

"Deke." Deacon's name got caught in his throat. He cleared it and tried again. "Deacon."

"Yeah?"

"C'mere and tell me if I'm hallucinatin'."

"You toke some spiked shit earlier?"

"Ain't toked a fuckin' thing all day."

"Bad Chinese?" His cousin surged to his feet and strode over to the desk.

"Ain't eaten shit yet."

"Maybe your blood sugar's low," Deacon suggested with a snort as he stepped around the desk. "Big asshole like you — *Oh fuuuuck.*"

"You seein' what I'm seein'?" Because in the last three days he'd been thinking about her a lot.

A. Lot.

Like close his eyes and nut in his Fleshlight, pretending it was the blonde's tight, wet pussy a lot.

Like whacking off in the shower to fantasies of those tits and ass a lot.

He'd been pretty much obsessed with her since the second he saw her in the municipal parking lot on Sunday.

And seeing her again in front of Walmart hadn't helped.

But now he had a good reason to let that obsession—and hope of getting a piece of that—go.

Damn.

Having a kid was baggage but like the carry-on size.

Having a kid and a husband was also baggage, but like a whole luggage set.

Having a kid *and* a bail-skipping husband was a shipping container full of shit. And of the loose diarrhea type. The kind you needed a half roll of toilet paper to wipe up.

"Well, there's the real reason you struck out, cuz. Wasn't your ugly mug and monster size. She ain't interested in your baby carrot dick 'cause she's already gettin' it elsewhere. Or she was before he got popped." Deacon leaned past him, grabbed the mouse and clicked on the court documents. "What he get busted for?" The document opened, blocking Cassidy Lange's, *wife* of Dennis Lange, picture.

Wife of Dennis the felon.

Judge skimmed the document.

"Oh damn," Deke murmured.

Judge sat back in his chair.

"There's low and then there's *goin'-to-hell* low. This fucker's gonna burn."

Judge brushed his palm slowly back and forth over the top of his head thinking the same thing.

"Wonder what happened to all the money?" Deke took a step back, then moved around to the other side of the desk, crossing his arms over his chest. "Want this job, Judge."

"No."

"Yeah, wanna catch this fucker. I'd even do it for free."

"No. We ain't doin' shit for free."

"Catchin' this fucker might keep me outta hell."

"It won't. Too late for either of us."

Deke blew out a breath. "Think she was in on it?"

Jesus. If she was... "Dunno. But gonna find out."

"Let me take it," he insisted.

"Got a job to finish first."

"Then I'm headin' back to Williamsport tonight and gonna hunt that fucker down so I can hop on this motherfucker."

"Shoulda been doin' that in the first place, you asshole," Judge growled at his cousin.

"Wasn't in a rush."

"You had three fuckin' days left, Deke."

"Yeah, *three* days. Plenty of time."

Judge shot him a look.

Deke shrugged and shot him a smile back. "Got motivation now."

"The money should've been motivation before."

"Fuckin' Dad died of the goddamn cancer, Judge."

Judge sucked air in through his nose and held it. "Was there, Deke."

"Yeah, and you know how bad it was."

Something he'd never forget. The cancer rotted his uncle from the inside out. It hit them all hard.

Even in the couple of years Judge lived with Deke's parents, his Uncle Walter ended up being a better father than Ox ever was. In fact, Walter practiced tough love and never once hesitated to knock some sense into Judge or Deacon.

Ox would get pissed because 5-0 brought Judge home, not because of breaking curfew. In contrast, Walt thanked the pigs for bringing him home, waited until they left and then taught Judge a lesson about breaking curfew. At sixteen, Judge had fought back once.

Once was all it took.

Judge never fought back again.

But it was those two years under Walt's roof that taught Judge a bit of respect and showed him a good reason to keep his ass out of jail.

He had Walt to thank for all of that. Because Judge had no doubt if it wasn't for Walt and his methods, he'd have ended up in and out of the joint just like Sig, the Fury's VP.

Walt also wasn't having any of Judge dragging his only son into trouble. Or teaching him bad habits.

So, any bad habits Deke had were strictly his own, nothing learned from Judge.

Judge wasn't the only kid in that household who got his ass whooped hard for doing shit he wasn't supposed to do. Though, it worked since Deke never landed behind bars, either.

Basically, by learning how to avoid Walt catching them taught them both not to be caught by the pigs. So, yeah, while at the time, those lessons sucked, he now really appreciated Walt's strict ways.

And so did Deke.

His cousin was now heading toward the door. "Headin' back to Williamsport. Take care of Justice 'til I get back, yeah?"

Judge raised an eyebrow. "When have you ever had to ask?"

"Never. But strikin' out with blondie has had you distracted."

Judge couldn't deny that. "Cassidy," he said under his breath.

"Yeah, Cassidy. Whatever. Doesn't fuckin' matter what her name is now. Now you know she's off fuckin' limits. Got a ball and chain who will soon be behind bars again."

"If we catch him," Judge grumbled.

"We'll get him if he puts one fuckin' foot in the Grove," Deke said with too much confidence.

"Right."

"Though, once he starts his sentence, the wifey might need a bit of comfortin'." Deke wiggled his eyebrows. "You got some pretty fuckin' big shoulders for her to cry on, cuz. All you gotta do is whisper somethin' sweet in her ear, pat her on the fuckin' back and maybe she'll let you stick your baby carrot cock in her snatch."

"Deke."

"Yeah?" he asked with a grin.

"Get the fuck outta here before I club you with my baby carrot of a cock."

Deke laughed and squatted down, patting his thigh. "Jussie, come say goodbye to your daddy."

Justice ran over to him, tail wagging. Deke planted a big kiss on his blocky head and got to his feet. "Be back soon."

"Sooner than later, Deke."

"Yeah." He disappeared from the office with a flick of two fingers.

Judge turned back to the computer and after reading through the documents more thoroughly, he opened Cassidy Lange's picture again.

Cassidy.

He wondered how involved the woman had been with her husband's crime. He wondered if she had more kids than just Daisy.

He also wondered why she'd skipped town and landed in Manning Grove. She never gave him her name, so she could be using a false one. Maybe it was just as he suspected, and she was in town to set up a place for hubby to hide. Or this was just a place to meet up before heading elsewhere.

Hell, a man like that with what he did, was facing up to twenty-five years. That was before he skipped bond.

Men like that were afraid of doing time.

Men like that were afraid of losing all their shit.

Men like that usually lost their wives and children.

So, men like Dennis Lange might have figured skipping out would be for the best.

Only problem was with men like that, they weren't really smart enough to do it well.

He'd probably want to head out of the country to hide. If he didn't have any connections, doing that wasn't easy. But Pennsylvania wasn't far enough away from New York to hide successfully, even if he changed his hair color and his name.

Nope. He was way too close to home.

So, maybe she was just in town temporarily. To try to have a normal holiday with her kid. Or kids.

Before they all went on the run.

Hell, maybe hubby was waiting on her somewhere else.

Or maybe Dennis Lange would show up for Christmas with the family.

And if he did, Justice Bail Bonds was going to get a nice fat deposit into their bank account after they caught his ass and handed him over.

Deke was right. Once hubby went down for twenty-five years, was Cassidy going to stick by his side and be the loyal wife? Or would she be looking to move on?

Dennis Lange might wear a suit, not have any tattoos, even drive some fancy fucking car. But if he did what he was charged with? He was scum through and through.

Looks could be deceiving.

Chapter Four

JUDGE SAT in his Expedition two houses down from 52 Fourth Avenue. It was late. It was dark. And he couldn't get Cassidy Lange out of his mind.

He was supposed to be there keeping an eye out for Dennis Lange, not his wife. But he'd never been so goddamn fixated on a woman in his fucking life.

And, of fucking course, she had to be married.

To a white-collar criminal.

And had at least one kid with him.

That sucked donkey dick.

Judge took in the Christmas lights strung around the windows and porch. In one front window of the small two-story home, he also noticed a decorated tree lit up.

The silver Honda CRV with New York plates was parked out front on the street because a couple of other vehicles were parked in front of the detached two-car garage. Probably belonging to Mr. and Mrs. Douglas, the couple who could be harboring a fugitive.

If not now, maybe soon.

Because how long could hubby stay away from his wife and kid? Especially during the holidays. Unless the man was just that self-centered and didn't give a flying fuck about them. Maybe he did his crime, got caught and then left her dealing with the mess left behind.

Because it had been a mess.

After Deke had left for Williamsport, Judge had done a bunch of online searches on the case.

Not only were the people of Rochester outraged, but all of New York, too. *Hell*, the whole fucking country seemed to be screaming for blood once it hit national news.

Judge didn't pay much attention to the news unless it happened to be about one of his clients. Otherwise, he was fine with living in his own damn little world. Just him, his cousin, his sister, and his aunt.

Though, that little world had grown a lot with the Fury being resurrected. And as the club grew with prospects, members and ol' ladies, his world continued to expand. They also needed more prospects and soon. Nothing better than having one to do any dirty work needing done.

Like sitting on a house all fucking night, keeping an eye out for a bail jumper named Dennis Lange.

Judge sat up slightly as a dark figure slipped out the front door. Was that fucking Lange?

He hit the button on his seat, powering it fully upright as his eyes stayed glued to that figure.

Yeah, it was a Lange, but not of the male variety. This one had curves he recognized even under the hip-length coat.

Where the fuck was she going at this time of night?

Where was she going dressed like that when it was this cold? From what he could see, as she headed to where she was parked near a streetlight, she was only wearing PJ pants and heavy slippers under that coat.

He watched as she climbed into her Honda. Maybe she was just grabbing something. Then the brake lights illuminated and a second later, so did the headlights.

And like that, she drove away. *What the fuck?*

Where the fuck was she going? It was after eleven and she was alone.

It wasn't like Manning Grove was dangerous, but still... A woman alone at night...

Plenty of those inbred Shirleys still remained up on that fucking mountain. And until they were all gone, Judge didn't think any woman in the Grove was completely safe.

He hit the Start button on his Ford and put it in Drive, not turning his headlights on until she had disappeared around the corner. He followed her at a distance, just staying close enough to keep her taillights in his view.

She circled a couple of blocks like she was lost—or maybe trying to lose a tail—and then ended up on Main Street. Close to the end of town, she pulled off into an empty lot.

A scowl pulled at his mouth. It was the lot where the Fury's warehouse used to be. The warehouse that used to house the Original's church. The developer who'd bought it from Trip had completely leveled the building.

Judge pulled over to the curb on Main Street and stared at the lone CRV parked in a place that, if he allowed it, brought back memories.

Some good. Some bad.

But she had no ties to it. She had no history with the Fury that he knew of, which made Judge want to know what the fuck was going on. Why she had stopped there. In a place where there were no lights or people. Where she was alone in the dark.

The reverse lights flashed as she put the Honda into Park and a second later all the cage's lights went out. That meant she might be staying a while.

Was she meeting her husband there?

Was she meeting someone for a late-night fuck?

Judge shut down the Expedition and waited.

And waited.

She didn't get out of the Honda and no one else drove onto the lot.

He waited almost ten fucking minutes.

Nothing.

He needed to know what the fuck was going on with her.

Which bothered the shit out of him. Why was he so goddamn obsessed over her? A woman who belonged to someone else.

He had a job to do, that was it.

"Fuck," he muttered, getting out of his Ford and locking it.

He walked the half block down to the former warehouse lot. He hadn't stepped on that property in over twenty years, so a chill slid down his spine the second he did so. It was almost like stepping into the past.

The property was bigger than it looked from the street and all that remained of the old warehouse was a large pile of scrap metal in a back corner, the large concrete slab where that metal used to be erected, a dilapidated chain link fence surrounding the boundary, and the parking lot with pot holes so large, they would become little frozen ponds once the weather turned colder.

The whole thing was dark and fucking depressing.

He stepped carefully over the unlit, damaged pavement, making sure he didn't step into one of those holes and break something. Because at six-foot-three and two-forty—give or take a few pounds—when he fell, he fell hard.

As he approached the rear of the SUV, he glanced into the driver's side mirror, trying to get a bead on what she was doing. The interior was dark, but it looked like her face was tipped down and hidden by her hair.

Was she talking to someone on the phone? Was she talking to her husband?

He crept closer, his brow furrowed as her hands came up and covered her face. And he could now see she was shaking a bit.

His heart began to pound.

She tipped her head back, slammed it into the headrest and screamed so loudly, ice shot down his spine.

He rushed to the driver's door, yanked it open and she screamed again, this time with her eyes wide open and looking straight at him.

Her hand went to her heart and her chest rose and fell quickly as she stared at him. Her voice held a shake when she pleaded, "Please... don't hurt me... I have a daughter..."

"Ain't gonna hurt you. Jesus fuck. It's Judge."

Her mouth dropped open and when she snapped it shut, it turned into a deep frown. "You scared the hell out of me."

"Should always lock your fuckin' doors."

She pursed her lips and when she reached for the open door, he blocked it. "Get out of the way and I'll lock them."

"Too late. Anyone coulda snagged your ass, dragged you outta your cage and..." He let that drop. So many things could've happened to her. Too many things.

"Why are you here?" she asked, her eyes narrowed and now sounding more annoyed than scared.

"Why the fuck are *you* here?"

"Are you following me?"

Fuck.

She glanced in the rearview mirror. "Where's your motorcycle?"

"Too fuckin' cold for that."

"Then where's your car?"

Shit.

"You can't be simply strolling through town this late at night."

Shit.

"Is this normal in this town, for people to be all up in your business?"

Shit.

Now she was getting pissed.

"Can't I ever get a fucking moment alone?" she yelled, her voice breaking, and her fists now clenched around the steering wheel.

"That why you're here?"

"What business is it of yours?" she snapped.

Oh yeah, she was fucking pissed.

"Just a weird spot where you're parked."

"Are you a meter maid?" she yelled, but her voice broke a little.

Judge frowned and yanked on his beard. "This used to be club property."

She shook her head. "What club?"

"My club. My father's club."

"Your motorcycle gang?"

His jaw shifted. The Fury might have been an outlaw MC once, but no longer.

"Then I'll just go somewhere else if I'm trespassing."

"Don't gotta go nowhere."

"Then leave me the hell alone. Let me have my meltdown in peace."

A meltdown? "Why you havin' a meltdown?"

Her loud inhale was broken by a soft sob. "N-no reason."

"Bullshit."

She reached for the ignition and started the car. "I have to go."

"No, you don't."

"Yes, I do. I don't know you. You don't know me. I'm apparently trespassing. I'll go."

"You ain't trespassin'. If you need to have a meltdown, then fuckin' have it. Ain't gonna stop you."

She blinked at him. "Well, I'm not going to do it while you're standing there inside my car door. Why are you here?"

"Saw your cage and got worried."

"Cage?"

"Your Honda."

Her brow furrowed. "Why do you call it a cage?"

"Because it ain't a bike."

"I don't get it."

"Not for you to get."

"Why are you worried about me?"

"Because it's late, you're alone and upset."

"Right. The only one of those you should know about is the first one. You shouldn't be aware I'm alone *or* upset. That's none of your damn business."

"Here to meet someone?"

"Again, none of your business."

He was making her his business. "Why you havin' a meltdown?"

"Again, none of your business."

Jesus fuck. She could go suck her fucking husband's dick and choke on it for all he cared.

"You're fuckin' right, woman. Ain't none of my business. I'll go fuck off." He slammed the door shut and spun on his heel. He strode quickly through the dark.

Fuck that bitch.

That was what he got for giving a fucking shit. Kicked in the fucking nuts.

Judge had to jump out of the way when she put it in reverse so fast, she fishtailed and almost hit him.

"What the fuck!" he shouted at her.

She slammed on the brakes and powered down the driver's window. "I'm sorry."

"Ain't done nothin' to you and... Just... Fuck you." He

kept moving, a muscle popping in his jaw as he clenched his teeth.

He heard the driver's door open. "Hey!"

Without turning around, without stopping, he yelled, "Get the fuck in your car, lock your goddamn doors and get the fuck outta here."

"I'm sorry!" she screamed. "I'm... I'm..."

Then he heard it. A loud sob.

Another one.

And then a third.

His pace stuttered.

Fuckin' keep going, asshole. Don't let her get to you. She ain't nothin' but trouble. She's fuckin' married to your target. She's gettin' his dick, she don't want yours, you big dumb fuck.

"Thank you for checking on me." It wasn't loud, but he heard it.

Goddamn it. He stopped, dropped his head, took a deep breath and, after waiting a few seconds, he turned.

She was standing by the back of her CRV looking lost.

So fucking lost.

She looked the way he felt the day 5-0 took his parents away and Jemma clung to him, expecting him to be her hero.

He wasn't a fucking hero. He'd been nothing but a dumb fucking kid who had no idea what to fucking do.

He'd been lost, too.

So, *for fuck's sake*, he knew that feeling. That feeling where life just slammed you in the chest so hard that you couldn't take a breath.

But you do anyway. And you figure it the fuck out.

Maybe Cassidy just needed to take a breath.

She quickly swiped at her cheeks which meant she was crying.

Goddamn it.

"I didn't want Daisy to hear or see me. We share a

room right now at my sister's. If she sees or hears me having a meltdown, she'll ask a million questions. Like you."

Judge said nothing.

"Questions I don't have answers for. And the ones I do, I'd have to lie about. I don't want to lie to her if I don't have to." Her words ended on another soft sob.

"Sometimes lies are necessary," Judge said more quietly.

Cassidy nodded. "And sometimes those lies come back to bite you on the ass."

That was fucking true, too.

The crunch of tires on stones caught their attention and it was hard to ignore the bright spotlight being shone on them both.

Christ. Just what he needed.

He braced as the black-and-white cruiser stopped at a location where the spotlight blinded him.

Goddamn pigs.

He fucking hated that he had to make nice with them. But he did.

The spotlight went dark and the cruiser slowly moved forward until it was next to him with the driver's side window down.

Inside were two of Manning Grove's *finest*, Leah Bryson and Tommy Dunn. He knew them both well since they'd been on the force a while. Unfortunately, Judge knew the whole force better than he'd like.

"Leah. Dunn," Judge reluctantly greeted them.

"Judge," Leah greeted back from the passenger seat. "What's going on here?"

He jerked his chin toward Cassidy. "She's new in town and got lost."

"Yeah?" the redheaded Dunn asked. "Heard the club sold this property a while ago. Reason you're standing on it?"

"Like I said, Cassidy got lost and I was helping her get turned around."

"That right, ma'am?" he called out of the open window.

Cassidy moved closer. "Yes, that's right. I'm only learning my way around town and somehow, I ended up here. I'm heading home soon."

"Pretty late, Judge," Leah said.

He ducked down and caught her eyes. Was he suddenly sixteen again? He was fucking thirty-seven years old and didn't need to be in bed by a certain time. "Sure is. Was headin' home when I saw her, so figured she needed help."

Leah's eyes slid from him back to Cassidy. After a few minutes they sliced back to Judge. "Why is she crying?"

"Why do any women fuckin' cry?" Judge asked her.

Leah's lips twitched and she pressed her hand to her rounded belly over her maternity uniform shirt. "I have a good reason."

"Brysons keep having babies, Dunn, you're gonna lose your damn job. They're gonna turn it into the Bryson PD."

Dunn huffed, "I'll be retired before all their kids are old enough. They want to do this thankless job, more power to them."

"Turnin' out to be a clan like the Shirleys."

"Hey now," Leah Bryson said.

Judge snorted. "Okay, you all ain't inbred, so you got that on 'em."

"You going to be okay, ma'am?" Leah called out of her window.

Cassidy lifted a hand. "Yes, thank you. I'll be fine."

"He looks bad to the bone on the outside, but he's just a sweet little kitten on the inside," Dunn yelled out to her. Then he laughed and put the cruiser into reverse. "Head home, Judge," he said much more seriously.

Judge did not like being told what to do by someone wearing a fucking uniform. But he bit back what he wanted to say and said, "That's the plan," instead. Even though he had no plan to head home. At least, not yet. He wasn't a kid anymore, he no longer needed to stick to any curfew. So, Dunn could go fuck himself.

Then the cruiser was gone and the two of them were bathed in the dark once more.

"How do you know my name?" came from behind him.

Jesus fuck. He screwed up. "Told it to me when Daisy introduced us."

"No, I didn't."

He turned to face her. "Yeah, you did. How else would I know it?"

Cassidy chewed on her bottom lip as she studied him in the dark. "Are you stalking me? Should I be calling those cops back here?"

"Like I fuckin' said, ain't gonna hurt you."

"I'm sure serial killers tell their victims that, too."

His lips flattened out.

"If I would have told you my name, I would have said Cassie. No one calls me Cassidy except my parents. And my grandparents, when they were alive."

Cassie. Fuck.

"So, you want to tell me how you know my name?"

Sometimes lies are necessary.

And sometimes those lies come back to bite you on the ass.

Suddenly, sharp teeth gripped his ass cheek. "Small town. Everybody knows everybody."

She tilted her head. "No, that isn't it."

"Yeah, it is. I asked around."

"Why?"

"Asked you twice and you didn't answer."

"Maybe there was a reason for that."

"Afraid of me, that's why."

She didn't say anything for a few seconds. "I could lie like you are right now and say I'm not."

"But you are."

"I just..."

"What'd I do to make you scared?"

"Nothing."

"Right," he said softly.

"So, even if it was true that you asked around about me, why would you do that?" she asked.

"Just curious."

"What else did you hear?"

"Nothin'," he echoed her.

"Bullshit," she repeated his earlier response. Then she gave him a sharp nod and headed back to her Honda. And Judge watched her hips rock and roll even in that winter coat.

"Wanna tell me why you were cryin'?" he called out.

"If you tell me the truth on how you know my name," she called back.

Judge stood there and watched Cassie climb into the old CRV.

Cassie.

"Tell you over a beer."

"I don't drink beer." Her door slammed shut and she drove the Honda in a circle and headed out of the lot.

Cassie Lange.

Only problem with that was the last name belonged to someone else.

And the person it belonged to probably wouldn't be happy that Judge wanted way more than to share a beer with Cassie Lange.

Way fucking more.

Chapter Five

Cassie opened the heavy wood door and stepped inside.

She had seen the ad in the local penny shopper looking for servers or a bartender. She'd never done either, but she was pretty sure she could learn.

She'd prefer to get a job at the local vet and use her skills, but she knew there'd be no way the vet would pay her under the table. And that was what she needed, a job that could pay her cash for now. At least until the divorce.

Until she scraped off all of Dennis's shit.

Until then, her job prospects were limited.

She only hoped the owner of the bar would be willing to pay her in cash along with any cash tips she made.

It would be something. And anything she made, even a little bit, would be better than nothing. She needed to put cash aside so she could settle somewhere by getting her own place and finding somewhere to raise her daughter without the stench of the crime Daisy's father committed.

She could never take Daisy back to Rochester.

If she could get a permanent job in Manning Grove, she'd consider staying. If not, she'd move on. In the meantime, she needed money and a plan. And right now, she had neither.

To make things more difficult, she needed shifts in the evening and weekends when Tyler or Heather could watch Daisy for her. She hated to burden them with that, too, but right now, she had no choice.

She let her gaze slide through the bar. The music in Crazy Pete's was loud. It was surprisingly busy for a Thursday night and the tables were about half full. A couple of guys were throwing darts in one corner, and, in another area off the main floor, were two occupied pool tables. The clack of pool balls could be heard just over the music, which was rock.

Cassie recognized the song. *Gimme Shelter* by The Rolling Stones. She hadn't heard that song in so long, it made the corners of her mouth curl up just slightly.

A man was hustling behind the bar and a woman with long black hair and blue stripes, dressed like she belonged on the small empty stage in the corner singing her own song, was carrying a couple of full pint glasses to a table near the jukebox.

The woman's open smile was large as she set them down, said a few words to the patrons, then laughed. She patted one guy on the shoulder before heading back behind the bar.

Cassie had no idea who the owner was, the ad had only said to show up anytime they were open. No resume needed.

One empty stool remained along the long wood bar, so she headed there, settling on it.

The bartender quickly stopped in front of her and tilted his head. "New in town, right?"

What? How did he know that?

"Saw you on Sunday. You and your girl. Ended up talkin' to Judge."

Jesus, she couldn't escape that man.

Cassie's eyes slid over him. While she didn't recognize his face, she recognized the black leather vest he was wearing since it was similar to Judge's. Only his name patch said, "Dodge," instead.

Dodge.

That was odd. But then so was the name Judge.

"Yes. That was me."

"Girl's real cute. Just like her momma. What can I get you?" He threw a paper coaster on the bar top in front of her and it was hard to miss some of his tattoos. Heavy silver rings donned a few fingers and wide black leather cuffs circled each wrist. She also couldn't miss the huge bulky belt buckle that consisted of two letters: HD.

"The owner."

He pulled his chin into his neck and just about looked down his nose at her. "There an issue?"

"No, I... I saw the ad. I'm looking for a job."

He loosened a bit as he repeated, "What can I get you?"

"I... I don't... Water?"

Dodge shook his head and tapped a ringed finger on the shellacked bar top. "Nah. It's a bar. Beer?"

"I don't drink beer."

"Whiskey?" he suggested, his dark eyes twinkling.

"I don't," the rest of the words spilled out from her quickly, "have any money." Heat slid up her throat and into her cheeks. "Dodge, right? I just need to speak to whoever's in charge."

"Yeah. Dodge." He jerked his chin to the black-haired woman who was wearing a long-sleeved tee advertising Crazy's Pete's Bar. "Stel's half owner."

"Who owns the other half?"

"Our club. Blood Fury."

Blood Fury was what the patches said on the back of

Judge's vest. "Then who is Crazy Pete?" Was that Stella's husband?

"Stella's pop. Died from cancer a coupla years ago."

Shit. She might not get this job if the owner figured out what Dennis had done.

"So, she does the hiring?"

"For the most part. Or Trip."

Good lord, she just needed to talk to someone about a job. "Who's Trip?"

"Her ol' man. Prez of the club."

This was all information she wasn't sure she needed to know, especially since one of the owners was on the premises. "Can I speak with her?"

"Dunno. Can you?" His lips twitched. He turned and bellowed, "Stella!" He then moved away, grabbing a bottle of Captain Morgan and pouring a healthy amount into a glass before filling it with soda the rest of the way. He set it down in front of her, one side of his mouth pulling up slightly as he gave her a wink. He was really handsome, and he knew it. Unlike Judge's long bushy beard, Dodge's didn't hide his face. It was trimmed close. "On my tab. I'll get 'er."

"Thank you." Cassie lifted the glass and took a sip, doing her best not to cough. It was stronger than she normally drank. She was more of a wine drinker, anyway.

"Hey," came a deep voice from next to her.

To her right sat a man staring at her. "Hi."

"You from around here?" The dark-haired man, wearing a very worn flannel shirt, leaned closer, the whiskey on his breath smelling stronger than her drink.

"I—"

"Hey," came out on a breath from the black-haired woman as she stopped in front of her on the other side of the bar. She glanced at the patron sitting next to Cassie. "She's here for a job interview, not to be picked up, Lenny."

Lenny shrugged and grinned, showing off his dozen remaining teeth. "Can't hurt to be friendly."

The woman jutted out her hand over the bar. "I'm Stella. Dodge said you saw the ad."

"Yes. I—" Cassie noticed Lenny still staring at her. Leering, more like it.

Stella pressed her lips together and then jerked her head. "C'mon. We'll find an empty table to talk. Bring your drink."

Cassie grabbed the glass, climbed off the stool and waited for the slender woman to make her way out around the bar. Then she followed Stella to a table in the back by the stage, where fewer people were.

"Sit."

Cassie sat.

"Business is picking up and we need help. But to be upfront, I own half this bar, my ol' man's club owns the other half. So, you'd be basically working for an MC. Do you have a problem with that?"

"An MC?"

"Motorcycle club."

Ah, yes. There had been a square "MC" patch on the back of Judge's vest, too. "Should I?"

Stella smiled and it reached her light blue eyes, which were stunning, especially in contrast with her long black hair. "No. We run a tight ship, doing our best to make it successful. It's not a biker bar, just owned by a bunch of bikers. So, it's safe. It's getting to be more successful and I'm starting to need more help. Which is why I ran the ad, of course." She jerked a thumb over her shoulder. "Dodge is a member of the MC, lives upstairs and helps me manage the bar. So, you'd have to listen to him, too."

Cassie's eyes slid back to the bar where Dodge was still hustling, keeping everyone's drink full. "He lives upstairs?"

"Yes, so if you ever need help, he can be down here in a flash. Have you ever been a server before?"

"No."

Stella frowned. "Well, this isn't a fancy place, so it's really not hard. You just need to get everyone's drink order right and get it to them quickly. They aren't the biggest tippers in here, but it's something. Do you know how to bartend?"

"No."

"Are you willing to learn?"

Cassie nodded. "Yes. But..."

Stella lifted a brow. "But?"

"I... also need to be upfront about something."

Stella sat back in her chair. "*Ooookay...*"

Cassie leaned in a bit and lowered her voice even though she was sure no one could hear them over the music. "I'm kind of in a bind."

Stella's lips turned down at the corners.

Cassie attempted to swallow the lump in her throat. "I was hoping... I'm looking for employment that could pay me in cash."

The woman's frown deepened. "Are you on the run or something?"

"No." Not in the way one might think. She was not running from the law but from people who judged her harshly because of her husband's deeds. "I... I'm in the middle of a divorce and without getting into details... My husband's accounts were frozen and because we were still legally married, so were mine. He..."

Stella raised a hand. "Say no more. All of us have baggage." Her frown smoothed out. "Typically tips around here are paid in cash since not too many people pay with credit cards. Even so, I don't have a problem paying you in cash... For as long as you need... I mean, as long as you work out here. But I haven't hired you yet."

"I know. But I would appreciate a chance. It's hard to find a place to work where I can earn cash. And right now, that's important. Truthfully, I'm a certified vet tech and I'd prefer to find a job in my field..."

"But you're screwed until your divorce is finalized. I get it. I went through a divorce. It's not easy, I know." Stella gave her a crooked smile. "I also know how hard it is to get back on your feet when life cuts you off at the knees. I don't have a problem training you. I trained Dodge. And he has enough experience now to help you, too." Stella's smile widened. "Plus, you look smart enough to mix a rum and coke or pour a draft beer. Not too many people ask for anything fancy in here. If they want fancy, they go to the hotel bar on the square or a fancy restaurant. That isn't us. We serve more locals than anyone and, for the most part, everyone knows each other and is friendly."

"That sounds perfect." Now, she just hoped she'd be hired. She crossed her fingers under the table as she waited.

"I can't hire you full-time yet. But maybe part-time and you can work for tips. I can also slip you a bit of cash under the table, if that's what you need, but that would need to remain between us, of course."

"Yes, that's what I need," she breathed in relief. At least until the divorce was final and she could start from scratch again. "Are the tips better bartending?"

"Maybe not better, but you'd get tipped more often since most people sit at the bar. So, we can train you for both. Plus, Dodge tends to close almost every night and he needs a break. As soon as the club recruits some more prospects, we both should be able to get that break. Then we'd depend more on you and the prospects. You okay with that?"

Cassie's knee bounced under the table in her excitement of getting a chance to start making some money. "Yes. I appreciate the opportunity. I have a daughter——"

Stella's narrowed blue eyes hit hers. "You were the one walking across the parking lot with your little girl."

"Yes. Daisy. I'm staying at my sister's right now and they can watch her evenings and weekends. Those are the hours I'm looking for, if possible."

"Perfect. Those are typically the busiest times and you can also learn to close. I can only pay you minimum wage right now but whatever tips you earn are yours. And you being so pretty might bring you more tips. In fact, you might even draw more customers. They're probably tired of looking at my face." She laughed and her face lit up.

Cassie doubted any man would be tired of looking at Stella's face. And if she had to be extra friendly to get bigger tips, she'd do what she had to do. Well, to a point, anyway.

"How soon can I start?"

"What time can you be here tomorrow? The holiday season should be getting busy with family coming into town. They all get bored staying home, so I'm going to do a little advertising for some karaoke and a couple local bands. Anything to draw in a crowd. The bigger the crowd, the more you'll take home in your pocket at the end of the night."

That sounded so good. All this job had to do was get her over the rough patch until Dennis was found, signed the divorce papers and then went away for a long time.

Maybe once that all happened, she could get her life back on track. Until then, she could suck it up and serve some beer with a smile.

THE LAST COUPLE of days had dragged on way too fucking long. Judge spent time in the office during the day running the normal operations of Justice Bail Bonds while Deke sat on the Douglas house. At night, they'd switch. Deke would take the dogs back to The Barn and Judge would watch for Lange all night.

He missed his fucking bed. He missed sleep.

And he was getting crankier by the fucking second.

He needed to talk to Trip about using the two remaining prospects to help sit on the house. Even though they were in training at the pet crematorium, they should be the ones working long-ass hours instead of him. And anyway, he was fucking older. Sleep was important.

Those two prospects were both at the age where they could still party all night. Judge now struggled to party half a night.

He grunted.

Fuck, he was bored as hell doing a "stakeout," looking for Cassidy Lange's husband to pop his head up like a weasel.

Judge would gladly be the fucking mallet.

Easy and Shady wouldn't be able take the man into custody, but Deke or Judge were only a text or call away. And he'd have to remind Shady not to slice the fucker's throat first like he did up on the mountain to every inbred he stumbled upon when they were rescuing Autumn.

Judge wondered what the fuck was going on in that long-haired fucker's head.

He shook his own.

He knew why Trip, Sig, Rook, and Cage were the way they were. But Shady? He had no idea what his past entailed. And Judge didn't like that.

The rest of the members were pretty much an open book. That man, not so much.

Probably better not to know.

But those lower-than-dog-shit prospects could sit in a vehicle and keep an eye on the house because Judge's eyes were getting fucking blurry.

He tipped his head back against his seat and sighed. Patience was not his strong-suit and sitting in his Expedition for hours sucked. This was why he usually handed off the skip-tracing and bail-jumpers to Deke. His cousin had a lot more patience than him.

He simply needed to keep that twenty percent in mind. More scratch in his and Deke's pocket. That was the ultimate goal in all this.

Not getting a piece of Cassie Lange.

Though, she was a piece of pie he'd like to taste.

His eyes tipped down to Jury, who was curled up contently on the passenger seat. He usually didn't bring her along, but he'd said fuck it tonight. He was missing his girl. He reached out and rubbed her warm ears, drawing a low groan from her, but she didn't even bother to open her eyes.

Getting her was the best fucking decision ever.

With another sigh, he glanced up and his spine shot straight. Cassidy Lange wasn't slinking out the front door this time. No, she strutted right out. Not one tear running down her cheek in sight. No PJ bottoms or slippers, either. The only thing he could see under that coat was jeans and some sort of boots with a slight heel.

She didn't need much because the woman was fucking tall.

Which he liked.

A lot.

Just as much as the width of her hips.

He had also noticed the other day in the empty lot—because he made sure to look—she wasn't wearing a wedding ring. Which he found curious.

He figured most married women liked to wear them.

His wife had.

Until she threw it at him. Along with a shitload of other things.

Mostly because he'd been a dumb fuck and deserved it.

But it wasn't his ex-wife climbing into that piece-of-shit Honda. She was someone else's.

At five-thirty in December, darkness closed in quickly, which made it easier for him to remain undetected where he was parked down the street. When she pulled away from the curb, so did he, again keeping a good distance.

This time she didn't get lost. Fuck no. This time, with what looked like confidence, she turned down the alley that ran parallel to Third Street. He pulled past it, turned onto Third, drove past Crazy Pete's, hooked a left and slowly drove past the alley again. But she was gone.

What the fuck?

He checked the rearview mirror, and, when he saw it was clear, he slammed on the brakes, shoved the Ford into reverse and shot backward until he once again was at the end of the alley.

He turned left and took a slow crawl along the narrow passageway between the buildings. There it was. The Honda. Parked behind Crazy Pete's.

His brow dropped low. *What the fuck?*

Why the hell would she park behind Crazy Pete's where Dodge, Trip and Stella parked? Why wouldn't she park out on the street like the rest of the customers?

And why was she going into Pete's anyway? Was she meeting Lange there?

"Fuck," he muttered and spun stones as he sped out of the alley and looked for a place to park on the street, which wasn't easy since it was a busy Friday evening.

Good for the bar and the Fury's coffers, not so great for Judge.

Once he found a spot, he strode with Jury by his side down the sidewalk toward Crazy Pete's. Stella never cared when he brought in one or both dogs. And the dogs loved it since they ended up being fed popcorn and other shit by the patrons. Plus, there were plenty of pats and ear scratches to go around.

No one had ever complained and if someone did? Fuck them. They could take it up with Judge.

He paused outside the door, wondering if maybe he should just sit and keep watch instead of blowing through the door like 5-0 on a no-knock warrant. He released the handle and stared down at Jury who stared back at him, giving him a slow tail wag.

Yeah, his girl knew when he was being dumb. She liked to remind him.

"Goddamn it," he muttered. He jerked his head toward the Ford. "C'mon, girl. Almost rushed in there like a fuckin' bull on crack."

Then Cassie would really wonder if he was stalking her. And maybe even warn Lange. Judge knew better than to keep blowing his tail.

With another curse, he strode back down the sidewalk and opened the passenger door for Jury to jump in. Then he climbed into the driver's side and pulled out his phone.

He texted Dodge, which was a way better plan. *A blonde just walk in?*

It took about five minutes before he responded, since Judge guessed he was busting his ass slinging drinks big time with how many cars were parked on the street.

Yeah, was the prospect's answer.

Tall n curvy?

Hard 2 miss those fckn curves.

Judge's jaw got tight. *She in there meetn any1?*

Not yet. Soon.

What the fuck did that mean? *Keep an eye on her.*

Not gonna B a prob.

Judge always texted slowly because of his big fingers. And sometimes he didn't have the patience for it and would call instead. But he also didn't want Dodge answering him out loud inside the bar where Cassie might hear him. *Lemme know if she meets up w/ a man.*

It took a few more minutes for Dodge to respond. *Prolly gonna meet a lotta fckn men here.*

Wanna explain that? Judge asked, cursing when he had fixed all his misspellings to at least where they were readable. But his fingers gripped the phone way too tightly.

Stel hired her, came the delayed answer.

Judge blinked at the phone in his hand. He read that last answer again. Stella hired her?

He smoothed a hand down his long beard. Then again.

That could be good. No, not good, fucking great.

It would be so much easier to keep an eye on her in a place she was around MC members and ol' ladies. *Hell,* those were extra set of eyes on her which wouldn't make her suspicious. And, while she was working, he wouldn't need to sit and rot in his fucking Expedition half the night.

That also could mean she might not be skipping town as soon as hubby showed up, which was his original guess.

Maybe she was starting fresh instead. The only question was, was it with or without Dennis Lange?

No wedding ring. New town. New job.

Maybe Lange wasn't showing up at all?

And if not, where the fuck was he?

Chapter Six

Judge downed a double shot of Jack Daniels, slammed the glass on the bar and chased it with the rest of his beer. A whine and a scrambling sound at his feet made him turn his head.

Jury rushed over to Justice and licked his mouth in greeting before wrestling Deke's dog down to the wood floor as his owner entered The Barn through the bunkhouse door.

"Think they hadn't seen each other in a fuckin' week or somethin'." Deke shook his head as he strode up to the bar, nabbed the bottle of Jack and headed over to one of the bus benches that had been moved in front of the stone fireplace in the center of church.

With a sigh, Judge followed him, dropping onto the bench next to his cousin. After Deke was done drinking from the bottle, he passed it to Judge, who tipped it to his lips next.

"You dirty a glass, it stays dirty 'til one of the sweet butts gets her fuckin' ass in here to clean it. You drink from the bottle, nobody gives a shit."

True.

Deke kicked his boots up onto the stone ledge surrounding the circular see-through hearth and dug into his cut, pulling out a small tin. Out of that tin, appeared a hand-rolled, not of the tobacco variety.

Fuck yeah. Judge propped his boots on the stone, too, and settled in. Time to fucking relax until two am or so when he tailed Cassie back to her sister's home.

Judge hated her closing up the bar. But for now, she wasn't doing it by herself. However, what she *was* doing was leaving out the backdoor late at night into a dark alley and getting into her vehicle alone.

Because of that, he not only made sure she got home okay, he sat down the street from the Douglas house for a bit to make sure there were no signs of Lange.

There hadn't been.

Still didn't mean he wouldn't show up. They had no reason to give up looking for him in Manning Grove until the New York bondsman called to say his ass was captured.

When he was, he wondered if Cassie would stay or go...

Fuck.

Or if he was never captured...

Judge ripped the lit joint from Deke's lips as he inhaled and took a long hit himself, letting the smoke fill up his lungs.

He didn't even know the fucking woman. She could be a total cunt who only went for rich, entitled, white collar fuckers, who screwed over charities and thought they were too good to go to jail when they were caught.

Fuck that tie-wearing motherfucker. He needed to be fucking choked with it.

He took another quick hit before Deke snagged the blunt back. "Don't mind fuckin' sharin', but don't bogart the whole fuckin' thing."

After they finished their WrestleMania match, the dogs barreled back to where they were sitting and settled by the fire with grunts and groans. Then Justice hiked up a rear leg and began to lick his balls.

Deke passed the joint back over and lifted the bottle to his lips. When he dropped it back to his thigh, he said, "Thinkin' 'bout headin' to Rochester."

"For what?" Judge already knew the answer and didn't like it.

"To find that motherfucker."

"Only supposed to nab 'im if he shows up in the Grove, Deke." It was a reminder his cousin shouldn't need. He knew how it all worked, knew what their part in this whole thing was.

"Yeah, but it's a bit personal for me. And the scratch is just a bonus."

The scratch should be the main reason. They weren't the goddamn Avengers. They were the last fucking people to be the moral police.

"What're you gonna do? Land on the bail bondsman's doorstep and ask questions? Deke, he don't wanna part with twenty percent if he don't gotta. We wouldn't, either, if Lange skipped out on us. He ain't gonna let you walk into the area he's got covered already with his own bounty hunter and invite you the fuck in. In fact, it could fuck up workin' with him in the future. Either him with us or us with him. Don't fuck that shit up."

"Can go up there all quiet-like and just snoop around a bit. See who he and the wifey hung out with. Check out their friends. Maybe someone knows something. Maybe the asshole talked about where he'd go hide from the law if he ever got busted. You know, while he was drunk or somethin'. Most white-collar assholes tend to run their fuckin' mouths when they're drinkin'."

White-collar workers weren't the only ones. "Right."

"Can't fuckin' hurt."

Maybe, maybe not. But he also didn't want to step on

that bondsman's toes. And Deke doing all that work, plus the expense of him traveling, wasn't worth the twenty percent. All of it, maybe. But twenty? Fuck no. They would end up taking a loss.

"Ain't good business, Deke. You, of all people besides Red, are good with numbers. Run it by her and see what she says."

"Already know what she'd say. Don't need to hear it from her."

"Maybe you do."

"Fuck, brother."

"No, Deke. Know it's personal for you. It's personal for me. But what he did didn't do shit to us when you look at it close enough. It didn't touch us at all."

"It's low."

"Yeah, agreed. It's fuckin' lower than low." Judge swallowed another mouthful of whiskey before handing it back to his blood cousin and club brother. "And anyway, you go up there, you might fall deep into some snatch and not come back for days. Not 'til your nuts are wrinkled up and your dick's shootin' nothin' but exhaust fumes. Can't have you gone that long. Not with me tailin' Cassie when she's not at work."

"Just a couple days. Promise not to stick my dick anyplace which might be a trap."

"All snatch is a trap. Foolin' yourself if you think otherwise."

"Not all snatch is a trap, Judge."

Judge grunted.

"Just 'cause you fucked up once, don't mean we all fuck up."

"Just be glad you didn't. Don't mean you never will."

Deke grabbed the Jack bottle and took a swig. When he was done, he used the back of his hand to wipe his mouth. "Just gotta be careful is all."

Judge swung his head toward his cousin, his blood pressure already spiking.

Deke lifted his hand and faked a laugh. "Know it wasn't you at first, cuz. She fucked you. But then you fucked her. From there everythin' went to shit. Kinda like the Fury did. Had your own mini implosion."

"Wasn't a mini fuckin' implosion." It blew his life apart.

Deke sobered. "No. I get it. Might've missed the original Fury exploding to pieces, but didn't miss the shit that happened to you. Saw it. And, Cuz, I learned from all that shit. Never tie yourself to a sneaky goddamn cunt. Not a life to live."

No, it wasn't. And now he was extra careful about who he stuck his dick into.

Judge relaxed against the vinyl bench and stared into the dying fire. "Did a bunch of research on Lange and his case after you left for Williamsport the other day."

"Yeah, so did I."

"Tried to get a read on the whole thing."

"'Cause of her," Deke said.

"'Cause of the scratch."

Deke snorted softly.

Judge ignored it. "Most comments from the public demanded the man's head on a fuckin' pike. Most were fuckin' ruthless." He could understand why.

"Yeah, well, that fucker hadn't stolen money from just any fuckin' charity, it was one for kids dyin' of cancer." Deke inhaled loudly and shook his head. "You don't fuckin' steal from kids."

"No, not dyin' kids," Judge muttered.

"And that right there's why I want to head north."

He turned and studied his cousin's profile. It was hard and Judge got it. Cancer was a stickler for both of them. To think about kids suffering the same way Walt did...

Fuck, Judge didn't even want to think about it.

It was bad enough when it was an older man who'd lived a life. But some fuckin' innocent child who hadn't even had a chance yet to live?

Life was fucking goddamn cruel.

And then some asswipe comes along and embezzles three-hundred grand. At least that was what the investigators could prove. It might have even been more.

Judge wondered why Lange needed the money.

Had he stepped in some shit he'd been trying to buy his way out of? Or was he trying to live above his means?

Cassie didn't seem to be the high maintenance type. She didn't seem the type to live the glamorous life. But maybe he was wrong, and she had demanded luxury and, once her hubby fell, she tumbled along with it into the gutter with the rest of the regular folk.

Maybe she and Lange had the money hidden away somewhere so, once they escaped, they could go back to living the high life.

He hoped to fuck he was wrong about Cassie.

He'd been wrong about a woman before.

He needed to put on his blinders when it came to certain women. Some of their pussies were sticky like a glue trap. Once you were caught, it was difficult to break free.

Yeah, maybe Cassie was temporarily slumming it with the rest of the regular working folk by driving that old Honda and taking a job at Crazy Pete's. Just biding her time until she could hook up with Lange again.

Maybe.

Christ. Why the fuck should he even care? He didn't even fucking know her. He had no reason to want to know her.

And she came with too much fucking baggage between her little girl and having a wanted husband.

"Gonna give you two nights up there. That's it."

Deke turned toward him and his lips twitched. "Why? Is

the whole cancer thing botherin' you? Or is it the blonde herself?"

"Already spendin' too much time on this case for only twenty percent. Just wanna get it over with. Either he's showin' up in the Grove or he ain't."

Deke knocked a shoulder into his. "Maybe get close to her. Get her talkin'. Get a read on her, see what you can pick up from what she puts down."

"Yeah," he grunted.

"Hang out at Pete's. Perfect time to strike up some friendly convo."

"Get Trip, Stel and Dodge involved, too," Judge added. Not just more eyes looking for Lange, but more ears listening might make their job easier.

"Can't hurt. Maybe she'll let somethin' slip."

Yeah, maybe she would.

"And you never know what else you may get out of it." Deke smirked. "You should give that pocket pussy of yours a break. Pretty blonde like that would be a nice change of pace. Give you a few new fantasies for your Fleshlight."

He wasn't telling his cousin Cassie already gave him a few new fantasies.

Judge shook his head. "Know you're a fuckin' asshole, right?"

His cousin's grin widened. "Have to be to work with you."

Judge rose to his feet and so did Jury.

"You headin' over there to strike up a little convo with her?" Deke wiggled his eyebrows and pinched out the lit end of the joint.

"Fuck no. Not tonight. Gonna let her get a little more comfortable workin' the bar."

"So, tomorrow night, then."

Judge shot him a look. "Yeah, you go work Rochester tomorrow night, I'll work her."

"You're gettin' the better end of that deal."

Judge wasn't going to argue that.

Not one fucking bit.

―――――

Cassie almost dropped the two draft beers she was carrying over to the "pool room." She barely caught them in time, then forced her attention from the door—where Judge and two large dogs just walked in—to her job, which was more important.

Her job was *way* more important, she reminded herself. If she spilled the beer, she might have to pay for them, and she needed every dime she was earning. Stella was graciously letting her work Thursdays through Sundays, which were the busiest nights.

And she was grateful. So far, her tips had been decent, and Dodge paid her cash after her shift every night once they closed. She'd been squirreling it away in a shoe box at her sister's house. Every night when she added to it, she counted every dollar all over again. To see that pile grow, even a little, was satisfying. It made her feel not so hopeless.

From now on, she would be in charge of her and Daisy's destiny. Not anyone else.

Filing for divorce a year ago, getting out of Rochester recently and now getting this job were her first steps toward that. It might be a slow process, but at least she was moving forward.

Just like her feet were doing, as she entered the half-walled area off the main floor, where the pool tables were kept. Even on a Sunday, both were occupied, and quarters lined the rails as people waited their turn to play.

Dodge told her the pool and dart league nights during the week were also lucrative nights to work and maybe Stella would eventually adjust her schedule to include them. Cassie hoped so.

So far everyone had been friendly. For the most part. If any of the men got too friendly or handsy, all she had to do was whisper something to Dodge in passing and he'd have a "discussion" with whomever it was. Usually it was a very "serious" chat with a lot of quick head nodding on the listener's part.

And usually, the next time Cassie had to serve that table, the occupants were much more respectful.

When things slowed down later in the evening, Dodge— or Stella, if she was still around—would teach her how to work behind the bar. How to pour a draft without a lot of head. How to mix drinks without over pouring. And how to use the old, worn bartender's bible kept behind the bar. Not too many people asked for mixed drinks other than some liquor mixed with soda, like a simple rum and Coke. And those she could handle easily.

Stella told her to get to know the regulars, learn their names, learn a little about their lives and talk to them as if they were friends. That would help get her bigger tips.

And it did.

Even when her feet ached, she kept a smile on her face and kept the conversation flowing. She didn't have a problem with small talk, as she had to do it often with her previous job.

While being a "bar maid" was different than being a vet tech, it was also somewhat fun and staying busy kept her mind occupied.

Better yet, she was making cash money.

However, right now her mind was focused on Judge. She, out of the corner of her eye, tracked him heading to the bar and settling his big body on an empty stool.

Cassie put the beers down on a small high table in the pool room, grabbed the cash, and tucked it into the little server apron she wore to keep her tips and make change. Dodge had grinned and shook his head when she showed up with it on Saturday night, but it helped her be better at her job. She also kept a small notepad in one of the pockets in case she got a large order. She didn't want to rely on her memory, screw up the order and then lose out on a decent tip.

So, Dodge could tease her all he wanted, but she didn't care.

She picked up a few empties near the pool tables, and as she headed back to the bar, she stopped at a table, asked if she could get the two occupants fresh beers and then moved behind the bar, setting the dirty glasses into the sink and tossing the empty bottles into the recycle bin.

She ignored the giant of a man, whose eyes had followed her once she had hit the corner of the bar. He was watching her as he talked to Dodge, who was standing in front of him and serving him a full pint glass.

Cassie didn't like when Dodge's gaze slid toward her as Judge continued to talk. When it slid back to Judge, he wore a grin.

No, she didn't like that at all.

She sighed and, as she filled two more beer glasses at the taps, Dodge sidled up to her. "Wants you to serve him."

Cassie kept her eyes focused on the rising beer. "Why?"

"Why does any man wanna talk to a woman?"

"I'm not interested." She closed the tap and waited for the beer to settle as she added them to the customer's tab in the register, feeling Judge's eyes on her the whole time.

Dodge leaned into her. "Tips good."

Yes, but how much would those big tips cost her? "I'm okay with the customers I have right now."

Dodge straightened and, out of the corner of her eye, she saw him shrug and move away.

Cassie blew out a breath and took the two beers to the

waiting customers. She made a quick round checking on all the occupied tables and then froze as she saw Judge move to one, both American Bulldogs casually following him. With a satisfied look on his face, he folded his length into a chair and the dogs settled nearby.

Daisy would love those dogs, absolutely go bonkers over them. She was always begging for a dog, but she was too young to be responsible for one. Maybe once they found a place, she'd let her daughter have a guinea pig or something.

Until then...

Until then, she needed tips to get her own place where she could start fresh.

And to get tips, she needed to be nice to customers.

Being nice meant striking up a conversation.

Judge was no different than any other customer in Crazy Pete's.

Or that was what she told herself.

Because if she looked deep enough, something about the huge biker kept catching her attention.

Maybe it was the way he had talked to Daisy. Maybe it was the way he had been with her.

Maybe it was his larger than life presence every time she'd run into him.

Even so, she just needed to put her head down and work on moving forward.

Judge could be a huge speed bump. One she didn't need to hit right now. Especially since she was currently running with only one wheel instead of a whole set. And that one wheel had damage already.

The table was empty in front of him and she glanced toward the bar where he had been previously sitting. He'd downed the beer Dodge had served him at the bar and left the empty glass behind.

Just so she'd have to wait on him.

With a sigh, she braced herself and headed over to him,

stopping opposite of where he sat so they'd have the table between them.

She plastered on a smile. "Hi."

His eyes crinkled at the corners, locked on hers and he jerked up his chin. "Yo." His grunt was so guttural, it sounded like it came deep from within the cavern of his chest. She imagined he could be very loud when he needed to be.

But he didn't seem the booming type. More on the quiet side unless he had a reason to raise his voice. And most people probably hoped they weren't that reason. Because she was also sure when he yelled, he could be very scary. His voice, his height—which had to be six-two or six-three—his long, thick beard, those intense green eyes that probably missed nothing...

"What can I get you?"

"Just wanna talk."

Cassie quickly glanced around the interior of the bar. "I'm busy."

"Woulda talked to you at the bar, but you refused to wait on me."

"I didn't refuse."

He cocked an eyebrow. His head was covered with a dark gray beanie. Not once had she seen his hair and she wondered if it was as long as his beard. She didn't like beards that long. She liked them neat and trimmed, where it didn't hide a man's features. Maybe a little shorter than Dodge's.

Though, Judge's beard seemed to emphasize his nicely shaped lips and those green eyes. And his cheekbones.

He'd probably be really handsome without all that shaggy hair. The hair Daisy was determined to pet.

"I didn't realize Manning Grove was so small..."

He leaned back and crossed his thick arms over his very

broad chest covered in a snug dark gray thermal and his leather biker vest.

"That I'd run into the same people so often," she finished.

He still said nothing. But his eyes had a lot to say.

She just didn't speak that language.

"Or maybe it's not just coincidence."

She finally realized after talking to him now a few times, what his voice reminded her of.

Slow moving thunder.

"Could be that my MC owns half this bar. Could be that Stella belongs to the club and she owns the other half. Could be the reason."

"Could be. But I don't think that's it."

Both eyebrows shot up his forehead. "Then what is it?"

"I don't know. Only you know. You knew my name before I even gave it to you."

"Still haven't given it to me."

"That's right, I haven't. But somehow you know it. You know where I work, and I just started here."

"Just coincidence."

Cassie dropped her head slightly and stared straight into those green eyes. "Bullshit."

His lips twitched slightly before he pinned them together.

What the hell was he hiding?

Probably no more than she was.

Damn.

"Beer?" She didn't wait for his answer and spun on her heel to head back to the bar.

A few minutes later, she returned, mentally cursing the tremble in her hand as she placed the full glass down in front of him. She avoided his eyes. "Would you like to start a tab?"

As her fingers slid from the cold glass, he snagged them, making her gasp.

"Still afraid of me?"

It was no longer fear but more like worry he might know things about her that he shouldn't. He might know where she'd come from and why she'd shown up in this town. Why she'd been running away. Possibly even from whom.

"No."

His fingers were warm, long and strong as they held hers. But when his thumb brushed over the spot where her wedding ring used to be, ice slid down her spine and her breathing became hitched. It was like a ghost had walked straight through her.

She yanked her hand, but he didn't release it. "Let me go," she whispered, the shake in her words now unmistakable.

Did he somehow know she used to be married? Was it the same way he knew her name?

Who was he and why was he interested in her?

This wasn't just a man interested in a woman. This was more.

The hairs on the back of her neck stood.

His thumb slid over the spot on her ring finger again. She stared at the slow, precise motion. That little movement was him asking a silent question and he was hoping her finger would give him an unspoken answer.

No indication remained that she used to wear a ring. None. Her wedding ring had been gone long enough that no indentation was left. Her finger showed no evidence of her marriage at all.

None.

However, what kept her still tied to Dennis was his financial and criminal mess. And Daisy, of course.

Hopefully soon it would only be their daughter.

She just needed him to sign the damn divorce papers so

she could be free. Problem was, the attorney had stopped looking for him. With their assets frozen, she no longer could pay him. Not only couldn't her attorney locate Dennis, neither could Dennis's.

She was told he'd skipped bond.

That meant this whole thing would be dragged out longer than it should.

Even if she wanted to find him on her own, she couldn't. She had no funds to do so. She couldn't pay her attorney. She couldn't hire an investigator to find Dennis. She was in limbo.

Right now, she was hating with every fiber of her being the man she used to love. If he showed up, she'd kick him right in the damn balls for all the problems he'd caused her. For deceiving her. For betraying his family.

Husbands who loved their wives and children did not do the things he did. He should have walked away, or sought out help, when issues began to arise. Not dragged his family into it with him.

If he had loved them, that was what he should have done.

Which proved the only person he'd loved was himself.

He could've saved her and Daisy. He chose not to. He chose to keep her in the dark.

Until it was too late.

He finally released her hand. "Where's your ring?"

Her heart stuttered. She wasn't sure whether it was from his question or from that deep voice.

But either way, that simple question didn't have a simple answer.

And that answer wasn't one she was willing to share.

Chapter Seven

JUDGE WATCHED her face carefully as the blood rushed from it and she pulled the hand he'd released into a ball against her chest.

Like it had been singed.

Like his touch had burned her.

Her throat worked and his eyes followed the movement. He wanted to taste her there. Scrape his teeth along that delicate line. Groan against it when he came deep inside her. Grip his fingers around it as he stole the breath from her with his mouth.

That throat belonged to another man. But he wanted it to be his.

He wanted to be the only one to touch it.

He wanted it to be the "property of Judge."

"I don't know what you're talking about."

He jerked his head toward her curled up left hand, still held tightly against her chest as it rose and fell at a quick pace. "Your weddin' ring."

The pulse in that throat, the one he wanted to make his, pounded so hard, he could see it. "Where is it? Why aren't you wearin' it?"

"I'm... I'm not sure who you are, or who you think you are. Or even why you know..." She squeezed her eyes shut and dropped her hands to her sides, pressing them against her thighs. When her blue eyes opened, they seared him. "If you want a beer, I'll serve you a beer. But that's it. Just wave me down when you need something."

As she turned, he simply said her name. "Cassie." She froze in place. "We need to talk."

She turned her head, glancing at him over her shoulder. "No, we don't. Please sit at the bar and let Dodge serve you."

"Not here to drink." Which was true. He could drink at The Barn for free. *Hell*, he could knock a few back out in the courtyard or in his apartment. Or even burn a fatty in peace at the farm.

But that was not why he was there. He also shouldn't blow his cover. He didn't need Cassie telling Lange that someone was looking for him in Manning Grove. That would screw his chance at that twenty percent.

Though, suddenly it was no longer about the money.

And the reason it wasn't was because she wasn't wearing her wedding ring.

Not just that, but because there was no mark where a ring would be.

It hadn't been taken off recently.

It had been gone for a while.

It had taken some time before any sign of his own wedding band had disappeared. The ring he'd been forced to wear even though he hated most jewelry. He'd only worn it to keep the peace.

But that ring had left a mark.

In more ways than one.

"Why are you here, then?"

"To get to know you." That wasn't a lie.

"I'm not interested."

He tilted his head and let his gaze run over her from the top of her blonde head to her booted toe. "Kinda gettin' that."

"Then you can be a gentleman and respect that."

One side of his mouth curled up and he stroked his beard. "Oh, baby, I'm no fuckin' gentleman."

A flush rose into her cheeks and her mouth flattened. "Call me if you need me." She turned her head and began to head back to the bar again.

"Cassie," he called out, making her freeze once more. This time she didn't look back.

He rose from his chair, pulled a wrinkled ten from his front pocket and approached her.

When he stepped behind her—not touching, but close enough to feel each other's heat—her spine snapped straight. He leaned down and put his mouth near her ear, murmuring, "Said call you if I need you." He tucked the ten into a pocket of the little black apron wrapped around her waist.

It was hard to miss the goosebumps breaking out over her arms and the slight shiver.

She wasn't afraid of him.

Fuck no.

Her reaction had nothing to do with fear.

Judge's half-grin widened into a full one when she jolted as if jump-started and rushed back behind the bar to escape that heat.

As he moved toward the door, she was saying something to Dodge, who was doing his best to keep a straight face. But the prospect's eyes hit Judge's across the room and Judge jerked his chin up at him.

Then he walked outside to cool the fuck off.

———

Judge ignored the whimpers coming from the doorway. Jury and Justice would just have to wait for breakfast. He had something important to finish first.

He squeezed his eyes shut even tighter, ignoring the noisy dogs, and listened to the squish his generously lubed Fleshlight made as he slid it up and down his throbbing cock.

If he couldn't have pussy, it was the next best thing. Sometimes even better, since when he was done, he could put it away and not be nagged.

But this morning he was picturing Cassie. Her long, blonde hair being flung around as she called his name and rode him hard and fast.

Her pussy soaked and squeezing him tight.

Her big tits bouncing and her own fingers playing with her rock-hard nipples.

Her thick thighs squeezing his hips.

Her head thrown back and her breath puffing from between her parted lips, which were swollen from her sucking his dick and then him kissing her until she begged him to fuck her.

No begging was needed.

As one hand guided his Fleshlight, the other cupped his balls, squeezing and tugging. Kneading. Feeling the slight scrape of her nails over the delicate flesh, which was still damp from her mouth earlier.

Fuck yeah.

He was determined to make the fantasy a reality, especially if the no wedding ring meant no more marriage.

That meant Cassie was free.

And if she was...

He pictured her at Crazy Pete's last night in the snug jeans and fitted V-neck top that showed off her generous cleavage and hugged every one of her damn curves.

Every fucking one.

He wanted to suck those nipples which had become visible through the thin fabric after he whispered in her ear.

He pursed his lips as he relived her rushing away from him.

Those hips. That ass.

The natural sway of them as she escaped him.

How every man in that bar wasn't on his hands and knees following her like the Pied fucking Piper…?

But he was relieved they weren't.

Because if the husband was out of the picture, Cassie was his. She just didn't know it yet.

But she would. Soon enough.

Yeah, he wanted info from her about Lange. But while he worked on that, he'd work on her.

He blew out a breath and drove his dick deep into the slick hole. Rolling over, he pinned the Fleshlight between him and the mattress, imagining he'd bent Cassie over one of the tables and she wore a short skirt where it showed off her bare thighs and her ass when he shoved it up.

Fuck yeah.

He leaned over her back as she gripped the table's edge and he groaned into her ear about how tight and wet she was.

With little whimpers, she encouraged him to fuck her harder. He did.

To fuck her deeper. He did.

To fuck her faster. He did.

Over and over he drove harder, faster, deeper. His fingers digging into the flesh at her hip and fisting her long, blonde hair.

Jesus fuck. She was perfection.

Goddamn perfection.

The pressure built. In his gut, in his balls. He thrust one more time and spilled deep inside her, his dick twitching, his balls emptying.

And when he was done, he laid there, his face buried in his pillow, his fingers clutching the sheets, his breathing rough and quick.

Then he heard it.

A donkey braying.

Fuck.

He slipped out of the silicone pussy and rolled over, making sure his load didn't spill all over his sheets. He grabbed his cell phone and some tissues from the nightstand.

The donkey brayed again, and Judge answered the phone with one hand while cleaning off the majority of the mess on his dick with the other. "Yo."

"Whatcha doin'?"

Judge glanced at the cum-filled Fleshlight, which he'd propped upright on the nightstand. "Was sleepin'."

"Why you out of breath?"

"Why the fuck you callin' me?" He pulled his phone away and glanced at the time. *Fuck,* it was later than he realized. Following Cassie home every night around two-thirty in the morning sucked. It was fucking up his sleep.

Deke snorted. "Got news."

"Couldn't have waited 'til I got to the office?"

There was a long hesitation, then, "Coulda. But figured the dogs woulda had you up by now."

"Let 'em out this mornin' around three, after getting back."

"No sign of the fucker, right?"

That sounded like a question Deke wasn't expecting an answer to. Like he already knew that answer. "No."

"You chat her up?"

Not as much as he'd hoped. "Not enough."

"Maybe you need to charm her with that flavor savor of yours. Bet if you try hard enough you can still smell the last ten pussies you ate, along with the pepperoni pizza from last week."

"Deke," he muttered, tired of the endless shit he gave him about his beard. "Gonna hang the fuck up."

His cousin's laughter hit his ear. "The fuck you will."

Judge pressed the End Call button and the phone went dark.

He waited.

The donkey brayed again as both dogs came running into his bedroom and took a flying leap onto the bed.

Judge reluctantly answered the call and put the phone to his ear, making sure neither wet snouts ended up anywhere near his now soft, but still somewhat messy, dick.

He needed to shower, feed himself and the dogs, and get to the office. He had no time for lying in bed and chatting with Deke like two fucking teen girls.

"Got info."

"Said that once already. Still ain't heard it."

"Jesus fuck, someone's cranky. Call Billie or somethin'."

Billie wasn't going to cut it. Right now, Judge only wanted one woman.

Though that woman acted like she didn't want him.

She did. Again, she just didn't know it yet.

"Deke..."

"Did a quick search online. Found out where she worked up here. Went there and talked to another vet tech—"

Judge brushed his fingers over the buzzed hair on his head. "Another vet tech?"

"Yeah, Cassie's a vet tech. Or was. Good at her job. Seems she was liked well enough by the people there. At least 'til all the shit with Lange hit the fan."

Judge stared at the ceiling and propped a bent arm under his head. "Was she involved?"

"People think she was. Said there was no way she couldn't have known."

"Which is bullshit."

"Yeah," Deke agreed. "Turns out Lange had a gamblin' problem."

Jesus fuck. That would make sense. "Shouldn't be surprised."

"Yeah, but she didn't know."

"He musta hid it well." Unless she did know and lied about it to her coworkers.

"Some locals can't believe it wasn't obvious."

"Guess it wasn't obvious to Lange's employer, either, if he had a chance to embezzle all that fuckin' scratch."

"Any-fuckin-way, the tech—who's fuckin' hot as fuck—"

"Christ, Deke. You fuckin' did her?"

Silence.

Judge groaned. Of course he did. "Jesus, you fuckin' did her." The man was good at finding ways to get info. Even if he had to use his own dick.

Not that fucking hot pussy was a hardship for him.

"Pillow talk got me good info from her last night. Any-fuckin-way, Beth—"

"Beth," Judge muttered to the ceiling.

"*Beth* said Lange wanted to take out a second mortgage. Of course, Cassie woulda had to sign for it since the house was in both their names. She refused when he wouldn't give her a straight answer on why they needed the line of credit. When she got suspicious, she began diggin' and discovered their joint bank accounts drained. Their retirement accounts zeroed out, too. Their life savings? Fuckin' gone. He blew through it all like a cokehead with an eight ball. Cassie kicked his ass out after she confronted him 'bout the money. They didn't have a lot but what little they had was lost in online card games, and at the tracks. Played both the ponies and the hounds."

"Fuck," Judge muttered, he hit the speaker button on his

phone and placed it on his chest so he could reach out and rub Jury's ears.

Most of the time he didn't even realize he was doing it, but at that moment, he did it on purpose. He needed to keep his thoughts calm and clear. Jury always helped him keep his shit from spinning.

"Thanks," he muttered.

"For what?" came through the speaker.

"For talkin' me into gettin' Jury."

Silence filled the room for a few beats.

It wasn't the first time he'd thanked Deke for taking him along to pick up Justice and it wouldn't be the last, so his cousin was used to it. Deacon got it. Justice was everything to him, too.

"Yeah, so Beth said she kicked his ass out and filed for divorce coupla months later. She and the girl stayed in the house, just thinkin' her douchebag husband was only a gamblin' addict. Turned out to be worse. Found that out when her ass got dragged in by the pigs and questioned. Even threatened with time in the joint and loss of her fuckin' kid."

"Fuck," he muttered again, his fingers moving more quickly over Jury's soft floppy ears. She groaned and stretched out along his side. Justice head-butted his other side and flopped down, wanting attention, too.

Judge didn't deny him.

"Get this shit... The fucker was the finance manager for the Kids Can Do Foundation. Finance motherfucking manager."

"Fuck."

"Yeah, perfect place to feed your habit, *if* you can get away with it."

"Small amounts, maybe."

"Right, maybe if you're smart. But if your addiction's out of fuckin' control, you're not thinkin' straight. You're thinkin' about where your next fix is comin' from. *And* eventually someone's gonna notice when several hundred grand comes up missin'. Even a financial manager can't hide that shit. He coulda been pocketin' any cash donations, too. Long story short, his ass got caught and they seized everythin'. He bonded out and you know the rest."

"Don't get why she left Rochester."

"Because this was a charity for kids with cancer, the news spread like wildfire. Everyone was up in fuckin' arms about how he could do this, not only to a charity but one that helped kids with the big C. And, of course, even though they had separated, her name was dragged through the mud along with his by default. Cassidy Lange, wife of Dennis Lange. Shit like that's hard to scrape clean of, 'specially when they're still legally married."

Judge figured as much since Cassie was still listed as his wife in the documents the bondsman had sent. Without a divorce, she could be held responsible for his debt. Which for her—*hell*, for most people—was huge. "This Beth think she was a part of it?"

"No, she's one of the few who don't. Said most of 'em in the vet's office don't believe Cassie knew. Unless she's a good actress, it all came as a shock to her. She was actually devastated when she found out he'd gambled everything away, *before* findin' out the rest. But John Q. Public blames her for not warnin' the foundation that Lange was a gamblin' addict the second she found out."

"Thought she didn't know."

"Yeah, she didn't and by the time she did, she wanted nothin' to do with him and had no idea he was embezzlin' all that scratch. She wasn't seein' any of the money, so she had no fuckin' clue about it. He was takin' it and gamblin' it right away. Apparently, he was playin' online poker and making bets right in his office durin' working hours. Movin' money from one account to another. Feds went in, took the man's computer and they then had all the evidence nice and neat. Case closed."

Yeah, case closed if the fucker hadn't jumped bond. "Jesus."

"Yeah. Sounds like the addiction had a solid hold of him if he was doin' it right there in the office."

"Why he got caught. Got reckless, desperate even, to feed his habit."

"Prolly. But the board of directors had ordered an audit of the books without him knowin' and that's when shit didn't add up. Hired a forensic accountant who pointed a finger at Lange."

"So, the asshole had a secret fuckin' life he hid from his wife and kid."

"Pretty much. But the looks she got, the comments, the harassment... She even had people push her, spit on her, threaten her and the kid's life. Everyone thought she should help pay back the stolen money since she was still legally married to him. But she had nothin' left by the time he got caught since he'd spent it all. Actually, she had nothin' by the time he admitted to her he had a problem. By then, it was too late."

Judge's jaw got tight. "Goddamn bullshit."

"People see what they want to see. Push blame where they want to, whether it's right or wrong. We fuckin' know that, Judge. Hell, we see that every fuckin' day in our business."

That was too true. People saw what they wanted to see. Someone could be staring directly at the truth and still not see it.

Maybe that was how it was for Cassie, too. She didn't see the signs that her husband was addicted to gambling. Though, it was a high that could be hidden a little more easily than drugs or booze because it wasn't directly in her face. Especially if he was doing it online at work and not going to the track or a casino to scratch his itch.

Eventually, when the gambler hit rock bottom, the truth would come out. But unless there were other outward signs, something like that could be hidden for a while. Overdue bills, bounced checks, car repos, foreclosures were the big red flags. Getting arrested and charged for embezzlement? That shit was a flashing neon arrow.

By that time, it had been too late.

By that time, the asshole not only fucked himself but his family.

With what Deke was saying, it seemed Cassie didn't come to the Grove to hook up with her hubby and hide. It looked like she might have come to escape the bullshit Lange created.

She was trying to scrape off the shit her husband splattered all over her and her little girl. Which made him determined now more than ever to help catch that fucker.

Lange not only fucked over kids dying of cancer, but his own daughter, as well.

A minimum-security prison wasn't good enough, which was where a white-collar criminal like him would go.

Suddenly, the twenty percent didn't matter. Just like it became personal for Deke, it had become personal for Judge.

Fuck the money.

Dennis Lange had done wrong.

And Judge was going to make it right.

Chapter Eight

CASSIE PARKED her Honda at the curb in front of the house, shut off the engine and sat in the dark, her eyes glued to the rearview mirror.

Her feet hurt. Her back hurt. But she had made a decent amount of tips tonight.

Some of that money would have to go toward Daisy's Christmas presents. The holiday was coming up soon and she wasn't prepared.

She hated to use any of the money for anything other than a new place for them to live, but Heather and Tyler insisted they were in no rush for her to move out.

As kind as that was, she still felt bad being a financial burden on them and destroying their privacy, especially when they were trying to make a baby.

But that wasn't her immediate concern.

She glanced at the clock on the dash and yawned. 2:35.

Every night she worked at Crazy Pete's, she'd come home, quietly take a shower, then climb into bed with Daisy, curling around her daughter and falling asleep almost immediately because she was so exhausted.

Tonight was the first night she'd closed the bar on her own and, being a Saturday, it had been busy.

But she did it.

She did last call at ten minutes before two and everyone left without too much hassle with only one straggler. She quickly counted the cash, put it in the safe, wiped things down and shut off the lights.

Stella and Dodge had a thing tonight at what they called "The Barn," which they said was their MC's clubhouse.

Actually, it was a celebration because Dodge was getting "patched in" as a full member of the club and would no longer be a prospect. Which was a big deal she was told.

Soon the back of his vest would look like Trip's and Judge's and have both rockers and the huge center patch.

In the week or so she'd been working at Crazy Pete's, she was getting to learn some of the lingo of an MC. She also asked Dodge and Stella, even Trip, a lot of questions when things were slow.

Cassie found it all fascinating.

But she wasn't sure if an MC was like a family or brotherhood, or just a club of friends. But whatever it was, they took it seriously, that was for sure.

She'd met Ozzy, who was a little older, and Dutch, a grizzly man who was a lot older. And also Cage, Dutch's son, had stopped in once for a couple of beers. But Cassie pretty much figured word was getting around in their MC that she was the newest employee at Pete's, and everyone wanted to check her out.

Tonight, she'd been on her own, but she'd handled everything smoothly and now had a nice wad of cash in her purse. A nice, *thick* wad.

She smiled, but it quickly dropped when headlights bounced off the rearview.

She was surprised to see him tonight. She figured he'd be at the "patch party" for Dodge since the newest Blood

Fury member hadn't returned before Cassie locked up the bar. She figured that meant the party was still going strong.

But she should've known he'd be there. Parking down the street. Watching her.

Every night she left Pete's, he followed her home. Every single night she worked.

It took a couple of days to figure out it was him. While he kept at a distance, he didn't totally hide. It wasn't hard to miss his tail since traffic through town at the time she left Pete's was pretty much non-existent. It was a small family-oriented town where there wasn't much going on past dinner time.

She had left Rochester so she could live in peace. And now, here in Manning Grove, she had a stalker.

She grabbed her purse and dug for her cell phone. Hitting the power button, her finger hovered over the nine button.

She should call the police and report him.

She should.

But tonight, like every other night recently, he didn't stay long. The headlights cut through her CRV as he did a U-turn and headed back in the other direction.

She tossed her cell phone onto the passenger seat and started her SUV again, put it in Drive and did a U-turn of her own.

She followed him this time. Through town and to a road that led out into the country. She glanced at the street sign as she turned. County Line Road.

She kept a good distance, barely keeping his taillights in her view until they disappeared when he turned down a lane.

To a farm.

She stopped on the road at the end of the lane and watched his Expedition make its way past a large, old farm-house and then disappear.

Did he live at this farm?

She chewed her bottom lip, debating whether to follow him down the lane or just go back to her sister's house and climb into bed.

The latter would be the smart thing to do. She was tired and where he lived was none of her business.

But why he was following her was. That was what she wanted to know. Why the hell this man, who knew her name, who knew she'd been married, was following her home every night.

He'd only come into the bar that one time.

Just that once to talk to her.

When she refused.

But maybe it was time to get things straight with him.

She slowly made her way down the rough dirt and stone lane and as she passed the dark farmhouse, she noticed a bunch of other dark buildings. What looked like different sized sheds. Some huge, some small. But what caught her eye was the big barn.

Maybe that was "The Barn" they talked about. The MC's clubhouse.

As she drove closer, she noticed the building didn't have any windows on the lower level and the large ones on the second floor were dark.

Maybe the party was over.

But vehicles were still parked haphazardly around the outside. However, Judge's Ford was not one of them.

Where did he go?

She turned off her headlights, using the December moon to light her way around the building. She headed along the right side, away from what looked like a courtyard with 55 gallon drums scattered around the area and a pavilion.

The building was surprisingly long and another newer

looking building was attached to the back. Again, no windows except for a couple on the second floor.

She kept the Honda at a crawl as she got to the back corner and hooked a left. Then she slammed on the brakes as she almost hit a dark figure.

A big one.

With hands on his hips and long, endless legs spread apart.

Shit.

Before she could put the vehicle in reverse, he moved. She tried to move faster, her hand shaking as she shoved the shifter forward, but as her foot left the brake, the passenger side door opened, and he jumped in.

She slammed her foot back on the brake pedal. "Get out!"

"Why you followin' me?" His deep voice and his larger than life presence made her SUV feel tiny.

"Why are you following *me*?" she countered.

Damn, he smelled like pot, beer and... leather. Plus, a mix of other things. That combo should be a huge turn-off, but on him, for some reason, it wasn't.

It was better than cologne, hair gel and shoe polish.

So much better. Since it was real and not fake.

She swallowed down the lump in her throat. "Get out of my car."

"Cassie, why you here?"

"Because... Because I want to know why you're following me."

The only sound she heard was the beating of her heart in her ears.

He was so close.

Too close.

And he was so not her type. But her heart wouldn't stop pounding. "You... You had me worried."

"If you were worried, woulda called the pigs," he grumbled.

"Pigs?"

"Cops."

She tightened both hands on the steering wheel and stared straight out of the windshield. She couldn't look at him. She couldn't. He was too close. Just inches away. "Just tell me why. Tell me how you knew my name. How you knew I'd been married. Why do you know any of that? Why do you even care to know?"

"Where's your girl?"

She blinked, not expecting that. She took a breath, her lungs filling with his scent, and turned her head to face him. "In bed. Asleep." Where Daisy was every night when she got home from Crazy Pete's.

"She good for a bit?"

Cassie frowned, wondering why he'd ask that. "Yes. My sister and her husband are home with her."

"Means you got time to talk."

That wasn't a question, it was stated as a fact. "Only if you tell me what I want to know." And that was a fact, too.

"Gonna tell you that. And more." He reached over and shoved the shifter into Park, turned the key and pulled it from the ignition. Instead of giving it to her, he closed his fist around it and climbed out of the Honda. He leaned down into the open doorway and said, "C'mon."

She stared at him. Could she trust him? He was part of the same club as Dodge, Stella and Trip. And she would've hoped Dodge would have warned her about him the other night if he was untrustworthy.

Wouldn't he have?

Or was their brotherhood strong enough that they covered for each other? That Dodge wouldn't snitch on his "brother" about him being some sort of psycho stalker.

But Cassie's gut wasn't telling her any of that.

Though, she didn't completely trust her gut anymore. Not after finding out Dennis had hidden his gambling problem for years.

Years.

She had been that blind to it.

A total fucking fool.

"Where are we going?" Because that's what a normal person would ask, right? Not just get out of her CRV in the middle of the night, in the dark, and follow some biker without knowing where?

He straightened, shut the passenger-side door, and came around to her side. She could lock the doors, but since he had the key, that would do no good. And he wasn't going to hurt her. He could've done that in the dark lot that night. Or one of the many nights he followed her home.

He opened her door. "C'mon." He jutted his big hand into the Honda.

She stared at it for a second, then unlatched her seatbelt. She sat in the seat for another couple of breaths before she finally put her hand in his.

It was so big. She swore it was twice the size of hers.

His fingers curled around hers with a gentle strength and he helped her out of the SUV.

"Where are we going?" she asked again, thinking a sane woman would need to know this first.

"To talk."

"We can talk in the car."

"We could. But we ain't." Keeping a grip on her hand, he pulled her along with him toward the metal stairs at the back of the building. He stopped at the bottom, released her hand and jerked his chin toward the steps. "Up there."

Her gaze rose up the metal stairway. At the top landing were two doors and two large picture windows, both dark. "What's up there?"

"You always ask so many fuckin' questions?"

"Well, this situation kind of warrants a lot of questions."

"Not gonna hurt you."

"You keep saying that."

"And you don't believe it."

No, she did. But that didn't mean she should do something stupid and regret doing that stupid thing later.

"I'd take you into The Barn to talk but thinkin' that might not be the best place for privacy since there was a party tonight. Not sure who or what's left behind..."

"Dodge hadn't returned before I left."

Judge snorted. "Yeah. There's a reason for that. You and Stel might be runnin' the bar tomorrow by yourselves."

"Did he get drunk?"

His lips twitched. "Among other fuckin' things."

"A patch party's a big deal, right?"

"Big fuckin' deal," he confirmed.

"You didn't get drunk."

He said nothing.

"Because you had to drive."

Again nothing.

"Because you've been following me home every night after work."

Still nothing. He just jerked his head toward the steps again.

She sighed, took a deep breath and climbed them. With each step, her heart pounded a little more.

At the landing, he grabbed a folding chair from near the door on the right and moved it next to the single chair that sat by the door on the left.

"Warm enough to sit out here for a few?"

The night was crisp, but the wind wasn't blowing so it was bearable. Living in Rochester, she was used to the cold. "Yes."

"Then sit."

He dug into his pocket, pulled out a key and opened the

door on the left. "Just need to be quiet since Red and Sig are probably sleepin'."

She had no idea who Red and Sig were and he didn't explain.

One of the American Bulldogs he had with him the other night rushed out with a soft whine, nudged Judge in the crotch with its nose and an enthusiastic tail wag. "Go pop a squat," he ordered. The large dog rushed down the steps and into the dark.

He shut the door quietly and settled into one of the folding chairs, which complained under his weight.

She sat next to him, staring out into the dark, trying to find the dog. "Where's the other one?"

"With Deacon."

"Who's Deacon?"

"My cousin."

"Is he also a member of your gang?"

"Club," Judge grunted.

"Is there a difference?"

"A big one."

Though she was curious about that, it wasn't what Cassie wanted to know from him. She could get that clarification from Dodge or Stella at another time.

He dug his hand under his leather vest—a "cut" was what Dodge had called it—and pulled out a small container and a Zippo lighter. A second later he was lighting up a joint.

A joint.

Holy shit. She had a sudden flashback to her high school days.

He took a big inhale, held it for a surprisingly long time, then tipped his head back and blew the smoke up into the night.

He took another long hit, then held it out to her.

She stared at it like it was a copperhead snake. He was

offering her drugs? She wasn't sure about the legality of pot in Pennsylvania.

"I... I haven't smoked pot since I was... younger."

Even in the limited light, she could see his grin. "Quit tobacco years ago. Besides booze, this is my only vice."

"Most people nowadays wouldn't even call it a vice since it's used as medicine." The laws around marijuana had definitely loosened since she smoked it when she was younger. It wasn't that big of a deal anymore.

"Yeah, it's my medicine."

She raised her gaze from his hand holding the joint to his face to see if he was being serious. He was.

"It's good shit."

She stared at the hand-rolled in his fingers again as he held it out to her. She shook her head. She wanted to keep her wits about her while they had this "talk," so now was not the best time to smoke pot since she had no idea how it would affect her. She'd probably been about twenty the last time she smoked any. And even then, it was only when her friends had it. She never smoked it on a regular basis.

He was taking another hit when the dog ran back up the steps and went directly to her, forcing its way between her thighs and planting—Cassie did a quick gender check—*her* head on her lap. Her hands automatically began ruffling her ears. The bulldog groaned, her tail held up like a flag and wagging slowly, her eyes on Cassie's.

"What's her name?"

Judge pinched the joint out and tucked it away. "Jury."

"Jury?" That was a strange name for a dog.

"Yeah."

"Judge and Jury," Cassie whispered.

"Yeah. We're a team."

She smiled as she stroked the big blocky head. A man who loved dogs couldn't be all that bad, right?

"She's sweet."

Judge was staring at Cassie's hand as it slid over his dog's short, smooth coat. "Yeah. When she wants to be. She's got a good instinct about people. So does Justice."

"Justice?"

"Deke's dog."

"Were they litter mates? They have the same markings."

"Yeah."

She ran her hand down Jury's smooth back. "I used to be a vet tech," she whispered. Used to be. When her life was together. When she thought everything was set, everything was neatly planned. Her family. Her career. Her life.

How foolish she had been to think her life had been perfect. That her path had been set in stone.

His next words made Cassie's hands still. "I know."

Judge surged to his feet and Jury quickly pulled away from Cassie, watching her daddy's every move.

Judge tipped his head toward the door. "C'mon. It's fuckin' cold out. We both got questions that need answers."

Cassie wasn't sure she liked the sound of that. Even so, *she* definitely needed some answers.

She followed him inside into what turned out to be a small apartment. The open front room was a living area with a couch, a few tables, a large screen TV on the wall, an old stereo system in one corner and, toward what looked like a short hallway, a kitchenette. Probably the perfect size for a single guy.

Or a man she assumed was single.

The apartment was pretty sparse with no décor or photos, just the basics. It wasn't filthy, but it wasn't perfectly clean, either.

The first thing he did was shrug out of his cut and hang it on a hook by the front door, then slid his knit beanie off his head and tossed it on a nearby table, where he also placed his keys. But not hers. Her car key was still buried deep in his front pocket.

He brushed a hand over his hair, which was not at all what she expected. With as long as his beard was, she assumed he was hiding a bunch of hair under his beanie. He wasn't. Actually, she was surprised with just how short it was clipped.

She wondered how he would look with it in reverse, with longer hair and a much shorter beard. With the facial structure she could see, he'd probably be fighting off women.

Hell, maybe he was now. There were plenty of women who were into long beards like that.

Even Daisy, at five, was fascinated by it. Daisy's mother, not so much.

But that was not why she was there in this apartment.

That was *not* why she was there in his apartment.

Without his cut, the off-white thermal he wore hugged his broad chest and thick arms snuggly. He was clearly solid, without the beer belly she expected from a biker. She figured they did nothing but party all the time. But no, this man did not have any kind of belly at all.

Unlike hers, which was bigger than she'd like. She'd been a lot smaller before she became pregnant with Daisy. Motherhood had filled her out just about everywhere.

Dennis had suggested she join a gym after Daisy was born, but Cassie was too exhausted to work out after working full-time, taking care of the house and raising her sassy daughter.

For the first couple of years, Dennis was involved. With Cassie. With the house. With their daughter.

Then three years ago, he began to pull away and get distant.

Cassie thought it was her weight that bothered him. That he was no longer attracted to her. That having a child, and also her weight gain, had destroyed their intimacy.

Many nights when she reached out to him, he'd turn his back to her and say he was too tired. And every time that happened, she vowed to join that gym and get back into shape.

But she never did.

And they became more distant. Less like a married couple and more like roommates who weren't even friends.

"Cassie."

She mentally shook herself and saw he'd moved closer. Now just a couple of feet away, he was looking at her with concern, those beautiful green eyes searching.

"You okay?"

She nodded. "Yes."

"Not gonna hurt you."

"I know."

"Wanna take off your coat?" He stepped even closer, holding out his large hand. She studied it. No jewelry in sight. Unlike Dodge, Cage and Trip, who all wore a few bulky rings and sometimes leather wrist bands.

But as he held out his hand, the sleeve of his thermal slid up enough for her to see a tattoo circling his wrist. She wondered how many he had.

"Will I be here long?"

"Depends on you." His voice—that rolling thunder—rumbled and it made heat swirl through her belly.

"You're the one with my car key."

He stepped up to her until they were practically toe to toe and slipped his hands under her coat to slide it off her shoulders. The whole time his face was tipped down to hers. Unreadable.

She hid the shiver that brief touch caused, but it was impossible to hide her nipples tightening into hard peaks.

She noticed that he noticed. Though, he said nothing. Instead, he took her coat in one hand and dug into his front jeans' pocket with the other, pulling out her car key. He slipped it into her coat pocket, making sure she saw him.

Then he moved away to hang it right next to his cut by the door.

An unspoken assurance she could leave whenever she wanted to.

"Who are you?" she whispered, her throat convulsing as he moved back to stand in front of her.

He was so damn tall. She was tall for a woman at five-foot-eight, but she felt tiny next to him. Almost petite.

His thumb brushed over her forehead, pushing a lock of hair out of her face, then he buried his spread fingers into the hair above her ear. "Judge."

"Is that your real name?"

"No," he answered softly, his eyes pinned on her mouth.

She licked her lips. "What is it?"

"Judd."

The longer he stared at her lips, the harder it was for her to catch her breath. "And why Judge?"

"Why not?"

"Is there a story behind it?"

"It matter?"

She guessed it didn't. "You answered my question with something I already knew. What I want to know is who are you?"

"Who are you?"

She blinked up at him. His thumb was massaging her temple, his fingers gripping her hair. Not roughly, but, even so, holding her there. A prisoner to his touch.

"Why do you know things about me?"

He released her suddenly and Cassie was relieved he moved away, allowing her to think more clearly, letting her catch her breath.

"Promise you're gonna hear me out."

Well, that just put her on edge. And not a good one.

"Been on your feet all night. Get off 'em."

Huh?

"They hurt?"

What the hell was he talking about?

"Your feet. They hurt?"

She pinned her eyebrows together. "Y-yes."

"Take a load off." He jerked his chin toward the couch, where Jury was already curled up in one corner but keeping an eye on them both.

She moved toward the couch only because, yes, her feet hurt, and it would be nice to get off them. A hot shower usually helped somewhat with her sore feet and back. A soak in a tub would be better but filling the tub would take too long every night and might wake up everyone in her sister's house.

"Shouldn't wear a boot with a heel," he said, going into the kitchenette and opening the fridge.

"It helps with tips."

His head popped up over the open refrigerator door. "The boots?"

She waved a hand down her body. "The whole outfit."

His head disappeared again for a second and when he straightened, he slammed the door shut and had a beer in one hand and a bottle of water in the other. He handed the water to her.

He remembered she didn't drink beer. *Hmm*, a man that listened and remembered. Those were a rare breed.

"Sit," he grunted. "Jury, off."

The dog scrambled from the couch to the floor and Judge waited for Cassie to take the dog's place.

She did and put the water bottle on the floor at her feet.

Judge settled on the other end of the couch, cracked open the beer, guzzled half of it and put the bottle down on the floor. He twisted toward her. "Take your boots off."

She stared at him. "Why?"

"When's the last time someone did somethin' nice for you?"

"When's the last time someone did something nice for you?" she repeated the question back to him.

He shook his head. "Not talkin' 'bout me."

"Heather and Tyler letting Daisy and me move in was more than nice."

"When's the last time a *man* did anythin' nice for you?"

Why was he asking this? "I... I don't know."

"Take your boots off."

"I don't understand why—"

"Take your fuckin' boots off, Cassie."

This was just weird. Coming up to his apartment was a mistake. "I need to get home."

"Kid's asleep. Sister's home. You got time."

"I came here to find out why you're following me and why you know things about me that are none of your business. Not to get comfortable."

She froze and her heart seized when he surged forward, grabbed one ankle, pulled her leg up and unzipped her boot.

"Hey!"

He had the boot pulled off and tossed across the room before she could scramble away from him. Then he pulled her foot into his lap and began to work the sole with his big, strong fingers.

Oh.

Oh shit.

Holy shit.

A groan slipped from between her lips.

His lips twitched at her reaction. "Feel good?"

"Yes," she breathed, leaning back against the arm of the couch, getting more comfortable. "Oh... my... God."

He grinned. "Like that?"

"*Yesssss.*"

"Get your other boot off," he ordered as he continued to massage her foot.

She didn't hesitate this time. This time she quickly unzipped the other boot and plopped her foot right into his lap, so she was sitting sideways on the couch.

She groaned as he began to massage her feet with both hands. "Holy shit." She closed her eyes and dropped her head back.

Whatever he was doing felt like heaven.

Pure heaven.

Oh God, it was better than sex. *Way* better.

A little whimper escaped her as he dug his thumb deep into a sore spot.

She almost sounded drunk when she asked, "How'd you know my feet hurt like that?"

"Aunt was a waitress. My uncle, Deke's pop, used to massage her feet after her shift. Kept their marriage alive. Afterward, we'd hear them go into their room and bang one out."

Her eyes popped open and her head jerked up. "What?"

Was he expecting them to "bang one out" after he was done massaging her feet?

Judge wasn't looking at her but was concentrating on her sock-covered feet with a smile. "It was tit for toe."

Tit for what? "Tit for tat?"

"He got her tits after massagin' her toes."

Cassie slapped a hand over her mouth to smother the laugh. "Was that a joke?"

He grunted. "Kinda. But it was true."

"I take it they had a good relationship."

"Yeah."

"You were close with them?"

"Yeah."

"Family should be important."

"Should be."

She groaned as he hit another sore spot. "I agree. They should be. I'm thankful for my sister and her husband."

"Why'd you run?"

She lifted her head again. "Tell me why you know things about me first."

His fingers slowed and she wanted to complain, but she had no right to, so she didn't.

"Own Justice Bail Bonds."

Cassie shot up and jerked her feet from his hands, curling her legs under her. "What?"

"My cousin, Deke, and I run a bail bonds business."

"Okay..."

"Lookin' for your husband."

"You're not the only one."

His green eyes hit hers and held. "You lookin' for him, too?"

"Yes."

"You don't know where he is?"

"No. If I did..."

"If you did...?"

"I'd finally be divorced."

He nodded. "Kinda figured that."

"How?"

"Feet," he demanded, his hands held out.

She sighed and uncurled her legs, putting her feet back in his lap. She jerked as he peeled off her socks and tossed them to the floor. He began to rub her bare feet.

And, *holy shit*... It made her melt like butter.

If he was some psycho killer, he knew how to bring down her guard.

But instead of going all Ted Bundy on her, he began to talk. "Got a call from a bondsman in Rochester about your husband jumpin' bail. Told me you came to Manning Grove and to keep an eye out for Lange. We catch him, we make a little scratch."

"Why would he come here?"

"To be with his wife and kid."

She blinked. "He's not looking for me."

"Yeah, figured that out."

"How?"

"Deke went up to New York and..."

His cousin went to Rochester? "And?"

"And got some info up there. From someone you know. Found out you two had split a while back. Before he got charged. Assets were seized while you were waitin' for the divorce to go through."

Well, someone got their information right for once. "Yes."

"That's why your finger don't have a mark."

What? She lifted her left hand and glanced at her ring finger. "I removed it after I kicked him out."

"Wasn't gonna give him a second chance?"

It seemed he was being honest, so she might as well be the same. Especially since they were both looking for Dennis. And if Judge found him, it would benefit Cassie, too.

In fact, if Judge or his cousin found Dennis, she could get him to sign the divorce papers and it might be the first step in being free of her hopefully soon-to-be ex-husband's mess.

"I considered it. *If* he would have gone to counseling for not only our marriage but his gambling addiction, but he refused. So, I refused to let him back in the house. He spent every damn dime we had saved. He wanted to put a second mortgage on our home. He spent our entire retirement. Everything was gone. Just... gone." She flung her hands up. "Just like that. Any money we had disappeared into thin air. Everything we worked for. Everything *I* worked for. He just..." She shook her head. "He left me and Daisy with nothing. Nothing." Her throat tightened. "He left his *daughter* with nothing. Not even the little we had put aside for her college fund. He drained that, too."

A muscle ticked in Judge's cheek and his grip tightened on her feet. "Yeah."

"And that was before I found out about the embezzlement, which made it so much worse. Right now, I'm paying for his crime. His daughter is, too."

His fingers relaxed a little more as he massaged. "Bondsman thought maybe when he bailed and you left town, you were settin' it up to meet him here, or maybe somewhere else and this was just a stop on the way."

Of course. Because almost everyone thought she was involved. She was disappointed that so many people thought so little of her own integrity. "No. The only reason I'd ever want to see him again is to get him to sign those papers. To set me free."

"Your daughter."

She stared at Judge. Those two simple words, the child she and Dennis shared, made things way more complex. "Yes. My daughter keeps us bound. But he's guilty. They have too much evidence against him. And once he goes to jail, it'll be up to Daisy, once she turns eighteen, whether she wants a relationship with him. I will not take her to prison to visit him. Does that make me a bad mother?" She shrugged. "I don't know. Maybe. But he should have thought about her before he stole all that money from *her*. He had the opportunity to turn himself around before it got that bad. He chose not to."

"Addictions are rough."

While she understood addictions were difficult and could rip families apart, he refused to get help. She couldn't help someone who wasn't willing to help himself. And she had herself and her daughter to protect.

Plus, she was angry. At him, for hiding it so well for so long, and at herself, for not seeing it.

"Maybe so. But losing your daughter should be much rougher. That's how I see it. I would do anything for her. He proved he wouldn't. All he had to do was get help. He didn't even try. He didn't even want to make the effort. That's when I knew I was done. When Daisy was done. I told him if and when he got help, I'd consider Daisy having a relationship with him again. But that never happened because he got arrested and charged. And then my life... *our* life... began to crumble even further. Her father's name was in everyone's mouth. What he did was unforgivable. But worse was where he stole that money from. That foundation trusted him. He'd worked there for years. That was one reason I left, because I didn't want Daisy dealing with the shit her father left behind. I wanted to make a fresh start where people might not know us."

"Manning Grove."

She chewed on her bottom lip. "Maybe. My sister offered us a place to stay temporarily. To escape the shit show in New York. I jumped on it. Daisy needs family. More than just me. She wasn't getting that in Rochester. My innocent little girl was caught up in shit that she didn't even understand. So, I packed what little I had left, what hadn't been seized and we came here. A place where I could gather my thoughts and make a plan."

"Bet that plan didn't include workin' in a bar."

"No, it didn't. But I am grateful that Stella hired me. It's a start. And it's giving me more than what I had. Which was nothing."

"Somethin' is better than nothin'," Judge mumbled.

Cassie's head snapped up. "Yes. Something is better than nothing."

"It's a sayin' Trip lives by. He resurrected our fathers' club not long ago. It had been destroyed, burned to the ground, and he had a plan to rebuild. You remind me of him. Startin' with nothin' and tryin' to make your way. Takin' what little you have and buildin' on it."

"I thought my future was set." She shook her head. "I

was dead wrong. And it's hard to start again with what Dennis did still hanging over us. I need this divorce. I need to be able to start fresh without worrying if every dime I make will be taken from me to pay off Dennis's debts. I shouldn't be responsible for the crimes he committed. My only crime was being blind to it all."

"Wasn't your fault."

She sighed. "Yes? Well, tell that to everyone else."

Chapter Nine

HIS FINGERS SLID over her bare feet, over her warm, smooth skin. She had tensed while talking about the shit Lange had created for her and their daughter and he was determined to get her moaning again, even if it was just with his hands on her feet.

"So, you were following me to find Dennis, thinking he would search us out? Or that we might be planning to go on the lam with him?"

"Yeah."

"Now you know he won't. He isn't stupid. He probably figures someone would be watching us. Plus, I'm sure he knows I need him to sign those damn papers."

Judge traced his fingers around her ankles, moving up slightly to squeeze and massage her lower calves.

"*Oh,*" she groaned, her eyes fluttering for a second as he moved his hands higher. "Uh... So, you no longer need to follow me. Or sit outside my sister's home."

He moved back down to the soles of her feet and then worked his way partly back up her calves. "Started to follow you to find Lange. Soon as I knew your divorce was pendin', the reason changed."

She lifted her head from the armrest and searched his face. "What was the new reason?"

"Make sure you made it home safely."

She frowned. "Why? Why would you care about my safety?"

"Got a little girl to take care of."

"So do a lot of other women. Do you follow a bunch of women home?"

When he ran into her at the municipal parking lot that first day and then again at the old warehouse lot, he thought she may be shy and submissive. He was quickly finding out the woman had some bite to her. And exactly where her daughter got her sass. "You leave late at night."

"So? This town seems safe. Way safer than Rochester and sometimes I used to get home late at night while I lived there."

"Didn't have me to watch you."

She sat up and began to pull her feet from his lap, but he grabbed her ankles and held her there.

"It's not your job to watch me."

"Didn't say it was."

"How about you give me your number and, if I see Dennis, the first thing I'll do after I get him to sign those damn papers—and kick him in the nuts for all the shit he put me through—is give you a call so you can haul his ass back to the pokey."

Judge fought to keep his expression blank. "The pokey?"

He lost that fight. Especially when she asked all sassy-like, "What? You don't call it the pokey?"

He smirked. "Baby, no one calls it the pokey."

"I do."

"Yeah, got that."

"Okay, back to business..."

Yeah, Judge was good with getting back to business, but not the business Cassie was talking about.

Pulling on her ankles, he slid her down the couch until her ass was against his knee. Until she was nice and close.

"What are you doing?" she whispered.

"Gettin' down to business."

"I said back to business."

"Okay, then. Gettin' back to business. Whatever you wanna fuckin' call it."

"I didn't come up here for that."

"Didn't bring you up here for that, either."

"We were supposed to be talking."

"Done talkin'. Lange ain't comin' to Manning Grove. Nothin' left to talk about."

"This is more than that."

"Wasn't gonna be 'til you said you kicked his ass out a long time ago. He was a stupid fuck and gave you up."

Cassie's mouth dropped open. "I have a daughter."

"Yeah? And I have a son. Didn't you fuckin' notice? It's just me and you on this couch, Cassie."

"I need to go." But she made no move to get up.

He released her and held up his palms. If she wanted to go, he wasn't going to force her to stay. He wanted more from her than just conversation, but that would be up to her. "Then go. Key's in your coat pocket. Can go at any time. Ain't holdin' you here. Your choice."

Her throat convulsed. "My choice for what?"

"To stay or go."

"And if I stay?"

"Means you're interested in the same."

"What are you interested in?" she asked in a breathy whisper.

"Nipples are as hard as a fuckin' rock, Cass. Got heat in your cheeks. Eyes are holdin' some heat, too. You know what I'm interested in."

"I don't do that."

"What don't you do?"

She waved a hand around. "Sleep with strange men."

"Ain't strange. Know who I am now. Know what I do. Where I belong. Even know my real name. Also told you somethin' some of my brothers don't know."

"About your son?"

"Yeah. Somethin' I don't talk about. Now you know. Gave you a piece of me not many other people have."

"Why?"

"'Cause I want you to trust me."

"Why?"

"Cass... 'Cause I want more than words from you."

"I..."

Judge shrugged. "Got it. I ain't your thing. You like a man who wears a fuckin' suit and works a nine-to-five behind a desk. But figured the way you liked me massagin' your feet, you didn't mind my touch."

"I didn't... I don't... I..." She shook her head. "I just haven't... I haven't considered..."

"Goddamn grown woman, Cassie. Bet you got needs just like the rest of us. Know you got a young daughter and it makes it hard to get those needs met. Right?"

"You brought me up here to have sex with me?"

"Jesus fuck," he muttered, pushing to his feet and causing hers to fall to the floor. "Brought you up here to talk. That's it. You wanna go, go. See I don't do it for you. So go." He went over to the door, grabbed her coat off the hook and waited for her to get her ass off his couch. "Never massaged a goddamn woman's feet before in my fuckin' life. Not once."

She sat up, but only stared at him, her lips parted, her cheeks even darker now, her fingers curled against her denim-covered thighs.

Seeing her like that made her not wanting him all the fucking harder. "Ain't gonna lie, Cassie. You fuckin' do it for me. Been a long time since a woman has caught my eye like you. Long fuckin' time. Surprised the fuck outta me. That day in the municipal lot, when I saw you walkin'... Jesus Christ... Wanted you right that fuckin' second..."

She got to her feet. But instead of pulling on her socks and boots, she padded over to him barefoot, her face unreadable.

"But saw you were scared. Bothered me but got past it. Then again at Walmart and the old lot. Didn't give you any fuckin' reason to be scared of me—"

He could see her throat move again as she swallowed. "I just wasn't expecting—"

He set his jaw. This was exactly why the fuck he didn't ever go after what he wanted. Why it was easier to fuck a sweet butt or his fist. Or his fucking Fleshlight. None of them said no. None of them found a reason to. "Don't give a fuck. Just fuckin' go."

She reached out and took her coat from his hands. She stared at where she clutched the thick wool and said something so softly, he didn't hear her.

"What?"

She lifted her face to his. "Maybe I don't want to go."

He stared at her and just breathed for a few heartbeats. He wanted to be goddamn clear with her about what he wanted from her. She needed to see what he wanted crystal fucking clear. "Want you like a man wants a woman, got that?"

She swallowed hard again. "Yes."

Jesus. "Means naked in my bed."

"Got it."

She fucking *got it.* "You stay..." If she stayed, they were both ending up naked in his bed. He wanted to see her without a goddamn stitch of clothes on, spread across his fucking sheets. He wanted to see, taste and fuck that juicy pink center. He wanted to smother himself in her tits, in those thighs. Maybe even in that luscious fucking ass.

"I can't stay long," she said with a catch in her voice.

He didn't want to hear that. Everything he wanted to do to her would take a while. If he got her naked, he wasn't rushing. And he'd make sure she wouldn't want him rushing, either. "Your sister got somewhere to go on a Sunday mornin'?"

"It's the questions that will be asked."

"So, tell her the fuckin' truth. Hadn't had dick in a while, needed it, got some. Sure she'd understand."

She pressed her lips together, then said, "I'm not sure I'd explain it like that."

"Then explain it how you gotta. Been wantin' you since the second I saw you, Cass. Again... ain't gonna bullshit you about that. Now I know the husband's out of the picture, want you even more."

Uncertainty filled her eyes. "I'm not sure this is smart."

He lifted and dropped one shoulder. "Yeah, done a lot of dumb things in my fuckin' life. Fuckin' you ain't gonna be one of 'em."

"Smart on my part, I meant."

He tilted his head and stared at her. Then he nodded, went over to the couch, picked up her socks, gathered her boots and came back to where she was still standing.

He held them out to her with one hand and turned the key in the deadbolt with the other. But before he could open the door, she reached up and locked the deadbolt again.

"I won't be needing what you're holding for a little bit."

He stifled his grin, but let the boots and socks drop to the floor at his feet. "Means you won't need what you're holdin', either." He worked the coat out of her clenched fingers and hung it back up. "Scared?"

Her throat worked, but she shook her head. "Nervous, I guess. I haven't... It's..."

Jesus fuck, that was good fucking news. "How long?"

Her throat jumped and her gaze dropped to his chest as she whispered, "Years."

Fuck yes.

Was that fucking selfish of him? Fuck yeah it was, but he didn't give a fuck. That meant that marriage was over years ago. She was not pining away for her ex. There was no lingering bullshit between her and Lange to get in the way with everything he wanted to give her tonight.

"Gonna think this is a mistake afterward?"

Without hesitation, she answered, "Probably."

"Least you're fuckin' honest about it."

"You've been honest with me."

That he had. "Can you live with that mistake?"

She lifted her face to his again. "Won't know until I make it."

He pressed his lips together to keep from grinning. "Got a plan."

"What is it?" Her question held a little shake to it.

"Starts with your mouth." When her lips parted, he dropped his head, dug his fingers into the hair on both sides of hers, and whispered, "Then it goes from there."

Her ragged breath beat against his lips and he hesitated.

She was probably going to regret this in the morning.

He wasn't from her world.

He probably wasn't even close to her type.

The biggest issue she ever dealt with in her life was the shitty hand her ex-husband dealt her.

But none of that mattered right now.

He just wanted tonight. And so did she.

So, he'd take what he wanted and give her the same.

When the sun came up in the morning, she might see things differently than she did right now. But he had until then.

And he was going to enjoy every fucking second of it.

He closed the small gap between their lips and swallowed the breath that rushed from her.

And the groan that followed.

Fuck yes...

Her lips were soft and her mouth sweet as he explored every fucking corner of it. He expected her to be hesitant with her kiss, but fuck no, she wasn't. Her tongue clashed with his, fighting to explore his mouth instead.

But hell no, that wasn't how it was going to go. Not tonight.

He was taking what he wanted. At least, everything she was willing to give him.

He tilted his head and drove her tongue out of his mouth. By her giving him her mouth, he was claiming it. Tonight, it was his.

One of her hands was fisted in his thermal, the fingers from her other lost within his beard, holding on, keeping him close. He didn't care that it pulled at his skin, as long as she wasn't yanking him away, wanting him to stop.

And hell no, she wasn't. Her tongue was now toying with his as their mouths moved together. He had never been into kissing. To him it had been a waste of time and always preferred to get right down to business, especially with a woman who wasn't sticking.

But he couldn't get enough of Cassie's mouth. The way her lips moved against his, the way she tried to steal the power with her tongue, the little noises she made at the back of her throat.

It all made his hard dick ache for her.

He released her hair from one hand, sliding it down her neck, feeling the pound of her pulse, then around and down her back until he got to her ass. He curled his fingers around the generous curve and pulled her tighter against him.

Now, she had no doubt how much he wanted her. The

proof was unmistakably pressed into her stomach and when she whimpered softly into his mouth, he broke the kiss.

She pressed her forehead into his chest, and he could hear her gasping for breath. He was struggling to find his, too. Because he hadn't been this worked up over a woman in fucking years.

Years.

But it was when her hand, the one gripping his thermal, loosened and slid down his gut, over his belt and brushed over his jeans where his hard-on was caught... That was when he knew they were done standing by the door kissing.

If he didn't move now, he was going to fuck her against that door. Or on the couch. Or even on the floor. Maybe even all three places.

He only had one wrap in his chain wallet. He had a box in his bedroom.

They would need the box.

And again, he wanted to see everything, he didn't want one inch of her hidden from him.

He also wanted to take his time exploring her, not do a quick bust-a-nut. Those he could do with any woman, sweet butt or otherwise.

He blew out a breath as she continued to explore his erection over his jeans. "Cassie..."

Her hand stilled at her name.

Fuck. He wanted her to stop but he also didn't want her to stop.

They needed to move.

Like fucking now.

"Last chance to not make that mistake," he murmured into her hair, hoping like fuck she didn't change her mind.

"Why do you think it would be my mistake? How do you know it's not you making the mistake?" came the muffled question from his thermal.

Yeah, most men didn't see sex as making a mistake.

Unless the woman trapped him in some way. Then it was a big fucking mistake.

He'd made one of those. And it's why he always wore wraps, even if the female was on birth control. It was also why he would only use his own wraps. Ones which had been in his control the whole time, because, yeah... He learned that lesson the hard fucking way.

It only took once.

Now was not the time to dredge up that old shit. He had Cassie in his arms and his fucking fantasy was about to come true.

Instead of answering her, he released her ass and her hair, grabbed the hand she still had on his dick and pulled her down the short hallway to his bedroom at the end. He hit the light and froze.

For fuck's sake. He forgot.

He spun on his boot and blocked her view. "Wanna hit the head first?"

Her brow furrowed. "Uh, sure."

"Door on the left there."

She gave him a look, nodded and then went into the bathroom, closing the door behind her.

He rushed to the nightstand, grabbed the Fleshlight and hurried to the closet. He shoved into the far corner, keeping it upright so the last load he dumped in it—and forgot to clean out—wouldn't spill.

He quietly closed the closet door, went back to the night-stand, swiped the lube off the top and tucked it in the back of the drawer before pulling out the box of wraps.

He heard the toilet flush, the water run, and the door open.

He turned and waited.

And he lost his goddamn breath when she stepped through his bedroom door. She hesitated, her eyes going from him to the bed and back.

He glanced over his shoulder to check his sheets to make sure there wasn't anything stained on them and they were half-decently clean. The bed wasn't made but she was just going to have to live with that.

Jury pushed past Cassie and took a flying leap onto the bed. She was claiming her spot before they did.

"Jury, off," he growled and pointed to her dog bed in the corner. The only time he forced her to sleep there was when he had a visitor.

Jury gave him a *you-suck* look, jumped off and curled up in the expensive bed he bought her that she spent, at most, an hour of her time in whenever a sweet butt was up in his apartment.

Tonight, if it was up to Judge, she would spend more time than an hour in that bed. Because Cassie would be in his for much longer.

Cassie was no fucking sweet butt. There would be no kicking her ass out as soon as he shot his load.

"Just gonna stand there?" he asked.

"Are you?" she countered. He could see the shake in her hand as she brushed the hair out of her face.

Yeah, she was fucking nervous. She wasn't sure what to expect from him or how this would go.

Or maybe she was second-guessing her decision to stay.

If she was, he needed to make sure she had no reason to bolt. The only direction she should be taking is toward him, not toward the front door.

He couldn't wait for her to change her mind.

So, he didn't.

He took a couple of long strides to where she stood, her eyes glued to him as he approached, never stopping as his body knocked into hers, his arms grabbing her so she wouldn't lose her balance. The air rushed from her and her blue eyes lifted to his in surprise.

Then something changed, surprising him instead.

She grabbed the fabric of his thermal at his chest with both fists, pulled him in a circle and shoved him against the wall. With one hand, she grabbed his beard and yanked it so hard he had no choice but to lower his head. Then she took his mouth.

She took *his* mouth.

This woman was *not* having second thoughts.

This time he let her tongue take control of his mouth. He let her have all the control. And he was kind of liking it.

As she tried to climb him, he hooked his arms under her ass and lifted her enough to where she could wrap her legs around his waist and her arms around his neck, not once breaking their kiss.

He spun her around and shoved her back against the wall, pinning her there. With one arm he kept her up, the other he shoved between them, doing his best to free the buttons on her blouse.

But he was getting impatient and was afraid he was just going to rip it open, popping all of her buttons and ruining it.

Then she'd have to go home wearing one of his shirts. He'd grin at that if Cassie wasn't currently creating havoc on his mouth.

He thrust his hard dick against the heat between her thighs.

Fuck, he wanted to be inside her.

But he was liking what she was giving him. If she wanted to drive right now, he'd let her. Without complaint.

A few seconds later, she released his mouth, panting against his lips as she stared at him. Again, surprise in her eyes.

Yeah, she wanted his dick. She wanted him. She hadn't expected to want him like that.

"You done bein' a little Domme?"

Chapter Ten

She pressed fingers to her lips. "I'm not a Domme."

"Coulda fooled me," he teased.

She removed her arms from around his thick neck and planted both palms against his chest, feeling his quick heartbeat along with the rise and fall of his rapid breathing.

"I don't know what came over me. Why..."

His cocky grin made her want to take his lips again.

"'Cause you want my dick." He thrust his hips again and his erection pressed against where she was not only slick, but throbbing.

She couldn't deny she wanted his "dick," so she pressed her face against his neck, hiding behind the long beard, ground hard against him, and muffled her groan into his skin.

"Damn," he whispered.

Yes, *damn*.

She couldn't remember the last time she'd been so turned on like this. Wanting to rip a man's clothes off, demand he do things to her.

"I need you naked," she whispered.

"Think that was my line," he whispered back.

"Then what are you waiting for?"

He adjusted his grip on her thighs, holding on tighter, and pulled away from the wall, turning them and striding across the room. He didn't stop when he hit the edge of the mattress. Instead, he held on to her as they both fell, making her gasp.

Somehow, he managed not to crush her under his weight, but it pinned her to the bed, his erection, hard and hot against her thigh.

She pointed out the obvious. "We're still not naked."

"Good observation."

She pressed her lips together and he rolled off her to sit on the edge of the bed, unlacing his boots. Within seconds, he had both pulled off, his socks went flying, then he shot to his feet and tugged his thermal over his head, messing up his beard.

He drew a hand through it a couple of times, smoothing it back down.

While he did that, Cassie stared at his chest. There was no way she couldn't.

It wasn't because of how huge it was, because it was. It wasn't because of how muscular it was, because it was.

But because of the number of tattoos covering his skin.

They went up both arms, over his pecs and shoulders, down his ribs, across his lower belly and disappeared into the waistband of his jeans.

She sat up, taking them all in. Wanting to ask so many questions about them, starting with the meaning of each one.

But Judge didn't appear to want to discuss his ink right now. No, he was unbuckling his belt and unfastening his jeans at a rapid pace.

She began to unbutton her shirt where he'd left off and he made a sharp but deep noise that made her fingers still mid-motion.

"Sit right there 'til I'm done." It wasn't a suggestion, but a growled demand.

And he called *her* a Domme.

She didn't know much about BDSM. Probably just as much as she knew about tattoos.

Which was basically nothing.

She'd never dabbled in the Dominant/submissive lifestyle, or any kind of kink, and she'd never been with anyone who had tattoos. Not even a small one.

However, Judge's tattoos were not surprising, not with what she knew about his lifestyle. Every biker she met who belonged to the Fury had quite a few, including Stella. Her boss had a full sleeve and a huge tree of life piece on her back, which she had shown Cassie in the back room one night when she asked about it.

She could only imagine Judge had a few on his back, too.

He shucked his jeans and boxers quickly. And suddenly, she forgot about any and all tattoos.

She also forgot to breathe.

His hard cock hung heavy, like he had a weight hanging off the end.

And it was not small.

It wasn't scary big, but it was a lot larger than she expected. Apparently, the size was deceiving when he was wearing jeans. But maybe it looked bigger because, like the hair on his head, his dark pubic hair was trimmed short. Very short.

Unfortunately, she couldn't avoid staring.

The noise he made when she licked her lips forced her gaze up.

His nostrils were flared and his eyes dark as he grabbed the root of his cock and squeezed it so hard, the veins protruded.

He suddenly moved.

Cassie's heart pounded in her chest, in her throat, in her ears, as the big man approached the bed. He made her feel very small as he stood at the end and studied her as he stroked his cock slowly.

"Now... slowly unbutton your shirt. Want you to touch yourself as you do it. Pretend it's me touchin' you."

"Why do I have to pretend?" She quickly slipped all the buttons through the holes. "Touch me yourself."

She shrugged out of her blouse and threw it at him. It hit his chest and fluttered to his feet.

He stared at it for a second, then lifted his gaze. His eyes burned hot, his hand had stilled around the root of his cock, and then...

He moved again.

All the air fled from her lungs as his weight hit her, knocking her onto her back. He grabbed her wrists and yanked them up over her shoulders, shoving his face in her cleavage which had almost been knocked free from her bra.

She groaned as he sucked her and his beard scraped her skin. He clamped both her wrists into one hand and ripped one cup down far enough until her breast came out.

"Fuck," he growled a split second before sucking her aching nipple deep.

Her hips surged up at that pleasurable pull that shot from her nipple all the way to her pussy.

Which almost made her come. Surprisingly, in seconds. Just with his mouth on her like that. He was not gentle as he sucked hard and rocked against her even harder.

He pulled her other breast out and sucked that one, too. His fingers finding the slick nipple he'd abandoned and tweaking it hard.

She gasped and lifted her head, watching him take in as much of her breast as he could into his mouth.

Him tipping his green eyes to hers was all it took to make heat burst through her center, radiate out, goosebumps break out over her heated skin and cause her thighs to squeeze together and her toes curl. She breathed his name.

She tried to say Judge, but the only part that came out was Judd. But then, it only seemed right to call him by his real name when they were being intimate.

He released her wrists and her breast and rose up onto his hands, staring down at her. "Bra off."

She wedged her hands beneath herself and unclipped the wide strap on the strongest bra she could find to hold the weight of her breasts up comfortably. As she did that, he unfastened the button and zipper on her jeans, and as she slipped the bra off her arms, he jerked her jeans down her hips, her whole body jolting as he did so.

She planted her feet into the mattress just long enough to lift her hips so he could finish peeling the denim and her panties down her thighs and calves, and free them from her feet as she fell back to the bed.

And now they were both naked.

Finally.

She froze as he kneeled between her calves with her jeans and panties crushed in his hand. His gaze slid from her hair which was spread loose around her head, over her face and lower. He paused on her breasts, which ached for his touch, and, again, continued lower.

She tensed as his eyes roamed over her stomach—the one part on her Dennis complained about the most—but his face didn't change, not even in the slightest, as he continued lower. Past the stretch marks she earned from carrying Daisy, over her wider than desired hips, and her thighs that jiggled when she walked.

When he was done, he lifted his eyes back to hers. "Fuckin' goddamn beautiful. Just like I knew you'd be."

She wasn't expecting that. *Hell*, she wasn't sure what his reaction would be. But hearing that...

He threw her jeans and panties to the floor, grabbed her calves and pushed them toward her until her knees were bent, then he spread her legs even wider. He took his time staring at her *there*, too. She gripped the sheets so she wouldn't instinctively cover herself, because it was difficult not to do so.

Dennis had been so judgmental about her body changes. It was one reason she never tried to date after separating from him. Daisy was another. Having a young daughter, she had to be careful about anyone she met.

Plus, with all the shit going on in her life, she hadn't wanted the hassle. Once things settled, she'd consider dating again. But right now, she had a long way to go before she got to that point.

She was in no rush. She hadn't had sex in a few years, anyway, so what was waiting a couple more?

But Judge was reminding her about what she'd been missing. What she'd used to enjoy before she pushed her own wants and needs aside.

Tonight, she wasn't doing that.

Tonight, Judge wanted her, and she wanted him.

Yes, he wasn't her type. And never before in her life would she have thought she'd be sexually attracted to someone like him.

But it was more than that.

He was more than his size.

More than his long, shaggy beard.

More than the cut he wore on his back.

More than the tattoos which were permanently inked into his skin.

On the outside, he could look intimidating, maybe even scary, but Cassie was finding on the inside he wasn't so much. Proving the adage that looks could be deceiving.

Even so, Cassie figured Judge could be dangerous if he wanted to be. She had a feeling if someone screwed him over, he wasn't going to ignore it and would do something about it. And whatever it was would make a strong statement.

He seemed to be the type of man who could be gentle with one hand, deadly with the other.

He trailed his fingertips up both her calves, over her knees and they took a slow path along her thighs. The closer he got to his destination, the more she wanted to squirm. She didn't. She only fisted the sheets more tightly, instead.

His gaze flicked from his fingers to her face and back. He pursed his lips as he skimmed them over her pubis bone but went no lower.

She wanted him to touch her there. She was getting slicker by the second at the thought of where this was going.

And she was getting impatient.

"Judge," she whispered.

"You gonna get bossy?"

"If I have to."

He grinned, then in one motion, dropped down to the mattress and shoved her legs as wide as they could go.

Her hips shot up as his mouth circled her clit and he sucked it hard. He crossed one arm over her hips, holding her down, the other he stretched up and grabbed her nipple, pulling it hard and twisting it.

Holy shit...

She wanted to watch him, but she couldn't. She rolled her head back and closed her eyes, just enjoying everything his lips and tongue were doing to her.

And what they were doing was sucking, licking, biting, exploring.

Holy shit, he was *really* good at it, too.

Perfect.

Better than perfect. His fingers squeezed her breast as he thumbed her pebbled nipple.

Holy shit...

The heavy weight across her hips disappeared and two thick fingers slid through her wet folds, teasing.

"Please..."

She didn't have to ask again, he plunged them inside her without any resistance since she was so wet. Her hips shot up again and he stayed with her, not letting up as he sucked and flicked her clit and ate her like a starving man.

When he pinched her other nipple hard, she gasped, and the pleasurable pain exploded through her, rushing down to meet the orgasm radiating up.

And, *holy hell*, she hadn't had such an intense orgasm since...

She didn't know when. Not even with her vibrator. And those were some pretty intense ones when she was in the right mood.

When the last ripple disappeared, she melted into the mattress, staring up at the ceiling and just trying to breathe.

Her eyes tipped down to him as he sat up, his shiny lips curled up slightly in a grin as he wiped off, not only his mouth, but his beard with his hand.

That was probably one drawback to having such a long one.

When he twisted and reached out to the nightstand to grab a condom, Cassie let her gaze slide over him and it landed on his cock, which had a string of precum hanging from it. Reaching out, she caught it on her thumb before bringing it to her lips and sucking it clean.

"Fuck, baby," he breathed, the condom temporarily forgotten in his fingers.

She smiled around the tangy taste and began to curl up to a seated position. "I want to do to you what you did to me."

It was only fair, right? And it was something she'd always enjoyed. She was pretty damn sure he'd enjoy it, too.

"Yeah, would love for you to do that... Just not now.

Want my dick deep inside you, instead. You wanna suck me later, not gonna stop you."

Later.

They didn't have later. She needed to get back to her daughter. They only had now.

Her simple, "Okay," had him moving again, tearing open the wrapper, rolling on the condom and settling once again on his knees between her thighs.

He dropped to his hands, planting his palms on the mattress on either side of her head as he lowered his own, catching her eyes. "So goddamn beautiful."

His rough whisper sent a shiver through her.

His genuine words made her truly feel beautiful.

The intense look in his eyes caused her heart to skip a beat.

He sucked one nipple, then the other, took her mouth, swallowing her groan. He nudged her thighs higher with his knees and he settled his huge body between them. Putting all his weight on one arm, he grabbed his cock and slid it through her wetness until it caught.

This was happening.

She was having sex with a man who was not her husband.

She was having sex with a man she hardly knew.

Maybe she should feel guilty, but she didn't.

She had given everything to Dennis. She had given everything to Daisy.

For once she was doing something for herself.

For once she was taking what she wanted.

Getting what she needed.

And she shouldn't feel guilty about that at all.

She was a woman in her early thirties with wants and needs.

She wasn't dead.

Judge was making her feel very much alive and appreciated as a woman.

But he didn't enter her. He hesitated. Right there. At the spot which would only take a slight shift to connect them.

He deepened the kiss for a moment, then pulled away enough to search her face.

He was going to ask her if she was sure. If this was what she wanted. He didn't need to ask because she gave him a small smile as an answer.

And that was all he needed.

He grabbed her wrists, pinned them into the mattress on either side of her head, kept his eyes on hers and thrust inside in one move.

Oh... shit...

He filled her, stretched her as he drove deep.

He wasn't slow or gentle as she suspected he might be.

Hell no.

His grip tightened on her wrists and he kept their gazes locked as he powered up and into her over and over, a deep grunt escaping him at the end of each thrust.

"Fuck, baby," he growled.

The power behind his movements shouldn't surprise her, but they did. And maybe they should scare her, but they didn't.

No.

It was then she realized the couple of years after Daisy was born, Dennis had been only going through the motions. But that had been all it was.

He'd been doing his duty.

The passion they had when they dated and then first married, had somehow dwindled to nothing. Something she used to enjoy immensely, only became a mindless act.

Why hadn't she recognized it? Was it the same reason she never noticed Dennis was a gambling addict? Had she just ignored it all, put on blinders, not wanting to deal with it?

Had she just tuned it all out and lived life on autopilot?

She had wanted them to go to marriage counseling when he first confessed about being an addict. And now, as she thought back, she had been almost relieved when he refused.

It had given her an easy reason to walk away.

Easy at first, until things became messy...

"Cassie," his deep voice washed over her, bringing her back to the present.

Her getting lost in the past wasn't fair to Judge.

Dennis was her past. She needed to leave him there. Maybe Judge could help her do that.

"Okay?" he asked.

She gave him another small smile. "Yes."

"Ain't hurtin' you?"

"No."

"Need me to slow down?"

Her smile grew. "No."

"Want you to come."

They were on the same page about that. "I plan on it."

His pounding paused. "Tell me what you need from me."

Her smile disappeared. She'd never been asked that before. She had dated a lot of men before meeting Dennis, some were good in bed, some not so much. And while some cared if she came before they did, she couldn't remember any of them asking her how they could make sure to get her there.

She usually had to tell them first if they didn't know.

Was it weird that the man inside her right now—the man she had expected to just take what he wanted and not really care about how she got it herself—was more worried about her getting what she needed than anyone else she'd been with?

Maybe her type had been wrong for a long damn time. Maybe.

But she hardly knew Judge. She shouldn't make assumptions. He only asked her what he needed to do to make her come. It wasn't like it was some life-changing thing.

Her life had already changed enough.

When he had stilled, he had done it partially inside her and now his erection flexed. Maybe with impatience.

"Havin' second thoughts?"

Holy shit, by her losing herself in her thoughts, he saw it as rejection. That wasn't even close. "Sorry."

He shifted and slid free from her, his expression unreadable. "Yeah, me, too."

"No... Judge..." She squeezed her eyes shut. She was bungling this all up. "I'm not having second thoughts. I want you." She reached up and cupped his jaw. "I really want you," she whispered. "My head is just messing with me. That's why I apologized. Not because I don't want this." His jaw shifted under her palm. "I don't want you to stop. Please..."

If she expected a positive reaction from him, she didn't get it. Instead, he pulled away even further. "If you don't got second thoughts now, gonna tomorrow."

She frowned. "I'm here now. Naked. In your bed."

"Been distant. Not with me."

"Yes, that's on me, not you. And I'll say it again... Sorry."

As he rolled off her, moving to her side, she also moved, rolling with him. And when he landed on his back, she immediately climbed on top of him.

"Oh no," she said. "You're not leaving me hanging like that." She did her best to straddle his wide body with both her hands and knees, but, *crap*, he was *big*. "I'm not leaving you hanging like that, either. You don't eat the appetizer then skip out before the meal. That's just rude."

His hands gripped her hips as she hovered above him, her breasts hanging low enough that her nipples brushed against his chest.

She dropped all of her weight on him, figuring he could handle it. It seemed he could since he didn't complain or push her off.

She took his mouth and swept her tongue through it once before pulling back. "Now, I'm sorry I got caught up in my head. I promise I'm with you." She slid down far enough that the head of his cock was right there again. And she hoped he would take what she was offering.

"Would suck to waste a wrap," he grumbled and tilted his hips sharply while he pushed down on her hips.

Her eyelids fluttered closed as he filled her once again.

"With me?" he asked, sounding a little amused this time.

"I'm *sooooo* with you," she breathed.

"Good," he grunted. She squealed and her eyes flew open when he flipped them over and drove hard and fast into her again. "Like it like that?"

"Yes," she hissed.

"Want it gentle?"

"No."

He grinned. "Good."

She squeezed his hips with her thighs, grabbed his beard with both hands and yanked his head down until she had his mouth again.

While he controlled the pace and the angle of the thrusts, she controlled their kiss. But when his pounding slowed, the control of the kiss changed. He deepened it and forced his way past her tongue, claiming her mouth instead.

She let him because she was liking what he was doing a lot.

Especially with his hips.

And she could no longer think straight to control that kiss. He kept one hand planted in the bed so he wouldn't crush her, and the other snaked between them, snagging a nipple and tugging just the tip, then rolling it between his thumb and forefinger.

She groaned into his mouth, gripping his beard even harder. After releasing one hand, she scraped her nails down his back and his muscles rippled as she went. She could only reach the top of his ass, but she dug her fingertips in anyway, encouraging him to go deeper, even though that was impossible.

Even though he could go no deeper, she still couldn't get enough of him. They both adjusted the tilt of their hips and her eyes fluttered closed at how good that felt when he hit all the right spots.

She missed this. She had pushed it aside and now in this apartment with this man she was taking it back.

Judge had awakened what had been sleeping inside her for years. He had sparked a fire that had been reduced to cold ashes.

This man, who she never would've expected, had done that.

Maybe he was right and tomorrow she'd see this as a mistake. A misstep.

But tonight, it was anything but.

Her hips rose to meet his, her head rolled back, and her breath puffed like a steam engine from between her lips.

He did not let up. He did not slow down. He took her as he wanted to.

And she didn't want it any differently.

It was like her sexual self had been numb and with each thrust he brought all of the feeling back.

A deep grunt came from him and his pace stuttered. "Baby, ain't gonna hang on much longer. What d'you need from me?"

Again, he was making sure she was right there with him. And she was. Almost.

"Keep going," she panted, tilting her head to see his face.

He almost looked tortured. "I keep goin', gonna come."

"That's the point."

"Don't wanna leave you behind."

"You won't. Just tell me when you're about to come."

His hips almost slowed to a stop.

"Keep going," she demanded again, digging her fingers deeper into his flesh. "Almost there."

"Soon?"

"With you," she assured him.

With a tight nod, he continued making the pleasure swirl through her. "Want it hard?"

"Yes," she breathed.

"Fast?"

"Yes."

"Come with me," he growled and went back to giving it to her how she wanted it.

She would have smiled but the movement of his hips knocked it right off her face.

His pace stuttered again, and he released her nipple, planted his other hand into the mattress again and dropped almost all his weight onto her, pressing his face into her neck.

His beard was scratchy, but it also scraped over her heated skin, making her shiver, his lips sucked the skin on her neck so hard she was afraid he'd leave a mark. He snaked one arm under her shoulders and the other under her hips and then he powered up and into her.

Over and over.

And... *Oh...* That was all it took to shove her over that edge.

He was a big man, but somehow, he could move *just right.*

She was grateful for that.

So grateful she cried out when the orgasm exploded through her, curling her toes and causing her to hang on tight with her thighs, her heels and her fingers.

He didn't stop. He continued riding her wave, until finally...

Finally...

He tensed, drove deep one more time and groaned against her damp skin.

He came so hard, she could feel him pulsating within her and just those twitches sent her spinning with another mini orgasm.

And when that happened he lifted his head and stared down into her face, surprised.

It probably wouldn't have been a mini if he'd done what she asked. "You didn't tell me you were about to come." Even though her words were a bit breathless since she was still floating down from her high, she made sure he understood it was a gentle scolding.

"Didn't think you'd miss me comin'."

She didn't, but... "But I wanted to know beforehand."

"Why?"

"I like to know."

"Why?"

Oh boy, he was persistent. "I just do."

His green eyes narrowed. "Cass..."

She shouldn't be embarrassed about it, so what did it hurt to tell him? "It... it turns me on." Even so, heat rushed into her cheeks. *Damn it.*

Sometimes it also made her come again. Like she had with Judge.

"Yeah, well... Turns me on when a woman's pussy explodes around me like yours did. Drawin' me in, squeezin' my dick. Makin' me lose my fuckin' mind. That's why I didn't warn you, baby. Had no brains left to think."

That was a good excuse, she guessed. "I'll accept that."

His body shook and she could see him trying to fight a grin. "Will you now?"

She shrugged one shoulder. "Yes. Since I have no choice."

"Promise to do better next time."

Next time.

She wasn't sure how many *next times* they had before she needed to get back to her daughter.

But she wasn't opposed to at least one more.

Chapter Eleven

Next time.

It was actually after the third time, after he'd went to piss, clean up and bring her back a washcloth, that she mentioned it.

He handed her the warm, freshly rinsed washcloth, glanced at the clock to realize it was morning and they'd fucked three times in three hours.

He wasn't sure how this was possible, but he still hadn't had enough of her.

No other woman had been in his bed this long since his wife. Usually it was a once and done for the night. The woman in his bed was a means to an end. That end being his balls being emptied. And his restlessness being quieted.

Then she had to go. No lingering. Because after he was done with her, his loyal bitch would join him in bed.

Jury.

But, *fuck*, if he had it in him, he'd fuck Cassie a fourth time before the sun rose.

At his age, he was just glad he got it up three times in the same number of hours. He had been crossing his goddamn fingers and toes hoping he could. He did and he was damn proud of himself. Though the third time, his dick had been on the fence on whether to cooperate or not. With a little encouragement and Cassie's mouth, it had decided to play along.

Thank fuck.

He grinned as he approached the bed but lost that grin when she mentioned the colors on his back.

He'd had them done at Trip and Deke's urging but, at the time, he hadn't been sure if he should.

His father had died with those colors inked into his skin. Because of what those colors stood for, what they meant. Now Judge had the same and also held the same spot at the table.

It felt like a bad omen. He had wanted to avoid walking in his father's boots. Instead, he stepped right into them.

He thought his life would be different. He'd raise a family—even if it didn't start out the way it should—be successful with his bail bonds business, keep his ass out of the joint, and bullets out of his back.

Once the club disintegrated that temptation to be pulled into mayhem was gone, which made it easier. Until Trip came home and resurrected the Fury. He dug up the past and dragged Judge right back into it.

If it wasn't for his cousin being enthusiastic about it, Judge would've told Trip to go fuck off. He didn't need that shit in his life. He didn't need to relive the past.

He had been doing fine.

Perfectly fucking fine.

And somehow, he let himself get sucked back in.

Because of that, his back was covered with the Fury's colors. He'd had it done at the same time as Deke. His fucking cousin could talk him into doing shit he had no plans on doing.

Like buying Jury when Deke got Justice.

Like lying on that ink-slinger's table for all those fucking hours.

He'd almost stopped Crow—the best damn tattooist in western Pennsylvania, if not the whole state—from finishing several times.

But he didn't.

He laid there, gritted his teeth and let the man continue, even though his gut kept screaming at him to put a stop to it.

And when the Dirty Angels MC member was finished and Judge took one look at his back in the mirror, a sense of dread filled him.

The path he'd wanted to avoid? He was now following it.

But now Cassie's fingers traced those colors as she sat up in his bed, the sheet wrapped around her like a toga.

"That's a lot of ink. Were you required to do this?"

"No. Not a requirement but a strong suggestion. Loyalty is important in an MC. The tat shows you're willin' to be loyal to the club and your brothers."

"Has everyone had it done?"

"Prospects can't 'til they're patched in. The Originals, like Dutch and Ozzy, had it done a long time ago. Deke and I had it done recently. Trip did it before he resurrected the club as proof of how dedicated he was to makin' it all work. The rest? Don't know."

"So, no one might ever see it, but *you* know it's there."

Yeah, he knew it was there. Every time he saw it in the fucking mirror. It reminded him of the responsibility he had taken on as Sergeant at Arms. Which wasn't a light one. "It's a reminder."

"Once you're in, are you stuck?"

"Can buy out your membership, but you better have a good fuckin' reason. Or you can have your colors stripped if you do somethin' stupid. Either way, gotta get rid of your ink. And anythin' to do with the club."

Her warm palm pressed flat on his back directly over the center insignia. The bloody skull. While he liked her touching him, he wished it was for a reason other than what they were discussing. "How do you get rid of it?"

"Depends on how you're leavin'."

"What does that mean?"

"Either way, it ain't pleasant. You go voluntarily, gotta cover it with more ink. Black it out." He shrugged. "If it ain't voluntary... Then there are other methods." Methods he'd seen the Originals use.

Fire. Acid. Blades. The offending member got the choice, but none of the choices were an easy one.

"It would take a lot of ink to cover that up. Especially with the size of your back."

"Yeah."

"It's just easier to stay."

"Death's the easiest way out."

Her fingers curled into his skin and she sucked in a sharp breath. "But nobody wants out, right?"

"Right now? Everyone wants to stay. It's new. Shit ain't got twisted yet." He shouldn't be talking about this shit with her. Club business wasn't anyone else's business. Speaking in general was one thing. Telling her specifics was another. Even ol' ladies shouldn't know details, and Cassie was a complete outsider.

He moved away from her hand and settled on the bed next to her. "Gonna share that sheet?" He jerked his chin toward the sheet she was wrapped up in. "Or am I gonna have to cuddle with Jury to keep warm?"

Her eyes slid to the digital clock. "I need to go."

"Got time yet."

"I need to get back before anyone wakes up."

He didn't like the sound of that. "What time does your girl get up?"

She smiled. "Too early."

"How you dealin' with that when you ain't gettin' to bed 'til the middle of the night?"

Her smile dropped. "Not very well."

"Sister helpin'?"

Cassie sighed. "Yes. I feel bad she and Tyler have taken on so much of the responsibility. I need to find another way."

"Family's there to help." Family should always step in and help unless they were useless pieces of shit. If it wasn't for his aunt and uncle, Deke's parents...

She stared at her lap. "Yes. Family is there to help. Still, Daisy isn't their responsibility. And they're trying to have their own baby."

"She's good practice."

Her lips twitched. "They might decide not to have kids after helping out with my daughter."

"She's got a sassy attitude."

Her expression turned pained. "That's putting it mildly."

"She got it honestly."

She twisted her head toward him. "Are you saying I'm sassy?"

"Don't know you well enough yet." He wanted to. "But what I've seen so far? Fuck yeah."

She moved to the edge of the bed and began to unwind the sheet from around herself. "Okay, I really need to go."

"Should get some sleep here before you do. You go now, you'll get none. Let your sister deal with your girl this mornin'. She'll understand."

"I don't want to take advantage of—"

"Would you do it for her?"

Cassie hesitated and glanced over her shoulder at him.

The dark circles from exhaustion were easy to see. Keeping her up for the past few hours hadn't helped.

"Yes."

"She knows you're workin' long fuckin' hours. Not gettin' much sleep." Why the fuck was he working so hard to keep her in his bed? He never did this.

He was turning into a fucking goddamn sucker. Trying to keep this woman in his bed because there was something about her that he didn't want to let go of.

And if she left...

If she left, they... *he* might never get this opportunity again. Because later today when the sun was high in the sky, she was going to realize her mistake. It was going to hit her like a two-by-four square across the forehead.

She had a five-year-old daughter. An ex on the run. A temporary job and her life wasn't settled.

She didn't need to be adding Judge to that list. She had enough shit to deal with.

She had given herself a little detour with him for the past few hours. But Cassie seemed to be the type of woman to take that detour and then get back on track as soon as possible.

For that reason, he wanted to keep her there as long as possible. Because, again, once she walked out that door...

"I *could* use a couple hours of uninterrupted sleep." Her expression was wistful. "It's too early to call Heather, but I'll shoot her a text to tell her I'm okay and..."

"And you got some dick."

"I won't word it like that." She chewed on her bottom lip as she stared at the open bedroom door. "My purse is in my car."

"Know her number?" If she got dressed and went out to her car, she might keep going. He snagged his cell from the nightstand and held it out to her. "Send it from my phone."

Cassie took it and sent a quick text before handing it back to him. He tossed it back on the nightstand before he finished unraveling the sheet from her and pulled her luscious naked body against his.

"Sleep," he murmured into her ear, his arm holding her snuggly against him, his chest pressed to her back. He burrowed his nose into her soft hair and closed his eyes when she relaxed against him.

Goddamn, this felt too fucking good. He could get used to having a woman like Cassie in his bed.

Her husband had been a stupid fuck for doing shit to destroy their marriage.

Though, Judge had done the same shit. But the woman he fucked over wasn't a woman like Cassie.

Did that make it right? No.

Had he been happy? Fuck no.

If he could go back, he'd do things differently. But then, he'd been young and miserable. And didn't realize his mistake would fuck up shit so badly.

Judge figured Lange was old enough to know better.

Did he have a right to judge the man? Probably not.

Was he going to anyway? Fuck yeah. His name was Judge for a reason.

He was judging that goddamn motherfucker's ass. Especially when it came to a woman like Cassie. Judge could argue his wife, Jen, deserved what she got. Cassie did not.

What he couldn't argue was that his son and Cassie's daughter didn't deserve to be caught in the mistakes their fathers made.

Judge knew only too well about the mistakes of a father.

Not only him. But a lot of the rest of his brothers did, too.

So, yeah, he fucked up and some might say he got what he deserved.

Cassie and Daisy didn't deserve the shit Lange dealt them.

It put a lot of pressure on Cassie. So, if Judge could take some of that pressure off of her for a few hours, he was happy to do it.

Plus, it wasn't a sacrifice. Not at fucking all.

———

SHE FELT bad about leaving and not saying goodbye, especially after all that great sex. But Judge had been out cold, one long arm flung above her head, the other over her waist.

She had moved slowly and carefully to free herself as to not wake him. Then grabbed her clothes and quietly got dressed out in his living area.

She needed to get home, even though the two hours of uninterrupted sleep hadn't been nearly enough. Unfortunately, she knew as soon as she got back to the house she wouldn't get any more before having to get ready for work that evening.

But it was her last shift before her three days off. Three badly needed days of rest. She just hoped Daisy would let her have some.

As she turned the key in the lock of her sister's front door and opened it quietly, she heard voices.

And Daisy's excited, rapid conversation.

Her daughter always had plenty to say and was very opinionated about everything.

It could be amusing at times, and other times, it could get wearisome. Basically, her daughter was a five-year-old know-it-all.

Cassie snorted softly as she closed the door behind her and turned.

She froze when she saw a few pieces of luggage parked

at the bottom of the stairs in the foyer. There hadn't been any new cars parked out front, and it wasn't close enough to Christmas yet for Tyler's family to show up, so she had no idea whose they belonged to.

She headed past the bags and toward the back of the house and kitchen, where all the noise was coming from.

Tyler was at the stove, his back to Cassie as he flipped pancakes, and Heather was pouring juice.

Her daughter, with bed head and still in her jammies, was sitting at the table, with one of her Dr. Seuss books. She was pretending to read it out loud even though Daisy only knew a few of the words. Basically, her daughter was pointing to the pictures and reciting the book from memory since Cassie had read *One Fish, Two Fish, Red Fish, Blue Fish* to her five million and one times. Like Daisy, she could probably recite it in her sleep.

However, Daisy said *flish* instead of *fish*.

"It's *fish*, honey," Heather was correcting her as she placed a small glass of OJ in front of Cassie's daughter. "One fish, not one flish."

"Don't even bother," Cassie told her sister as she entered the kitchen. "She knows what it is. She chooses to destroy Dr. Seuss's greatest classic by choice."

"Momma!" Daisy squealed and scraped her chair back, jumping down and running at Cassie like a slo-mo Godzilla with exaggerated steps and flying arms. At least that gave Cassie time to prepare for the impact.

Daisy hit her legs, wrapped her arms around them and glanced up. "Where were *yoooooou*? I was all alone!"

"You were not. Aunt Heather and Uncle Tyler were here. And if they weren't, you'd be getting cereal and not pancakes from me."

"Then I'm glad you weren't," her daughter huffed. "Because pancakes are *waaaaay* better than cereal."

"That we can agree on." She peeled her daughter off. "Uncle Tyler has a plate ready for you."

Daisy did her dramatic slow motion run back to the table and scrambled into her seat. Tyler pushed her closer to the table and put the plate down in front of her. Cassie went over and plucked the Dr. Seuss book off the table so it wouldn't get coated in maple syrup. Right now, she didn't want to waste the little money she had on a new copy.

"Got your text," Heather said in a low voice as she shuttled past her with a couple more plates piled with an adult-sized portion of pancakes. "From an unknown number."

Heat immediately filled Cassie's cheeks and her sister shot her a knowing look with raised eyebrows.

"Late night, huh?"

"Mmm."

"Everything okay?" Tyler asked, his eyes holding amusement.

"Mmm hmm."

"Momma, you made me sleep *alllllll* by myself *alllllll* night. I was lonely."

She gave her daughter a dubious look. "I doubt you were lonely since you were asleep."

"Yes, it was a *very* lonely sleep."

Cassie rolled her eyes and sat down in the fourth spot at the table. After last night's activities, she was starved.

Tyler dropped his head to hide his laughter, then picked up his mug of coffee.

Coffee.

Yes, that was what she needed. Coffee would have to replace the sleep she really needed.

"Guess you forgot to take a brush to your sleepover," Heather asked with a smirk.

Cassie's hand immediately raised to her hair and she quickly combed her fingers through some of the knots. "Mmm. Yes."

"Aunt Heather said you had a sleepover last night with one of your friends," Daisy said around a mouthful of pancakes.

"Uh... Yes, sweetie, I did. But please don't talk with food in your mouth."

Daisy made a big display of swallowing it down, then opened her mouth to show Cassie it was now empty before asking, "Did you have fun?"

"Umm. Yes, it was fun."

"Did you play games?"

"We... uh... Yes."

"Did you win?"

A loud snort came from Tyler's end of the table. Heather shot up from her seat, almost knocking her chair over. "I'll get you some coffee, sis."

"Did you win?" Daisy repeated in a scream this time.

Cassie winced. "Inside voice, young lady."

"This *is* my inside voice."

"No, it isn't, and you'll go up to your room without finishing your pancakes if you don't find it."

Daisy's mouth dropped open, snapped shut and then she whispered, "Sorry."

"Apology accepted."

"Did you win?" Daisy asked again in a loud whisper.

Cassie wrapped her hands around the mug Heather set in front of her. There wasn't enough caffeine in the world for her to come up with a good answer, so she simply said, "Yes."

"What did you play?"

Oh good God.

"I think it's a game called slap and tickle, Daze," Tyler said, struggling to keep a straight face.

"I never heard of that game before," Daisy said with all seriousness, then shoveled a stuffed forkful of pancakes into her mouth, syrup dribbling down her chin.

"That's good," Heather said, tears escaping the corners of her eyes and her face turning red from trying to contain her laughter. "It's a game for adults."

"Why? I like being tickled!" Daisy declared loudly. "No slapping though. I don't wanna be slapped."

"That's good," Cassie said, setting down her mug and eating a mouthful of pancakes. She needed to change the subject. And fast. "Why is there luggage by the door?"

"We're goin' on a trip!" Daisy announced.

"We are?" She turned toward Heather.

"No, *we're* going on a trip. I texted you several times last night."

Cassie frowned. "My phone... Uh..."

Heather raised her palm. "We got a call late last night that Ty's dad fell and broke his hip. He's in the hospital and his mom is really upset."

"Holy shi—*er*, moley! Is he going to be okay?"

Ty shrugged. "A broken hip is always a concern at his age."

"His age?" Cassie frowned. "He's not that old."

"Old enough to make it a worry, apparently. I tried to text you but—"

Daisy cut her aunt off. "But Momma was *toooooo* busy winnin' at slap an' tickle."

Cassie shot Tyler a glare and mouthed, "This is your fault."

Tyler's lips twitched and he ate another mouthful of pancakes.

"So, wait... Are you headed down there, Ty?" Cassie asked him. "What about Christmas?"

"Yes," Heather answered. "John won't be able to travel for a while. Tyler's whole family decided to have Christmas at the family home instead of coming out here. We'll do Christmas here next year."

"That's all been decided already?" Cassie asked in shock.

"Sorry," Tyler apologized. "But you're welcome to come. My mom said you can come down and stay at the house with us. There's plenty of room for you and Crazy Daze."

"Yeah!" Daisy screamed, plunking down her glass so hard, OJ splashed over the rim and onto the table.

She couldn't do that. She just couldn't pick up and leave. She not only just got to Manning Grove, she now had a job. "I just got this job, I can't leave. And I don't want to uproot Daisy already. Even if it's only for a couple of weeks."

"It's not a permanent job, Cass," Heather reminded her. "You can probably get it back later or find a new one. Maybe you-know-who will be found during the holidays and things can get back to normal for you."

"Who got lost?" Daisy asked, her head spinning around the table.

"No one got lost," Cassie assured her, then shook her head. "I'm not ditching this job. It's paying me cash. Even you said one like that would be hard to find."

Her sister sat back and nodded. "Yes, you're right."

"And I need the money," Cassie needlessly reminded her sister.

"What will you do about Daisy? Do you want us to take her with us?"

What?

Heather continued, "It would only be for a little more than two weeks. Until after New Year's Day."

After New Year's Day? She couldn't live without her daughter for that long. It was bad enough Daisy's father disappeared from her life. Not only that, she couldn't stick Heather and Tyler with her—as Judge called her—sassy daughter.

That also wouldn't be fair to Tyler's parents, especially since John was currently hospitalized and would need time for recuperation. An active, loud five-year-old would not help.

"Yeah, Momma, I'll get more presents that way."

"No, you're not going down to North Carolina. You're staying here with me."

"I don't wanna stay with you," Daisy huffed. "I'll lose at slap an' tickle. Maybe Uncle Tyler's momma will play with me an' I'll win."

She shot Tyler another deadly glare. "Again, it's not a game for kids, Daze."

She could just imagine what a nightmare it would be once Daisy went back to school and asked the other kids to play slap and tickle. She could be the first kid in history to be expelled from kindergarten.

Daisy crossed her arms over her chest, made a mad face and huffed, "Fine."

"Finish your breakfast," she told her daughter and turned toward Tyler. "When are you two leaving?"

"We decided to drive, so tomorrow morning. We'll take turns and drive right through."

Cassie grimaced and nodded.

"Momma, can I go watch cartoons?" Daisy hopped out of her chair. "*Pweeeeeeze.*"

It was no surprise her five-year-old was tired of the adults talking. "Please," she corrected her daughter.

"Please," she harrumphed with a sharp head nod.

"Yes, you *may.*"

Daisy squealed loud enough to make everyone but her wince and she dashed from the kitchen.

"At a reasonable volume," Cassie called out to her daughter. Of course, she didn't get an answer.

"At least the decorations are already up, but I still feel bad leaving you two alone for the holidays," Heather said.

"We'll be fine. We were alone last Christmas at the house."

"I thought Mom and Dad came over."

Cassie's lips thinned. "They went on that *cruise*, remember?" She lifted her eyebrows.

Heather frowned. "Oh, yeah, I forgot about that cruise since we spent the holidays last year at Tyler's brother's."

That trip was conveniently booked when Cassie suggested they get together for Christmas. Her parents took a last-minute two-week cruise in the Caribbean.

"My only concern is what to do with Daisy when I'm working. Any suggestions?"

Paying for a babysitter—if she could even find one— would cut into her small pile of cash. It would delay her leaving her sister's house. Even so, she had no choice but to find someone to watch her daughter. She couldn't bring her along to the bar.

"It'll have to be someone old enough to stay overnight," Ty suggested, "since you roll in sometime after two."

"Do you mind a stranger staying in your house?" Cassie asked.

"Do you mind a stranger watching Daisy?" Heather countered.

Shit.

"There has to be someone we know. Someone we trust." Tyler rose from his seat and gathered the empty plates and dirty silverware. "A neighbor? That would be convenient. Someone who could go home as soon as Cass returns from work."

"But who?" Heather pursed her lips. "It would have to be someone without a day job, I would think."

"Well, after tonight I'm off until Thursday afternoon. So, we have until then to find someone."

Heather smacked her hands together sharply. "How about a college kid home from school for the holidays? No job. Needs the dough. Same attitude as Crazy Daisy. Doesn't mind being up late at night..."

"A *responsible* college kid would be perfect. If we knew one," Cassie said. "Maybe make sure it's a girl, too, since Daisy might ask to play slap and tickle. Thank you very much, Ty. Can't wait until you have one of your own, so I can pay you back in spades."

Heather whacked Tyler in the gut, quickly getting rid of her husband's smirk. "Okay, who's got a college kid home in the neighborhood..." She tapped a finger against her lips.

"A female one, Heather," Cassie reminded her. "Just for my peace of mind."

Heather inhaled sharply and her face lit up. "The Martin's daughter might have come home for Christmas. I swore I saw her car out in front of their house. I'm going to go call them." She dashed from the room almost as quickly as Daisy. Then a second later, she peeked her head back in. "I'll change the sheets in our room before we go, so you can have the master bedroom and you don't have to share the spare bedroom with Daisy." Then her sister was gone.

Sleeping by herself would be like heaven. Though, she wouldn't doubt Daisy might try crawling into bed with her very early in the morning. The only other person she might want climbing into her bed...

"Anyone we know?" Tyler asked, wiping down the table with a sponge.

Cassie's gaze slid from where Heather disappeared to her brother-in-law. "Hmm?"

"Was he anyone we know?"

"Nope. Just someone I met at the bar."

"So, nothing serious."

"No."

"Sometimes a little random slap and tickle is good for you."

Yes, sometimes. Earlier this morning seemed to be one of those times.

But that couldn't happen again.

Nope. It couldn't.

Or shouldn't.

Because if it did, it would no longer be so random.

Right?

Chapter Twelve

JUDGE POUNDED on the door with the heel of his fist and dropped his head to stare at his boots.

He twisted it to the right for a second to glance at the CRV and one other car in the driveway.

Yeah, he hadn't been invited but he really didn't give a fuck.

He forced himself to leave her alone yesterday. But he'd checked with Dodge in a roundabout way to make sure Cassie had shown up for work. She had.

And, of course, he couldn't text her because he didn't have her fucking number. He definitely wasn't asking Stella for it. Or Trip. Because that would throw red flags and his ass would be ridden until it was chapped.

What they did early Sunday morning in the dead of night was their fucking business and no one else's.

He hadn't followed her home Sunday night, either, for the first time since he found out she was working at Crazy Pete's. He'd fought the instinct to do it and somehow won. Because if he had, she might have ended right back in his bed.

He needed some sleep so he could think clearly today and so did she.

He gave her some time and now, there he stood, on the porch of her sister's house, banging on the goddamn door.

He should just fucking leave.

It was stupid to chase her.

He never chased women.

Never.

Through the lacy curtains, he saw a little tornado rushing toward the front door.

If he could see Daisy, she could see him. Now he couldn't fucking leave even if he wanted to. Especially when she screamed, "It's Judge!" at the top of her lungs and continued running down the hallway, sounding like a herd of buffalo.

Just as she flung the door open—he'd have to have a little discussion with her about doing that—he saw her mother peek her head out into the hallway from a room at the back of the house, possibly a kitchen, and her mouth drop open.

Yep, he was definitely not expected.

The door whipped open so quickly, it banged into the doorstopper making it twang loudly.

"Hi, Judge!" was squealed at dog whistle frequency.

At least somebody was happy to see him.

He stepped back but she kept coming and she ran right up to him, her little sneakered feet pressing right against the steel toes of his boots. Her head fell all the way back as she stared up at him, her eyes—the same blue as her mother's—snapping with excitement. "Pick me up."

Jesus, she wasn't asking, she was demanding. Like a mini tyrant.

His eyes slid to Cassie, who was now coming down the hallway, not at the same pace as her daughter. Fuck no, much more slowly, not bothering to hide the suspicion in her expression.

Daisy pounded on his thigh, drawing his attention, when he really wanted to watch Cassie's hips rock like a boat in stormy seas toward him instead.

"Pick. Me. Up!"

"Daze," Cassie began.

But before she could get the rest of her words out, Judge scooped the little girl up in his arms and she just about made him deaf with her shriek of excitement.

Then she grabbed his beard with a tight tiny tyrant fist. He winced when she yanked on it. "It's *soooooo* scratchy!"

The five-year-old yanking on it was not the same as her thirty-something mother doing the same.

He'd admit he preferred the latter.

Judge grabbed her little fist and pried her fingers open. "Don't need bald spots, kid."

Daisy laughed like a little maniac and released her hold, wrapping her arms around his neck and her little legs around his waist. She began to bounce and kick him with her heels. "Giddyap, horsey, take me inside."

"Daisy!" Cassie yelled, reaching for her daughter.

"I got 'er," Judge told her and stepped inside. It was a good excuse to get his ass in the door.

She closed it behind him, probably only because it was cold out and not because she wanted him there. "Please, put her down. She can't just climb all over strangers."

"He's *not* a stranger, *Mommmma*. We know him. He's Judge."

He met Cassie's annoyed blue eyes, his lips twitching. "Yeah, you know me. I'm Judge. We've... *met.*"

The woman rolled her eyes at his smirk. "It's late. You need a bath and to get ready for bed."

That sounded like a good plan to him.

"Judge just got here!"

Damn. Maybe Cassie meant that for her kid, not him. "Not stayin' long, kid, just needed to talk to your momma."

"Will you read me a story 'til I'm sleepy?"

"No, he will not," Cassie said sharply.

Daisy pouted. "My momma is *soooooo* mean."

"Doubt that." Judge put the little girl on her feet. "Always gotta listen to your momma. She knows best."

"She don't know poop."

"I'm sure she knows poop." Judge did his best to strangle his laugh and not encourage Daisy's behavior.

Cassie sighed. "Okay, then. I need to get her upstairs. Is this going to take long?"

Probably not as long as he'd like. "Get done whatcha gotta get done. I can wait."

"She needs a bath and a story before she falls asleep."

Judge would love Cassie to give him that bath and read him a story, too. Not the same kind of story she was going to read to Daisy. "Got time."

Cassie's mouth opened, then she shut it and pursed her lips. Color rose into her cheeks as he stared at that mouth. The one that had sucked him hard not even two days ago.

"It's going to be at least an hour, if not more. If you only have something quick to say..."

"Do whatcha gotta do, Cass. I'll wait. Or I can come back if you'll let me back in."

Her hesitation didn't give him a lot of confidence she'd let him back in.

"Tell you what, gonna run to Pete's and grab a beer. Be back in about an hour and a half to make sure she's settled in for the night. This way we're undisturbed."

Daisy stomped her foot. "But I want Judge to read me my story!"

Judge glanced down at the little hellion in pink sneakers. "Not tonight, kid. Next time maybe, if your momma says it's okay."

Cassie's lips parted and her brow furrowed.

"Know how to read, you know," he teased her.

She rolled her eyes. "Fine. Go get a beer. Don't pound so hard when you come back."

"Don't know how to *pound* any other way, baby," he whispered close to her ear.

Her cheeks exploded in color as he pulled away.

With a grin, he left.

———

STELLA GRINNED at Judge as he settled on a stool at the bar. "Cassie isn't working tonight."

"Know it. Didn't come here for her."

"What did you come here for?"

He shook his head. "A fuckin' beer. Last time I checked this was a fuckin' bar, right?"

Stella laughed and moved away, grabbing a pint glass and filling it at the tap.

The newest patched member, who normally bartended, was nowhere to be seen. "Dodge still down for the count?"

Trip came around the left side of the bar to stand behind it. "Fell into some pussy. Figured I'd help Stel tonight and give him that. The man works fuckin' hard. A few nights off in a row to let him finish celebratin' ain't gonna hurt."

"Must be some pussy," Judge muttered.

"Mmm hmm." Stella slid the full glass in front of him.

He met Trip's ol' lady's eyes. "Coulda offered Cass an extra shift. She could use the money."

"I did," Stella answered him. "She turned it down."

Judge frowned. "Why?"

"She didn't tell you?" Stella asked.

"Why the fuck would she tell me?"

"Oh, I don't know... Maybe because someone saw her sneaking out of your apartment early Sunday morning?"

His frown deepened. "Who?"

"Does it matter?"

Fuck no, it didn't. Not really.

But, *shit*, that meant the word already spread if Trip and Stella knew. The club was full of gossips who couldn't keep their fucking mouth shut. Just like in high school.

Stella leaned over the bar toward him. "Don't scare away my newest employee, Judge. We need her and she's good at her job."

"She needs this fuckin' job, she ain't gonna scare easy."

"How's he gonna scare her away? With his big dick?" Trip wrapped an arm around his ol' lady.

"Oh, you have a big dick?" Stella wiggled her eyebrows at Judge, then bumped her shoulder into Trip's. "Is it too late to switch ol' lady cuts?"

"Woman, my dick might not be as big as the Jolly Green Giant's here, but I got a golden fuckin' tongue." He stuck it out and wiggled it.

Stella elbowed the club prez in the gut and he dropped his arm from around her. "So, what are we talking here, Judge? A one-night thing?"

"Why you care?" Trip asked her.

Stella shrugged. "Just want to know if I need to be prepared for a scorned, broken-hearted employee."

"What we did had nothin' to do with hearts."

Trip grinned.

"Done talkin' about that shit. Ain't no one's biz. Need to talk to you about something else, prez."

Trip's grin flipped upside down. "Need to set up a meet?"

Judge took a long sip of his beer. "Not yet. Wanted to talk to you about it first. Give you a heads up."

Stella straightened. "I'll go wipe down some tables."

"Stel," Judge stopped her. "Don't care if you hear this."

"Is it club business?" she asked.

"Yeah. But might need your help convincin' your ol' man."

Stella's blue eyes narrowed. "Convince him to do what?"

"Not likin' this," Trip grumbled.

"Yeah, well. Not likin' what happened to Autumn. We fucked up. And it's been eatin' at me. *I* fucked up as your brother sittin' at the table to your left. Didn't want to take the Sergeant at Arms spot, knew how dirty it could be. Ignored my gut instinct, anyway. Became my job to protect the club's property, but fucked up. Autumn got snagged on my watch."

"She wasn't the club's property, Judge," Stella reminded him.

"The fuck she wasn't. Sig claimed her the second he brought her back to the farm. We all knew it. Just wasn't official."

"Did our best," Trip said softly.

Judge knew Trip didn't believe that, and he shouldered a lot of the guilt, too.

They both did.

"Shoulda had someone on her ass at all times. We got sloppy. No, I got fuckin' sloppy. This is all on me. It's my responsibility."

"She's fine," Trip assured him.

"Yeah, now. Thank fuck. But what if they had..." He tugged on his beard. "Those motherfuckers had enough time to really fuckin' hurt her. Kill her, kill that baby."

None of them said a fucking word because it was true. That also weighed heavily on him.

"'Cause of all that shit, she ended up havin' Levi early."

"Only two weeks, Judge. He was fine. They both were," Stella reminded him.

"Again, thank fuck. What if it had been two months early? What if he woulda died? What if she did?"

"Judge."

Judge threw up a hand. He was done talking about it.

He'd failed.

It was his job to keep everyone safe and he'd failed.

He finally said what he'd been wanting to say since they came off the Shirleys' mountain that night. "Need to find a new enforcer."

"Bullshit," Trip growled, his body tightening up. Stella put a hand on her ol' man's arm and he visibly loosened a bit.

"Ain't like my pop. Ain't a job for me. Told you that when you originally came to me about it."

"Judge—"

"Trip, ain't for me."

Trip shook his head. "Not acceptin' you leavin' the club."

"Not leavin' the club. Just that spot at the table."

"Not acceptin' that, either. You're the goddamn perfect person for it. Your pop was the Fury's enforcer and you saw how he handled shit."

"That's the fuckin' problem, brother. Look what fuckin' happened to him. Promised myself and Jemma I wouldn't follow in his fuckin' footsteps and here the fuck I am." Not only wearing the Fury cut, but his father's patch, sitting in his goddamn seat.

"And I said the same fuckin' thing about me followin' in Buck's, Judge. And here we the fuck are. Doin' it right this time. Rightin' all the fuckin' wrongs."

"Are we, though? What fuckin' wrongs are we rightin'?" Judge asked him.

"We're buildin' a brotherhood that's unbreakable."

"You try hard enough, brother, everything's breakable."

Trip shook his head, hooking Stella around the neck

with his elbow and pulling her into him. She was his rock. She was who kept his temper to a low simmer when it could easily become an erupting volcano.

Trip found his woman and Judge was happy for him.

But even though Stella was Trip's ol' lady, Judge was responsible for keeping her safe. Just like he'd been responsible for Autumn. She'd been on club property, sleeping in their VP's bed for months. That made him responsible for her.

And he was about to take on the responsibility for Cassie and her daughter. She didn't know it yet, but he already knew it in his gut.

It was on him to protect her.

To find that fucking husband of hers.

To free her of that mess that asshole splattered all over her.

He could've just taken that night of pussy and moved on.

But he couldn't.

Cassie wasn't just another pussy.

The second he saw her at the municipal lot, he knew that. He knew it deep in his gut.

Maybe she wouldn't be interested. Maybe she wouldn't want anything to do with him because of him being a biker and her having a young daughter.

But being a biker was one thing. Being a club enforcer was another. It could be a violent job. There could be shit he'd never want exposed to a young kid. There could also be possible blow-back.

It was another reason he wanted to rip off his rank patch.

But it wasn't the only reason. He'd only known Cassie for a couple of weeks, if that. Hardly spoke to her before sleeping with her the other night.

He shouldn't even go back to her sister's house tonight. He should just walk away like she did.

He was hoping for something he shouldn't be hoping for.

The woman's life was a cluster right now and he shouldn't add to it.

He shouldn't.

But maybe he could help. Do some good.

It wasn't the reason he went over to her house earlier, but it would be the reason he'd go back. Plus, he needed to know why she left without a word.

Though, he probably knew why already. She'd regretted fucking him, waking up next to him.

He thought he'd been prepared for it. Expected it.

But he hadn't.

He glanced up from his beer to see Trip had disappeared. He was so lost in his fucking thoughts, he hadn't even noticed.

What kind of Sergeant at Arms didn't even keep an eye on his prez?

That was his fucking job.

Jesus fuck.

He was thinking more about his dick than his club.

Stella stood staring at him, her eyebrows pinned together. "He had to step outside for a sec."

"He thinks I'm fuckin' him over."

"No, he doesn't. But he needs you, Judge. You have a good head on your shoulders and you aren't a hot head. I mean, you have Trip sitting at the head of the table who struggles every fucking day. He's afraid he'll turn into Buck. He needs someone to remind him not to do that. Then you got Sig sitting on his right. A man who's fucked up in the head. His temper is worse than Trip's. You have those two leading. He needs someone solid in the number three spot. There's no one better than you."

"Deke."

"Deke wasn't a part of the club back then like us. He has no idea how bad shit can get. You three do. You three need to make sure it doesn't head down that path again. If you step back..." She shook her head. "He needs you, Judge. He's not going to beg because he isn't that type of man. *We* need you. What happened to Autumn wasn't your fault. You guys wanted to take care of the problem neatly. It ended up not being so neat. You learn, you move on."

"Ozzy."

Stella planted her hands on her hips. "Didn't you just hear everything I said?"

"Yeah, Stel, I did."

"I know you didn't want the spot. I know Trip and Deke pressured you into it. But you took it. You have that patch on your chest," she pointed at the rectangular patch that read *Sgt at Arms*, "so own it. Do the job without making the mistakes your father made. Trip has to do his job as president and not make the mistakes Buck made. We're all in this together." Her eyes got shiny, which surprised Judge. "We all lost our family, Judge. All of us, in one way or another. We're now family. Trip trusts you to be the club's enforcer. We all do. Don't bail on him. Don't bail on us. *Please.*"

Judge closed his eyes for a moment. Stella was a strong fucking woman and for her to get emotional over him stepping down from his position...

"I asked Sig to do better. He's doing his best. And I know it's a struggle for him. If it wasn't for Autumn, I doubt he would've stuck around. Trip said Sig probably would've rolled out in a few months, if not sooner. Maybe you need your own anchor. Something besides the club. Like Trip and Sig. Someone like Cassie."

"Stel, we fucked one time."

She grinned, those hovering tears long gone. "Once is all it takes sometimes. She's got nowhere to land. Maybe we need to convince her to stay in Manning Grove." Stella leaned over the bar again. "Maybe you need to convince her."

"Not lookin' for an ol' lady." He tried to make that sound believable but by the look Stella shot him, she wasn't buying it.

"Yeah, well, neither was Sig. Look at him now."

"Ain't Sig."

"Thank fuck for that. One Sig is enough. Anyway, I'm asking you to stay sitting in the seat to Trip's left. I feel better knowing it's you. Give it a year. If you want out then? I'll encourage Trip to take it to the table for a vote."

"You're only supposed to be an ol' lady, Stella."

Her grin widened. "Times have changed, Judge. This isn't the Originals' club anymore. And it's a good thing it's not. Let's keep it that way."

That Judge could agree on. "Make you a fuckin' deal. I stay sittin' at the table for now. I fuck up again, I'm rippin' this patch right the fuck off my chest and handin' it over to someone better."

"Like Trip said, no one's better than you. And you're not going to fuck up. You know why?"

This should be good. "Why?"

"Because even though Trip wants this club to remain legit—and I agree—what happened on that mountain opened our eyes. If we need to get our hands dirty to protect what's ours, to protect our family, then that's what we're going to do. No regrets. We just need to do it smart."

"Stel..."

"Yeah?"

"You're a goddamn badass bitch, know that?"

She smiled. "My father was Crazy Pete. It's in the genes."

"Trip couldn't find anyone more perfect for him than you."

She threw her arms up. "I fucking told him that when we were kids. He just didn't listen!"

Judge snorted, dropped his head and shook it. "Yeah, he was a dumb fuck back then. We all were."

"Yes, we were. We lived and learned. And that's why that damn patch is staying on your cut." She slapped her hand on the bar top. "Now, I'm done with this foolishness of you stepping down as the enforcer and I'm getting you a fresh beer."

"Don't bother. Got somewhere to be."

"Does it have to do with a blonde?"

Judge pushed to his feet, dug a ten cut of his chain wallet and threw it on the bar.

"Don't want your money, Judge. We're doing okay now, and the club owns half the bar. No reason to pay."

"Then sneak it into Cassie's tips next time she's workin'."

Stella snagged the ten spot and snapped it between her fingers. "You got it. Tell her I said hi."

Judge pressed his lips together, shook his head and headed out.

Chapter Thirteen

As Judge parked the Expedition at the curb, Cassie dropped the living room curtain where she'd been peeking out and pressed her back to the wall.

Her heart thumped so hard, she was afraid he'd be able to see it trying to escape her chest. She pressed her fingers to her mouth and realized they were shaking, too.

What the hell was wrong with her?

How could this man make her react like this? She hardly knew him. Okay, maybe not hardly... She *did* end up getting naked with him.

His face—and that beard—had ended up between her thighs...

Maybe they knew each other a little better than she wanted to admit.

But still...

She hardly knew *who* he was. Besides being a biker and a bounty hunter or bondsman or whatever he called himself.

A light tap on the door had her pounding heart doing a somersault.

She needed to keep herself together. She couldn't let him see how he affected her.

She cleared her throat and nervously tugged her baggy sweatshirt down to make sure her tummy pooch was covered. It was stupid because he'd already seen her without clothes, but it was also habit. One she wasn't sure she'd ever break.

She moved to the door and, with her hand clutching the knob, blew out a deep breath before opening it. When she did, her eyes immediately landed on his broad chest, covered in a snug dark blue thermal with a white T-shirt peeking out at the collar and his black leather cut.

She slowly raised her gaze, sliding it over his too-long beard, those lips that had made her lose her mind and his strong, straight nose until she met his green eyes.

Unreadable. That was what they were.

"How tall are you?" she managed to get past her tight throat. Because, of course, that was how you answered a door, right?

Dumb.

His lips twitched. "Six-three. How tall are you?"

"Not six-three." Not even close.

"I'm thirty-seven and weigh about two-forty. Now... You gonna let me in? Or you need to know my boot size, too?"

She stepped back and he pushed past her. But before she could close the door, he had it done for her and she was pinned against it with that six-foot-three, two-forty body and his hands cupping her jaw and tilting up her face.

"Now you know."

Good lord, that voice just did all kinds of things to her insides. "Know what? Your height?" Damn the shake in her own.

"That it was a mistake."

"I needed to get home, Judge."

"Didn't even fuckin' say goodbye. Or 'Thanks for the dick.' Or 'Sorry for the huge wet spot on your bed, Judge.'"

Heat shot through her at the memory of how that wet spot was made. Honestly? She wasn't sorry about it. Not in the least. "I didn't want to wake you."

"Bull-fuckin-shit."

"While, yes, maybe it was a mistake, it had been one I was willing to make."

His chin jerked back, and he quickly masked his surprise. He dropped his head until she could feel his warm breath sweep over her parted lips. His eyes followed her tongue as she licked them slowly.

Those Caribbean Sea green eyes turned very dark and heated. "You learn from that mistake?"

"Mmm hmm."

"What d'you learn?"

"That I really liked what we did to make that wet spot." Truth be told, she would love to make another one.

"So, it's a mistake you're willin' to make again?"

"Mmm... maybe."

"Thank fuck," he murmured against her lips, then took her mouth.

She groaned as his tongue tangled with hers. She grabbed the sides of his face and pulled him deeper into the kiss.

A few seconds later, and with what felt like a steel pipe pressing into her belly, he pulled back. "Keep temptin' me like that, you're gonna end up naked in your foyer, so if your girl or sister wakes up, they're gonna get a sight they might never fuckin' forget."

"It's probably a good idea if we move, then," she whispered.

"Yeah." He stepped back and they both dropped their hands. She already missed his heat against her. And that hard-on which was making the crotch of her yoga pants damp.

If she didn't know better, she'd think she was having a hot flash.

"Where we goin'?"

To her bedroom if it was up to her, but she'd be afraid of waking Daisy. And he wasn't here for that.

Or was he?

No. He'd been ticked she'd left Sunday morning without a word. That was why he was here. Right?

Though, he was a big, bad biker, why would he care about that? "Do all the women you sleep with say goodbye before they leave?"

"If I give 'em a chance. Sometimes I'm kickin' their ass out the door so fast, they're lucky they're wearin' clothes."

Cassie stifled her laugh. "That's rude."

"Yeah? They know the deal."

Suddenly, what he'd said wasn't so funny. "Do they? How would they know?"

"'Cause they're..." He grimaced. "'Cause they do."

"Because they're what? Hookers?"

His brow rose. "Hookers?" Then he dropped his head and shook it. When he lifted it again, his face still held amusement. "Never had to pay..." He frowned. "No, that ain't right. Had to pay once, but never got what I paid for."

"You paid a hooker?" she practically squeaked.

"Not a hooker. Just a whore. A patch whore who was willin' to pop my cherry."

What? First of all, what the hell was a "patch whore" and secondly... "Pop your cherry? How old were you?"

"Old enough to want a taste of pussy, young and stupid enough to be willin' to pay for it."

"And it never happened?"

"Let's just say it was for the best. Bitch had crotch rot that could burn your fuckin' nose hairs."

Cassie slammed a hand over her mouth. She wasn't sure

if she should find that funny or appalling. Or maybe a little of both.

After a second, when she could breathe again without wheezing, she dropped her hand.

He grabbed it. "Where we goin'?"

"Somewhere we won't wake Daisy."

"We gettin' loud? Not opposed to that, just to be clear. Got my Ford out front, no one's gonna hear us in there."

Her eyes slid toward the door, tempted.

No, she couldn't leave Daisy alone in the house just so she could scratch an itch. That wouldn't get her a Mother of the Year trophy. Not that she had a mantle to put it on, anyway.

"Living room, I guess." She used the hand he didn't have a death grip on to point in the direction they should go.

"Your sister got one of those plastic-covered couches like my gramma had?"

It took her a second to figure out what he meant. "I thought you were here to talk."

"Yeah, 'til you said you don't mind makin' mistakes. Thinkin' since I'm a big one, you might wanna try again."

When they entered the dark room, she flipped the switch as they passed it, turning on the lights. He collapsed onto the *not-covered-in-plastic* couch—which actually creaked under his weight—taking her with him. Not quite pulling her onto his lap, but close. As she tried to make some space between them, he yanked her closer.

She was going to have a hard time having any kind of conversation with this man while being pinned against him. "My daughter's upstairs."

"She asleep?"

Good lord, Cassie hoped so. "Why are you here, Judge?"

"Been thinkin' about your problem."

"Welcome to my world, that's all I think about."

"Even the other night in my bed?"

Heat filled her cheeks. "No, not then. But I've been thinking about this, too... I want to hire you to find Dennis. Since you now know he's not coming here to Manning Grove, I know he's no longer on your radar. Since you were only supposed to capture him if he showed up here in this area, correct?"

"Still on my radar since he ain't caught yet and that don't mean he ain't gonna wanna see his girls. Fugitives can be unpredictable. But even so, bail bondsman up north is still lookin' for 'im."

"But he hasn't found him, and I... You're good at finding people, right? That's your job."

"Ain't my main job. My job's bailin' people out, which is basically loanin' people scratch to get their asses outta jail. Get paid well to let 'em borrow that scratch. Only gotta chase their asses down when they skip town or miss their court date. Truthfully, when it comes to findin' people, Deke's better at it than me. He's good at skip tracin'."

"Which is what Dennis did. Skipped. Can I hire Deke to find him outside of Manning Grove?"

He leaned back against the couch and twisted his big body to face her. "You hire him, you get me. Package deal."

"I don't think I can afford both of you."

"Don't think you can afford either of us."

Well, that was a bucket of ice-cold water thrown in her face. "You're right." She squeezed her eyes shut and curled her fingers against her thighs. "I can't even afford to move the hell out of this house and get out of Heather and Ty's hair." Her voice caught. She kept her eyes shut until the sting subsided somewhat.

Fingers on her chin had her reopening them, but she focused on her lap. He jerked her chin up so she'd look at him.

"Why'd you turn down the extra shift at Pete's tonight?"

She hadn't wanted to. She needed every dollar she could get. "I didn't have anyone to watch Daisy."

He frowned. "Where's your sister and her man?"

"Gone."

His head snapped back and his scowl became somewhat scary. "What d'you mean, gone?"

"While we were..." she flapped a hand around, "the other night, they got a call from Tyler's mother. His father broke a hip and they're headed down to North Carolina to visit, help his mom, and then spend the holidays there instead of doing it here since his parents will no longer be able to travel."

"Means you're here alone?" He did not look happy about that at all.

"Yes. With Daisy."

"So, alone."

She frowned. "With Daisy."

"Alone for Christmas."

"And New Year's." What was his point?

"Don't like you bein' here alone."

She didn't remember asking his opinion on it. "I'm used to being alone. It has just been Daisy and me for a while now. Even when Dennis lived with us, I was alone. It's nothing new."

"Still don't like it."

It wasn't up to him. "And anyway, you've been watching me like you're my guard dog."

"Was watching for Lange."

She cocked an eyebrow at him. "That's all?"

His lips flattened out. "Can't help you got an ass that won't fuckin' quit. Tits I wouldn't mind being smothered to death with and a pussy that made the goddamn angels sing."

Cassie rolled her lips under for a moment to gather herself. "Is that all I am? Tits, ass and pussy?"

"Got all that fuckin' blonde hair, too. A length good for fisting. And those baby blues that make my nuts tight. *Fuck.*" He ran his hand along his bulging zipper.

"Well, now I know what to put on my Tinder profile."

"What the fuck's that?"

She grinned and shook her head. "Nothing. I'm kidding." The last thing she needed to deal with right now was online hookups or even dating. She needed to be free of one man before she even considered another.

Instead, she considered the man sitting next to her. No, it was not a good idea. She had a man she was trying to divorce, a daughter to raise and a life to get settled.

Though, this man probably wouldn't want something serious, right? Just a few rolls in the hay, or on the mattress? He didn't seem to be the type to want anything more. Being a biker and all that...

Plus, Daisy liked him. So, she wouldn't have to sneak around and worry that Daisy might see him.

Hmm.

Wait. Was she seriously considering this?

Oh God. They'd take away the Mother of the Year Award she won last year. Just revoke it.

But being a mother did not mean she was no longer a sexual being. What was wrong with wanting what she wanted if she went about it the right way?

"Cass..."

"Hmm?"

"You're starin' at my fuckin' dick."

Yes, she was. She lifted her gaze to his grin and amused green eyes.

"Ain't helpin' my hard-on by doin' that. But if you want my dick, I'm pretty fuckin' accommodatin'."

She rolled her eyes. "Do you tell that to all the girls?"

"Fuck no."

"Oh, then, I should feel special," she teased.

"Yeah, baby, you should." Again, his words came out like low, rolling thunder and a shiver shot through her, making her nipples peak. "Got a wrap burnin' a hole in my wallet. Need to use it before it self-combusts. Wanna help?" He added a sexy grin.

"Daisy's upstairs," she whispered, her breathing becoming ragged at his suggestion.

"Yeah, know that. Told me already. Just gotta be quiet. She wake up easily?"

"No, she sleeps like the dead until about four or five in the morning. Right when I'm finally in a deep sleep after working all night, she's waking me up since we're sleeping in the same bed."

"Sharin' a bed now?"

"No, not now. They gave me the master bedroom while they're away. I finally got some decent sleep until Daze came crashing into the room way too early this morning, demanding French toast."

Judge lifted a thick eyebrow. "She get it?"

"She got Cheerios while her mother drank a whole pot of strong coffee and contemplated running away to join a circus."

Judge snorted.

"Anyway, I *was* hoping to get some sleep tonight."

"'Til I showed up."

"You only came to talk, remember?"

"Yeah, *talk*."

"Is that biker code for doing everything *but* talking?"

"No, that code word is fuckin'."

"No code ring needed to decipher that."

"Nope."

"We go upstairs, we not only have to be super quiet, but you'd have to be gone before she wakes up."

"Promise I'll be out of your bed before she wakes up. Difference is, I'll say goodbye first."

Damn. "Rude."

"Yeah, it was. Really fuckin' rude."

"Honestly, I didn't think it would bother you," she admitted.

He lifted one eyebrow but said nothing.

Of course, that made her feel worse. "Sorry."

"Can make it up to me."

"By using that condom before it 'self-combusts?'"

"That's one way."

"What's the other?"

He dragged his thumb over her bottom lip. "Forgot to list one of your other assets earlier."

"What, that I'm highly intelligent?"

"Haven't tested that IQ but have tested that mouth."

"So, you don't care if I'm as dumb as a rock as long as I'm good at oral sex?"

"Thinkin' I need to shut the fuck up now before you kick my ass out."

"That would probably be a good idea," she agreed.

"A better idea would be for you to find a way to keep me quiet. 'Cause if I get kicked out, my dick comes with me."

"Do you think I'd only want you to stay because of your dick?"

"It's a pretty damn good reason. But if you only want me for my dick, you ain't gonna hear me cry about it."

"You'd just let me use you for sex?"

"Yeah, 'cause I ain't stupid and you ain't the only one benefittin' from it."

"Well, that's true."

"Which part?"

"Both?" she asked.

"Don't like that fuckin' question mark."

"Okay, then. Both."

"Better, baby."

"Do you always call women baby?"

"Just ones I'm fuckin'."

"You really know how to melt a woman's heart."

He shook his head. "Yeah, I need to shut up now."

She climbed onto his lap and her pussy brushed over his erection. "Yes, you do."

He grabbed her hips and kept her from grinding down onto his lap. "Baby, wanna kiss you, wanna fuck you. Wanna make you gush like a geyser. What I do not wanna do is look up and see your mini-me watchin' me doin' it. Your sister's door got a lock on it?"

"Yes."

"Then why the fuck are we still on this couch?"

That was a very good question.

Two seconds later, they weren't.

———

CASSIE STRETCHED, groaned, ran a hand down her stomach and...

Shot up in bed.

She was naked.

She *never* slept naked.

Ever.

She twisted her neck to see the other side of the bed empty and the sheets wrinkled.

Oh, thank goodness. He did what he said he would. Disappeared before morning.

She flopped back down, blinked up at the ceiling and realized the insides of her thighs were a bit tender from his beard and her pussy was a lot more tender from that beard, his mouth, his fingers and his cock. Her nipples were also a little sore from all his rough, but welcomed, attention.

Not once had she told him to slow down or take it more

gently. He was pretty damn good at knowing what she needed and when. It was actually refreshing and unexpected. She figured the first time, at his apartment, could've been a fluke. After last night, she knew it wasn't.

She tipped her head back to see the towel they had jammed between the headboard and the wall, so the pounding didn't break the headboard, damage the drywall or wake up Daisy. She turned her head to see the blue bandana he had pulled from inside his cut and tucked between her teeth—with her approval, of course—to keep from not only waking up her daughter, but the neighbors.

She grinned at the sight of it. Until her gaze landed on the clock next to it.

She sat straight up in bed again.

Holy shit!

She tilted her head and listened carefully.

Nothing but quiet. Complete silence.

That can't be right.

Where the hell was Daisy and why hadn't her daughter come barreling into the room yet?

A quiet daughter could mean trouble. Especially with the little blonde hellion that had sprung kicking and screaming from Cassie's loins.

Jumping from the bed, she grabbed her sister's silky robe that was a little tight on her since her sister still had that firmer pre-baby body. She secured the tie enough to make sure she was half-decently covered, flung the door open and hurried down the hall to the spare bedroom.

The door was open. The bed empty but a complete mess.

She spun around, opened her mouth to holler her daughter's name, and snapped it shut. Her nose wrinkled at the smell wafting down the hallway.

Was Daisy cooking? Was she using the stove?

Oh no!

The burst of panic she first felt when she saw her daughter's empty bed swept through her again. And the images of Daisy burning down Heather's house had her almost tumbling down the steps.

Following her nose, she noticed it didn't smell like anything was burning. It actually smelled pretty damn good.

What the hell? She didn't even trust Daisy to make toast. What the hell could she be cooking?

She slid to a stop at the entry to the kitchen and blinked.

Daisy was sitting at the table stuffing her face with what looked like French toast, syrup dribbling down her chin and plopping onto her PJ top. A half glass of milk sat in front of her.

Movement caught her attention and she slowly turned her head to see Judge standing by the stove, a pile of French toast on a plate next to him on the counter. The man knew how to make French toast?

Why was that her first thought? That wasn't the point. He was supposed to leave, not stay and make her daughter breakfast!

"What are you doing?" She did her best to keep that question at a respectable level and not scream it across the small kitchen like she really wanted to.

He leaned back against the counter and crossed his thick arms over his even broader chest. "Makin' your girl breakfast."

Suuuure... That was normal, right? Some big bad-ass biker she just boned woke up, went downstairs and made her five-year-old breakfast.

Yep, happened all the time.

Completely normal.

"Judge made me French toast, Momma. No cereal today."

Her eyes slid to her daughter, who wore a very smug expression, and back to the man who did something he had no right to do. The man whose expression was blank as he studied her carefully.

He was judging her reaction.

Which he should be.

Because he was supposed to be gone. He clearly was not.

With a set jaw, she rushed over to where he stood, grabbed his beard in her fist and yanked him along behind her through the kitchen. She told her daughter in passing, "You stay in that seat and finish your breakfast. Judge and I need to talk."

"'Kay, Momma," her daughter answered, like she was used to seeing a leather-clad biker being dragged out of the kitchen by his whiskers.

Cassie continued to steer him out of the kitchen and into the living room.

He hadn't fought her or said a word. Until they were out of Daisy's view.

He wrapped his fingers around her fistful of beard and growled, "Don't fuckin' mind you tuggin' on it when we're fuckin' but this shit ain't—"

"You were supposed to leave," she hissed, cutting him off. "You weren't supposed to be here when my daughter woke up. You were *definitely* not supposed to make her fucking breakfast!" She bit back a frustrated scream.

"Wanna let go of my fuckin' beard?" he growled again.

Oh, was he not happy? Good. Welcome to the club.

She released it, took a deep breath to cool her anger, but when she stepped back, he didn't let go of her hand.

They both stared at each other for a few seconds. He was probably waiting for her temper to settle before opening his mouth again. That was smart on his part.

Until his gaze raked her from the top of her messy bedhead over the gaping too-small robe, catching on her cleavage and getting stuck there. She yanked at one edge of the fabric with her free hand, but that didn't help much.

His nostrils flared and he caught his bottom lip between his teeth for a second. "Didn't mean to cause a problem. Was tryin' to help."

Her anger was quickly dissipating at the heated look in his eyes. She needed to stay on point, *damn it*. "How is it helping when my daughter now knows you slept over?"

He pulled her into his chest and tipped his head down to her. "She don't know."

Cassie frowned and narrowed her eyes. "What do you mean she doesn't know? How does she not know?"

"Got up, got dressed, waited on the steps for her to come out, soon as she did, scooped her ass up and took her downstairs to get her fed. Wanted to let you sleep a little longer. Your fuckin' ass was exhausted. Me stayin' last night didn't help that, so wanted to find a way to help make up for the sleep you lost."

She stared at him, her mouth hanging open. A moment later she snapped her jaw shut. Well, that was sort of nice, but... "You promised, Judge."

"Promised to be out of your bed before she woke up. Did what I promised."

Cassie smacked her free hand onto her forehead. "Wow, talk about semantics." She glared up at him. "You knew exactly what I meant."

"Yeah, baby, I did. But never promised to leave. Don't like you here alone and told you that."

"But that's not up to you."

"The fuck it isn't."

She pinned her eyebrows together and opened her mouth to argue. But as soon as he began talking, her argument was somehow forgotten.

"Whatcha gonna do about Daisy when you go back to work Thursday since your sister and her man ain't gonna be back?"

Huh? "A college girl down the street will watch her while I work."

He frowned. "More money spent."

"Yes, but I'm between a rock and a hard place. I need to work to make money and I need money to pay a sitter so I can work. It'll just put me behind for a while longer. Heather and Tyler offered to take Daisy with them. But I..." She sighed. "I can't."

Judge squeezed her hand gently. "Can't be away from your girl that long."

"Yes. And she's my responsibility, not theirs. I feel bad enough squatting under their roof. I don't like relying on anyone like that. Even if it's my sister."

"Told you, that's what family's for. Help you out of a jam."

"Yes, and I appreciate everything they've done, but I need to get back out on my own."

"Ain't gonna do that by payin' a babysitter."

She tilted her head. "What, are *you* going to watch her?"

"Nope. But gonna help you best way I know how. Gonna find that son of a bitch, get him to sign those fuckin' papers, then hand him over to New York. Will make my money that way and you don't gotta pay a dime. And hopefully you'll get out from underneath that fuckin' mess."

"Judge, while I—"

"Also gonna bring Jury over. Have her stay here while your sister's gone. Your girl will love her. Jury will love the attention. She'll help keep you protected."

He wasn't asking. He was telling.

"You don't have to do that. Just like I love Daisy and don't want to be away from her, you love your girl, too. It'll be hard being away from her like that and Jury will miss her Daddy."

"Who said I ain't gonna be with her?"

She blinked. "Um..."

He grinned.

She frowned.

His grinned widened.

Her frown deepened. "No."

"Ain't askin'."

Her eyebrows shot up. "Did you really just say that?"

"Pretty sure those words came outta my mouth."

"I'm not sure why you think we can't stay here alone, but—"

He took her mouth, stopping her flow of words. Well, that was a good way to stifle any objections. Her body, the traitor that it was, melted against him as she remembered all the things he had done with that mouth last night.

Good lord, a little sex and she was losing her damn spine.

She snapped it straight and broke free of his kiss. "No."

He grinned again. "No what?"

Shit, now she couldn't remember. "No. Just no."

"No what, baby? No to more of my dick? No to Jury bein' here? No to me bein' here to take care of Jury?"

"Having Jury here is just an excuse for you to sleep in my bed every night."

"Ain't gonna lie. That's true. And with every jury comes a judge." His grin turned into a smile. "That's me. The judge in this case."

The man must think he was a freaking comedian. "Then I'll skip that trial, thank you very much."

"Why?"

"Because I don't need a man to stay in this house. There's no threat, the town is safe, why do we need protection?"

"You got a five-year-old little girl whose father's a fugitive."

"Dennis is a lot of things, but he would never hurt Daisy. Or me for that matter. He did something very stupid but he's not a violent man."

"Not gonna be here every night, but Jury will. Need to find Lange, so I'll be out lookin' for him. Deke, too. If Deke's out, Justice will be here, too. Those two will not let any fucker in this house."

"You bring two dogs in this house and Daisy will never stop riding my ass for a dog."

"Then when you get settled in your own place, you get her one."

Was he crazy? He was damn crazy. "You sure like to make decisions that aren't yours to make."

"A dog will teach your girl responsibility."

She sighed. "No, it'll create more work for me. I'm a vet tech, remember? I know how much work a pet can be. And Daisy is already a handful on her own. I'll get her a turtle. Or a fish."

"Nothin' like a loyal dog. Or a loyal man."

"Not looking for either. But thank you for the suggestion."

"Just dick."

"Dick is enough for now. Unless it's attached to someone who is trying to run my life for me."

"Ain't tryin' to run your life."

"No?"

He lifted his gaze from her exposed cleavage to her face. Then he smiled.

Cassie did not like that smile.

Well, she did. But not at that moment.

"Ain't gonna lie. Got a thing for you, Cass. That shit don't normally happen to me. You're makin' it happen. Ain't gonna ignore it."

"Do I have a say in this at all? Or because you want to sleep with me you suddenly feel the need to control my life so you can do that?"

He cupped her face and tipped his down. "You act like this is a one-sided fuckin' thing. You did not kick me outta your bed last night after I fucked you. You know what you fuckin' did?"

Did she need to answer that? Because yes, she was there and knew what she did. She really didn't need a reminder.

He answered it for her, anyway, like she hadn't been in that bed. "You fuckin' curled around me, put your head on my chest and fell the fuck asleep. More than dick. You don't do that shit with only a fuck."

"And you know that how?"

"'Cause as soon as I'm done bustin' a nut in... in... whoever the fuck's in my bed, their ass is out the door. Said that already. Thought you saw the difference."

"So, let me get this straight... You think this could possibly be more than just sex?"

"Ain't it?"

Her heart was thumping as she jerked her face from his hands and stepped back, covering herself better with the robe and tightening the tie more securely. "I don't..." *Breathe.* "I can't..." *Swallow.* "I'm not sure..." *Think.* "I have a daughter."

"Yeah, Cass, I fed her fuckin' breakfast. Pretty sure I'm aware of that."

"I need to protect her."

"From what?"

"From a man we hardly know burrowing into her life. With everything that happened with Dennis, with us splitting, and then us moving and her father disappearing..." She shook her head. "I'm worried how this will all affect her."

"Just gotta give her a steady home. You settle in Manning Grove, you got family here to help with that. Get a place. Get her into school. Let her meet some friends. Kids will bounce the fuck back, Cass. I've seen it."

"How?" What experience did he have with kids? Was it about the son he mentioned briefly and never mentioned again?

What kind of father didn't talk about their child? Not just a father, but what kind of man?

"My sister was your girl's age when a whole bunch of shit went down. Lost our parents, lost our home, lost everythin' we knew. She did okay."

Holy shit. That had to be difficult. "And you?"

"Not talkin' about me."

The way he said that made it sound like he wasn't going to talk about it, either, which made her even more curious. But she wouldn't pry. If he wanted to tell her about his past, that was on him. The same way it was if he wanted to tell her about his son. She wasn't going to demand things from him like he was doing with her.

She needed to go check on Daisy. It was not like her to sit still for this long. And she could only imagine what mess she'd find when she went back into the kitchen. Maple syrup art on the walls, most likely.

"My concern is letting a man into our life, her getting attached and then him disappearing like her father did. She misses him."

His jaw shifted enough she could see it even through that bushy beard. "You miss him?"

"No. But I miss him for her. No matter what, he's her father. He loved her and wasn't a bad father, he just made bad choices."

"Ain't askin' to be her pop, Cass. Just askin' to bang her mother."

Cass threw up her hands and rolled her eyes. "*Ah*, okay, then. Well, that settles it. Go pack a bag, I'll make some room in the closet for you." She shook her head. "I need to check on Daisy." As she turned, he grabbed her wrist and spun her back toward him.

"Didn't let me finish."

"Oh? There was more? Sure sounded like you were done."

His lips flattened out. "Yeah, there's more."

"I'm all ears."

"Did you use 'em to hear the fuckin' part where I said I got a thing for you?"

"I figured you just meant a hard-on."

"Cass," he growled.

"Look, I like you. I do. But I have so much shit going on right now."

"Yeah, and gonna help you with some of that."

"And while I appreciate that, I'm not sure getting involved with you is smart right now."

"*Mommmmmaaaaaa!*"

She grimaced. "I'm surprised that didn't happen sooner. Which makes me wonder what the kitchen looks like right now."

"I'll check on her. You go shower in peace. You're done, I leave. I gotta go to work and talk to Deke. Make a plan to find Lange. Will drop Jury off later. Maybe even Justice. Either way, gonna let you know, so I need your number."

"*Juuuuuuuuuudge!*"

"You okay, kid?" Judge yelled out. "All limbs still attached? Not bleedin' out or anything?"

"I'm *fiiiiine*. But you're takin' too long an' I'm tired of sittin' in this seat. My butt hurts!"

"Be there in a sec," the man told her daughter, but still held Cassie's eyes.

Holy crap. He was just stepping in like he belonged there. Who the hell was this man? "I can get her."

"No. You do your thing while I'm here to watch her."

"Judge..."

"Cass, just accept the help and don't bitch about it."

"It's not that simple."

He leaned in, brushed his mouth over hers, his beard tickling her chin, and when he lifted his head, he said, "Yeah, baby, it's just that simple." He released her, ordered her to "go," smacked her hard on the ass and strode out of the living room to go check on her daughter.

Cassie stood there, rubbing the sting on her ass, staring in the direction he disappeared.

What the hell just happened?

Did she just agree to have Judge and his dog move temporarily into her sister's house without actually agreeing?

That might have just happened.

Chapter Fourteen

JUDGE STUDIED the Blood Fury insignia carved into the center of the table. He sat in the same seat his father used to. To the left of the club prez. Sig, as VP, sat to Trip's right. They were the two top spots in the executive committee after the president. Positions that held almost as much responsibility.

Both the VP and the Sergeant at Arms were supposed to help the prez run the club. Make sure shit was being done and it was done right. Judge was to keep order within the club, make sure no one was being disloyal, and no one was being stupid, which could cause blowback on the MC.

He hoped there never came a day where he had to plug a .45 into the forehead of one of his brothers like Ox had.

Judge's gaze circled the table. Besides Trip and Sig, Ozzy as Secretary, Deacon as Treasurer, and Cage as Road Captain sat at the table where important decisions were made.

And sometimes not so important ones.

But right now, Trip was talking about Shady, one of their prospects. Judge needed to pay attention.

He hadn't liked the man when he first showed up. He

was quiet. He didn't jump on any pussy. He was sort of a loner. And that wasn't normal within an MC.

That bugged the fuck out of Judge.

Without telling anyone, Judge had run a background check on him and besides the same kind of shit everyone else had been busted for in the past, nothing weird jumped out at him.

Judge's respect for the prospect had bumped up a few notches after dealing with the Shirley Clan. He'd gone up there with the rest of them and quietly "dispatched" several Shirleys without blinking.

Maybe that should worry Judge. That emotionless, calm slicing of a throat. But for some reason it didn't. To him, it was a man showing loyalty and dedication to his future brothers. And their women.

Because it never was only about the members. Ol' ladies needed to be protected, too.

That was one of the reasons why guilt laid heavily on him. Letting the Shirleys grab Autumn right from the farm, right from under their noses, was a big fuck-up. She could've been hurt badly or even killed.

Thank fuck she wasn't.

Thank fuck she didn't blame him because that would've made it even harder.

But Autumn—or Red, as Sig called her—showed Judge nothing but love. She was awfully goddamn forgiving for a woman who dealt with as much trauma as she had.

But then, she just wanted to put all of that behind her.

They all did.

Judge just needed to keep his finger on the pulse of those armed inbred hillbillies on that mountain. Because if they fucked with the club or the Fury family again, what happened up there the last time, when they went to rescue Autumn, would be like child's play.

The next time, as Sig had told those fuckers, no one would survive.

They'd been warned.

His name being called pulled him from his thoughts and he glanced up to see everyone staring at him. Jury's head was in his lap and he had been rubbing her ears mindlessly. He did that a lot when he was lost in thought. Or ready to snap.

The Fury prez was frowning at him. "You with us?"

"Yeah," he grunted.

"You wanted Shady's time as a prospect to be longer than six months. But instead of extendin' it, thinkin' we should patch him in a couple weeks early for his part in the shit that went down on the mountain. He proved himself."

"Yeah, he did," Sig agreed. "Guy's got some big balls on him. Though, he could be scary as fuck. Those silent killers usually are."

"He got military time? Some special ops shit or somethin'?" Ozzy scratched at his beard.

"If he does, hasn't said a fuckin' word about it," Cage said. "He mention anything to you, Prez?"

"Nope. Not to me," Trip answered. "And he knows I served."

"Those silent types can be fuckin' crazy," Cage said. "I get why Judge was wary about him, but he did kick ass up there. Was fuckin' impressive."

"Yeah, he was," Judge muttered.

"That's why I'm thinkin' we shouldn't wait. Show him our thanks by votin' tonight. Get him his rockers. And have the bash on Sunday."

"Just gotta call a vote, Prez." Ozzy sat back in his seat and crossed his arms over his chest. "I'll make the motion."

"Second," Sig said.

Trip's eyes slid to Judge's. "You okay with this?"

"Yeah," he answered.

Trip nodded. "All in favor?"

All five officers voted *aye*, except for Cage, since the Road Captain didn't get a vote unless another officer was missing and he needed to fill in.

Trip smacked the gavel on the table. "Motion passed. Shady's gonna be our newest fuckin' member." He smiled. "Shit's comin' together, brothers. Club's growin', the coffers are growin' and everyone's takin' care of business."

"Twelve of us now, but with Shady patchin' in we only got one fuckin' prospect left. We need more," Cage said.

"Yeah, Easy can only shovel so much shit," Deke said.

Trip spoke up next. "And like I say every fuckin' meetin', keep your eyes open and ears to the ground. Thinkin' after Easy, all prospects gonna do a year sentence. Let's vote on that, too."

Unanimous *yeahs* went around the table when Trip called it to a vote.

"A whole fuckin' year of bein' dog shit. That's gonna suck." Cage shook his head but wore a grin. The man liked giving the prospects shit.

Cage needed to watch that because prospects became members and once they were members they might want revenge.

"Then you better thank the sperm gods you came from Dutch's wrinkled, hairy nut sac, and that your momma took his load in her twat and didn't swallow you," Ozzy told him. He opened his mouth and, using his fist, made the motion of a blow job.

Cage flicked his lit hand-rolled at Ozzy, who batted it away. "How you know what Dutch's nut sac looks like unless you were fuckin' up close and personal? Got somethin' to tell us?"

"Don't ask, don't tell," Trip ordered, trying to keep a serious face. "When it comes to dick, nobody gives a shit if you suck it or fuck it."

"Wonder if Shady leans that way?" Sig asked.

"Don't give a fuck as long as it doesn't affect the club," Trip answered his brother. "Anyway, Sig, set up a party for Sunday. Keep it on the DL what the party's for. Gonna surprise him." He turned toward Deacon. "Get a pig from the Amish since I don't want our VP anywhere near them."

"Need Deke with me," Judge told Trip.

Trip frowned. "With you where?"

"Gonna head up to Rochester. He already did some groundwork, but we need to dig deeper."

"What the fuck's in Rochester?" Ozzy asked.

"That's where Cassie's from," Deke answered.

"Yeah. And?"

"Yeah and we gotta head up there," Judge answered the club's secretary. "Try to track down her ex."

"Ain't her ex yet," Trip muttered.

Judge turned toward him. "And that's the reason we're headed up there. Gonna find his fuckin' ass, scrape her free of him."

"She got the money to pay you? Know she's hurtin' financially," Trip asked.

"She ain't got shit. And now her sister and brother-in-law left town, she's gotta hire a babysitter while she's workin' at Pete's. Gonna set her back even more."

"Get one of the sweet butts to watch the kid," Cage suggested.

"Fuck that," Judge said. "Cassie don't know what a sweet butt is. She finds out and one of 'em is watchin' her girl...?" He shook his head.

"Then he might lose out on a piece of that sweet, sweet pussy," Deke finished for him in a sing-song voice and with a grin.

"Cuz," Judge growled.

"Oh fuck, you tappin' that?" Ozzy asked, his grey eyes wide. "She's got it goin' on." He smirked and used his hands to make an outline of a woman in front of him, indicating how curvy Cassie was.

Judge ignored him.

So did Trip. "Who's watchin' the dogs? Want me to keep 'em up at the house?"

"Nope. Stayin' with Cassie and her girl. Figured the girl will love 'em and they'll love bein' spoiled. Plus, they can protect her while we're gone."

"They need protection?" Trip asked, eyes narrowed. "She hasn't said anythin' to me about bein' worried."

"Nope. But they'll be there alone." It was his job to protect his club and everyone in it. That protection extended to Crazy Pete's since it was owned by both the club and Trip's ol' lady. By default, with Cassie working there, it put her under his protection.

He didn't give a fuck what anyone else thought about that. He would protect her like club property whether she was or wasn't.

Whether she would be or not.

He'd let nothing happen to her on his watch. He already had enough guilt eating at him.

Sig was studying him way too closely. He almost lost his woman because of them not being watchful enough. Because of Judge not taking his position as seriously as he should have. Having Autumn kidnapped had driven Sig to a breaking point. *Hell*, it almost drove a lot of them to the breaking point. So, the man understood Judge's concern.

"Want them up in your apartment while you're gone? Red and I can keep an eye on 'em." Sig glanced around the table. "Hell, we all can."

Judge shook his head. While he appreciated the offer... "Don't wanna uproot her girl again so soon. And there's only one bed in my place. Neighbor girl's gonna watch Daisy while Cass works."

"You two be back before Sunday?" Trip asked.

"Leavin' tomorrow mornin' and hopefully be back way before Sunday. Don't wanna miss a fuckin' patch party," Deke said. "Missed the last one. With loose liquor comes loose lips. You know which ones I mean." He smirked.

"Can't leave the business that long anyway," Judge told Trip.

"Want someone to check on Cass when she's not at the bar?" the prez asked.

"Don't think she's in any danger. Ex ain't violent, just a crook who gambled away everythin' they had. Dogs should be good enough."

Trip nodded and spun the gavel within his fingers. "Any other business?"

"Yeah," Deke spoke up. "All the paperwork's finally settled with the crematorium. Easy and Shady know what they're fuckin' doin' now. Everythin's movin' forward. It's all ours now. The vet said he'd be available if any questions come up."

"Good," Trip said. "More scratch in our pockets."

"And a good way to dispose of any evidence," Sig said under his breath.

"Let's hope to fuck we don't need it for that. Anything else?" Trip's head swiveled around the table. When no one else said a word, he slammed the gavel against the table. "Meetin' a-fuckin-djourned."

———

As THE DOGS pushed past him and rushed into the house, he heard an ear-splitting squeal, a thunder of feet both four-legged and two-legged as they bum-rushed each other from two different directions.

"Yo!" he yelled as he hurried inside and dropped the shit he was carrying at his feet, worried the two big dogs would plow right through and over Daisy, scaring or hurting her.

As he quickly made his way into the living room with Cassie on his heels, he saw that did happen. But Daisy was rolling around on the carpet, maniacally laughing her little ass off as the dogs licked her face.

"Momma!" she laugh-screamed. "Are these my new dogs?"

"No," Cassie said. "Judge asked if we could watch them while he goes away."

Daisy's blonde head popped up between two blocky bulldog heads. "Where ya goin', Judge?"

"Got some business to attend to, kid." He clapped his hands. "Jury, Justice, settle."

Both dogs flopped to their bellies next to the five-year-old, their tongues hanging out and both wearing "smiles."

"Guess they like kids?" Cassie asked with eyebrows raised.

"Haven't eaten one yet."

"That's reassuring."

He peered down into her face. "You worried?"

"I'm a vet tech, remember? American Bulldogs are not a breed I'd worry about around her. And they both seem well-adjusted and well-trained."

"Best dogs ever," he assured her.

"Maybe when she's older I'll get her a dog."

"Want one *noooooow*, Momma!" demanded the little hellion.

"Well, you have two right now to deal with. Let's see how well you do taking care of them for Judge. Then we'll see."

"How long are they stayin', Judge?" Daisy asked as she laid flat on her back, one hand on each dog, petting them.

"'Til your aunt and uncle get back."

Daisy's smile got so big it practically lit up the whole room. "When you leavin'?"

"In the mornin'."

"So, you're gonna make me breakfast?" came the high-pitched question.

Judge smiled down into Cassie's face. "Depends if your momma lets me."

Another ear-piercing squeal filled the room as she sat up. "*Pleeeease*, Momma! Judge can make me French toast since you won't."

"I make you French toast," her mother exclaimed.

"His is better."

"Doubt that, kid."

"It is," Daisy insisted.

"Maybe we'll have your momma make us both French toast and we can see whose is better."

Cassie narrowed her eyes up at him. "Wow," she mouthed.

He grinned at her and she shook her head.

"Time for you to get ready for bed."

"Sounds like a plan," Judge said under his breath just loud enough for Cassie to hear.

She whacked his stomach with the back of her hand and he smothered his laugh.

"Can they sleep in my room?" Daisy asked, climbing to her feet.

"No," her mother answered at the same time Judge said, "Yeah."

Cassie frowned. "You don't want them with you?"

"Them bein' a couple doors down ain't gonna be a problem," he murmured. "Won't be room in your bed for 'em, anyway."

Color exploded in Cassie's cheeks and she quickly glanced at her daughter, who was now having the dogs chase her around the living room in a circle.

"I wasn't planning on having them in my bed, anyway. I've never slept with a dog of the four-legged variety and I wasn't planning on starting."

He cocked an eyebrow. "Slept with one of the two-legged variety?"

She returned that cocked eyebrow. "You tell me."

"Get your girl ready for bed. Will put the dog beds in her room. Though, doubt they'll use them. Where you want their food and stuff?"

She sighed. "Kitchen, I guess." She turned to her daughter. "C'mon, Daze. Time to get ready for bed."

"But I wanna play with them," Daisy whined as she and the dogs continued their endless circles around the living room like a NASCAR race. Judge was waiting for the twenty-car pile-up.

"You can do that tomorrow out in the backyard where you have lots of room and won't break anything."

"It fenced?" Judge asked Cassie.

She nodded. "Yes."

"Good." That relieved the worry of Cassie having to walk the dogs. They were strong, and though well-trained, preferred their freedom to do their business, that was why being out on the farm was perfect for them.

Judge hauled the dogs' stuff to the kitchen, then the beds upstairs and, once Daisy and both dogs were settled in her small bed, he gave them a last thorough head scratch and left Cassie alone with her daughter to read her a story.

He grabbed his duffel from the hallway where he had dropped it at the top of the steps and went into the master bedroom to wait.

And wait.

He was beginning to lose his patience when the door finally opened and she slipped inside the room. "Well, having the dogs here is the same as giving her a two-liter bottle of Mountain Dew. She's so hyped, I didn't think she'd ever close her eyes. I put the dogs to sleep with my story-telling long before her."

"They in bed with her?"

"I'll give you one guess."

"You care?"

"She's pretty active in her sleep. I worry more about them than her."

"They don't like it, they'll move."

Her gaze dropped from where he was sitting on her bed, leaning against the headboard in just his jeans and a black wife-beater, to the foot of her bed where he'd piled his duffel, his cut, and his boots.

"I guess you were planning on spending the night?"

"Didn't realize that was in question."

She glanced over her shoulder at the closed door. "Well..."

"Think she cares that I'm in your room?"

"I care."

"Don't want me here?"

"I worry about what she'll think about it."

"Not for nothin' but did you plan on stayin' celibate 'til she's eighteen?"

"I just don't..."

He surged from the bed and stalked toward her, not stopping until they were toe to toe.

"Want a revolving door," she finished softly, staring up at him.

"You plannin' on another man comin' through that door," he jerked his chin toward the closed one behind her, "tomorrow night?"

"No."

"The next night?"

"No."

"One man in your bed don't make a revolvin' door, Cass."

"No men would be better."

"For who? You?"

"For Daisy."

"Why? What's wrong with teachin' your girl that women have certain needs and there's nothin' wrong with gettin' those needs fulfilled?"

"I don't want to be a bad mother," she whispered.

"Baby, if you think wantin' sex makes you a bad mother, you'd be fuckin' wrong. You wanna know what a bad mother's like? I can have you talk to a few people who'd make you think you're the best fuckin' mother in the world." He slid his fingers into the hair above her ear, tipped her head up and his down until their mouths were close but not touching. "Wantin' my dick don't make you a bad mother, makes you a normal woman."

"What about tomorrow morning?" she whispered.

"Be outta your bed early. Will get her and the dogs up and let you sleep. Yeah?"

"Undisturbed sleep sounds better than an orgasm," she breathed, her fingers fisting the cotton of his tank.

He grinned. "Guess I gotta work harder on those orgasms, then. Musta been fuckin' slackin'. Guess I'll start now."

He bumped his chest against hers, making her take a step back. He did it again until her back was to the door. Pushing his knee between her thighs, her legs widened slightly. His right hand, which was still threaded in her hair, slid around to the back, bunching it within his fist. He tugged the handful until her face was tilted up and her neck arched and exposed.

The pulse in her throat pounded as hard as the pulse in his dick. He needed her naked. He wanted her to plaster her palms against the door, tip her ass out and wanted to take her hard and fast from behind.

But that's not what he did.

Instead, he ran his lips over that pulse, feeling it speed up even more.

He jerked up the bulky sweatshirt she wore, which did

nothing for her curves, to find her wearing some bullshit sports bra. Something that crushed her tits to her chest. He yanked one side up and snagged her peaked nipple between his fingers and twisted it until she whimpered. Her throat moved under his mouth as he drug it across her delicate skin up to behind her ear. After sucking on her earlobe for a few seconds, he caught it between his teeth, just biting it hard enough for her to feel it.

He did not miss the shiver that shot through her, which made him smile.

Releasing her hair, he gathered her wrists in one hand and pulled them over her head, pinning them to the door. He took her mouth, sucking her bottom lip, scraping his teeth over it, then exploring inside.

He captured her groan, shoved her sweatshirt and sports bra up farther, seizing the other nipple and rolling it between his fingers until it was diamond hard and she squirmed against him. Then gripping it tighter, he twisted it until he knew it would cause a sharp pain.

Like her groan, he caught her gasp and tangled his tongue with hers, not letting her take control of the kiss.

He kissed her harder, drove his tongue deeper, releasing her nipple, sliding his hand down her stomach and into the loose cotton pants she wore. Again, something that did nothing for her curves but hide them.

He hated that.

She needed to show off how fucking luscious she was. Her hips, her ass. Those tits.

He knew what she was hiding under those baggy clothes. He'd seen it. He planned on seeing it again.

He planned on seeing it a lot.

He only hoped Cassie wanted the same thing as he did.

His goal was to find Lange to scrape Cassie clean of him. To let her move on.

No matter what, he wanted to help her.

And, yeah, he was also being selfish. Because he wanted what Lange held onto legally.

But Judge wanted her free and clear. No piece of her still belonging to another man.

He wanted all of her to be his.

It was fucking crazy.

There were plenty of women who didn't have baggage. An ex, who wasn't an ex yet. A kid with that ex. And one financially broke because of that ex.

But none of that mattered to him.

The only thing that did was the ex. The rest he could live with.

He would do his best to deal with Lange and then help her deal with the rest.

Why he gave a fuck...?

When his hand slipped into those loose cotton pants and through the dark blonde wiry hairs until he found her clit, she whimpered again in his mouth, driving her tongue more frantically against his. He pressed, circled and teased it before sliding his middle finger lower to test how wet she was. His answer? Very fucking wet.

He didn't give a fuck because he wanted to fuck her. He gave a fuck because he wanted *her*.

Her body bowed away from the door, but his knee kept her open to him, his hand kept her and her wrists against the door.

Slick. Hot. Soft.

He wanted to shove his face there, lose himself in her scent, lose himself with the sounds she made, the reactions to his actions.

He wanted to hear her call him Judd. Because when she did, she herself was lost. With what he was doing to her.

And affecting her in that way affected him.

How she had burrowed so quickly under his skin in such a short amount of time, he didn't know.

Did it bother him? It did and it didn't.

It did if he was just a dick to ride. It didn't if he could be more.

In all of his thirty-seven fucking years, he never wanted more from a woman. Not once.

Not even Ry's mother.

Not even her.

And that had become a problem.

He shoved his past out of his head and concentrated on the now. On the woman he had pinned against the door, who was encouraging him with the noises he muffled with his own mouth, with the responses to his touch.

He slipped a second finger inside of her, and she bucked against him as he didn't let up, not for a second.

His hard-on was throbbing, his brain urging him to just take her. But this orgasm was for her. Not him. Her.

His thumb circled her clit and she ground against his fingers, trying to break free of his kiss, but he didn't let her go.

Did he want to hear her call his name? Fuck yes, he did. But if she did, it would wake up Daisy.

Every muscle on her tensed, and he swore she stopped breathing. Her tongue retreated and her back arched, her hips slamming into his as she tightened around his fingers and a gush of warmth surrounded them.

He released her mouth, pressed his cheek to hers and they both just breathed as she melted against him.

His dick was aching, his need to fuck her strong. But he waited. Letting her have that moment because he was sharing it, too.

With his mouth to her ear, he asked, "Sleep better than that?"

"I'm not sure yet," she panted.

He released her wrists and it took a few seconds for her to drop her arms and when she did, she dropped them around his neck and pulled him into another kiss. Much shorter, much less intense, but just as good.

"Need to try again? To prove my point?" he asked against her lips.

"Mmm hmm. Just to be sure." Her eyelids were heavy, her face flushed and relaxed, her lips slightly curled up.

She was so fucking beautiful that it scared him.

She had sucked him in. Stolen his fucking soul.

Just like that.

Almost instantly.

Now he was more determined than ever to find Lange.

Because Cassie was no longer his, she was Judge's.

And that man wasn't getting her back.

Not fucking ever.

Chapter Fifteen

THE RATTLE of the doorknob and sound of a small fist pounding on her bedroom door made her heart jump into her throat. Wide-eyed, she stared up at Judge whose, amongst that thick beard, lips twitched.

"It isn't funny!" she mouthed and glared at him.

She tugged at his hand, which was still down her pants and stroking her gently. He slowly removed it and stepped back so she could adjust her clothes.

The knob shook again and a *"Mommmmmma!"* came through the door loud and clear.

Had they made too much noise?

It didn't matter now; her daughter was awake.

She made a "shooing" motion to Judge, indicating he needed to hide.

"Momma!" came the yell and pound of fists again. "Heard a noise. Why's the door locked?"

"The door isn't locked, sweetie. It's probably just stuck. Give me a second."

Judge stepped behind the door as she unlocked it and opened it a crack to stand in the opening, blocking Daisy from rushing in.

Her daughter pushed on her thigh with both hands, trying to move Cassie out of the way. She didn't budge. "Why are you out of bed?"

"I woke up and couldn't fall back asleep."

"You need to go back to bed."

Daisy pushed against her legs again. "Wanna sleep with you."

"No, we should sleep in our own beds. You're not a baby anymore, you're a big girl."

"Then Judge can tuck me in."

"Judge isn't here." She winced at her own lie.

"Yes, he is. He's in your room. Judge! Tuck me in!"

"Daisy..."

Her bottom lip pushed out in a pout and she stomped her little bare foot. "Momma, I want Judge to tuck me in. Jury and Justice wanna say goodnight to him."

"They said that?"

She nodded like her neck was broken and just flopping around. "Yes. They told me to get him."

Heat pressed against her back. Cassie tilted her head back and saw him standing over her. "Gonna tuck her in and say goodnight to the dogs."

"Told you he was in your room! You lied, Momma! You said lyin' is bad!"

Shit. "Lying is bad. I was mistaken. I wasn't aware he was in here."

Her blonde mini-me shot her a scathing look.

Cassie sighed, opened the door wider, and grabbed her daughter's shoulders, turning her toward her room. "Let's go."

"Judge, you comin'?" Daisy yelled over her shoulder.

"Yeah, kid," came the grumble behind her.

They got into the spare bedroom, saw the dogs remained curled up on the bed, their eyes open and watching, but undisturbed. When they saw Judge, their long wagging tails whapped the bed loudly.

"In bed, sweetie. We all need to get some sleep."

Daisy climbed in between the dogs. "Put your legs under the covers, kid," Judge instructed. She scrambled to tuck her legs into the narrow space between her hairy bunkmates. "Don't need to tuck you in. Jury and Justice got you tucked in good."

Daisy smiled. "You gonna tuck in Momma?"

Cassie avoided looking at Judge. If she did, she'd probably turn bright red.

"Yep. She's next, kid. If you go to sleep now, morning will come sooner and then we can judge your momma's French toast before I leave, yeah?"

"Yeah," Daisy answered, then she whispered, "Yours is better."

"We'll find out once we wake up in the mornin'. But mornin' will never come if you don't fall asleep."

"Goin' to sleep now." The girl squeezed her eyes shut and pretended to snore.

"You get outta bed again and your momma's gonna cancel that French toast and feed us stale cereal with skim milk."

Cassie turned her head away and slapped a hand over her mouth.

Daisy eyes popped open. "She can't do that!"

"Yeah, she told me if she don't get sleep, she's gonna be too tired to make us breakfast and will be stuck with Lucky Charms without the marshmallows and spoiled milk." Judge wrinkled his nose.

Daisy screamed, "NO!" and wrinkled up her face, too, before laughing.

"I'm actually considering feeding you two dog food."

"Momma, no!" Daisy giggled and pulled the sheet over

her head. "No dog food! Then what's Jury and Justice gonna eat?"

"French toast."

The sheet flipped down. "You're mean!"

"Go to sleep," she told her daughter. "Judge is right. The sooner you sleep, the sooner you wake up, the sooner you'll be eating my French toast which is *way* better than Judge's." She leaned over, swept the hair off Daisy's face and placed a kiss on her forehead. "'Night, sweetie."

"G'night, Momma."

"Don't kick the dogs too much."

"I won't."

"G'night, Judge."

"'Night, kid." He ruffled her hair, both dogs' heads, then headed back out the bedroom door.

"Gonna tuck Momma in now?" Daisy asked his retreating back.

Without missing a step, Judge tossed, "Yep, soon as she's done with you," over his shoulder.

"If you marry Judge, Momma, the dogs can sleep in my bed every night."

Oh boy. "Judge doesn't own Justice."

"Then Jury can."

"How about just being happy Jury will be here until your aunt and uncle return."

Daisy huffed.

"Sleep," Cassie ordered. Blew her daughter a kiss, turned out the light and left her bedroom door open a crack, even though the nightlight was on.

She stood in the hallway outside the doorway a few minutes to make sure Daisy didn't immediately climb out of bed. She listened to her daughter chatter to the bulldogs for a couple of minutes, then her speech slowed and she became quiet. Cassie pushed the door open slightly, peeked in and saw all three occupants of the bed with their eyes closed.

She breathed much easier and decided to close the door completely. She tiptoed down the hallway and back into the master bedroom. As she closed the door behind her, she glanced up and froze.

Judge was in her bed wearing nothing but a smile. "Don't come near this bed wearin' any of that shit."

She reached behind her to lock the door. She did not want her daughter to be scarred for life. And seeing her mother bumping uglies would leave a lasting impression. As a child she had walked in on her parents doing the exact same thing and it was a hard memory to wipe clean.

She and Dennis rarely had sex after Daisy was born, so it hadn't been an issue with them. This last week was the most sex she'd had in *years*.

Damn, that was depressing. She didn't stop being a woman once she became a mother. Judge was right, she was a woman with needs and she shouldn't ignore them.

Admittedly, it was very hard to ignore the naked six-foot-three, bearded biker in her bed. Especially since his fist was wrapped around all that hardness and he was stroking it.

"You have a lot of tattoos." *Gah*. That was a dumb thing to say. He already knew that. So did she.

"That's what you fuckin' notice?"

"Was I supposed to notice something else? Your tattoos are hard to miss."

He squeezed the root of his cock, making it turn dark and veiny. "Nothin' else hard to miss?"

She raked her gaze over him. "Let me look closer... Mmm. No. Just your tattoos and the beard that needs a good trimming."

His free hand went immediately to his beard as his eyes went wide before quickly narrowing. "Woman! Don't be sayin' shit like that."

She made a snipping motion with her fingers. "I can trim it short for you. Let me grab my scissors."

"Gotta rethink this shit."

She kept her expression serious. "What shit?"

"Givin' you my dick."

"Well, who else are you going to give it to?" She made a point of glancing around. "I don't see anyone else in this room."

He released his cock, bounded from the bed and she bit back her squeal just in time as he grabbed her and growled, "Someone needs a spankin'."

Her eyes went wide, and a thrill rushed through her. "Don't you dare!" she hissed.

"See exactly where your girl got her sassy mouth."

Cassie pointed at her lips. "You mean this one?"

"Yeah, that's the fuckin' one. Told you to take all that shit off."

"You told me, huh?"

"Yep. And you didn't listen. Still gave me lip. Now I gotta get that shit off you myself."

She bit her bottom lip, fighting back her smile at his fake grouchiness. "I mean, I don't want you to strain your fingers doing it or anything. That would be a shame."

He dropped his head and their eyes locked. "Yeah, it would, especially after you came all over them when I used them to fuck you."

Good lord, that caused a spark inside her. Almost like she'd stuck a fork in a socket.

She'd never been spoken to like that before. Not once with a bossy, growly, alpha male tone. It shouldn't excite her, but it did.

However, she could be bossy, too. "Get me naked."

His lips curled slightly, and his green eyes became dark and hooded. "No." He released her and stepped back.

No?

His broad, naked back with the colors of his club permanently inked into it retreated and she let her gaze slide lower to his ass and long legs as he went and settled on the bed in the same position he'd been in when she walked through the door.

"Get naked," he demanded in his low rumble that made her nipples peak painfully. As she stepped toward the bed, he lifted his palm and shook his head. "Right there."

Her heart pounded and her throat tightened at the thought of standing there, where he could see everything and just stripping.

"Cass," came the grumbled warning.

She lifted her gaze from the hem of her sweatshirt, where she was gripping it so hard, her knuckles were turning white.

"Do it." He watched her closely as he began stroking his cock again.

How could that simple act be so damn mesmerizing? So sexy? Make her so wet?

This time his low, thunderous, "Cass," made her jerk into motion, yank the sweatshirt over her head and toss it, shove her lounge pants and panties down to her ankles before working her snug sports bra over her breasts.

Then she stood there naked. Completely exposed.

At her most vulnerable.

But it hit her then. Right between the eyes.

He looked at her without an ounce of judgment.

His heated gaze which slowly slid down her body made her feel nothing but wanted and desired.

That right there made him even sexier in her eyes.

That made her want and appreciate him even more.

It was difficult to appreciate him from across the room.

So, she didn't.

• • •

FUCK.

Judge didn't know where to eyeball her first as Cassie approached the bed. He had noticed when she first got naked, she looked unsure, then something changed as she stood there.

Her spine had become straighter and her shoulders pulled back, drawing his attention to her amazing fucking tits. She released the bottom lip she'd been chewing on as she stripped, and finally she fucking smiled.

It wasn't a normal smile, but a naughty, *I-might-just-fuck-out-your-brains-tonight* smile.

And that was the best fucking kind.

It also made his dick twitch in his hands and his balls pull a little tighter.

Because, *fuck yeah*, if he was brain dead in the morning, he might be A-fucking-Okay with it.

His fingers itched to touch her, he wanted to taste her on his tongue, make his lips slick with her arousal and hear her whimpers in his ears.

Just to start.

But they needed to keep the noise to a low roar. He did not want to be interrupted. Because once she landed in that bed, she was not leaving it until he was done with her.

Until she was done with him.

Until they were both boneless, drained and satisfied.

When she got to the side of the bed where he sat waiting, he held out his hand and she accepted it, but he didn't help her onto the bed.

Not yet.

"Turn around, baby."

That fucking insecurity popped back up in her blue eyes and he frowned. There was no reason for her to be like that.

None.

She was goddamn perfect.

He moved to sit on the edge of the bed and planted his

feet solidly on the floor. "Turn around, Cassie." Not a request but a demand. When she still hesitated, he growled, "Turn the fuck around."

A flush ran up her chest, but she slowly turned, her jaw set, her fingers clenched.

Which he didn't fucking like at all.

She needed to understand that the only opinion which mattered in that room, at that moment, was his. No one else belonged in that room with them.

"Lift your hair up. Hold it on top of your head. Don't want it coverin' anything."

"Judge," she whispered.

"Do it," he said more softly. He wanted to throat punch whoever made her unsure. Especially if it was a man who hadn't appreciated everything about her.

She did it. Slowly gathering all her thick blonde hair with both hands and holding it to the top of her head, exposing the long line of her neck, the curve of her shoulders, the indentation of her spine.

"Keep it there."

"Judge..."

"Quiet."

Her fingers twitched in her hair at that, but she remained silent.

Using his fingertips, he traced her spine from the top of her neck down, only stopping when he reached the top of her ass crack. Then he slid them back up, leaned forward and repeated it using his warm breath against her skin, the occasional skim of his lips, the scrape of his beard. All the way down, all the way back up.

A shudder moved through her, bringing out goosebumps all over her skin and causing the fine hairs on the back of her neck to stand.

But she stayed quiet and didn't move.

"Fuckin' beautiful," he murmured when he next placed

his mouth at the very top of her neck and tasted her skin with the tip of his tongue. He dragged it down the curve of her spine to the curves of her ass where he sank his teeth in gently.

She jerked slightly and he heard a rush of breath. So, he did it again with the other cheek, this time a little harder, making sure the sharpness of his teeth could be felt.

"Judge." His name caught in her throat, and she began to tremble.

"Don't move," he told her again, grabbing her hips and sliding his hands to her front, skimming his palms over the small patch of hair at the top of her cunt, and up over her belly. He palmed the weight of both tits before squeezing them. And while he did that, he pressed his lips again to the top of her spine. "Don't." He pinched both nipples, causing a breathy gasp and then he thumbed one and took his other hand back down, over that soft patch again, where he hesitated. "Move."

He sank his teeth into her neck at the same time his middle finger slid between her folds and inside her. She swayed and he braced her against his chest.

She was so fucking wet as he slid his finger in and out of her, listening to her breathing become more and more ragged, feeling the way her body responded to his teeth, his touch.

Without warning, she surged forward, pulling away from him, spinning around, and shoving both of her palms into his chest, knocking him onto his back. Without hesitation she climbed over him, grabbed his dick and was about to impale herself when he grabbed her waist, using all his strength to keep her from doing so.

"Wrap," was all he said with a jerk of his chin toward where he had placed it.

She blinked as if she had come back to reality and her head twisted toward the nightstand. Without a word, she leaned over, snagged it, tore it open, threw the empty wrapper over her shoulder and rolled it down his cock in record time.

Once she rolled it to the root, she held it in place, hovered over him and sank down.

It wasn't slow. Hell no, she wasn't fucking around.

"Fuck," he groaned as her tight, wet heat surrounded him. When he was fully inside her and couldn't get any deeper, she ground hard against him. "Jesus fuck."

She planted both her palms on his chest and began to rise and fall. Not slow, but like she was in a race she was determined to win. If she kept that pace, that race would be over sooner than he wanted, and no one would be the winner.

He squeezed her hips. "Baby, slow down."

She either didn't hear him or was ignoring him because she continued to ride him like she was using his dick to desperately scratch an itch she couldn't reach.

And while he was impressed by her enthusiasm, he had to grit his teeth and think other thoughts just so he wouldn't blow his load.

Watching her face didn't help. Neither did watching the heavy bounce of her tits. Or focusing on where they were connected as his dick disappeared inside her again and again.

For fuck's sake. He turned his eyes to the ceiling, and inhaled long breaths through his nose. Desperate to keep his heart from escaping his chest and keep his cum in his nuts.

He just needed to let her do her thing and do his best to wait her out. Then he could do his. He folded his arms behind his head—because he couldn't touch her either— and began to recite some of the lyrics for Guns N' Roses song *Patience* in his head. He didn't know them all, but he knew the most important ones, the lines he needed to concentrate on.

He just needed a little patience.

And willpower.

He'd had women ride him like a manual handle on a well pump before, but none of those women had been Cassie. None of them could compare.

And that was the problem.

Cassie twisted shit inside him no woman had before. It wasn't a bad twist, just one he wasn't familiar with.

With a whimper, she slammed down on him one more time, a grunt escaping him from the impact. She threw her head back, tightened up and...

He bit his inner cheek and held his breath as she exploded around him. He almost detonated, too.

Somehow, he managed to gather his shit and hang on.

He kept himself perfectly still until her head dropped forward and her hair covered her face. Her tits rose and fell just as fast as when she was fucking him.

He wanted his face between them when he came deep inside her.

And that wasn't going to happen in their current position.

She lifted her head, wearing a lazy, relaxed smile, her eyes unfocused and soft.

Jesus. For him, Christmas had come early.

And it was the best fucking Christmas ever.

"You done?" When she didn't answer, he growled, "You're done," as he slammed his hips up, knocking her off balance. He dragged her up the bed, settled between her soft thighs and plunged inside her only stopping once he hit the end of her.

"You're not," she breathed, wrapping her fingers around the back of his neck and giving him her baby blues.

"Fuck no. You ain't, either."

She'd already had it hard, now he would give it to her soft. He would take his time and appreciate everything about her, starting with her mouth and ending with his face between her tits.

She didn't try to take control of the kiss this time and she let him set the pace. With a tilt of her hips, she accepted him completely. And when he couldn't concentrate on their kiss anymore, he buried his face between tits that were now his as he drove slow and steady into her slick, hot sheath.

Her pussy squeezed him, rippled around him so strongly, he could even feel it through the wrap. He wished he didn't have to wear it, but the harsh reality was, he did.

He learned from his past, even though he hoped Cassie was his future. But there was no guarantee of that. Because of that, he wouldn't risk it. He wasn't going to have a misstep destroy what he wanted with her before it even really began.

Her nails scoring the skin of his back brought him back to the bed, back to being inside her, where he never should have left in the first place. He lifted his head only enough to see she had covered her own mouth with her hand, her eyes were closed, and her head tipped back in a pool of blonde hair.

When her eyes popped open, they caught his and with the way she tensed, he knew she was about to come again.

Without a wrap, he'd feel that warm gush. Without a wrap, he'd feel even the smallest of responses around his dick.

"Gonna come," he managed to warn her before snagging her nipple into his mouth and sucking it deep as he drove inside her one more time, finally letting go. And when his mind finally unclouded and his dick stopped twitching, he stayed right there, planted inside her to the root.

"Fuck," he panted after releasing her puckered, swollen nipple. He drew his tongue across the very tip, then tilted his face up to hers.

She wore a smile again.

And that smile twisted everything inside him even tighter. So tight, he'd never be able to loosen it. Never be able to be free of it.

But she'd never be his completely until she herself was free.

He was determined to help her before this, but now?

Now, he couldn't fail.

Not again.

Chapter Sixteen

HE *MIGHT* HAVE SLIGHTLY PURRED as she combed her fingers through the long wiry hairs of his beard. She was doing it mindlessly with her cheek pressed to his shoulder and a small curve to her lips.

The urge to take her mouth was strong, but he liked what she was doing and didn't want her to stop. If she wanted to pet him the way he petted Jury, he wouldn't do anything to disrupt that.

Until she asked, "How long have you been growing your beard?"

That simple question pulled him out of his euphoria, and the deep satisfaction that had seeped into his bones quickly evaporated.

It wasn't her fault.

She didn't know.

Almost no one did.

Seeing and feeling the length of his beard was simply a reminder for him. "Since I lost my son."

With a sharp intake of breath, her fingers stilled. "I'm so sorry."

He squeezed them gently. "He didn't die, if that's what you think."

She lifted her head. "Then I don't understand. How did you lose him and what does one have to do with the other?"

He normally didn't talk about it because every time he did, he got angry. Every time he did, he was overwhelmed with regret and frustration.

And of goddamn helplessness.

She went to sit up and he pulled her back down, pressing her head back to his shoulder. He combed his fingers through her hair. Unlike his beard, her long hair was soft and silky against his skin.

"Decided not to cut it 'til I saw him again. Just a reminder of what I lost. Think of him every time I look in the mirror and see it. Reminds me of just how long it's been."

His long beard wasn't the only reminder of what had been his and who he had lost. His son's name, Henry, was tattooed down his right side. If he couldn't be with Ry in person, Ry could be with him always. And he didn't want one day to go by where he didn't think about him.

Not one fucking day.

Because that would make him feel like a failure more than he already did.

One day he also hoped his son realized how much Judge loved him and wanted to be his father. How it wasn't his choice to be separated. One day Judge hoped Ry gave him a chance to get to know him.

One day.

Once that damn evil bitch was no longer controlling his son's life.

He just hoped by then it wasn't too late.

She tugged gently on his beard, pulling his face and his attention toward her. "Why don't you see him?"

His jaw shifted and he beat back his anger, so it didn't

spill onto the woman in his arms. "His mother won't let me."

Her blue eyes narrowed. "What do you mean, let you? Did you fight for visitation?"

"Sure as fuck did. Got it, too. Then she fuckin' bolted."

Because he didn't love Jen, she felt the need to hurt him by stealing his son. She was too stupid to admit, by taking Ry from him, she was hurting their son, too.

She didn't care because she was petty. She hated Judge and wanted to do anything and everything she could to make his ass suffer.

But separating a man from his child for no good reason should be inexcusable. If she wanted to hurt him, she should've found another way.

"Why?"

"To fuck with me."

"Why?"

"She was pissed, so she used my son to get back at me."

"For what?"

He blew out a breath. "It's a long fuckin' story, Cass." One he didn't really want to tell. He had been relaxed, had a hot as fuck woman in his arms, had empty balls and was now tired.

He also needed to get up and get on the road early.

What he didn't need to do was relive his personal hell.

The only people who knew the whole story was his aunt and Deke because they lived through the bullshit with him. Everybody else who asked, he told to fuck off.

"I want to know."

And here was this woman he was thinking about making a future with—even if she didn't know it yet—asking him to rip off that fucking scab and bleed once more.

Yeah, she had no fucking clue what she was demanding, so he couldn't be pissed at her about it. He also couldn't tell her to fuck off. Not if he didn't want her to crumple up that possible future into a ball and toss it in the trash can.

So, yeah, he needed to decide how much he would tell her, if anything.

But if whatever was between them was more than a casual thing, if this went somewhere more than just a few orgasms, she would have to know anyway.

She would also need to know why it all happened. How he fucked up and how he failed his marriage and his son. Because maybe that shit wouldn't sit right with her.

Maybe what he revealed would make her look at him differently.

Maybe she wouldn't want him around her daughter.

Maybe she wouldn't even want to stick in Manning Grove.

Worse, maybe she only wanted him for his dick and nothing more. Just like men, not every woman wanted something other than sex.

He was one of those men. Not once had he been with someone where he wanted anything more.

Not even Ry's mother.

That was why every time he had hooked up with Jen, he wore a wrap. Every fucking time. So, when she came up pregnant, he doubted the kid was his.

She insisted it was.

Turned out she was right.

Judge also figured out Jen had trapped him because he didn't want to commit to her. She had poked holes in the fucking wraps she kept in her bedroom.

Goddamn holes.

That was why he now always used his own. That was why he still used wraps even when a woman insisted she had birth control "covered."

Never fucking again.

He didn't want a kid with Jen. *Hell,* he didn't even want

anything long term with her. He had always been up front about that and never let her believe anything different.

"Even though it wasn't what I wanted, I was determined to do a better job at it than my parents. There was no way I was gonna desert my kid, there was no way I wanted him to think he wasn't wanted."

"When did you find out?"

"When it was too late. She waited to tell me on purpose."

"Damn. She had a plan," Cassie whispered.

"Yeah, she had a fuckin' plan. But you can't force someone to love you. And that's where her plan failed. But I also failed when I fucked up, pissed her off and ended up not bein' a better parent than Ox or Trixie."

"You still haven't said how you fucked up, Judge."

"Never shoulda married her. Another mistake after the wrap shit. Don't like bein' forced to do shit. Was forced, was pissed, and besides that piece of paper legally bindin' us, really wanted nothin' to do with her. Marriage was rotten from the start. No fuckin' sex 'cause I hated her for doin' what she did. No relationship existed at all."

Cassie remained silent, so he continued.

"Waited a year or so after Ry was born, hopin' maybe I could feel somethin' for her. That maybe somethin' would grow. It didn't and I couldn't. Began lookin' elsewhere to get my needs met because I wasn't gettin' them at home."

Cassie tensed against him. "You cheated."

"Technically, yeah. Was young, not dead, so yeah, found it elsewhere, but came home every night to my kid. He was the only thing good that came out of fuckin' that scheming bitch. Ry was the only reason to stay. Shoulda left before that, then maybe I'd still have my son. But I didn't. Figured stickin' around and just fuckin' around was better for him than leavin' his mother. I was really fuckin' wrong."

"How did she find out?"

He stared up at the ceiling. "When I wasn't home, the woman I was fuckin' on the side decided to come knockin' on our door to introduce herself."

"Guess that didn't go well."

"Bingo. Jen fuckin' clocked the woman in the face and knocked her out. When I got home, unaware of what I was walkin' into, got kicked in the fuckin' nuts, found all my shit burned in the backyard and their bags packed. If she couldn't have me, she thought nobody else should, either. She stayed with her parents 'til the divorce, 'til custody was set."

So far, Cassie hadn't kicked him out of her bed, so until she did, he was going to keep talking, lay it all out. Let her form her own opinion about him.

He wouldn't make excuses.

Jen fucked up. He fucked up.

His kid suffered because of it.

"Funny how my cheatin' was the final straw for her, not the loveless, sexless marriage we were sufferin' through."

"Maybe she loved you. Why else would she trap you?"

"Truth? Think she's got mental issues. Didn't know it when I was fuckin' her 'cause I never stuck around long enough to notice. But after Ry was born, and we were livin' together, started to see signs. She was never diagnosed so I ain't sure. Never was violent or did anythin' too crazy where I could force her to see someone but had my suspicions. Somethin' was off, just couldn't put a finger on it. My priority was Ry. Problem was, she used my cheatin' against me in the divorce and custody case. 'Cause of that, got visitation but not any kinda custody, which was bullshit. Have a feelin' I got fucked there, too. Thinkin' her father, or someone she knew, had some sorta connection with the judge. 'Cause not only did I not get custody, that fuckin' judge allowed her to take him outta state. She went to the west coast and took my son with her. So, there went the fuckin' visitation I fought for. She claimed she had family out there and Ry would be raised around cousins and shit. Fuck bein' raised by his father, though, right? Cousins were more important?" His jaw tightened. "Fuck her. She didn't even think twice about rippin' my heart right out of my fuckin' chest and crushin' it under her goddamn heel. Hated her so fuckin' bad, had to force myself not to fuckin' kill her. Because, believe me, it was close. Me endin' up in prison wasn't gonna help my son and I swore to never follow in my father's footsteps like that."

Though, in some ways he had. With the club and his spot within the club. But he would do everything he could to stay out of prison. He didn't want Ry to lose his father the same way Judge lost his.

"But you could still see him, right? You were awarded visitation whether he was in PA or not. Am I wrong about that?"

"Never flew on a goddamn plane in my fuckin' life. Never wanted to. And for me to drive across the country a couple times a year..." He sucked air in through his nostrils. "Did it once. Took almost a week on my sled. She knew I was comin' 'cause it was planned and when I finally got out there... She left. Just fuckin' left." He could feel his blood pressure rising as he remembered that day. It might have been years ago, but it still felt like yesterday.

"Please tell me it was for an emergency of some sort and not on purpose."

It had taken everything he had not to fall to his knees on that porch and just lose his mind. He sat there for hours, hoping it had been a misunderstanding.

Deep down he knew it wasn't. That she'd done it on purpose.

If his son hadn't lived in that house, he would've burned it to the ground. But he refused to lower himself to her level. He had to convince himself to be the better person.

But sitting there alone, he'd gone through every fucking emotion a person could have.

From disbelief, to rage, to disappointment.

He never told anyone, but he sat on that porch and fucking cried like a goddamn baby.

He wanted to know his son and he wanted his son to know him. And he was denied that all because the woman who bore him that son was on an evil power trip.

He had sat there until he got his shit together and, once he did, he went knocking on doors.

"Neighbor said she'd flown to Orlando to take her son on vacation. *Her* fuckin' son. She took the son I hardly knew on vacation to avoid me. Damn sure Ry had no idea his father was standin' on the porch of an empty house dyin' to see him. Rode all that fuckin' way. The whole trip, kept in touch with that bitch, too. Told her when I'd get there, so it wasn't a surprise. She had the whole thing planned. Now that was a damn cunt move." He drew his hand over his eyes, tamping down that anger. "Never answered one goddamn text or call. She even went so far as to block my number when I blew up her damn phone. Guess she figured eventually I'd give up."

"You didn't."

"Fuck no. Not then, at least. Scared as fuck to fly. But the second time I went out there, got on a plane. Had Deke go with me. Don't mind two or four wheels, but no wheels ain't for me. Wasn't born a bird, was never meant to fly."

"Fear of flying is a real phobia," she said softly.

"Know it. But did it anyway. Only puked twice when I flew the fuck out to California. That time I didn't let her know I was comin'. Kept it a fuckin' secret. Waited 'til summer, for the month I was supposed to have him accordin' to the visitation agreement. Got out there, thought I was finally gettin' a shot at seein' my boy and that cunt had us arrested for trespassin' when we showed up at the door.

Told the pigs we tried to hurt her and force our way into the house. Luckily, the charges didn't stick but by then, the damage was done. By the time we got released, she had time to split town with Ry and I never got to see him."

"I don't understand it."

"Yeah, me neither. It's just her bein' a petty bitch."

"Petty? Oh no, it's more than that. She trapped you into marriage by getting pregnant. You do the right thing, then realize it's the wrong thing. That drives you to do the wrong thing and she blames you for everything."

"Basically. Not blameless in all that shit, though."

"No, you're not."

Judge grimaced. "Like I said, the marriage was bad but that's still no excuse for what I did. Even so, would let her kick me in the fuckin' nuts every fuckin' day just to see my kid, raise him, watch him grow. Got fucked outta all of that." He closed his eyes because they got that sting in them when he thought about what he missed out on with Ry.

Cassie cupped his cheek and waited. As if she knew he was struggling.

He kept them closed when she traced the tattoo of Henry's name on his side. She took her time and ran her fingertip around the outline of each letter. She outlined the last two letters of his name twice. Ry.

It wasn't his choice to name him Henry. It was Jen's because it was her father's name. So, Judge never called him that. He made the name his own.

When she was done, she asked, "You don't talk to Ry at all?"

"She shut me out for the longest time. When he was eight, I mailed out a prepaid cell phone for his birthday so I could talk to him. Know Jen got it 'cause she signed for the package but no one ever answered it. Now he's older, I call him for his birthday and Christmas and leave a message. I send a text once a month. I tell him he can call me anytime.

He can reach out if he needs anything or just needs to talk. I let him know my address every time I move. I ask him to call me back, to just respond so I know he's gettin' the messages."

"And he doesn't?"

"Not once." Jen wanted to fuck up Judge's relationship with his son out of spite. She succeeded.

"I'm sorry."

"My fault, too. Should've pushed harder. But I let her win. She wanted me out of her life because I wanted her out of mine. The problem was, Ry got caught in the middle."

"How old is he now?"

This was when the knife always twisted the most painfully. "Seventeen." Jen had taken off to California before he'd turned one. He was now at an age where he could think for himself. And that was what hurt the most.

Well, that and missing out on all those years. No pictures, no phone calls.

Nothing.

Cassie whispered, "Holy shit."

"Yeah, it's his senior year. Told him I'd pay for his college if he wanted to go."

"Can you afford it?"

"I'd find a way, even if I had to borrow the scratch. Want his future to be a good one, even if I'm not in it." But he hoped to fuck he'd be in it.

He was just waiting for his kid to turn eighteen and graduate high school. Then he was inviting him to come back to Manning Grove. Even if it was for a short trip. Just to open that door toward some sort of relationship. He missed watching his boy grow up, he didn't want to miss out on the rest of Ry's life.

He just needed to get his son out from under Jen's thumb. Let him make his own decisions. Let him form his own opinions about his father, too.

Judge only wanted a fair shot at him.

"I can't imagine having Daisy stolen from me. And here I am crying about Dennis stealing all our money and gambling it away. At least I still have her. What happened to you makes me realize that every minute I have with her is precious." She rolled back into his side and planted her chin on his chest, staring up at him. Her face twisted. "Except when she's being a bossy little monster. I don't know where she gets that from."

Judge shot her a look. "Right. Got no clue, huh?"

Her expression became a mask of innocence. "Nope. My mother is very opinionated. Maybe it skips a generation."

"Yeah, sure it does. Just didn't skip yours."

She pretended to be insulted. "Are you saying I'm bossy?"

"Sayin' you try to be bossy. But I ain't lettin' you boss me around. You wanna be bossy in bed, might allow it. To a point. Beyond the bed? We might have a serious discussion about it."

"Will we?"

"Fuckin-A-right."

Her sassiness disappeared when she stretched up and planted a kiss on his mouth. "Sorry about your son. I wouldn't wish that pain on anyone. I never understood how a parent could use their children as pawns to hurt the other one. Nobody wins in those types of situations. I only hope he'll give you a shot. He needs to know you're a good man, Judge."

"Glad you think it, but you don't know me enough to say that."

Her eyebrows rose. "I know you enough to be naked in bed with you. You're one of a select few who has had that privilege."

Judge snorted and he fisted her hair so he could stare into her blue eyes. "A privilege, huh?"

"Well, of course!" She waved a hand over her naked body. "Not everyone gets to experience all this goodness. You should feel lucky."

He barely managed to keep a straight face. "You're right, baby, consider myself lucky to have you lying here next to me."

She grinned. "See?"

"Even luckier you didn't kick my ass out after hearin' all that."

She frowned. "Why? We've all done things we're not proud of. Should that define the rest of our lives? The whole time you told it, I watched your face, I felt your body react, I heard your voice. There's no doubt you love your son. I only wish he had the opportunity to see that and to get the chance to give you some of that love in return. The only thing you can do is keep reaching out like you are, so he knows you haven't forgotten about him. One day he'll see it and realize what it meant. You never know, one day he might just return the call or text. Never give up hope."

Christ, this woman.

That was a pep talk he needed. He kept that shit buried deep and sometimes it ate at him to the point he felt like giving up. That the whole situation was hopeless. That he should just move on and accept the fact he lost his son and would never get him back.

But he'd always had that thin thread of hope.

And Cassie just turned that thin thread into a rope he could grab onto.

If she believed it, maybe he needed to keep believing it, too.

"Baby?"

"Hmm?"

"Think I gotta fuck you again."

"I thought you needed sleep for the drive in the morning?"

"Will get Deke to drive. Right now, you're more important than sleep. And I'm feelin' pretty lucky. Lemme show you just how lucky..."

———

CASSIE GROANED as she rolled over, pushed the hair out of her face and glanced at the digital clock.

How could she be so sore from sex?

A smile spread across her face as she stretched.

Because it was super awesome sex and loads of it. After years of not having it, she couldn't get enough.

It helped that Judge was game to make sure she got everything she needed.

She wiped the sleep out of her eyes and sat up. She was supposed to make breakfast this morning, but Judge was already gone from the bed and she couldn't hear any kind of racket. Maybe he left and couldn't wait for breakfast.

Once again, he hadn't woken her up.

She thought again about his son and that satisfied smile she wore disappeared. While her daughter was a handful, she couldn't imagine not having Daisy in her life. Daisy was a piece of her. Just like Ry was a piece of Judge.

He was heading up to Rochester this morning to help her. She only wished she could help him heal that wound in return. But not only was it not for her to fix, she wouldn't even know how or where to begin.

The frustration she felt from that probably wasn't even a fraction of the frustration Judge dealt with and had dealt with for years.

Years.

Years of not seeing his son. Of no communication. Of being totally cut from Ry's life out of pure spite.

Jen was evil but also smart to leave Pennsylvania and move across the country. It made it easier to fuck Judge over. Because if she had stayed, he could've forced his rights as a father.

Seeing the way he was with Daisy made her believe he would've been a great father. Ry lost out on all of that. That was sad and shameful. She could only hope his ex-wife was hit with the karma bus.

Cassie would be glad to be behind the wheel.

She normally didn't wish ill on anyone, but right now, she had two people on her shit list.

She needed to get up and check on her own child. Because if Judge had left, she wouldn't put it past Daisy to have her butt planted in front of the TV, watching cartoons and on her way to a sugar high by eating Heather's stash of Hershey Kisses for breakfast.

Cassie groaned at the thought of having to tie Daisy to a chair so she didn't bounce off the walls like a ping pong ball.

Plus, she had no idea where the dogs were and if they'd even been outside yet.

After pulling on the stuff she had worn last night, she peeked into Daisy's room, finding it empty—as she expected—and headed downstairs, listening for any kind of activity.

She heard it coming from the kitchen. Her daughter was either chatting a million miles a minute and having an in-depth conversation about her Barbie dolls to the dogs or to Judge. She hoped it was the latter so she could say goodbye before he left.

And maybe a little selfishly, she wanted one more kiss from the man. While she disliked the shaggy beard, she had a lot of appreciation for his lips amidst all that wiry hair.

With a smile, she stopped in the entryway to the kitchen where Judge and Daisy were sitting at the table. His back was to her since his chair was turned toward the kitchen window where he could monitor the dogs outside. Her daughter was in his lap and he sat patiently while she did something to his face.

Whatever she was doing, he was allowing her to do without complaint. And that right there, squeezed her heart.

"Momma sometimes braids my hair just like this," she was saying, with her blue eyes lit up and face animated as she spoke. "I *tryyyyyy* to do it with my dolls, but their hair isn't long enough. But I don't need my dolls anymore since I have you, Judge. Your beard isn't as soft as the dogs. It's scratchy. It tickles my hands. Does it tickle your face? I don't like bein' tickled because sometimes it makes me pee. Do you pee when you're tickled? No! Don't move. I'm not done yet! I *neeeeeeed* to make you pretty for your trip. I'm gonna miss you. Are you gonna be gone long? When are you gettin' back? When you come back are you stayin' with us? Can you make me pancakes next time? Are you movin' in with us? Can Jury be my dog if you *dooooo*?"

She wasn't sure if she should continue to stand there and be entertained, or to save Judge from the hands of her chatty little stylist. The poor man was being more than patient.

Suddenly Daisy sat back, cocked her head and studied Judge with a critical eye. Her little girl smiled at the big man. Then she caught Cassie standing in the doorway. "Momma! Come see how I braided Judge's hair!"

The chair scraped back, and Judge put Daisy on her feet as he rose to his own. Cassie held her breath as he turned around. Then she held it some more so she wouldn't burst out in laughter.

"How do I look?" he asked her, his green eyes wrinkled at the corners.

"Gorgeous," she managed to get out without choking.

Daisy had attempted to braid his beard into about a half dozen braids. However, her little fingers weren't dexterous enough to do so. Instead, she had twisted the wiry length of facial hair into what almost looked like loose dreadlocks. Actually, it made the lower half of his face look like Medusa.

"Wow. I—" She slapped a hand over her mouth just as a giggle escaped.

"Judge said Jury could be my dog when he moves in."

That sobered her up quickly. Cassie hadn't heard him answer Daisy during her ramble, so she knew that wasn't true. "I doubt that. And what did I say about lying?"

She huffed and planted her hands on her narrow hips. "It's not a lie, Momma. Maybe I'm just *mistaken*."

Oh boy. She was in trouble. If she was like this at five, she couldn't wait until Daisy was fifteen. *Fiveteen.* That was what she was right now.

"Jury is Judge's dog and he's not moving in. We don't even live here, Daze. We're only staying with Aunt Heather and Uncle Tyler until we find our own place."

"When we find it, we can all move in together so Jury can be my dog."

Out of the mouth of babes...

Her gaze hit Judge's and he wore a slight smirk. She rolled her eyes and decided it was best to end that conversation before it became too uncomfortable. Instead, she made her way into the kitchen and asked loudly, "Who's ready for the best French toast in the whole wide world?"

She smiled when a loud "Me!" came from both of them at the same time.

Chapter Seventeen

IT SHOULD BE a goddamn happy occasion, but Judge wasn't feeling it. Not one fucking bit.

He and Deke kicked the bushes in Rochester for almost three days—three *long* fucking days—and they came home with nothing but a pile of steaming dog shit to show for it.

Deke was almost as frustrated as him. Even though Judge didn't want to stop searching for Lange until he found him, he had no choice. They had run out of time. He had a fucking business to run and their search up in New York kept running into dead ends.

The man had simply fucking disappeared.

Usually a trace was left. Something. But even Deke—as good as a skip tracer as he was—wanted to give up.

The man had left no paper trail at all. The Langes' credit cards and bank accounts had been frozen. Their vehicles had been repossessed.

Dennis Lange couldn't have gotten far unless he had someone financing him in cash. The local bondsman said he'd already talked to all his friends and his sister, plus a few cousins, and he couldn't find shit, either.

The only thing him and Deke could guess was Lange

had stashed some scratch somewhere, just in case he needed to make a quick getaway. Even so, they both had a tough time believing a gambling addict could save enough money before spending it. Gamblers usually chased the high of the next bet, thinking they would hit big enough to cover their previous losses. They never did, because on the slim chance they won big, they doubled down on the next bet.

Only one more bet.

Just one more.

And one more.

Until there was nothing left, and they hit the bottom of the empty barrel.

But Judge wasn't giving up. It would just take longer than expected to find Cassie's husband and make him an ex.

He also hated seeing the disappointment in her eyes when he came back to town late Friday night and went immediately to Crazy Pete's to let her know. By the time he got there, the Friday night crowd had thinned, the local band had packed up and left and she had time to talk to him as he sat at the bar, having a few beers and watching her work.

He couldn't keep his eyes off her ass, tits and her smile as she moved around the bar, working on making some big tips.

He had been impatient to give her his tip after her shift.

As soon as she'd closed up, he followed her home, they both checked on a sleeping Daisy and when she wasn't looking, he slipped cash out of his own wallet to pay the babysitter. Then he fucked her once, and only once, before they both fell asleep exhausted.

The next morning, they woke up with Daisy and Jury between them because they, in their impatience to get naked, had forgotten to lock the door. Luckily, Cassie's daughter hadn't slipped under the sheet because neither of them had thought to pull on any clothes after they collapsed. Which could have been more uncomfortable than the hand Daisy had fisted tightly in his beard as she slept.

Saturday night, both of them double-checked the lock. And both a dog whining and a child bellowing outside the bedroom door the next morning not only woke them up but gave them time to cover the important shit.

Now here he was, freezing his nuts off as he sat on his sled with his brothers in a formation of two lines. Being late December, it was too fucking cold for a run to celebrate Shade becoming the newest fully patched member.

Yeah, *Shade*. Because Shady decided to change his road name—which had been given to him specifically as a prospect because it was an insult—to Shade. And the man owned it.

Quietly, of fucking course.

Cage, as Road Captain, gave the signal and they all revved their engines as Shade strode between both lines. When he got to the front door of The Barn, Trip stood there and handed him his cut with all the rockers and patches. As soon as the prez and Shade clasped hands and bumped shoulders, they all cheered and shut down their sleds.

Even though Judge was not in the mood, it was time to party.

But first he'd warm up his fucking nuts by the fire. He'd prefer to be warming up in bed next to Cassie, but she was working the bar while Dodge, Trip and Stella were at the celebration.

It sucked for Judge. Yeah, he'd prefer to have his woman by his side, but she had a job to do and needed the money. Plus, Stella had no one to take Cassie's spot and until she did, Cassie was stuck working during the club parties.

But Judge was going to make sure that changed. He might have a plan for her—where she wouldn't have to work late nights anymore—*if* she was willing to stay in town. And by staying in Manning Grove, that meant staying with him.

He hadn't talked to her about it yet. *Hell*, he hadn't even talked to Trip or the exec committee yet. But he would. Right now he needed to concentrate on finding Lange. Once Cassie's divorce was final, she'd be free to plan her future.

Hopefully, with him in it.

Because, fuck him, he'd been on the edge the whole time in Rochester, being away from her. At first, he thought it was because he was anxious to find Lange. Then Deke laughed at him and told Judge why he was being a cranky motherfucker.

It took a couple more days before he admitted Deke was right. Though, he didn't tell Deke that. No fucking way. He was not getting ridden raw by his cousin.

After putting his sled away in the shed, he made his way back to The Barn with Jury on his heels. He thought about leaving her with Daisy while Cassie worked but he'd missed his damn dog when he'd been away.

As much as he missed Cassie.

And her little hell-on-wheels was growing on him, too.

The first stop inside the busy clubhouse was to grab a beer, then he sat by the roaring fire in the center circular fireplace, kicked up his boots and lit a fatty.

The music was blaring, the club's sweet butts were making their availability known by making rounds, and Shade was banging down shots at the bar with a bunch of their brothers.

Nobody was getting through the night without getting fucked or, at least, fucked up. Including Judge.

He was giving himself the night off, then tomorrow he'd be back in the office taking care of his business, as well as making some calls to try to put out some feelers around the country for Lange. He wasn't sure it would do any good, but it was better than doing nothing.

Trip dropped down beside him on the bench and held out his hand. Judge passed the joint and watched his prez take a long hit, hold it for a good ten seconds and then blow it at Angel, one of the newest sweet butts, when she approached, her eyes focused with a purpose on Judge.

"Get lost," Trip growled at her.

Angel, who had to be barely twenty-one, if that, and way too thin for Judge's taste, shot the prez a scowl and then headed toward the crowd at the bar, looking even more determined to get her claws into someone wearing a cut tonight.

Trip twisted his head toward him. "Figured you weren't interested in hittin' that. I wrong?"

Judge snagged the joint back after Trip took a second hit. He took another one himself and after he blew it out, said, "Nope. First off, too young. And she don't have anythin' to hang on to when she's ridin' my cock. She ain't enough to smother me. If I ain't strugglin' for my next breath when my face is between her tits or thighs..." He grinned.

Trip returned the grin. "Didn't think that's the reason you wouldn't be interested. Was thinkin' it was 'cause she ain't blonde and her name ain't Cassie."

Judge passed the pot back to him and picked up his beer from the floor near his feet. He tipped the bottle to his lips. "Might be another reason." He let the cold beer slide down his throat.

"No luck in New York?"

"Fuck no."

"Now what?

Judge lifted and dropped one shoulder. "No fuckin' clue. Asshole left no trace. Just disappeared."

"Feel bad for her, tryin' to raise her girl and in some

fuckin' limbo 'cause her husband fucked her. And not in a good way. Screwed his family, then split. That ain't a man, that's a fuckin' coward. She's left holdin' the flamin' bag of dog shit while he could be on a tropical island somewhere livin' off the scratch he skimmed, drinkin' a Corona and suckin' on a fuckin' lime wedge."

"If he is, hope the fucker chokes on that lime."

"Never know, maybe he's dead."

Judge thought about that possibility. "I'd be all right with that if—and that's a big fuckin' if—Cassie got a death certificate. That might free her of his debt."

"Or as the widow, make her responsible. Not sure. Don't know how any of that fuckin' shit works."

He didn't, either, and a lawyer might have to get involved if that was the case. However, a lawyer cost a good amount of scratch. Money Cassie didn't have.

"If that's true, need to find his ass alive and get him to sign those divorce papers." In truth, he wasn't even sure that would clear her of all the debt, but Cassie seemed to think it would.

Trip sipped on his own beer as they both stared into the flames. "When I was down in Shadow Valley with the Dirty Angels, met a few guys, not sure if they were mercenaries or not, but definitely some kind of former special ops. They worked for the DAMC's enforcer at In the Shadows Security. Do all kinds of jobs. Diesel, the enforcer, said they're the best. Remember Slade who just came up here? My Marine buddy? He vouched for that crew, too. Said they could find or *lose* anyone. Got a problem? They could make that problem disappear."

"Yeah?"

"Yeah. Rub is, they ain't cheap. Gotta take a goddamn mortgage out to hire 'em, but they get the job done. They could probably find his ass, in case you and Deacon can't."

"You know she don't have the scratch for that."

He hated to drop that kind of dough, but he would if he needed to. He'd put a little money aside in case Ry ever took Judge up on him paying for college. Even if his son wanted nothing to do with him, Judge still wanted to make sure his son's future was set.

Trip flipped his baseball cap off his head, then jerked it back on. One of the habits the man had when he was thinking hard. Or hardly thinking. "Yeah, know it. Feel bad for her, gettin' fucked like that. She's workin' really fuckin' hard at Pete's. Workin' that bar again tonight by herself. Stel trusts her completely and knows she'll get the job done."

"Yeah, she's exhausted every night. Daisy keeps her on her fuckin' toes, too. And with not havin' help 'cause her sister and her man are gone..."

Trip's lips twitched. "Apparently she's got you. Sig said you haven't slept in your apartment all week."

Fuckin' Sig. "Was up in Rochester."

"Before and after." When Judge didn't answer, Trip continued, "Anyway, the Shadows are an option, even if they're an expensive option to hunt that fucker down."

"If I keep runnin' into dead ends, will give it more thought." Judge took a deep breath. "Wanna run somethin' by you."

Trip paused his beer bottle at his lips. "Shoot."

"Know she's a vet tech, right?"

"Yeah, Stel said she was."

"Once she's free of that asshole, thinkin' she's gonna need a better job than workin' at Pete's. Needs to make some real scratch for her and her girl."

"Yeah. And?"

"We now got that pet crematorium..."

"Don't need a vet tech to flip the switch on an oven or scoop the ashes into a bag. Ain't much better than what she's doin' now."

"Thinkin' we could expand the business."

Trip set his beer bottle on his thigh and frowned at Judge. "You were *thinkin'*? Did it hurt when you did it?" He snorted. "What kind of expansion? You run it by Deke?"

"Not yet. Wanted to run it by you first."

Trip slowly turned the sweating bottle within his fingers. "Hit me with it."

"Not sure if she'd be willin' to do it, but it could make her and the club some decent scratch and it goes along with the crematorium." He cringed as he stared at Jury crashed at his feet, soaking up the heat of the fire. The whole crematorium thing just gave him the fucking creeps.

"You gonna spit it the fuck out?"

"Thinkin'—"

Trip snorted. "There you go again. Gonna fuckin' hurt yourself doin' that."

"That we could start a mobile pet euthanasia service. She's good with people, she's got the experience workin' with pets. She's certified. She could use the van, go to people's homes, do it in their house so the dog or whatever ain't freaked out because family's there. She does what she needs to do, comforts the family, and then brings the pet back to the crematorium. Full-service euthanasia."

Trip shuddered. "Christ."

"Yeah, bugs me, too, but it's a growin' service and there's good money in it. Pet owners are leanin' more and more that direction instead of draggin' their dog, cat or whatever into the vet to get it done. Jury hates goin' to the vet, stresses the fuck out. When it comes time..." He didn't even want to finish that sentence. It turned his fucking stomach. "It's somethin' I'd use. Deke, too. Figure a lot of people might and there ain't one around here."

"You already did the research."

"Couldn't sleep in Rochester. Sat up and surfed the net on my phone, tryin' to figure out how to help her."

Trip stared at him, not hiding his surprise. "Seriously stuck on her. That was fuckin' quick, brother."

Yeah, Judge agreed, it was quick. "Not any quicker than Sig with Red."

"Yeah, well, that whole thing with them was fucked up and not typical. Still ain't. Might never be."

"They make it work. Better together than apart," Judge murmured.

"Think that's you and Cassie, too? Think she'd make you a better man?"

He wasn't sure.

"Damn well know my ol' lady makes me a better fuckin' man. No doubt 'bout it and got no problem sayin' it. Will get it tattooed on my fuckin' forehead." Trip turned his head until he found Stella standing over by Dodge and Cage, laughing at something. Probably at those two being assholes. "Fuckin' woman got me good. Couldn't do this shit without her."

"Your fuckin' queen," Judge murmured.

"Yeah," Trip whispered. "My fuckin' queen. No fuckin' doubt."

"Just don't turn this into Buck's kingdom."

Trip, with his eyes still glued to Stella across the barn, nodded. "Yeah. Workin' too damn hard to destroy it all like he did. Hopefully, the good men sittin' with me at that table up there," he pointed to the ceiling, "won't have any problem tellin' me if I start slippin' toward the dark side."

"You givin' me permission to knock you upside the fuckin' head if you do?"

Trip grinned and picked at the corner of the bottle's soggy label. "Fuck yeah. Told Stella she could have you kick my ass if I ever do anythin' to hurt her. Same with this club. I fuck up with this club, kick my fuckin' ass. Means I deserve it. Wanna do this right. Wanna raise my sons on this farm, in this club, in our family of brothers."

Judge would love to have his own son here on the farm with him. He never told Trip about him and wasn't planning on doing it anytime soon.

"Gotta knock her up to have sons."

Trip grinned again. "When she's ready."

"Probably have daughters instead."

The prez's grin widened. "Then gonna raise a coupla badass girls. Won't cry about what Stella gives me, long as she gives 'em to me."

"And if she don't?" Judge knew Stella had lost a child; he just didn't know the details. If Trip or Stella wanted him to know, they would tell him. Otherwise, wasn't his business. Just like Ry wasn't anyone's business, either. Brothers or not. They all had secrets. Every fucking one of them.

Trip's grin flipped upside down. "Then I gotta live with her decision. She comes first, the rest is just a fuckin' bonus."

Judge watched the prez's ol' lady, dressed in curve-fitting jeans and her normal rock-star clothes, grab a drink from behind the bar, then head in their direction. "She'll give you babies, Trip. She loves you too much. Loved you since you were a fuckin' asshole kid. Back then she said she was gonna marry you and she was fuckin' right. You both just took a crazy ass path to get there."

"Yeah, nobody felt right 'til her. Knew it the second I spotted her at the bar that day. When I realized who she was, it was like goddamn fate clubbed me right in the head."

Just like Sig knew it the second he rescued Autumn in the woods that morning.

Just like Judge knew it the second he saw Cassie walking through the parking lot in town.

It had probably hit Sig and Trip in the gut, just like it had hit Judge's.

"So, about that idea I mentioned?" Judge asked as Stella

reached them and settled in Trip's lap, giving her man a soft smile.

"Wanna go back to the bar, baby, then walk back to me? I could watch that show all over again," Trip told his ol' lady.

She lifted a dark eyebrow. "I could, but I'm comfy right where I'm at now."

"Soon you won't be when my dick's pokin' your ass 'cause you make me hard as fuck." He turned his head toward Judge. "Yeah, will think on it. Do a little research of my own. The more scratch we got comin' in from different avenues the better. To do that we need successful businesses with reliable help. Lemme talk to Deke about it, too, since he's got a good business sense. Don't wanna do it just to give your woman a job and then it ends up bleedin' funds from the club."

Stella glanced from Trip to Judge and back. "What business are you talking about and by saying 'your woman' I assume you mean Cassie? And if so, does that mean I might be losing her?"

"Was only just temporary, Stel," Judge said. "She told you that. Woman's got a fuckin' degree she's not usin' right now. Needs more than tips."

"She knows how to work the crowd, Judge. She makes good money in tips."

"But don't want her closin' the bar late at night. Don't really want her workin' the bar at all."

Stella's eyes narrowed. "Why?"

"'Cause I don't."

"Not your call," she reminded him.

"Not yet. But will be." He grimaced that he let that slip.

"Does she know that?" Stella asked with a deep frown.

Judge flattened his lips and stared at the flames.

"Does she know what you're planning?" Stella prodded. "Just a word of advice, women like Cassie don't like a man stepping in and making life decisions for her." She turned her face toward Trip. "Right?"

Trip put his beer bottle to his lips and kept quiet. Smart fucking man.

"Right," she answered her own question.

"Just workin' on givin' her options," Judge said.

"Sounds like you're putting your boot down about her working at Pete's. That's what it sounded like to me. She can handle herself just fine. She knows how to handle the men getting out of line."

Judge's spine snapped straight. "Assholes are gettin' outta line with her?"

"It's a bar, Judge. With booze," Stella reminded him like he was Daisy's age.

"Just proved my point, Stel. I see someone gettin' handsy with her, gonna break some fuckin' fingers."

Stella smiled and whispered, "Damn. You got it bad."

Trip finally spoke up. "Yeah, he does. Can see Cassie bein' claimed at the table soon."

"No claimin' 'til she scrapes off that fuckin' ex of hers."

"Lemme go find a fuckin' chisel," Trip said. "Like her. Think she's a good woman and would make a good ol' lady."

"*Weeeellll*, big guy," Stella started, leaning over and patting Judge's thigh. "First she'd have to decide to stay in Manning Grove. Then she'd need to decide if she wants to be with you. *Then* she'd need to decide whether she'd want to be an ol' lady. See how I said, 'she would need to decide,' and not 'you?' *You* can't force her to do anything. Being an ol' lady takes a special type of woman." She shot Judge a smile. "But I agree with my ol' man. She'd make a great ol' lady. Woman's got a spine and the right attitude. And bonus, she'd keep you in your place."

"Ain't lookin' for a woman to keep me in my fuckin' place," he grumbled.

Trip snorted. "With her, that's what you're gonna get."

Stella laughed. "It's not as bad as you think. Right, Trip?"

Again, Trip tipped his almost empty beer bottle to his lips to avoid answering.

"Anyway, it would be nice to have another sister. But let it be her choice, please. Speaking of sisters, I'm going to go talk to Autumn and save her from Lizzy, who is talking her damn ear off. Give me a kiss, baby, while you're sober since I have a feeling you'll be passed out cold later." After a thorough kiss, she climbed out of Trip's lap and grabbed his empty. "Want another beer?"

"I'll get it."

Stella nodded and headed back over to the bar. They both watched her go.

"There's a joke in there somewhere... A redhead, a blonde and a black and blue haired woman walk into a bar..." Trip laughed.

"Those women ain't a joke, though."

Trip sighed. "No, they ain't." He turned and studied Judge for a moment. "Once you claim Cass, we'll discuss that other shit, but not 'til then. Don't wanna make plans that might not pan out."

"Yeah."

"She's only been in town a few weeks. Give her a chance to settle in. Her sister's here and if you keep giving her good dick, you might convince her to stay."

"Ain't good. It's fuckin' great. Tongue, too."

Trip laughed again. "Take your word for it. Now, gonna go have a shot with our newest brother and get shit-faced. You comin'?"

"Fuck yeah."

Chapter Eighteen

Cassie stepped through the front door of what Judge had called "The Barn." It truly was a two-story barn that looked like it had been restored into a ski lodge or a rustic country bar.

Besides the inside looking cool, it was unexpected.

The circular stone see-through fireplace sitting in the center of the room caught her eye first. The interior walls were rough wood boards just like the outside. The floors made of wide, worn planks. Various motorcycle items and signs decorated the walls. And the Eagles' song *Take It Easy* filled her ears.

Like at Crazy Pete's, the crack of pool balls could be heard above the music. But out of the two tables only one had a couple of men, both wearing cuts, playing a game of pool. She didn't recognize either of them.

She pursed her lips as she noticed Dutch, a local garage owner and member of Blood Fury who she met at Crazy Pete's, passed out on the other table with an empty whiskey bottle knocked over next to him. Only, he wasn't alone.

Sprawled on top of the older man, like a blanket, was a naked woman. Calling her a woman was debatable since she barely looked legal, but it was hard to tell and Cassie wasn't getting closer to inspect her or ask her age, even if she had been awake. But she couldn't imagine Trip, the club's president, would allow underage girls—or boys, for that matter—to hang out at a party like this.

She hoped she wasn't wrong.

She wasn't sure where Judge was, but he had texted her just before closing Pete's and told her to come. He gave her the address on County Line Road to plug into Google Maps on her phone, since she'd only been out there that one night when they first hooked up and wasn't quite sure where the farm was located.

Crazy Pete's had been busy, so she was exhausted and questioned whether coming here was a good idea. But being tired paid off. With Sunday Night Football on the big screens, and tables full of patrons who were being especially generous with Christmas coming up, she had earned a huge wad of cash in tips. And while she was happy about that, she needed to sit down and put up her aching feet.

After getting Judge's invite, she had texted the babysitter and asked if she would stay the night. Melanie said she would, but, of course, those extra hours would dip deep into Cassie's hard-earned tips.

Like Judge, Trip and Stella were nowhere to be seen, but then, it was after two-thirty in the morning. They were probably in bed, as were most people at this hour.

Exactly where Cassie should be. Back at the house, checking on Daisy and taking a hot shower to relieve her tight and sore muscles before crawling in between the sheets.

But, instead, here she stood, just inside a motorcycle club's clubhouse, the sudden awareness of how her life had changed so drastically smacking her upside the head.

Loss of a husband. Loss of financial stability. Loss of their family home. Loss of her stable job. Loss of her hometown.

Loss of her parents' emotional support.

The only thing that remained constant in her life was her daughter, her sister and her brother-in-law.

Everything else around her was new. Judge, a job at a bar, and spending time with bikers. Bikers! Both at Crazy Pete's, in her bed, and now at a barn outside of town.

Utterly crazy.

It also proved just how quickly things could change. Not by choice, her life's motto had become "expect the unexpected," so nothing should surprise her anymore.

Even so, she needed to buckle-down, figure out her path and give Daisy some stability. Her daughter came first. Always would. That meant, a bit of guilt was eating at her for wanting to see Judge instead of going straight home to her little girl.

In a short amount of time, the bearded, tattooed biker had somehow crawled beneath her skin and, even more surprising, she was finding that something about him soothed her soul. Which was desperately needed after all the turmoil and upset she'd been through in New York.

High-pitched female giggling coming from her right drew her attention. She hadn't realized there had been a female lying naked on the bar at first because of the male bodies blocking her view. But, yes, there certainly was a woman on the bar and those men—two wearing Fury cuts, the other two not—were doing shots off her naked body. Or at least, that was what it looked like from where she stood. She wasn't sure she should move closer to make certain she was seeing it right. As long as the woman was consenting to it—and by her laughter, it sure sounded like it—then it wasn't her business. Was it?

And none of the men were Judge.

Thankfully.

Though, if it had been, did she have any right to be jealous? They'd only known each other for three weeks, if that.

She had no claim to the man. And she wasn't even sure if she wanted him in that way.

But still...

She was relieved it wasn't Judge licking salt off the woman's breasts, sucking tequila out of her belly button before plucking a lemon wedge from her pussy with his teeth.

Cassie grimaced. Well, that seemed extremely hygienic...

She hoped that method of serving tequila shots didn't become a weekly "special" at Crazy Pete's.

She sighed. She needed to find Judge. He had to be there somewhere. She hoped if he had left, he would've texted her first. He wouldn't have made her drive out to this farm in the middle of the night for nothing, right?

She stepped away from the door and headed to the left of the fireplace to avoid the bar since it was clear Judge wasn't in that mix. And as she rounded the fireplace and passed a knocked-out Dutch and company to her left, she saw movement in the back corner of the barn.

Her step stuttered, her heart thumped, and her feet froze in place.

She rubbed at her eyes. Was she so tired that she was seeing things? Did these types of things really happen in this place?

Apparently so, if what she was seeing wasn't her imagination.

Ozzy, who she had also met at Crazy Pete's, sat on one of those bus benches that lined the walls with his jeans down around his boots. He gripped a handful of long dirty blonde hair in his fist as the head, attached to that hair, rose and fell in his lap.

That alone should be enough to make Cassie think twice about being there. But wait, there was more!

Dodge—yes, Dodge, who she had to work with and look directly in the eyes when she did—stood behind the same woman, who was on her knees and bent over, as he was fucking her. Her denim skirt was pushed up and her top pushed down until they were gathered at her waist. Dodge was also smacking the woman's ass as he thrust into her.

As if in slow motion, Ozzy's gaze rose and caught Cassie's. He shot her a warm, welcoming smile, released the nipple he was pinching and lifted that hand in a greeting toward her.

Before she could catch herself, she automatically lifted hers to return the wave. She quickly dropped her hand, broke eye contact and scrubbed her sweaty palm along her thigh.

What was she doing? Why was she even here? This wasn't normal at all! Why would she want anything to do with people or a place like this? Where they shared women in public. Where the sex wasn't special at all and women were treated like...

Objects.

Toys.

Sex toys.

These weren't her people. She didn't know who they were.

It surprised her because she had no idea Trip and Stella were a part of something like this. She thought the MC was a club, a group of men who rode motorcycles and were friends, not a sex free-for-all.

Would she even want her daughter to be around this? To see this?

She needed to leave.

As she turned, she noticed a door propped open at the back of the building and, from what she could see, it led to a long, dimly lit corridor. Where it went, she had no idea and wasn't about to find out.

But her eyes narrowed on dark figures down that hallway. She could make out two people—a male and a female, the man not nearly tall enough to be Judge—pressed against the wall. And like the rest of the women she'd seen so far, she wasn't being held there against her will.

Cassie grimaced as she stood watching the woman down that corridor get nailed to the wall. Nope, she wasn't struggling to get free at all.

Maybe these women didn't have it wrong. Maybe it was Cassie who needed to pull the stick out of her own ass.

These women were free to come and go. They chose to be there. They chose to do the things they were doing. No one seemed to be forcing them.

In truth, she had no right to judge.

Absolutely none.

Consenting adults and all that.

And, anyway, was she any better? She had been sleeping with Judge only two doors down from her own daughter. Not just once, but a few times.

Even with questions about her own morality, heat flickered in her belly at the thought of Judge taking her against the wall the same way that man, whoever he was, was taking that woman.

It looked hot and spontaneous.

Spontaneity had never been her thing. But with this new life she was building, maybe it needed to be.

Apparently, predictability and having normal life expectations—getting married, having a child and working hard—had been a mistake. Or at least, living a boring, typical life had made her oblivious to changes going on beneath the surface of her marriage. Or lack of marriage.

Judge was certainly not typical or boring. And nothing surrounding her right now in this barn was normal, that was for sure.

Where the hell was Judge, anyway?

She dug into the pocket of her winter coat, grabbing her

cell phone so she could text him. If he didn't answer, she was leaving.

As her fingers moved across her keyboard, she saw more movement out of the corner of her eye. Lifting her head, her heart seized as Judge came out of that hallway with his head tipped down and was talking to a woman with short, dark hair, who hung onto him with an arm wrapped around his waist.

As he walked, the woman with heavy, dark makeup had her face, wearing an inviting expression, lifted to him. He was so focused on her, he didn't notice Cassie standing there, her phone dangling precariously from her fingers.

"Yo!" came a male shout from the bar. When Cassie's head spun in that direction, she saw Cage giving Judge a look but pointing at her.

Judge's head slowly swiveled from Cage to Cassie, his brow dropping low and his mouth turning downward. He jerked the shorter woman's arm from around his waist and said something to her quickly as he began taking long strides in Cassie's direction, leaving the other woman in his wake.

Oh no.

Nope.

She didn't want to hear any damn excuses from him.

He came from the back of the building, which she could only assume had private rooms, and had a woman hanging on him. She didn't care if it was or wasn't what it looked like.

He texted her.

He wanted her to come here.

He wasn't even around when she got there.

He came out of the back with another woman.

Why did that piss her off?

Why did that make her stomach turn?

Why should she even care?

Because, *damn it,* she did.

But she wasn't the type of woman who would be spread naked across the bar or bent over a bus bench between two men or have sex in a hallway where anyone could see it.

She wasn't one of them at all.

Didn't he know that?

Shoving her phone into her pocket, she spun on her heels and practically sprinted toward the exit. As she reached for the handle, a sob bubbled up her throat, but she quickly swallowed it back down.

Strong arms hooked her around the waist, and she was yanked against a tall, hard wall of muscle and leather.

"Know what you're fuckin' thinkin', but you're wrong." Cassie's heart pounded in her throat at his low growl in her ear. "Believe it or not, glad you're here, babe."

Babe.

That was new. The overwhelming smell of pot and whiskey permeated from him.

"Are you?" Damn the shake in her voice.

His arms tightened around her waist, immobilizing her against him, and his beard and potent whiskey breath tickled her cheek. "Wouldn't've told you to fuckin' come if I didn't want you here, Cassie."

And that was true, but... "Are you excited to see me, or did she give you that?" If he denied he had an erection, she would elbow him in it. Then there'd be no denying what pressed against the small of her back.

"You think I fuckin' want her?"

She was glad he couldn't see her face when she asked, "You ever sleep with her?" And, *damn it,* her voice broke asking that.

She shouldn't feel betrayed that he was touching another woman, even if it was the woman who had her arm around his waist and not the opposite.

Even so, she didn't like that deep-seated hurt. She had felt it once before, before she lost almost everything. She was about to lose again. And disappointment once again saturated her down to her bones.

She had to remind herself she came to Manning Grove to collect herself, straighten out her life, not complicate it even further.

Judge, his club, and his way of life was a complication.

"Ain't gonna lie, fucked her in the past, but..." His jaw shifted and he growled, "I sleep with *you*, Cassie, and there's a fuckin' difference."

Oh, was he getting a little angry? Good.

"Is there?" She pulled free from his arms and spun on him, pressing her hand to his gut under his cut. "Tell me what the difference is."

"Cass... Was in the head takin' a piss and she followed me in."

Why was he avoiding her question? "And you let her."

"Had my fuckin' dick in my hand and was pissin'. Walked out soon as I was done. She followed me out and offered herself up. Told her you were comin' and she needed to land in someone else's bed tonight."

"If you didn't know I was coming, would she have landed in yours?"

He set his jaw. "No."

"Are you sure?"

"Fuck, baby." With his eyes narrowed, he shook his head. "You don't fuckin' get it, do you?"

"Get what?" She flung her hand out. "What don't I get? What's going on in this place? How you guys just fuck women whenever and wherever? I can't imagine tonight is the first night of this type of party. It's pretty eye-opening, actually."

His jaw moved again like he was grinding his teeth. "You're fuckin' right. It's not the first goddamn time and won't be the last. It happens a lot. It's a fuckin' celebration. This is the way we celebrate."

This is the way we celebrate.

So, this was normal to them. To him.

The whiskey smell on him was so overwhelming, it made her nose wrinkle. "Are you drunk?"

"Don't gotta drive, baby, so fuck yeah."

She'd never seen him intoxicated before. Not even on the nights he'd hung out at Crazy Pete's, waiting for her to finish her shift.

"My apartment's upstairs around back. Remember it? You followed me home that night. That first night we spent together."

She didn't need a reminder. She'd never forget.

"You ghosted before I could show you the place. Remember that, too? I fuckin' do. But if you want, will give you a fuckin' tour now before you ghost this time."

Before you ghost this time.

That still bothered him. Or it could be the alcohol talking.

Either way, she should be leaving. "Not sure I want a tour right now. Not with what I've seen so far tonight. We could come across more surprises I don't need to witness. It's bad enough I won't be able to look Dodge in the eye ever again. Doesn't seem like anyone's shy."

"Yeah, nobody's shy here, Cass. The point of life is to fuckin' live it. That's what we're doin'. There ain't a right or a wrong way, long as no one's gettin' hurt."

Long as no one's gettin' hurt.

Problem was, seeing that woman with her arm around Judge hurt.

"Do you do this type of stuff?" She waved her hand toward the bar and then the bench where the woman was sandwiched between two bikers, except Dodge had now switched places with Ozzy.

"Now?"

She looked up at him, her mouth gaped open. "Ever."

He rubbed a hand over his mouth and stared at a spot above her head.

Well, that answered her question, so he no longer needed to. She lifted a palm when he tried. "Never mind. Why did you want me here, Judge?"

"Wanted you to see this part of my life. To know what it's about."

"For what reason?"

"Just in case."

"In case of what?" she prodded.

"In case you decide to stay in Manning Grove. And this is the part you ain't fuckin' gettin'... In case you decide you wanna stay," he grimaced as if what he was about to say was painful, "with me."

Once again, she found herself gaping up at him. Stay with him? "Stay with you? In what way? I thought... I... I wasn't expecting you'd want more than what we have."

Especially after seeing the casual sex tonight. It had cemented the realization that might be all they had. Something fun but not serious.

The problem was, after getting jealous about that woman made her realize it had become more serious for her than it should have.

"You mean the fuckin' sex?"

"Well... yes." Should they even be talking about this here? Now? "I figured we were just enjoying what we had... *have*. I wasn't expecting anything more."

Oh yeah, he was getting a little angry. Just slightly. "Why the fuck you here, Cass?"

Her eyebrows pinned together. That was a dumb question when he already knew that answer. "You invited me."

"No, Cassie, why the fuck are you here?" He jabbed his index finger toward the floor. "Right now. In this fuckin' clubhouse at almost three in the fuckin' mornin' instead of home in bed under the same roof as your girl?"

She didn't get why he was asking that. "Because you asked me."

"Coulda said no."

"I could've but I..." *Oh shit,* now she got it.

"'Cause you wanted to see me. Fuckin' asked you 'cause I wanted to see you. Got it?"

"Yes," she breathed. He wanted to spend time with her, not just have sex with her. That meant he wanted something more than just a casual relationship. "I'm not even divorced yet," she whispered.

"And I'm workin' on that. But you got shot of his ass a while ago, Cass. That wound ain't fresh and you have no plans on takin' his ass back."

"Well, no. It was over with Dennis a while ago. But you never answered my question. I need to hear the answer, Judge."

"You wanna discuss that here? Then we'll discuss that here so there's no fuckin' mistake about it." He dropped his head and kept his voice low. Enough so the angry grumble sent a shiver down her spine. It wasn't just his rough, deep voice causing it, it was his words when he said, "'Cause when I'm inside you, it's different. When I fuckin' come deep inside you, I ain't finished. Would normally push a woman away afterward. I draw you closer, hold you tighter. Just a fuck? Want 'em out of my bed as soon as fuckin' possible. With you? Don't want you leavin'. That's the damn difference between a fuck and you."

She stared up at him.

"Get it now?"

Oh yes, she did. She got it.

She *so* got it.

However, it wasn't only her. She had her daughter to think about. And this environment was not the best to raise her around.

Before she would even consider letting things get serious

with Judge, she would need to think long and hard about what Daisy might be exposed to. She would need to talk to Judge about what it was like as a child growing up in a club like this. And she would need to have a serious conversation with Stella since she was a little girl when her father was a member of this very club. She, if anyone, could tell her the good and the bad. The absolute truth.

She didn't want Daisy growing up thinking women were only property. That they could be used as sex toys. She wanted her daughter to know women should be respected, not used. That they were an equal.

"Baby, you didn't answer me."

She stared up into his green eyes. Concern. That's what she saw in them. "I understand now."

"Still gonna make it clear. Want you and only you. From the second I saw you, haven't been able to get you outta my head."

"So, you haven't been with any other women since that day in the parking lot?" She had a hard time believing that. Not with what she'd seen tonight.

"Just said I couldn't get you outta my head, woman, even though I wasn't expectin' you to give me a shot. Thought you'd only be my spank bank fantasy."

"Your what?"

His angry expression was gone and a grin quickly replaced it. "Every fuckin' time I closed my eyes, saw your face."

Great. "When you were with other women?" Did she really want to know that answer?

"No, when I was—"

A drunken male voice from over by the bar yelled, "Judge, you want a shot?"

"Yes, Judge," Cassie arched a brow at him, "do you want a shot?"

His grin twisted and his green eyes narrowed. "Do you?"

"You'd probably like that, but I prefer my tequila served in a glass and not on a human, so I'll have to pass."

"Got regular glasses."

She never drank at Crazy Pete's. She didn't want to take advantage of Stella's generosity of allowing her to drink for free. Nor did she want to go home to Daisy even slightly buzzed. But she originally hadn't planned on going home tonight, figuring she'd end up upstairs in Judge's apartment. That was why she came.

"Baby, do a shot with me. It'll loosen you up some. Get rid of that jealousy you're hangin' onto 'cause of Billie wantin' your man's dick. She ain't gettin' it, only you are. So, let's have a fuckin' drink and then I'll give it to you."

She blinked up at him, then snapped her mouth shut. "Do I even know you at all?"

"Yeah, you do, Cass. And you're gonna know me better after tonight and after every other fuckin' night we spend together."

"I haven't decided if I want anything more than sex with you, Judge," she said smartly.

"Yeah, you do. Not only is the dick worth it, but the rest of me is, too."

Her eyebrows shot up. "Do you have any references?"

"Nope, 'cause nobody got the rest of me. Just the dick."

"While I'm tempted to say that's a good answer, I'm not sure if it is."

He cupped her cheeks and lowered his head. "Got it. You don't like thinkin' about your man bein' with other women."

It had to be the pot or whiskey putting him on this "your man" kick. Because that, like "babe," was the first time she was hearing it. "You're really pushing it right now."

"That jealousy's awful cute on you."

He took her mouth as she opened it to argue and she let him, even though the pot-whiskey mix was not her favorite.

But it was something she'd probably have to get used to if things developed between them.

Because she doubted he would change.

This was his life and he was inviting her in. He said he wanted her to come out there tonight to see how he lived, how this club was a part of him. Either she could accept it, or she could reject it.

And by rejecting his lifestyle, his choices, she was rejecting him. She couldn't have Judge without getting everything that came along with him.

Just like he couldn't have her without her sticky situation and her daughter. By looking for Dennis on his own time and dime, he was willing to help her clean up the mess Dennis made. Plus, Daisy loved him already and, so far, he was great with her.

Even so, thinking about any kind of future with the man wasn't an easy decision. Or one that would be made tonight. She had to seriously consider the impact of his lifestyle on Daisy.

His tongue tangled with hers as his fingers tightened, just short of painful, in her hair. The heat that swirled through her earlier when watching that couple in the hall returned, making her press her thighs together as her pussy pulsed with need, and her nipples ached for his touch. She couldn't deny she wanted him sexually.

But life wasn't only about that.

Hoots and hollers from the direction of the bar made Judge break the kiss but he didn't pull away. His lips hovered over hers, their breaths mingling as they both tried to slow down their breathing.

Damn, she wanted him. And the evidence he wanted her was pressed against her.

After a few seconds, he grabbed her hand and led her over to the bar where he introduced her to Rook, Easy and Rev, since she had already met Cage. He also introduced the human shot glass, Crystal, who gave her an easy-going smile and a friendly wave as she was still sprawled naked across the bar.

She now had whipped cream covering both breasts with cherries where her nipples would be. Across her stomach someone had also written, "Congratz, Shady fucker," on her stomach ending with three crooked exclamation points. Another whipped cream arrow pointed to the woman's shaved crotch.

"Where the fuck is Shade?" Rook yelled drunkenly, a beer raised in one hand, a lit joint in the other, as he swayed on his feet.

Judge snagged the joint from Rook's fingers and tucked it between his lips. "No fuckin' clue."

"Is it Shade's party?" Cassie asked. She glanced around, too, but had no idea what the man named Shade looked like. *Hell*, he could've been the man in the hallway.

"Yeah, the quiet fucker disappeared a while back and haven't seen him since," Judge answered, turning his head to blow the smoke away from her.

He offered the joint to her and she shook her head. She didn't have anything against someone smoking pot, but she had no clue how it would affect her, since it had been a while since she smoked it and wasn't prepared to find out tonight.

"Maybe he fell into some really good pussy," suggested Easy. The lower rocker on the back of his cut read *PROSPECT*, just like Dodge's had when she first began working at Crazy Pete's. Cassie assumed he'd be having a similar party whenever he got patched in.

"Been savin' Crystal for 'im," slurred an obviously well-baked Rook. "Can't let 'er go to waste." He leaned over, sucked one of the cherries off her breast and kissed the woman, transferring the cherry into her mouth. He then ran a finger through the whipped cream until just her nipple was exposed and shoved the cream-covered digit into his mouth, sucking it clean. "Man don't appreciate the cake we made for him."

"That looks more like a sundae," Cassie informed him.

Rook blinked at her for a long moment, then smiled. "Yeah. A fuckin' sundae. You want a lick?"

"Sorry, I'm lactose intolerant," she answered, even though she wasn't. "Nothing personal," she said to Crystal, who simply shrugged.

Judge snorted, moved behind the bar, slapped two shot glasses on the wood top and grabbed the almost empty bottle of tequila at the end of it. He poured what remained in the bottle into the glasses and came back to where Cassie stood, handing her one. She stared at it in her hand.

She hadn't drunk tequila since she turned twenty-one and that was in the form of a Tequila Sunrise. Not straight.

Judge leaned close and whispered in her ear, "One shot and we're goin' upstairs."

"Do you really need another shot?"

"What I need is you. So, hurry up and drink it." He grinned, clinked his glass with hers and upended it, drinking the whole thing down in one swallow.

She followed his lead, put the glass to her lips and downed it all at once, too. Then she held her breath as her insides lit on fire.

"Gotta breathe, baby."

If she breathed, she would cough. He drank it like it was water. To her it was like swallowing turpentine. She grimaced and blew out a slow breath.

Judge laughed and pulled the glass from her fingers. "'Nother one?"

She surprised him by nodding. He was right, she needed to loosen up a bit and tonight was the perfect time to do it. She had zero responsibilities right now. She didn't even have to get up for work tomorrow since it was her day off. And if

Melanie was willing to stay even longer, she wouldn't rush out of Judge's bed when the sun rose.

Once again, she reminded herself she was more than only a mother. She needed time to rediscover herself as a woman. She could do that with Judge. He made her feel like a woman. Feel wanted. Feel beautiful. Even sexy.

She missed that. She didn't realize just how much until that first night with him.

Shit, that tequila was already going to her head and making her think permanent thoughts about the man who handed her another shot. He had opened a new bottle, but there was no way she was drinking more than two. She'd end up passing out and not getting "her man's dick." Or at least remembering that she got it.

That stick up her ass was already loosening up some.

Yep, two double shots were her limit. Any more and she might end up on that bar, on one of those green benches or against the wall down that hallway. Dick over dignity. Dignity be damned.

As she tipped it to her lips and let the liquor slide down her throat and into her already warm belly, her eyes caught on a cut hanging on the wall near the bar.

She handed Judge the empty glass back and moved over to it, sliding her fingers over the worn, dirty leather and patches. It had been attached to the wall with the vest wide open, so the front patches, as well as the back could be seen.

One rectangular patch said *Crazy Pete*.

Heat pressed against her back as Judge put his hands on her shoulders, squeezing them.

She leaned back into him, her head against his chest. "Stella's father?"

"Yeah, he was an Original."

"Just like yours."

"Yeah."

"Where's your father's cut?" Pete's was the only one she saw displayed on the walls. She wondered why.

He hesitated and when he finally spoke, his voice was rougher than normal. "Wearin' it. Normally, when a member dies, he gets buried in it. Stella didn't get home in time to do that with Pete. She was dealin' with another crushin' loss. Mine was in prison when he was killed. Had no fuckin' clue where his cut was 'til I found it a while later at the old warehouse."

The warehouse. That had been located on the lot where he followed her the third time they met. The Fury's old clubhouse.

"What was he in prison for?"

"Murders."

She turned her eyes up to him, finding his expression grim. "As in plural?"

"Yeah. More than one."

"Were you ever in prison?" That was an important detail she should know.

"No."

"Have you ever done anything that could've put you there?" When he didn't answer, she turned to face him directly. "I need you to answer that truthfully."

"It's in the past, Cass."

The blood drained from her face. "But I need to know. I need to know if what you might do in the future would get you arrested. Get you taken from me. From us. It's already happened once, Judge. I'm dealing with a cluster because of a man who committed a crime that I had no knowledge about and who was also yanked from my daughter's life because of it. I can't risk Daisy going through that again." *Hell*, she couldn't risk it, either.

"On the day Ox was arrested, promised myself and my sister I was never goin' to prison."

His sister? She didn't even know he had a sister. She'd

have to circle back to that at another time. "You can't guarantee that if you're doing things that could put you there."

"Ain't doin' shit to put me there."

"Smoking pot."

He shook his head. "Ain't goin' to prison for that. Get a citation at the most. Cops around here don't give a fuck about dope. Hard shit? Yeah. Some grass? No. Gonna be legal for everyone one day soon, anyway. They got bigger fuckin' fish to fry than someone smokin' a joint, gettin' mellow and eatin' an order of fuckin' loaded fries from Dino's."

Maybe that was true—though, she hadn't tried the famous Dino's Diner loaded fries yet—but she had done some Googling of what a Sergeant at Arms did in an MC. She had read several articles on motorcycle clubs. Not only because she worked for one but because Judge had been staying in her bed and spending time with her daughter. Before coming to Manning Grove, she knew nothing about MCs. She still didn't know a lot, but she did know what a club's enforcer did for the most part.

"You enforce the rules."

"What?"

"You're supposed to keep everyone in line and punish those who don't follow those rules. Do what you need to do to protect your club and brotherhood."

"Where'd you hear that?"

"I read about it," she admitted. Though, she never would have if it hadn't been for this conversation.

"Yeah, baby, that's my job as the enforcer."

"It's dangerous."

"Could be."

"It could get you arrested."

"Could, if I do somethin' stupid."

"Like murder?"

His silence was telling. She turned but stayed toe to toe with him.

"Like assault and murder?" she asked again.

"Gotta do what needs to be done, Cass," he said way too seriously. He grabbed her chin and tilted her head up higher. "Not just for my brothers, but their ol' ladies and their kids. Current and future. The club's one big family. They're responsible for their own, but I'm responsible for all of them. Took my father's former spot. Didn't want it, took it anyway. Take the job seriously. Wanna do better, be better than him. Will do what I gotta do but keep my ass out of jail."

"You can't guarantee that."

"Just gotta be smart."

"Judge…"

"Baby, trust me. Ain't gonna do shit to land behind bars. Swore to Jemma, I wouldn't."

"Who's Jemma?"

"My sister."

"We need to talk about her, too." She needed to know everything about him. Not just bits and pieces.

"Not now."

"Then soon."

He stared down at her. "Yeah, soon. Right now, wanna fuck you. Got the babysitter stayin', right?"

"Yes, until morning."

"Want you to stay with me tonight."

She wanted that, too, even though there wasn't much left of the night. Sunrise was right around the corner. "Only…" Heat flooded her cheeks. This heat wasn't from the tequila.

"Only what?"

"Only if you take me against the wall just like that couple back there."

"Back where?"

"Where you came from with that woman."

His head twisted in that direction. She knew the exact moment he realized what she was talking about.

Especially when he shot her a big grin. "Got plenty of wall space upstairs."

"We also need to finish this conversation."

"Promise we will. After."

After. If she was still awake. After one round with Judge, she might not be able to stay that way.

"Then let's hit it." *Holy crap*, did that just come out of her mouth? It had to be the exhaustion and the tequila combo. "I'm fading fast. Especially after the booze. Where's Jury?"

"Probably with Justice sleeping in Deke's bed. Will grab her on the way upstairs."

"He lives here, too?"

"Yeah, one of the rooms in the bunkhouse."

"Guess I'm getting that tour anyway."

"Gonna be quick and we'll avoid the closed doors."

"Your brothers actually close their doors?"

He snorted and tugged on her hand, directing her to the back corridor. "Sure they won't mind if you wanna watch."

"Only if you want me to compare."

"Can compare all you want. Only one Judge."

"Is that a blessing or a curse?"

"Blessin' to other men, curse to all the other women out there who can't have me."

Cassie didn't bother to smother her laugh. She let him hear it loud and clear.

But that laugh quickly disappeared once they got upstairs and he showed her just how right he was.

Chapter Nineteen

ANOTHER FUCKING WEEK AND NOTHING.

Christmas flew by and even though he loved spending every fucking minute of the holiday with Cassie and her girl, including watching Daisy's face and reactions during the Christmas parade in town, all he had wanted to give Cassie for Christmas—besides his fucking dick—was her freedom from Lange.

He couldn't give her that until he found the fucker. So far, he'd failed. Every time he tried, he came up empty and it made no sense how a financial nerd and gambling addict had turned into the Invisible Man.

Time was running out on him shacking up with Cassie in her sister's house, too. The homeowners were coming home the day after New Year's since both had to get back to work. That meant Cassie was back to sharing Daisy's bed, unless he could find a place for her and her girl. They hadn't discussed it, but it would need to be a discussion to have. And soon.

He considered moving them into his apartment temporarily, but it was too damn small for three people.

Even with Daisy being pint-sized, her attitude was full-on adult.

Three people, one tiny bathroom and one bed wasn't going to cut it. Plus, he doubted Cassie would agree since Melanie was heading back to college after the holidays and she'd be relying once more on Heather and Ty to babysit the kid while she worked.

This all added to his fucking frustration.

No Lange. And soon, for him, there'd be no Cassie.

And if he had to, he'd admit the sassy-mouthed Cassie clone had grown on him, too. He actually didn't mind her waking his ass up to demand he make her dog-shaped pancakes or watch cartoons with her.

There was that, too. Jury had been sleeping in the kid's bed every damn night. The girls, both two- and four-legged, had bonded.

It got him in the gut every time Cass went to check on Daisy, and he went with her to check on Jury, that Cassie's girl slept with her arms wrapped around Judge's girl.

Fuck. He might be losing all his girls. He definitely needed to do something about that.

His eyes tracked Cassie as she came out of the bathroom wearing something he never saw her wear before. Had she been holding out?

"Jesus fuck," rumbled deep from within his chest.

She stopped in the center of the room, put a hand on her curvy hip and jutted out not only that hip, but those fucking tits. If that didn't catch his attention, nothing would.

She tilted her head as she took him in lounging on the bed. "Is that a complaint? Shall I return it?"

"You spent scratch on that?"

"Well, I had wanted to give you something for Christmas. You're just getting it a little late because I had to order it online and shipping got delayed."

Early, late, that wasn't the fucking point. He was just

surprised to get anything at all, especially after telling her not to spend her money on him.

"You spent scratch on that," he repeated. She bought that for him, even though she was counting her pennies. She didn't already have that outfit tucked away somewhere, she went and bought it for *him*.

For Christmas.

Best fucking Christmas gift he'd ever unwrap.

Hell, best Christmas gift ever.

The only thing better would be if she became his ol' lady and it was his cut she was wearing over her naked body.

If she did agree to being claimed at the table, it would solve the housing issue. He'd have to move out of the apartment and get a place big enough for three of them. With space for Jury, too.

And maybe a second pup for Daisy so he could get Jury back.

That was another discussion they needed to have.

But they'd only known each other for about a damn month. And he knew Daisy would be her greatest concern. Rightly so.

He couldn't have Cassie without Daisy. And he was all right with that.

But right now, the kid wasn't on his mind. Right now, her mother, who looked sexy as fuck, was.

Because, fuck him, the silky baby doll negligee that hardly corralled her tits, and definitely didn't hide even one of her curves, had made him hard as fuck.

Her blonde hair was piled on top of her head, with just a few long tendrils falling around her face, her eyes held a naughty look and she wore a wicked smile.

He was torn between ripping that fucking thing off her or keeping it on when he threw her on the bed and fucked her until that mouth wasn't curved in a smile, but in a big-ass *O*.

Or he could do both.

Yeah, fuck it. It was his Christmas present, right? He could fuck her with it on, then fuck her with it off. "Door locked?"

Her head twisted in that direction and she rushed over to double-check. "Yes."

"Stay there."

She turned to face him, the white door a perfect backdrop for his beautiful woman. Blue silk that matched her eyes touching every part of her he himself wanted to touch.

"Jealous of that fucking thing right now."

"This thing?" She slid her hand over exposed upper curves, then the covered underside of her tits.

"Keep goin'," he demanded, pulling himself upright against the headboard. He was getting comfortable for this show.

"Where do you want me to go?" The huskiness of her voice made his dick throb.

"You know where."

"Here?" She touched the fabric at her stomach.

"Show me what's beneath it."

She pulled the hem of the baby doll top up slightly, exposing the little matching panties. "Like this?"

Fuck, she was a damn tease. "You horny?"

A flush covered her chest and cheeks, and her eyelids were heavy. Yeah, she was fucking horny.

"Are you?" she asked, staring at his hard dick which he was now stroking slowly.

"Slide those panties off and bring 'em here."

She rolled her eyes and sighed. "You're awfully bossy."

Nothing but a game. He played along. "Ain't begun to show you bossy."

She bit her bottom lip, slipped her hand into her panties and began to play with herself.

The woman wanted him to lose his fucking mind. "Told you to take them the fuck off."

She didn't answer him. Instead, her eyes closed, and her hand moved restlessly under the small scrap of silky material. She let out little gasps just loud enough for him to hear.

Damn wicked tease. She knew exactly what she was doing.

"Baby," caught in his throat. "Gave you an order. Gotta listen."

She still ignored him and releasing her bottom lip, her mouth gaped open and her head fell back. A low, soft moan reached his ears.

Despite being annoyed at her for not listening, a smile crept across his face anyway. "Baby," he said in a warning tone, as he heard her breathing turn to little pants. He stroked faster, watching her get herself off. "Cassie…"

Every muscle on her locked, her tell-tale sign of an impending orgasm, and she whimpered softly, but she jerked her hand out of her panties like she'd touched fire.

Her head snapped up, she shoved her panties down, and rushed over to the bed.

His fist had frozen mid-motion when she had stopped just before orgasming. And now he was scrambling to get a wrap open and over his dick as she climbed onto the bed and over his lap.

"Fuck, baby. Gimme——"

She knocked the wrap out of his hand and sank down on his dick, drawing both a groan and a bit of panic from him.

"Cass," he growled, even though he did nothing to stop her riding his dick like he was a bucking bronco and she was hanging on for those eight seconds, because, *fuck*, her fucking him bareback was mind-blowing. "Cass," he tried again. "Fuck!"

She sank down onto his lap, taking him as deep as he

could go. Her blue eyes opened and she stared right into his. "The teddy isn't your only Christmas present."

What the fuck was she talking about? He certainly wasn't looking to get her pregnant. They had a long way to go before he'd even consider that. Plus, he was thirty-seven now. Babies weren't even in his plan.

He already had a son he didn't see and, if it was up to him, a future "daughter" who wasn't his. As much as he wanted Cassie in his life, he hadn't even considered babies with her.

She wrapped her arms around his neck. "Remember after Shade's party when I asked you to get tested and I told you I'd do the same just to make it fair?"

"Yeah," he grunted as her luscious ass ground into him.

"We gave them my email address to send the results."

Fuck, between Christmas and all the Lange shit, he forgot about that.

"I read the email this morning."

"Guess we're good to go?"

"Yes." She rose slowly, until the head of his dick was barely inside her.

"Ain't the only reason to wear a wrap, baby," he reminded her.

She slowly slid back down his length, then ground once more against him, making it hard for him to concentrate on her words. "You never asked because we were wearing condoms and I thought it was smart to continue, but... Merry belated Christmas. I've been on birth control since right after Daisy was done nursing."

He dug his fingers into her hips, holding her still, and pulled his head back to get a good look at her face. "Baby, it's more than that, it's..."

"I know. You got burned." She cupped his cheek. "I trust you, Judge. One hundred percent. Do you trust me?"

He stared at the woman on his lap. The one he was considering taking as his ol' lady. The one he wanted to get a place together with. The one he wanted to build a life with.

He couldn't do that without trusting her.

He needed to trust her in this. To trust her in all things. They had nothing without it.

And he wanted something with her.

For fuck's sake, he wanted everything with her.

Maybe even babies.

Christ. He closed his eyes for a minute. That last thought had been totally unexpected.

Fingers sliding over his cheek and down his beard made him open his eyes. Made him see the woman he was connected to. And not just because she was currently sitting on his dick.

"Yeah, baby, I trust you." That came out a lot easier than he thought it would.

"You sure? Because you look a little pale." She grinned at him, then circled her hips.

"Just a little? Pretty fuckin' dead right now."

She dropped her forehead to his chest and her body shook against him. When she lifted her head, she said, "Well, you are pretty stiff."

He thrust his hips up. "Everythin' about you makes me fuckin' hard."

"I love everything about you, too." With that, she began to move again, drawing him in and out of her wet heat, her pussy pulsing around him.

Wait. She fucking just dropped that bomb and then continued like the world just didn't tilt on its axis? Like it was something she casually said to him every fucking day?

He needed to add that conversation to his ever-growing list of discussions.

Right now, he wanted to fuck, not talk. His thoughts

would be a lot clearer when her pussy wasn't squeezing his dick.

He sat back against the headboard and watched as her beaded nipples lifted and fell behind the slippery blue fabric. He bet that sensation turned her on even more. Ripping the clip from the top of her head, he let her hair fall around her shoulders and over her tits. He grabbed a handful and tugged her head back, exposing the curve of her throat.

When he latched on and sucked her heated skin hard, her whimper rose up her throat and vibrated against his lips. He scraped his teeth along her pounding pulse, along her jaw and pressed his lips to her ear. "Gonna come, baby. Need you to come soon."

He wasn't lying that he was about to blow. Yeah, it was way too quick, but they had all fucking night.

This first time he'd consider a warm-up. Especially now with no wrap and just the two of them. Nothing between them except that sexy nightie.

That was fucking hot as fuck.

But no wrap also made it harder to keep from coming. Even though this was supposed to be his gift, he didn't want to leave her in his dust.

The thought of coming inside her didn't help the pressure that was building, the tightening of his balls and the urge to fill her completely. To know, when she was sleeping beside him, she'd still hold a part of him inside her.

It was crazy. He'd never had that need before. But in his mind, it was another step toward making her his, including her permanently in his life.

She would belong to him and he to her. Because going without a wrap, birth control or not, meant neither of them would be with anyone else.

Only one damn obstacle remained.

Her slamming herself down on his cock and muffling her cries by pressing her mouth into his shoulder, drew him out of the thoughts that had helped delay his own orgasm until she got hers.

Once she melted against him, her ragged breath hot and damp against his skin, he flipped her over, buried himself between her soft thighs and drove hard and fast into her, quickly chasing what she had achieved.

"Givin' you my cum." He grunted into her hair as he powered deep one last time and held, spilling inside her, his pounding heart skipping a beat.

And once his balls were empty and his dick done twitching, he began to move lazily in and out of her as he took her mouth and kissed her gently. Continuing to enjoy the connection they had until he had no choice but to slip from her.

As he rolled to his back, she began to get out of bed. He grabbed her arm to stop her. "Stay. Don't move."

"But I should clean up…"

"No. Gonna fuck you again as soon as my dick wakes up. Gonna get some good use out of that nightie tonight. Just gonna keep fillin' you up again and again, 'til I can't get hard anymore."

"That'll leave a big wet spot."

He grinned. "Might have to buy them a new mattress."

Her lips twitched, too. "Are you going to explain to them why?"

"Yep. Gonna tell 'em you can't get enough of my dick."

"I can't wait to see their faces when you do."

"Can't wait to see *your* face when I do." She whacked his arm and he rolled out of bed. "Gonna get you a washcloth, then we have to do a bit of jawin'."

"*Jawin?*" she echoed.

"Got some shit we need to discuss," he threw over his shoulder as he went into the master bathroom, cleaned himself up, took a piss, and ran a washcloth under the faucet.

When he came back out, he was relieved she was still wearing that nightie. That was his present to unwrap and he was going to take his time doing it.

He handed her the wet washcloth and climbed in next to her. While she was taking care of business, he said, "Gotta thank you for my gift. Was a complete fuckin' surprise. Best gift ever."

"You never got anything cool for Christmas as a kid?"

"Nothin' as hot as you. Always had some crazy fantasies and you're one that came true."

Her face softened as she rolled into his side, wrapped her arm around his waist and propped her chin on his chest. "That might be the best compliment I've ever received."

"It's true. And, believe me, I jerked off a lot as a kid." Still did. But his Fleshlight was going to get a lot less use if Cassie stayed in his life.

Her face twisted. "Should I still take it as a compliment?"

"Yeah, if you can empty a man's nut sac that easily, take it as a compliment."

She sighed and he grinned.

But that grin quickly fell. "Gotta apologize, Cass."

She turned surprised eyes up toward him. "For what?"

"Wanted my gift to you to be you free of your ex. Did my fuckin' best, my best wasn't good enough."

"Judge—"

"Wanted to at least give you that. Failed you."

She sighed again. "You didn't fail me. You didn't cause any of this. And, really, it's not your responsibility to free me of this mess."

"Wanted to do it for you. For your girl. Make it a good holiday."

She traced his nipple, making it bead. "It was a great one. I've got a roof over my head. I have a healthy, happy daughter. And..."

"And?"

"I've got you."

Damn. "Ain't goin' nowhere." He combed his fingers through her hair. "Didn't miss what you said. Just like the nightie, wasn't expectin' that."

"To be honest, I wasn't, either. It just… I just said what I felt… what I feel."

She was the first woman who told him that and he believed her. His ex-wife said it often, but he never believed her. Not one time. Her actions had spoken louder than her words.

The same with Cassie. Even if she never said it, he felt it. And that right there was everything and made him want her even more. "Ain't a hard woman to love, Cass."

"Oh, another compliment!"

He smirked. "Ain't bad to look at, either."

"Mmm hmm."

"Got a smart mouth sometimes, though. That's a con."

"A con for what?"

"For lettin' you move in with me."

"Letting me?" she squeaked.

"Yeah. 'Cause now I'm gonna have to find a bigger place for all of us."

"Judge… I'm not sure I'm ready for that. With Daisy…"

"Yeah, get that. We got time. Just wanna know you're okay with the idea."

She gave him a smile. Soft just like the way her eyes looked. "I'm okay with the idea."

"When you're ready."

Her fingers shifted to mindlessly trace the tattoos on his chest. "When I'm ready."

"Like soon." He knew he was pushing but he wanted her to know how important she was to him. Daisy, too.

It took her a few moments before she said, "When you find a place."

"Want you and your girl in my life."

"*Ain't goin' nowhere*," she echoed his earlier response.

"One of the best things I ever heard besides you lovin' me."

"Oh, wait. That's what you heard?"

"Swore that's what I heard." He wiggled a finger in his ear. "Do I need to clean out my fuckin' ears?"

"I don't know…" She pulled herself across his chest and put her mouth to his ear. "I love you." She pulled back. "Did you hear that?"

"Not sure. Try again."

She smiled and did it again and when she drew back the second time, he captured her face and pulled hers to his. He gave her a slow kiss, taking his time exploring her mouth and sliding his tongue over her lips.

When he released her mouth, she asked, "What did you hear?"

"I love you."

"That sounds about right," she said with a grin and a tug on his beard.

"Yeah, it does." He wouldn't argue that.

Because it was true.

Chapter Twenty

JUDGE SAT BACK in the folding chair outside of his apartment and blew the smoke up toward the night sky while the fat snowflakes fell down around him.

Sig sat next to him, his feet kicked up on the railing and sucking back a beer. "My fuckin' balls have gone into hidin'."

Yeah, a late-night January snowfall wasn't the best time to sit outside and get high, but Sig didn't smoke inside his apartment because of Autumn. And Judge came outside while Jury was somewhere out there in the dark doing her business.

He offered the half-kicked joint to Sig, who took it and tucked it between his lips, taking a couple short puffs, then blowing the smoke out of his nose like an angry bull.

"Red sleepin'?" Judge asked him.

"Nah. Readin'. Soon as I'm done out here, gonna go in, find my balls and fuck her. Then she'll be sleepin'."

Judge snorted and shook his head.

But he wished he could say the same thing. Cassie was still living at her sister's house and sharing Daisy's bed. Which sucked the fucking big one. But it was what it was until she was ready to share a roof. Though, he'd first need to find a roof big enough to fit them all so he was ready for when she was.

He'd talked to Trip about building a little house somewhere on the farm and Trip seemed to be okay with it. However, mid-January in northern Pennsylvania wasn't the best time to start building and he wasn't waiting until the Amish could build him what he needed. He needed to find something else in the meantime.

Again, once she was ready.

Judge didn't think she'd be ready until Lange signed his fucking name on those divorce papers. Which made him more determined than ever to find the fucker. He had even called Diesel, a Dirty Angels MC member and fellow enforcer, to see how much it would cost to hire one of his Shadows to find Lange.

His asshole had puckered when he heard.

He had a decision to make: build a fucking house or find Lange. He couldn't afford both. *Hell*, if he paid for a Shadow, he wouldn't even have enough to temporarily lease a place for him and his girls.

It fucking sucked. His business did well, but not well enough to plunk down the kind of cash needed to hire an expert from In the Shadows Security. Justice Bail Bonds had a lot of overhead and Deke also had to live off whatever they made.

He ground his molars at the thought of Lange getting off scot-free and leaving Cassie behind with the mountain of debt and a valid marriage certificate.

His girl ran up the steps, squeezed under and between Sig's legs and jammed her nose right into his junk. "Jesus fuck. Savin' that for Red, Jury. Damn dog."

Judge grunted. "Maybe she was lookin' for your lost balls."

Jury gave Sig's beer bottle a lick before coming over to him for an ear scratch.

"Did she just lick my fuckin' beer?"

"Better than lickin' your dick."

"Know that for a fact?" Sig cocked an eyebrow as he took another big hit off the blunt before passing it back over.

Judge studied the lit joint in his fingers, watching the smoke swirl into the air from the tip.

Sig took a long chug of beer and belched loudly when he was done. "Whatcha doin' about Cass and the kid?"

"Not sure yet."

"Claimin' her, right?"

"Plan on it."

"She's into it?"

"Fuckin' hope so."

"Nice havin' pussy in your bed every night."

Judge twisted his neck toward the man sitting next to him. "That what Autumn is? Pussy?"

"Know what the fuck I mean."

Yeah, he knew what Sig meant. It was his delivery that sucked. Sig would be the first to admit Autumn saved his ass. But then, Sig saved hers, too.

Just like Stella saved Trip's.

Two of his brothers had found women who fit them perfectly.

So did Judge.

But he wasn't feeling settled like them. He was feeling goddamn restless.

He missed Cassie. He missed having her curled against him as they slept. He missed waking up in the middle of the night and fucking her. He missed Daisy pounding on the door in the morning with her tyrant demands.

He missed it all.

For the past two weeks, it had been just him and his

Fleshlight in his apartment and it was lonely as hell. Cassie's sister agreed to watch Daisy overnight a couple of times, but it wasn't nearly enough for Judge.

Not enough for Cassie, either.

She missed him as much as he missed her.

Fucking crazy for him to fall so fucking hard for a woman he'd only known for about six weeks. Cassie said the same.

That's why she was in no rush to move from under her sister's roof. Plus, she was still putting money away. He hoped it was so they could get a shared place and not one on her own, but it would be up to her.

He wouldn't rush her. Not only because of her but because of her girl.

He got it.

But it still sucked.

He had hoped she'd spend the night tonight since she was on days-off from Crazy Pete's, but her sister and brother-in-law had some work thing to go to and couldn't watch Daisy.

So, he'd gone over after closing up Justice Bail Bonds for the night, had dinner with her and Daisy and left once his girls had settled in to watch *Frozen* for the millionth time.

He could do a lot of things but watching *Frozen* again was not one of them. Especially when Daisy, while dressed like Elsa, sung at the top of her little lungs to the point where he wanted to jam pencils in his eardrums.

He sighed. It was time to go inside, thaw out his own balls and maybe spend a little quality time with his Fleshlight and his imagination.

As he rose from his seat, his cell phone went off, playing Cassie's ringtone, which was not the fucking song *Let It Go*. He swiped the screen and put it to his ear.

Maybe she was calling to have phone sex. He could get on board with that.

"What's up, baby?" At first, she didn't answer, making the back of his neck tingle. "Cass."

But it was her whisper that made his heart stop. "He's here."

"Who's there?" he shouted, already knowing who the fuck she was talking about. He glanced at Sig. "Take Jury in with you."

Sig dropped his feet from the railing to the metal landing and stared at him with concern.

"Dennis," came the shaky whisper.

"Jesus fuck. Where?"

"In Daisy's room. He's sitting on her bed, talking to her."

"What? Did you let him in?"

"No!" she whisper-shouted. "I have no idea how he got into the house. But he's in there. I went to check on her and he was just... there."

"Where are you?"

"I closed the bedroom door before he saw me and called you right away."

"Where are you?" he barked as he ran down the steps, Jury on his heels. "Get Jury!" he shouted up at Sig.

The man ran down the steps, grabbing the bulldog by her wide collar and holding her as Judge jumped into his Expedition, which was parked at the bottom of the steps.

"In Heather's room."

Judge pressed the Ford's Start button and the engine roared to life. His cell phone's Bluetooth automatically hooked up. "Will he hurt her? You?"

"No, I don't think so," came her shaky voice through the vehicle's speakers. "He's just talking to her, but I have no idea what he's saying."

He shoved the shifter into Reverse. "Fuck."

"Yes, fuck, Judge! What do I do? Call the cops?"

"No, I'm on my way. If he tries to take Daisy with him, you hang up with me and call 9-1-1. You got me?"

He could barely hear her "Yes."

"Keep your shit together. If you approach him, stay calm, yeah? If you can, try to keep him in the house 'til I get there. If he leaves, do not let him leave with Daisy. If he tries leavin' without her, make sure you get the description of his vehicle and plate, yeah?" He sped down the rough farm lane, past Trip and Stella's house and toward County Line Road.

"Okay."

"Only stop him from leavin' if you can do it safely. Do not put yourself at risk. We don't know what his fuckin' mental state is."

"He's upset. I think he's getting Daisy upset, too, because he's crying."

"He's fuckin' cryin'?"

"Y-yes. I think so."

Jesus Christ.

"Want you to text Deke right now. Don't hang up with me, but text him and tell him what the fuck's goin' on. You keep the line open with me so I can hear everythin', okay?"

"Okay. I'll text him now."

"You get his vehicle description, text it to both of us."

He got no answer, so he assumed she was doing what he told her. A few seconds later, she returned with, "Okay, I texted him."

"He text you back?"

"Not yet."

"He will. Don't worry. Gonna shut up now so you can listen for him. Make sure he does not take Daisy, Cass. Do not let him leave the house with her." He could not say that enough. Judge was worried Lange might use her in a stand-off. Or for ransom. Or, worse, as a shield like his father did with Jemma that night over twenty years ago.

"I won't. He's not taking her. No way."

In the dark interior of the Ford, he nodded to himself at her answer as he sped toward town.

"I'm going to get him to sign the papers," she whispered after a few minutes.

"Fuck the papers, Cassie. Wait 'til I get there."

"This might be my only shot."

"Cass, just stay put and keep an eye out for what he's doin'."

"I need to be free of him. So does Daisy."

"Cass…"

He got no answer.

"Cass!" he shouted into the dark interior of the vehicle. "Jesus fuck!"

"I'm here."

Oh, thank fuck.

"The papers are in our room."

"Fuck the papers."

"He's still here. I can convince him to sign them."

Judge ground his teeth. "I'm almost there."

"Okay, then I'm hanging up."

"No—" The phone disconnected. "Call Deacon!" he yelled the voice command, and a ringing filled the interior.

"What's up?" his cousin answered.

"Where are you?"

"Headin' out. Was face first in pussy when—"

Judge cut him off, not needing to hear about Deke's latest fuck at a time like this. "Head toward Cassie's."

"Headin' there now. But—"

"Will give you an update when I get there."

"Got it," came the answer before the phone went dead again.

"Call Cassie," he shouted. The phone rang and rang and a few seconds later her voicemail picked up.

He jammed his boot harder on the accelerator, making

his Ford scream as it did fish-tails in the snow that was starting to accumulate at each corner he took.

When he got to the house in record time, the driveway was empty and Cassie stood barefoot in the snow with her arms wrapped around her waist.

She was probably fucking freezing, standing there like that.

He rolled down the window as he pulled in. "What's he drivin'?"

"Light colored, maybe tan, four-door Dodge sedan. I don't know the model."

"Get the plate?"

She shook her head. "When I went into her room, he pushed me down and ran out of the house. I had to chase him." Tears were sliding down her cheeks. "He didn't sign the papers."

For fuck's sake, those goddamn papers.

He put his arm out the window. "Give 'em to me."

She lifted her empty hands. "I don't have them. I threw them in the car when he was escaping. He has them."

"Gotta go catch his ass. Text Deke the details. Get in the house and lock the doors."

She nodded again, shivering and wrapping her arms around her waist once more. He jerked the shifter into Reverse and the Expedition fish-tailed again as he smashed on the gas pedal to back out of the driveway. As soon as he regained control, he headed in the direction of the disappearing taillights he'd seen when he'd come around the corner.

Thank fuck there were also the tire tracks in the inch of snowfall. They would help unless Lange turned onto heavier traveled Main Street. And, of course, that's where the fucker went. Luckily, between the snow and the late hour, no one else was driving through the middle of town. Up in the distance, he saw what looked like the Dodge's taillights. He blew through the red light in the square—since, luckily, no one else was around—and down the slushy road.

As Judge raced to catch up, the Dodge slowed up ahead, the brake lights glowing bright even in the falling snow. The cage turned.

Fuck me. This was déjà vu all over again.

But this time he didn't park at the curb and walk into the empty lot where the former Fury clubhouse used to stand. Fuck no. He pulled in behind the parked Dodge, which now had its lights out and was sitting in the dark.

He blocked it in as best as he could since Lange had parked in a back corner of the lot near the fence. Where no one would see him from Main Street.

Where shit could go very fucking wrong and no one would know right away.

He quickly sent a text to Deacon, then shut off his lights, but kept his engine running. He reached under his seat, where he kept a holstered 9 mm Glock and shoved it into the back of his waistband.

With one eye on the Dodge and its occupant, he shoved his door open and climbed out. He took cover behind the door for a few seconds, just in case Lange was armed and willing to take a shot at him.

When no shots were fired or threats yelled out, he cautiously approached the car. And, of course, the window was still wound up. Lange had both hands firmly on the steering wheel and stared straight ahead. Judge noticed the divorce papers lying on the dash.

"You've got to be fuckin' kiddin' me," Judge muttered under his breath. Louder he said, "Roll down the window, or I'm bustin' it out."

Lange slowly turned his head and stared at Judge through the closed window, his eyes vacant and tears running down his cheeks. The back of Judge's neck tingled again. Something was definitely off with this fucker.

He did not turn into the old warehouse lot to escape. He pulled into the vacant lot to hide.

Why?

"Get the fuck outta the car," Judge ordered. Even though the man was a fugitive and it was Judge's right to take him into custody, he could not use his gun to do so. While he had a license to carry a concealed weapon, it was for personal reasons and not for his business. To use it for business, he would need his Act 235 certification, which he and Deke never completed. Because of that, they used non-lethal options when capturing a bail jumper instead of a firearm.

But if Judge had to shoot the fucker to keep himself from dying, he would. That would be a last resort since too many questions would arise if he killed Cassie's husband. Especially since he was fucking the man's wife and planning a future with her.

That might appear a bit suspicious.

The window powered down and Cassie's estranged husband stared up at him. "Who are you? Why are you bothering me? Just leave me the hell alone."

That wasn't going to happen. "You skipped on bail and have a warrant. You're comin' with me."

Lange's eyes went wide and he shook his head. "No, I can't go to jail."

"Ain't your choice. Just like you gave Cassie no choice by stickin' her with all the debt after you stole from a kids' cancer charity. What kinda fuckin' man does that shit?"

"Just leave me alone and she'll be free of me."

"Not if you don't sign those fuckin' papers, she won't. And the fuck if you're livin' free while she suffers. You're gonna get what's comin' to you."

"I can't go to jail! I can't! I'll never survive."

"Ain't goin' to jail. Goin' to prison. But you're the type of asshole who'll go to a country club prison, nothin' fuckin' hardcore. You'll be playin' tennis durin' the day and at night, some rich daddy will make you his bitch. Promise it'll only hurt the first coupla times."

"I only wanted to see my daughter one more time. I needed to apologize to my wife, my daughter. I didn't mean for any of this to happen to them."

"An apology will never be enough to fix your fuck up. You lied to her. You not only lost everything she had, your actions destroyed her life. Now she's left pickin' up the pieces. She lost everything, Lange. Her marriage, her home, her job, her security, all because you gambled away all your shit, then turned around and, bein' such a selfish mother-fucker, you stole from kids with cancer. That ain't a man, you asshole. That's a selfish pig. Instead of the money goin' to help families with dyin' kids, you lost a hand of poker. Or a round of blackjack. Or by bettin' on the wrong fuckin' horse. Whatever your poison was, it affected a lot more people than you. So, fuck your apology."

"I know, I—"

"You didn't even have the balls to tell her. Could've admitted your weakness and asked for help. You fuckin' didn't. Instead, you brought Cassie and Daisy down with you. Was thinkin' more about yourself than your family. 'Cause of that, can't leave you alone. Law's after you and so am I."

Lange covered his face with his hands. "I can't go to prison," he whispered.

This conversation was getting old. And Judge was losing what little patience he had. "It's over. Get outta the car."

"I can't let you take me."

"You didn't wanna get caught, you never shoulda broke into that house. Never shoulda upset your girl."

Judge reached for the door handle and Lange screamed, "All right. I'll get out." He shoved open the door and climbed out, leaving the door open as he faced Judge.

The man wasn't much taller than Cassie. Maybe a couple of inches. His hair was longer than the picture Judge had of him, his coat dirty, his pants wrinkled. And from what Judge could see inside the open door of the Dodge, it was full of fast food wrappers and trash.

The man had hit rock-bottom.

But that wasn't Judge's problem. Cassie and Daisy were his problem. He didn't give a fuck about Lange, he gave a fuck about them. "You're gonna sign those goddamn papers and do somethin' to help Cassie for once instead of fuckin' her over. Then I'm takin' you to Rochester."

"I can't go."

"Got no fuckin' choice."

"We always have a choice." The man's voice sounded eerily vacant.

"And you made some fuckin' bad ones. Now do somethin' for the woman who once loved you 'til you fucked her over."

In a sudden move, Lange pulled a gun from his coat pocket and pointed it directly at Judge. Right at his goddamn chest. *Fucking motherfucker.*

"Don't come any closer."

Judge wasn't planning on dying tonight. He needed to distract the man so he could get the gun away from him. "Gonna kill me, motherfucker? That what you're gonna do? Think of your fuckin' daughter. She's gonna have to live with her daddy being a fuckin' murderer."

"I am thinking about her. I'm setting her and Cassie free."

"No, you're thinkin' about yourself again. Just like when you stole that money from a goddamn kids' cancer charity. Was all about Dennis Lange. Fuck everybody else."

"That's not true!" he screamed into the still night.

"Then prove it. Give Cassie what she wants, the fuckin' divorce and you out of her life."

Lange nodded. "Fine. I'll sign. I'll sign and then you'll let me go."

The gun in his hand shook and his finger was way too close to the trigger. The man probably didn't know the first thing about guns. That could be a good thing or a very bad thing, depending if things went sideways.

But Judge wasn't going to wait for that.

Lange jabbed the gun in his direction. "Step back. I need to go to the other side of the car."

Judge took a step back, giving Lange space to move around the Dodge. He followed the man, staying a few feet away but close enough to make a grab for the gun if he got the opportunity.

And he needed to get it. Because there was no way Lange was going on the run again. Judge was delivering his ass to the bail bondsman in New York, getting his cut and giving that scratch to Cassie. It would hardly make a dent in what she lost but it would be a start.

She'd get some money, get her divorce and finally be free of the man who was reaching for the passenger-side door handle.

And as he did, Judge saw his opening. He interlaced his fingers and lunged at Lange, bringing both connected fists down on his wrist. As he struck it, Lange cried out and dropped the gun. Judge put his boot on it so Lange couldn't recover it, then snagged the surprised man by the throat, shoving him against the car.

Judge squeezed hard enough to make the man's mouth open and close as he struggled for air. He leaned in until his face was in Lange's. Then he gave Cassie's ex a little lesson. "I am the Judge. I am the jury. And I am the fuckin' enforcer. I alone decide what happens to you." He flexed his fingers around the man's throat. "Right now, I have your life in my hand, and decide whether you live or die. Not you."

He pulled the Dodge keys from Lange's coat pocket and

shoved them into his. There was no way he was letting this man escape.

Cassie's life would turn around with what happened tonight in this very goddamn empty lot. A lot that held history for the Fury. A lot that held more recent history between Judge and Cassie.

The night he found her crying because of the fucker he was currently strangling. He reluctantly loosened his fingers and let the man breathe.

"Gonna let you loose. You do somethin' stupid, you're gonna regret it. You get me?"

"I'll sign the papers if you let me go."

"You'll sign those fuckin' papers 'cause I said you're signin' those fuckin' papers. I'm tired of this shit. You're wastin' time. Now get in there and do it." Judge yanked Lange away from the car, opened the passenger side door and shoved him toward the open doorway. Lange stumbled but caught himself on the door frame and while he was climbing into the passenger seat, Judge kicked the man's gun away, spinning it into the dark and out of reach. He'd deal with it later. Right now, he needed to watch Lange do what Cassie needed him to do.

Lange, now sitting in the passenger seat with the stack of papers on his lap, said, "I... I have a pen in the glovebox. I'm going to reach for it."

"Do it slow and don't do anything stupid," Judge warned him.

Lange opened the glove box and dug around with Judge watching his every fucking move.

And once he pulled out that pen, he began to sign those damn papers Judge never wanted to hear about again after tonight. Thank fuck it would finally be over.

Lange flipped through the pages, signing on every line one of those little plastic arrows pointed at. When he was done, he put the pen back in the center console instead of the glove box and when he pulled his hand back out, he had another gun in it. This time what looked like a fucking snub-nosed .38 revolver was pointed at Judge.

For fuck's sake. He should've strangled the motherfucker.

"Back off," Lange shouted at him. This time the man's finger was securely on the trigger and the hammer was cocked, too.

Lange was desperate and desperate people were dangerous, so Judge reluctantly took a step back. But gun or not, Judge wasn't allowing Lange to escape.

"You were wrong. You don't decide whether I live or die." He put the barrel of the handgun to his own temple. "I do."

As Judge fell forward to grab the man's wrist, the crack of the gun going off made every inch of his body flinch and he stumbled, landing hard against the Dodge. He caught himself, his ears ringing and his mind spinning, trying to make sense of what just happened.

And then everything went still and deafeningly quiet.

With his own heartbeat pounding in his ears, Judge straightened and stared over the roof of the car into the dark. To where only the memory of the Original's club-house remained.

His past.

He sucked in a deep breath of frigid winter air, and, with his gut twisting, dropped his gaze to the car's interior.

To his and Cassie's future. Now marred by what he saw.

Fuck.

Fuck.

Fuck.

Fuck.

Lange's head had fallen forward. Blood and brain matter covered the inside of the car and windshield. The hand holding the gun sat lifeless on Lange's lap and under it was Cassie's signed divorce papers. Splattered with dark, shiny spots. Soon to be soaked to the point they were unreadable. When ink and blood eventually blended into one.

But it didn't matter. None of that mattered.

What mattered most to Judge was Cassie was now free.

But not entirely. Because this was not how Cassie wanted it to go. Neither did he. And this might haunt her for a while. If not forever.

Judge turned and slid his back down the side of the vehicle until he sat with his knees cocked on the cold, rough pavement. He drew his fingers over his face, finding and smearing warm blood on his skin that was not his. He dropped his head into his hands and just breathed.

Fuck.

He'd have to tell her. And then she would have to explain it somehow to her little girl.

Daisy was too young to understand the wrongs Lange did. No matter what choices the man had made, he was still her daddy. A father she would never see or hold again. And that was going to hurt.

After a few more minutes, when he had pulled his shit together, he scrolled through his cell phone and found a saved number.

Not looking forward to making this call, he closed his eyes and put the phone to his ear. "Chief…"

JUDGE STOOD BACK but kept his gaze forward, keeping an eye on the activity in the distance.

Rochester had a few inches of snow last night and the wind was biting. He worried his girls would be cold since they'd been out there for over a half hour now. He was getting impatient for this to be over.

She said he didn't have to come, but there was no way he was letting her come back up here alone.

Holding Daisy's pink-mittened hand, Cassie guided her to the casket and helped her daughter put a flower on the top, then placed her own on there, also.

His woman, wearing a black dress and long black winter coat, turned and spotted him. Even from where he stood, he could see her eyes and nose were red since she'd been crying during the whole service.

She was still so damn beautiful even with her face ravaged with grief. Knowing that she could forgive the man that fucked her over and could come here today and pay her respects to him and his family killed him. But he understood it and supported her in doing so.

She didn't think it would be good for him to stand by her and Daisy's side at the service or the gravesite, so he didn't. He stayed close but just far enough away to not intrude.

Even so, he had a difficult time not going to her and curling her into his side when she had been surrounded by Lange's family and they pretty much ignored her. They mostly spoke to Daisy. He got it. She had left her husband a while ago and they probably didn't consider her part of the family anymore. Or they blamed her for not sticking by his side during his troubled times.

Normally, he might agree with that, *if* she hadn't asked Lange to get marriage counseling and help for his gambling. She gave him that shot, that way back in, but he'd turned it down. Cassie leaving his ass was all on him.

As was his choice of death over prison. He chose to take what he thought was an easier route, not caring his decision wouldn't be easy for everyone else around him. The living left behind had to grieve and make sense of it all.

After Lange's parents said a few more words to Daisy, Cassie squeezed her daughter's shoulder and turned her in

Judge's direction. Without pointing him out, Daisy spotted him anyway, and her little tear-stained face lit up. She broke free of her mother's grasp and ran across the rows of snow-covered graves, darting around headstones to get to him.

Daisy came toe to toe with him, dropping her head back and staring straight up at him. Seeing her red-rimmed eyes, he was reminded that Lange had done this to her. The man had made his daughter cry.

"You said you were stayin' in the motel."

He was being scolded by a five-year-old. "Yeah, I did. Missed you two, though."

He didn't want to be too far from Cassie in case any of Lange's family gave her shit. If he had to, he would've stepped in. With him being the club's Sergeant at Arms, and now that Cassie and Daisy were what he considered club property, it was his job to protect them.

He took that job very seriously.

Before the little tyrant could demand it, Judge scooped her up into his arms and she took a hold of his beard like she always did.

Using a knuckle, he wiped a stray tear off her chin. "You okay?"

Daisy nodded. "I'm sad. I miss my daddy."

"I'm sure you do, kid. You will for a long time. Sometimes I still miss my daddy, too."

Shiny blue eyes blinked at him. "Did he die?"

"Yeah. A long time ago."

"How'd he die?"

Judge wasn't sure how to answer that. "He went to prison, Daze, because he did a bad thing. He died when he was in prison."

"Oh. Someone said my daddy did a bad thing, too, an' was goin' to prison. But he died 'fore he got there, right?"

Christ. "Yeah, kid."

"Momma said he got *reeeeeeally* tired an' just went to

sleep. An' when he was asleep, he flew *aaa!llll* the way up to Heaven. Just like an angel."

Judge knew that wasn't exactly the explanation Cassie told her, but today was not the day to correct her. "Yeah, that's what happened."

"Is your daddy in heaven, too?"

Judge doubted it. "Yep. He'll be waitin' for your daddy there."

"They can be friends."

He gave her a squeeze. "Yeah, baby, they can be friends."

Judge lifted his gaze to where Cassie broke herself free from saying her goodbyes and headed in their direction. He was relieved to see she was no longer crying as she stared at the two of them waiting for her.

When she reached where they stood, she pressed her forehead to his shoulder and he curled his free hand around the back of her head, holding her close.

"I shouldn't cry for him," came muffled from his thick leather jacket.

"Yeah, baby, you should. You loved him enough to marry him and have his baby. Things just got twisted is all."

"I don't even know if I'm a widow or a divorcee."

"Free. That's all you need to know for now. The rest we can figure out later," he reminded her, adjusting Daisy's legs around his waist more securely. The little girl's cheek pressed to his other shoulder.

Cassie tipped her face up to his, her blue eyes red-rimmed and her mascara a little smudged. Still beautiful as fuck, though. "Free to be yours."

Yeah, he wanted to shout that, but he didn't. "To start new."

"Free to put down fresh roots. Settle in and get our life in order."

He knew she meant her and Daisy's life, but he was pretty damn sure "our life" also included him.

"Sorry it happened this way," he whispered into her hair which had been pulled back into a tight bun and not loose like he normally preferred it.

"Me, too." Pulling her head back, she looked up at him again. "Let's go home," she whispered, running her fingers over Daisy's fist which was still gripping his beard tightly.

If the kid needed that, he'd let her have it. He wanted to give both of them whatever they needed, whenever they needed it.

"Yeah, baby, let's go home."

Epilogue

THE BEGINNING

Almost six months later

IT DIDN'T GO unnoticed that the nails on Judge's hands and toes were painted several different colors. Someone had gotten into Cassie's nail polish again and Judge, as patient as he was with her daughter, had suffered through Daisy practicing on him.

"I guess I need to stock up on more nail polish remover. I hope I have enough for you to remove that before your uber-manly poker run today. Otherwise, the guys won't miss all those shades of pink and red. I have to say, though, those colors do look good on you."

"If you can talk, woman, ain't doin' my job," came the low rumble from his chest into her back.

"What job is that?"

"Of making you come."

"Work harder, then."

She bit her bottom lip when those brightly colored nails disappeared from her breasts and a thick arm wrapped around her hips as those fingers dipped between her thighs.

She braced one hand against the shower wall and the

other gripped the strong arm across her belly, which held her like a vice. His nose was pressed into her wet hair, and the hot water beaded on their eyelashes and ran in wide rivulets down their connected bodies. They had installed a large hot water heater for this very reason. It was worth every penny because they took a lot of showers. Especially since the bathroom was a good place to muffle the sounds of them having sex.

Which was often.

Two of those long, thick fingers slowly slid in and out of her, the pace quickening slightly with each thrust. But it wasn't nearly fast enough since she was close, but not quite there. And they didn't have a lot of time to spare.

His steel rod of an erection pressed into her back and she knew as soon as he got the result he was working toward, he'd be taking her from behind, so he could come deep inside her. That thought took her one step closer to the edge.

He liked the idea she would spend all day carrying a little bit of him inside her. If she was being honest, she liked it, too.

It was simply another way to mark her as his ol' lady. Just like the "Property of Judge" cut he had made for her after officially claiming her at the table and in front of his brothers.

They had a busy day ahead of them since today was the First Annual BFMC Poker Run with all the proceeds going to the Kids Can Do Foundation. Cassie had wanted to help make up for all the money Dennis stole from the charity. She suggested it to Judge, and he took it to the table, where everyone agreed it was a good idea.

Just last month they had gone down to Shadow Valley to a fundraiser run by the Dirty Angels MC to help raise money for the Walker Foundation, a charity for amputees unable to afford prostheses. The DAMC was deeply involved with it and the whole club helped out. While there, Cassie had taken lots of notes and asked Ellie Walker numerous questions. Thankfully, the woman had a lot of patience.

Besides raising money for Kids Can Do, doing charity work would also help build good relations between the Fury and citizens of Manning Grove. Over the last few months, Cassie learned about the bad history between the club and the town. And how Trip was determined to not let history repeat itself.

But she shouldn't be concentrating on any of that right now when her ol' man was driving her to the brink of an orgasm. It would also help if she focused on what his fingers were doing rather than what would happen later that day.

She dropped her head back to his wet chest, leaning on him instead of the wall, freeing up her hands to cup her own breasts and thumb her own aching nipples.

"Fuck, baby." Those two words and the way he groaned them made everything inside her tighten.

"Thumb," she moaned, and he didn't delay pressing that digit against her clit.

She rode his fingers and ground into his thumb, closing her eyes and letting him work his magic.

"Come on my fingers. Wanna taste you."

She shuddered and breathed, "God."

"Judge," he corrected her. "Nobody but me doin' this to you."

As she opened her mouth to say something smart, the words became lost and turned into a whimper as she did what he wanted—what she needed—and came. He continued to lazily slide his fingers in and out of her until the last wave of the orgasm waned.

He held her tightly as she became boneless and a languid, satisfied smile spread across her face.

When he slipped his fingers from her, she turned her

head in time to watch him tuck them between his skilled lips and suck them clean.

Everything squeezed inside her once more. She wished they had time this morning for him to give her beard burn on her inner thighs. The discomfort would make her think of him all day and remind her of how lucky she was to find a man like Judge.

Completely unexpected and far from perfect, but perfect for her.

"How do you want me?" she asked him.

"Any and every way you want to give me. Long as I got you, I'm good."

Long as I got you, I'm good.

When he said things like that it was just as good as him saying he loved her. He didn't say those three words often but all the other things he said made up for it.

She reached back and cupped his wet, bearded cheek. "You got me." And that was so true.

Life wasn't quite settled yet, but it was getting there. Slow and sure. They were putting down roots together as a family and those roots were beginning to burrow deep.

Building a house on the farm and moving in together was one way. The club giving her a piece of Tioga Pet Crematorium was the other. With the help of Easy and Shade, they had set up a mobile service to help pet owners when the time was right to send their beloved family member over the rainbow bridge.

Was it heartbreaking at times? Often. But the appreciation she got from the owners for the gentle care she gave their old or ill pet outweighed the sadness. If she could ease the owners' pain as she relieved their pets', it was worth it.

But today wasn't about the growing business and moving forward. Today was about beginning to heal the past.

"I want to face you." She wanted to see his face this morning when he came inside her. She wanted that connection. It would be a long, tiring day and seeing him always gave her strength. Even if it was only in a recent memory.

As she began to turn toward him, she froze.

A nose pressed against the steamy glass wall of the large, multi-jet shower. It wasn't a human nose because it was black. Though, the color didn't mean anything. Cassie had to scrub off marker and paint on her daughter's face and body countless times.

But she recognized that nose. "Uh... How did Jury get in here? Didn't you lock the door?"

"Fuck," came the deep mutter behind her.

Before either of them could separate and double check that the bathroom door was closed and locked, a loud, "Momma, I—"

"Get out!" Cassie screamed in a panic, her heart in her throat. "Oh my God! Saylor!" She elbowed Judge in the gut since he was shaking against her. "This is not funny!"

He pulled her tightly against him to hide his raging hard-on, so her daughter wouldn't get an eyeful. *And* ask questions neither of them would want to answer a soon-to-be six-year-old. At least, not this morning.

"Saylor!" Cassie called out again. Where the hell was she? Their house mouse was supposed to be making Daisy breakfast. "Come get Daisy!"

A female voice came from way too close. That meant not only were Jury and Daisy now in their oversized master bathroom, but so was Saylor. Cassie covered her breasts with one arm and her nether region with her hand, just in case Rev's barely eighteen-year-old sister could see them through the steamy glass.

"Sorry! Sorry! Daisy, c'mon. Your mom's taking a shower and needs her privacy."

Why did it sound like the girl was trying not to laugh? Why was everyone finding this funny except for her?

"Momma, is Judge in the bath with you?"

Technically, they were in the shower, not the Jacuzzi tub that sat in the corner, so she wasn't lying when she answered, "No."

"You're lyin'. He is so! Why can't I play in the bath, too?"

Saylor made a choking sound so loud, Cassie could hear it over the running water.

"Saylor!"

"Daisy, let's go. Your waffles are getting cold."

"Yes, go eat your waffles," Cassie instructed her daughter. "We have a big day ahead of us and I need to get ready."

"Lock the door behind you," a low baritone voice instructed.

He just couldn't keep his mouth shut, could he? Cassie sighed and elbowed Judge again.

"See?" her daughter huffed. "Momma was *mistaken* again. I get in trouble when I'm mistaken, she don't."

"That's because she's an adult and adults make a lot of mistakes, so they'd be in trouble *all* the time." Saylor's voice became faint as they left the bathroom.

As soon as they heard the door slam shut, Cassie unfroze herself and turned to face Judge. Her forehead hit his chest as she groaned, "Oh. My. God."

A deep rumbling laugh rose from that broad chest and she smacked his arm.

"You know what? You think it's so funny? I'm leaving it to you to explain the birds and bees when it's time. Which might be soon if she keeps walking in on us."

"Can we finish?"

She stepped back and glanced down at his now semi-aroused cock.

"It looks like you're finished."

He grabbed her wet hair and tugged it back to lift her face to his. "With you it doesn't take much to make me hard. Pretty fuckin' sure I can get your motor runnin' again, too."

"We don't have much time."

"Ain't gonna take long."

Her lips flattened out and she *mmm*'d.

"Gonna prove it to you."

"I don't need proof of how fast you can come. I already have all the evidence I need."

"Funny, woman," he growled.

"But true," she told him smartly.

"Then gonna take my time and we can be late—"

"We can't be late!"

He ignored her interruption. "Then you can explain to everyone you're late 'cause your ol' man was givin' you good dick."

"Good is a relative term."

Judge dropped his head and shook it. When he lifted it, the corners of his eyes were crinkled. "You want fucked?"

She pursed her lips. "The water's getting cold now."

"We can heat it up."

She smiled. "That we can."

And they did.

It had been a good fucking day. The early June weather had held out and the poker run was a huge success. Not only did all his brothers participate in the ride, two ally clubs—the Dirty Angels MC and the Dark Knights MC, along with Diesel's six Shadows—took part, too. Judge was even surprised to see a few bikers wearing Blue Avengers cuts, a law enforcement MC. He never expected pigs to join in an event held by the BFMC, but some showed up, as well as other bikers not affiliated with any MC from across Pennsylvania and surrounding states.

Cassie's idea to raise money for Kids Can Do was a huge success, but then, she and the ol' ladies had put a lot of work into it. Tents had been set up for food and booze. A couple of pigs—four-legged, not two—roasted on spits. An area had been set up away from the adults for the children to hang out and play games. They had a silent auction earlier. And pool and dart tournaments were currently happening inside The Barn.

Best of all, they raised way more scratch than expected. Way more than anyone expected. From what Autumn said, who'd been keeping track of the donations from individuals and local businesses, plus the event fees, it was close to fifty grand.

Fifty fucking grand.

Kids Can Do would be getting a nice fat check.

Now it was getting late and everyone was gathering inside and in the courtyard to eat, drink and party for the rest of the night.

He stood near the barn and out of the way of the women moving like worker ants under the pavilion. Cassie, along with Stella and Autumn, were getting the evening activities organized for the participants. A bunch of the Dirty Angels' women and the wives of Diesel's Shadows were helping her, too.

Yep, it was a good fucking day. Evidenced by the tired smiles everyone wore on their faces.

He also knew an almost six-year-old whose ass was dragging and had hit her limit for the day. The tiny tyrant had turned into a cranky complainer. And after Cassie made sure her daughter ate a decent meal, instead of only junk food, she handed her off to Saylor for the rest of the night.

Judge's eyes sliced over to their house mouse, who was holding Daisy's hand and walking across the field back to the modest ranch house he hired the Amish to build. Right now, it was big enough for the four of them with the ability to expand in the future, if needed. Hugging the tree line, it was still close enough to The Barn so they could walk there, but also far enough away so Daisy couldn't see or hear shit happening outside in the courtyard during parties. Plus, they put her bedroom on the back side of the house, just in case.

Saylor had her own room, too, since she was there to help with the house, the meals and Daisy. Rev's teenaged sister ended up in juvie during high school for a bunch of different shit and when they released her the day she turned eighteen, their parents wouldn't let her back into the house. She had nowhere to go, and since Rev lived in the club's bunkhouse, she couldn't stay with him.

Judge didn't think Cassie would be on board with an eighteen-year-old troublemaker moving in with them. But she shocked the shit out of him when she was willing to give the girl a chance, as long as certain rules were laid out and Saylor followed them. Even though it had only been a couple of months, so far, so good.

The arrangement was actually perfect. They had someone to watch Daisy while they worked, Saylor had a roof over her head and a job to keep her out of trouble, and Rev was close enough to keep an eye on his little sister.

And not just to keep her on the straight and narrow, but because she was young, outgoing and gorgeous. Which was a dangerous combination.

Rev and Judge hadn't been the only one keeping an eye on her today, a lot of the single bikers had, too. Not for the same reason. However, Judge now considered her not only Fury property, which put her under Judge's protection, but as if Saylor was his own sister.

That meant if anyone fucked with her, they would have to deal with him as judge, jury and enforcer. Or even execu-tioner, depending on what they tried or did.

Trip, walking up behind him and whacking him on the

back, pulled him from his thoughts. "This is the kinda shit I wanted for the club. All this right here."

Judge glanced at the man at his side. "Well, you're fuckin' gettin' it."

"This fuckin' club's turnin' into the family we all need. All of us. Not just for our brotherhood but our women and kids, too. Gotta thank you for you and Cass takin' a chance on Saylor. Glad to see it's workin' out."

"Yeah." Judge's gaze slid back over to the house where Saylor and Daisy disappeared.

"Businesses are in the black, too. Good time to expand."

"Get Deke on it."

"Already got him searchin'. The more scratch this club makes, the better off for everyone."

Judge was financially upside down right now because of that house. Even with using the Amish, building it hadn't been cheap. Any funds he had put aside for Ry's college fund were now gone. Any money he made with Justice Bail Bonds was used to support a four-person household and the rest went back into the club account since Trip had let him borrow the remainder he needed for the house instead of trying to get a bank loan.

Cassie running the pet crematorium helped, but not enough.

Even so, they were living good. His girls were happy and that was all that mattered to him. If he had to bust his ass and scrounge for every penny to keep them happy, he would.

"That's not why I came to find your ass."

Judge turned toward his prez. "What's up?"

"Got some kid in the barn lookin' for you."

He frowned. "Kid?"

"Not a little kid like Daisy, but one about Saylor's age."

As those words sank into Judge's brain, his heart began to thump heavily in his chest. "Boy?"

"Yeah. A tall one. Looks an awful lot like you. Not as gangly as you were as a teenager, though. Probably got no problem gettin' laid, unlike you."

Judge ignored all that. "He ask for me by name?"

"Askin' for Judd Scott. Most people in there don't know you by that name. Just a couple of us."

"Deke in there?"

"Yeah, he's talkin' to him now, keepin' him occupied."

"Fuck," Judge muttered under his breath.

"He yours?"

Judge stared at Trip and answered honestly, "Got a boy 'bout eighteen."

The Fury president's eyebrows rose. "His name Henry?"

Without warning, Judge's knees wobbled enough that Trip grabbed his shoulder.

"You okay?"

"Don't fuckin' know," Judge managed to get out. His feet were frozen to the ground, his heart was pounding out of his chest, his pulse raced like he'd just snorted an eight-ball of coke and his brain spun like a Tilt-A-Whirl.

"What d'you need me to do?" Trip asked. "Want me to have Deke take him somewhere? If he's yours, not sure if The Barn's a good place to meet with him right now. It's packed and loud. When's the last time you saw him? Didn't even know you had a kid."

Judge continued to stare at Trip, unable to wrap his head around what might be happening. "Yeah. The mom fucked me sideways right out of his life. Haven't seen him since he was almost one." Not since he was a baby. A fucking baby.

"Damn," Trip whispered, yanking off his baseball cap and scraping his fingers through his hair before jerking it back onto his head. "Like I said, kinda looks like you, brother. Just ain't as big yet. But close."

Jesus.

Why the fuck was he still standing there instead of

rushing to see his boy? Why couldn't he move? His eyes slid back to the pavilion, where Cassie was speaking with Stella.

"Want me to get her for you?"

Judge shook his head. "Get Deke to take him up to his apartment. Will meet him up there in a few."

Trip continued to stand there staring at him with his hands on his hips, like he had a million more questions. Problem was, Judge didn't have the answers. After a minute, the man nodded and headed toward the propped open double doors on the courtyard side of the barn.

Judge wasn't sure if he should have Cassie with him or meet Ry on his own. *Fuck*, he wasn't sure of anything right now.

Everything on him right now was tight. He was worried he'd be unable to get out the right words he needed to say to his own son.

Judge didn't even know him.

And Ry didn't know him.

Judge squeezed his eyes shut and when he opened them, Cassie was heading in his direction, worry marring her face. Dodge was standing where she previously stood, also looking in his direction, a frown on his face.

Her walk turned into a jog as she rushed over to him. "Judge..."

She didn't need to say anything more. Just his name and the way she said it was enough. "Yeah."

She reached down, snagged his hand and squeezed it hard. Then she tugged him out of his frozen spot and toward the back of the barn.

"Don't know what to fuckin' say to him, Cass." His chest was getting so fucking tight he was struggling to breathe.

"Just be you."

"Probably fuckin' hates me."

"You don't know that."

"How can he not?"

"I know you, Judge. Just let him get to know you, too."

"Don't even know if that's why he's here. Maybe he's here to put a bullet between my eyes."

Cassie sucked in a breath and yanked on his arm. "Don't even say that!"

He followed his woman to the back of the barn and up the metal steps to his old apartment, the one his cousin moved into the second Judge moved out. At the top of the stairs, Cassie hesitated.

She turned her face up to him. "Do you want me in there with you?"

He didn't know. He was having a tough time making any kind of decision right now.

She shook his hand which was tightly clasped in hers. "I'll come in with you. Then if I need to slip out, I will."

Judge only stared at her and nodded.

"You okay?" she asked.

"Fuck no."

She smiled. "You haven't seen your son in seventeen years. It can't get worse than that."

"Shit could always get worse."

"It won't in this case." She put her hand on the door-knob and glanced over her shoulder at him. "You ready?"

"Been ready for seventeen years, just didn't realize how hard it would be."

She turned the knob. "Just be you," she repeated in a whisper.

As they stepped inside, Deacon immediately approached, stopping shoulder to shoulder with him, but with him facing the door. "Christ, this was totally unexpected," he said under his breath just loud enough for Judge to hear him.

No shit.

"Not sure why he's here, but he is. That's the first step."

"Yeah," Judge breathed.

Deke whacked him on the back and walked out, closing the door behind him.

"You Judd Scott?"

Judge stared at the kid… boy… no, the young man who asked the question. When he didn't answer, Cassie whispered a sharp, "Judge," that shook him loose.

"Yeah."

Trip was right. Ry was tall. Over six foot already. And his hair was dark blonde like his. But Trip was also right about his son not being gangly. Not at all.

He tried to blink away the sting in his eyes, but it didn't work.

"Judge," Cassie said again, squeezing his hand until it almost hurt. Then she released it and moved a step further into the living area, closer to where Ry stood by the kitchen counter.

"You're not Judd?" Ry asked, suddenly appearing confused.

He swallowed, trying to loosen his throat so he could talk. "Judge is my nickname."

"You know who I am?"

"Yeah. Know who you are," he answered the boy who was no doubt his son.

Ry began to fidget, suddenly looking very unsure of himself. "Didn't mean to just show up like this. I… I… wasn't sure if you'd want to meet me. Figured you might be pissed that I never responded to any of your calls or texts."

Judge couldn't breathe. He couldn't. Was this really happening? "Cassie," he whispered.

"Yes?" came from behind him and he hadn't even realized he had taken steps closer to his son and Cassie had backed away.

"Am I awake?"

Cassie made a soft noise, then said, "Yes, baby, you're awake. That's really Ry standing there."

Ry turned his head toward Cassie. "Ry? How do you know my nickname?"

"'Cause I gave it to you," Judge answered, taking another step closer. He now was only a few feet away from his son. His fucking son.

Finally.

"You did?"

"Yeah."

"I hate the name Henry."

No surprise. "Me, too. Refused to call you that."

His boy smiled. "Mom would only call me Henry. It pissed me off." That smile dropped. "She died a month ago."

Judge wasn't sure whether to be sad or fucking happy about that. "Sorry."

"I... uh... was going through her things with my aunt and I found something in my mother's closet." He dug into his front pocket and pulled out an old flip phone.

It was the one Judge had mailed to him ten years ago, hoping to make a connection with his son.

"I wondered why she kept an outdated phone, so I found a charger and charged it. I figured the account had been closed since it was so old, but it wasn't."

No, he'd kept it open and paid for it every month. Just in case.

Just in case a day like today ever came.

"I listened to the voicemails and read all the texts."

That had to take a while since there were hundreds of them. "You never saw any of them." He didn't make it a question because he already knew the answer.

His son shook his head. "I had no idea you were even alive." Ry scrunched his brow. "She told me you died in a car accident when I was a baby. That's why she left Pennsylvania and went to California. She said she was devastated and couldn't live with the memories."

Lying fucking bitch.

He knew it was fucking wrong, but he couldn't help hoping Jen died a slow, painful fucking death. Because no matter how she fucking suffered, it wasn't nearly as bad as Judge having his son stolen from him. He'd suffered for seventeen fucking years.

"I'm sorry."

Jesus fuck. His kid was sorry, and it wasn't even his fault.

"So am I," Judge said. "Just glad you know the truth now. So glad you found that phone. Glad you're here." He ran a hand over his mouth and down his beard, trying to keep his shit together.

"I didn't want you to think I ignored all those messages. I didn't. I would've responded. I asked about you. Mom always said it was too upsetting for her to talk about you."

Christ.

"I wanted to meet you in person, not talk to you over the phone. So, I began driving here right after graduation. I'm going off to college at the end of August, but I figured, if… if you want to, we can use my summer break to get to know each other?"

Judge closed his eyes and once again wobbled a bit.

"Would that be okay?"

The uncertainty in Ry's voice was like a knife to his heart. He opened his eyes. "Nothin' I'd want more."

"I can find a place to stay nearby, maybe get a summer job while I'm here—"

"Yeah, got you covered on all that. You can help me in my business, got a bunkroom downstairs with only a couple prospects in it. Got plenty of room."

He didn't think an eighteen-year-old boy staying under the same roof with an unrelated eighteen-year-old girl was smart. Letting him stay in the bunkhouse was smarter. Ry could still be close, but independent.

Judge took another step closer and their eyes locked. Ry

had green eyes just like his old man. *Fuck*, it was almost like looking in the mirror when he was that age.

But his kid seemed smarter and better looking.

Thank fuck.

He needed to touch his kid. To make sure he was real. Even if it was just a fucking handshake.

Or a fist bump.

Something.

Anything.

Jesus fuck, his son was standing just out of his reach. His fucking son.

Fuck the handshake.

Judge took two long strides to Ry and the last thing he saw was the kid's eyes go wide as he grabbed him and pulled him into his chest, enveloping him in his arms.

And fuck the burn in his eyes. Fuck the tears that came.

Fuck them. He didn't give a shit.

If there was a time to cry, this was it. And fuck anyone who thought differently.

He swore he stood there for at least ten minutes, refusing to let his son go.

Afraid if he did, he'd just disappear.

But when he finally let Ry loose, his son still stood in front of him. His kid's eyes and nose appeared a little redder as he swiped at his cheeks.

Yeah, this was worth crying about. For both of them.

Hell, he heard Cassie sobbing softly behind him, too. *Shit.*

"You good?" he asked Ry.

His son nodded and sniffled.

"Yeah, me, too." Judge stepped back and held out his hand to Cassie. She moved closer and when she reached him, she placed hers in his. "This is my wo— ol'—your future stepmother, Cassie."

Cassie bumped her shoulder into him and laughed

through her tears. "Hi, Ry, it's great to meet you. I'm so glad you came. Sorry for crying like a baby."

"Me, too," Ry said with a laugh, rubbing his forearm over his eyes.

"Have you eaten?" Cassie asked him.

He shook his head.

"Why don't we get you boys some food and you can start catching up while you eat? You two have plenty to talk about."

"Sounds good, baby," Judge told her. He turned to Ry. "Why don't you go on out? Need a sec with Cassie."

His son's eyes slid from her to him, then he nodded and headed toward the door.

"We'll just be a second, Ry," Cassie assured him.

As soon as the door closed behind his son, Judge said, "Waited seventeen years. Never thought this day would come, so another second shouldn't kill me, but it is."

Cassie smiled up at him. "I know. But he's here. He came to you, Judge. That's huge."

"Yeah." Ry seeking him out gave Judge a lot of hope for the future. That maybe they had a chance to build a relationship between them.

"What did you need to say to me?"

"Just wanted to thank you for bein' here. For bein' a good woman. For lovin' me. Today had already been a great day and it just got better."

Cassie nodded, her lips trembling. She was struggling with her own emotions. "The future might not always be easy, but we'll get through it. We can work on fixing the past and building a stronger future. All of us. Together." She reached up and stroked the length of his beard, giving him a shaky smile. "Now you can cut it all off."

He jerked his head back. "Bite your fuckin' tongue."

"I'll borrow some clippers."

"Woman..."

"Hey, let's go show him how great you are." As she moved away, he grabbed her arm to stop her. She tipped her face up to him again. "You know, I was walking through a parking lot one day and I came across a whole bunch of bikers. And one in particular was huge and scary looking…"

"Your girl wasn't scared."

"No, she wasn't. She knew better than her momma."

"Yeah, took you a bit to catch on."

Cassie laughed. "Did it?"

"Yep. But now you love me."

"That I do," she whispered.

"And are stuck with me."

Her face twisted. "I guess I am."

"Don't act like you don't like takin' my dick."

"Meh." She shrugged. "It's alright."

"You beg for it."

"Let's not get carried away."

He dropped his head. "Love you, baby," he said against her lips, then brushed his lightly over hers. They didn't have time for him to claim her mouth like he wanted to.

"And I love you." She patted his chest. "Now let's go get your son to love you, too."

He grunted. "Shouldn't be hard since I'm so fuckin' lovable. Like a giant fuckin' teddy bear."

"Speaking of teddy bears, last night Jury ate the eyes off Daisy's."

He guided his woman out of the apartment and began the long journey of getting to know his son.

Their story was only just beginning.

And he looked forward to discovering how it all played out.

———

"Failure is only the opportunity to begin again, only this time more wisely." ~ Thomas Edison

---

Want more Judge, Cassie and Daisy? They attend the Manning Grove Christmas parade in
<u>Brothers in Blue: A Bryson Family Christmas</u>

Sign up for Jeanne's newsletter to learn about her upcoming releases, sales and more! https://www. authorjeannestjames.com/

Sometimes a challenge comes along that can either make or break you...

Deacon has a great life. A loyal brotherhood within the Blood Fury MC. A successful bail bonds business he runs with his cousin, Judge. A faithful dog. He's also an expert at seducing the ladies. He's got the looks. He's got the charm. And he's got the skill.

Or at least he thought he did. Until he met his match. A woman who not only resists him, but challenges him at every turn.

As an expert bounty hunter, he's been hired to capture a violent fugitive. Dealing with a dangerous man is one thing, but dealing with a stubborn woman is quite another. And the victim just happens to be her younger sister.

For Deacon, winning over a woman has never been this difficult. The more she fights his "charm," the more determined he is not to give up. This is one war he can't afford to lose, not only for her, but with locating the fugitive before he finds his victim.

It's a challenge he's willing to take on, as long as it doesn't destroy him first.

**Turn the page to read the prologue of
Blood & Bones: Deacon**

Blood & Bones: Deacon

Prologue
Nothing Stays the Same

DEACON STOOD ON THE PORCH, watching the plain tan four-door sedan turn into the driveway. Without a word, his father and mother left him there as they went out to meet the dressed-up woman climbing out of the driver's side.

They exchanged words Deacon couldn't hear. Though, he wanted to. He wanted to know what was being said between the three of them and how it would affect him.

His mom had said his Aunt Trixie and Uncle Ox had gotten into trouble and were in jail, so his cousins now had nothing and no one.

Deacon didn't know much about his aunt and uncle because his mother didn't want anything to do with her brother and his wife. He'd heard his parents talking about them in the past, and the word "trouble" always came up. Along with some other words he wasn't allowed to say unless he wanted to be grounded.

So, he didn't really know his cousins—the ones who no

longer had parents to take care of them—even though they hadn't lived far away at all.

He was only told this morning, while he was eating his Corn Pops, that his cousins, Judd and Jemma, were coming to stay with them.

People, who were practically strangers, were coming to stay in their house.

When his mother told him that, he dropped his spoon into his cereal bowl and splashed milk onto the kitchen table. He quickly used his napkin to clean it up before his father saw it. But Deacon said nothing until he was told he'd have to share his bedroom with Judd.

"What? Why?" How was that fair?

His mother had narrowed her brown eyes on him. "Because they have nowhere else to go except into the system. And we only have three bedrooms in this house. One needs to be for Jemma. That means you'll have to share yours with Judd."

"Why can't they go into the system?" He didn't want to share his room with anyone else. He didn't want to share his parents with other kids.

He was happy the way things were.

And, anyway, Judd wasn't even his age. He was like a million years older. Why would the teenager want to share a bedroom with a ten-year-old?

"Because despite the way my brother lived his life, they are family," his mother said. "They didn't choose this, they are victims of circumstance."

Whatever that meant.

Deacon jutted out his jaw and pounded his fist on the table, making the cereal bowl jump. "But I don't wanna share my room!"

Deacon's heart began to thud as his father took three long strides over to him and cuffed him upside the head. "Boy, you have everything. They have nothing. You will share your room, your toys and everything else you have with your cousins. And I don't want to hear a word about it. They've already been through enough and they don't need to hear you whining like a damn crybaby."

"But Dad—"

"Not another damn word about it, boy. They're coming here because we're all they have. What if it was you, huh? What if something happened to me and your mother and no one gave a shit enough about you to take you in? You'd end up in some foster home and probably spend the rest of your life in and out of the system. They've had no guidance in their life. They need that and a roof over their heads. And we're going to provide it."

Deacon's bottom lip had trembled as he stared at the sweetened yellow puffed corn floating in the lukewarm milk.

But now, not even an hour after choking down the last of that soggy cereal, he stood on the porch and watched as his cousins got out of the back of the car and, when the woman popped the trunk open, his father grabbed two small garbage bags from it.

They didn't have suitcases? That was all they had?

As his mother reached to pick up a five-year-old Jemma, Judd pushed past her, grabbed his sister and lifted her up instead. Jemma clung to her sixteen-year-old brother with her tear-stained face buried in his neck.

Why was she crying? She was getting her own damn room. Unlike Deacon. And his room wasn't even big enough for two beds.

His father, carrying the black plastic bags, headed toward the house.

Judd stood in the driveway, his sister in his arms, staring at Deacon's father's back, then his gaze landed on Deacon. He couldn't tell if Judd was mad or sad, or what, because the kid's expression never changed.

It remained blank.

His mother wrapped an arm around Judd's shoulders and steered him toward the house. She said something to him, but Judd didn't respond. He just walked, holding on to Jemma tightly. Like he was afraid someone would steal her from him.

Just like he was about to steal Deacon's room. Deacon's life.

As his father climbed the porch steps and passed him, he muttered, "You better drop the attitude, boy. I can see it on your face and so can they. You might not have asked for this, but neither did they. I'm sure they would've been happier staying where they were, not getting uprooted like this. So, you better think twice before you say something stupid to either of your cousins, you hear me?"

Deacon couldn't unglue his gaze from those two cousins, who were approaching *his* house. Neither of them would even be fun to hang out with. Judd was too old. Jemma too young.

"You hear me, boy?"

"Yes," he forced out between clenched teeth.

His dad gave a sharp nod and went inside, the springs on the wooden screen door squeaking as it slammed and bounced against the frame behind him.

Deacon spread his feet wide and crossed his arms over his chest, refusing to move out of their way as they stepped onto the porch.

His mother released a disappointed sigh as she went around him, but Judd stopped right in front of him. He waited until Deacon's mother went inside, then his cousin, much taller than Deacon, said, "Think I wanna share a room with a spoiled, snot-nosed shit like you? You think I got a choice to be here? I'm only doin' it for my sister, that's all." Judd leaned down and sneered right in Deacon's face. "So, get the fuck over it, twerp. What's mine is mine and now what's yours is mine, too. Get used to it. Now, get the fuck outta my way."

Deacon stared at him for a few seconds longer. Then he moved, but not fast enough. Judd clipped Deacon's shoulder as he pushed forward, knocking Deacon to the side.

Judd paused in front of the door and said over his shoulder, "You do anything bad to my sister, I'll beat the shit outta you."

"You touch me and I'll tell my Dad."

"Then he'll beat the shit outta you, too. Your pop told me he's glad I'm not a pussy boy like you." Judd jerked open the screen door and carried Jemma inside.

Before the screen door slammed shut, he saw Jemma's face peek out from Judd's neck and she stuck her tongue out at Deacon.

Deacon rubbed at the burn in his eyes and the sting in his nose. He tore down the porch steps and out to the shed, where he grabbed his prized BMX bike, which he refused to share, and hopped on it. He pedaled until he couldn't pedal anymore, until his lungs were burning and he lost track of time.

By the time he got home, it was dark and past his curfew. After he put his bike back in the shed, he came around the corner of the house to find his father waiting for him on the porch in the rocking chair. Rocking and waiting. Probably getting more ticked by the second.

His dad was usually fair, but Deacon knew he not only broke the rules, but missed dinner. He'd also somehow torn a hole in his new jeans, so now his mother would have to repair them.

"I'm sorry, Dad," he mumbled as he slowly climbed the porch steps.

His father stopped rocking and got to his feet. "Yeah. You're going to be."

The sound of his father's belt being unbuckled made him freeze.

"Go to your room and wait for me there."

Deacon flicked his eyes up to his father's. "Is Judd in there? You gonna let him watch?"

"He's going to see what happens when he doesn't follow the rules. Just because he's sixteen doesn't mean he'll get away with pulling stunts like this. You know the rules. You broke them."

Deacon began to tremble as heat filled his cheeks. "But Dad!"

His father slid the belt from the loops of his jeans. A familiar sound that made the hair on the back of Deacon's neck stand. "One more word and I'll add another six on to the six you already earned. You don't disrespect me, your mother, your blood or this house. And you did all of that today. Now go."

Deacon blinked quickly and wiped away the tears that were already starting to fall as he jerked the screen door open and ran inside.

———

DEACON WINCED as he pulled his PJ bottoms up over his still stinging butt.

Judd sat on Deacon's bed, his back against the headboard and his ankles crossed as he studied him.

The whole thing had been embarrassing. Not only because his butt had been exposed as he kept his feet on the floor and his hands planted on the bed while his father struck him with the belt, but because he had let a few whimpers escape and he couldn't stop the tears.

All with his cousin, who was a stranger, watching.

But his father used Deacon's discipline as a warning to Judd. Letting the older boy know that he needed to keep in line, that he wouldn't tolerate Judd becoming like his father, Ox. He would respect the law and his family. He would become a productive citizen and not some out-of-control convict.

Now it was just the two of them in Deacon's room. And Deacon had nothing to say. All he wanted to do was climb into the bed Judge was settled on and pull the covers over his head.

But he had a feeling he wouldn't get to sleep in his own bed tonight. Someone would be sleeping on the floor in the sleeping bag that was rolled up against the wall. Of course, it would be him.

Judd had already staked his claim on Deacon's comfortable bed. And if they got into a fight about it, his father wouldn't hesitate to come back into that room and dole out some more "respect."

"You picked a hill not worth dyin' on, kid."

Deacon sniffled and wiped the back of his hand under his running nose. "What's that mean?"

"Means you just need to not do stupid shit and if you do stupid shit, you need to know how not to get caught."

"And you're going to show me how not to get caught?"

"You bet I am and for that, you're gonna be my bitch 'til I'm old enough to move out."

"What does that mean?"

"Means when I need you to do somethin' for me, you're gonna do it. And you ain't gonna whine like a little pussy about it, got it?"

Deacon nodded, though he wasn't quite sure if he "got it." But if there was a way to avoid the belt, Deacon was on board with that.

Judd grinned. "If you haven't figured it out yet, kid, I'm takin' the bed. And that sweet little BMX bike you rode off on? That's mine, too, 'til I get a set of wheels."

"But—"

"Did you enjoy pullin' your pants down in front of me and gettin' hit with that belt?"

"No."

"Then you stick with me, kid. Watch, listen and learn."

Watch, listen and learn.

He could do that if it helped him avoid his father's belt or a cuff upside the head. Or even getting grounded.

So, maybe his cousins moving in wouldn't be such a bad thing.

As long as he got his own bed back.

Continue Deacon's story here:
https://books2read.com/BFMC-Deacon

If You Enjoyed This Book

Thank you for reading Blood & Bones: Judge. If you enjoyed Judge and Cassie's story, please consider leaving a review at your favorite retailer and/or Goodreads to let other readers know. Reviews are always appreciated and just a few words can help an independent author like me tremendously!

Want to read a sample of my work? Download a sampler book here: BookHip.com/MTQQKK

About the Author

JEANNE ST. JAMES is a USA Today, Amazon and international bestselling romance author who loves writing about strong women and alpha males. She was only thirteen when she first started writing and her first published piece was an erotic short story in Playgirl magazine. She then went on to publish her first romance novel in 2009. She is now an author of almost 70 contemporary romances. She writes M/F, M/M, and M/M/F ménages, including inter-racial romance. She also writes M/M paranormal romance under the name: J.J. Masters.

Want to read a sample of her work? Download a sampler book here: BookHip.com/MTQQKK

To keep up with her busy release schedule check her website at www.jeannestjames.com or sign up for her newsletter: https://www.authorjeannestjames.com/

www.jeannestjames.com

Newsletter: https://www.authorjeannestjames.com/
Jeanne's Down & Dirty Book Crew: https://www.facebook.com/groups/JeannesReviewCrew/

Get a FREE Sampler Book

This book contains the first chapter of a variety of my books. This will give you a taste of the type of books I write and if you enjoy the first chapter, I hope you'll be interested in reading the rest of the book.

Each book I list in the sampler will include the description of the book, the genre, and the first chapter, along with links to find out more. I hope you find a book you will enjoy curling up with!

Get it here: BookHip.com/MTQQKK